SILENCE FALLEN

SILENCE FALLEN

PATRICIA BRIGGS

ACE
NEW YORK

ACE
Published by Berkley
An imprint of Penguin Random House LLC
375 Hudson Street, New York, New York 10014

Library of Congress Cataloging-in-Publication Data

Names: Briggs, Patricia, author.
Title: Silence fallen / Patricia Briggs.
Description: First edition. | New York : Ace, 2017. | Series: A Mercy Thompson novel ; 10
Identifiers: LCCN 2016046323 (print) | LCCN 2016055943 (ebook) |
ISBN 9780425281277 (hardcover) | ISBN 9780698195813 (ebook)
Subjects: LCSH: Thompson, Mercy (Fictitious character)—Fiction. | Shapeshifting—Fiction. |
Werewolves—Fiction. | Vampires—Fiction. | BISAC: FICTION / Fantasy / Urban Life. |
FICTION / Action & Adventure. | GSAFD: Fantasy fiction.
Classification: LCC PS3602.R53165 S55 2017 (print) |
LCC PS3602.R53165 (ebook) | DDC 813/.6—dc23
LC record available at https://lccn.loc.gov/2016046323

First Edition: March 2017

Printed in the United States of America
1   3   5   7   9   10   8   6   4   2

Cover art by Daniel Dos Santos
Cover design by Judith Lagerman
Map by Michael Enzweiler

*To Libor, Martin, and Jitka, who suggested that
Prague should have its own pack of werewolves.
I hope you enjoy them. Good luck.*

*Also to Shanghaied on the Willamette, who brought out a
new album (finally) so I don't have to do anything drastic.
Seriously, gentlemen, thank you for your music.*

*And finally, for Richard Peters,
who provided "Sodding Bart"
with his new favorite swearword.*

ACKNOWLEDGMENTS

Thanks are due to all of those people who have helped with the writing of this book: Collin Briggs, Mike Briggs, Linda Campbell, Caroline Carson, Dave Carson, Katharine Carson, Deb Lenz, Ann Peters, Kaye Roberson, Bob and Sara Schwager, and Anne Sowards.

As always, the mistakes that remain are mine.

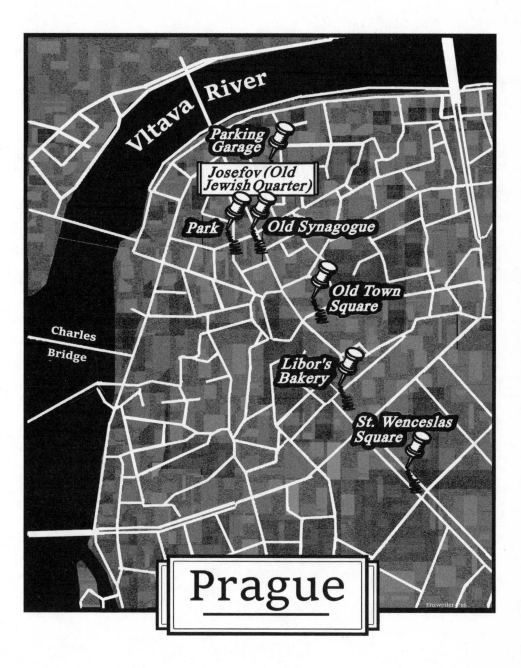

Dear Reader,

For the best reading experience, please pay attention to Mercy's notes at the beginning of each chapter. Fair warning—the timeline is not completely linear. My imaginary friends made me do it.

All best,
Patricia Briggs

1

MERCY

This wasn't the first time chocolate got me in trouble.

I DIED FIRST, SO I MADE COOKIES.

They were popular fare on Pirate night, so I needed to make a lot. Darryl had gotten me a jumbo-sized antique mixing bowl last Christmas that probably could have held the water supply for an elephant for a day. I don't know where he found it.

If I ever filled the bowl entirely, I'd have to have one of the werewolves move it. It ate the eighteen cups of flour I dumped into it with room for more. All the while, piratical howls rose up the stairway from the bowels of the basement.

"Jesse—" Aiden began, raising his voice to carry over an enthusiastic if off-key whistling rendition of "The Sailor's Hornpipe."

"Call me Barbary Belle," my stepdaughter, Jesse, reminded him.

Aiden might have looked and sounded like he was a boy, but he hadn't been young for a very long time. We had assimilated

1

him, rather than adopted him, as he was centuries older than Adam and me put together. He was still finding some things about modern life difficult to adjust to, like the live-action-role-playing (LARP) aspect of the computer-based pirate game they were playing.

"It only works right if you think of me as a pirate and not your sister," Jesse said patiently. Ignoring his response that she *wasn't* his sister, she continued, "As long as you call me Jesse—that's who you think of when you interact with me. You have to believe I'm a pirate to make it a proper game. The first step is to call me by my game name—Barbary Belle."

There was a pause as someone let out a full-throated roar that subsided into a groan of frustration.

"Eat clamshells, you sodding buffoon," Ben chortled. His game name was Sodding Bart, but I didn't have to think of him that way because I was dead, anyway.

I got out my smaller mixing bowl, the one that had been perfectly adequate until I married into a werewolf pack. I filled it with softened butter, brown sugar, and vanilla. As I mixed them together, I decided that it wasn't that I was a bad pirate, it was that I had miscalculated. By baking sugar-and-chocolate-laden food whenever I died first, I'd succeeded in turning myself into a target.

The oven beeped to tell me it was at temperature, and I found all four cookie sheets in the narrow cabinet that they belonged in—a minor miracle. I wasn't the only one who got KP duty in the house, but I seemed to be the only one who could put things in the same place (where they belonged) on a regular basis. The baking pans, in particular, got shoved all sorts of odd places. I had once found one of them in the downstairs bathroom. I didn't ask—but I washed that motherhumper with bleach before I used it to bake on again.

"Motherhumper" was a word that was catching on in the pack with horrible efficiency after "Sodding Bart" Ben had started using it in his pirate role. I wasn't quite sure whether it was a real swearword that no one had thought up yet, one of those swearwords that were real swearwords in Ben's home country of Great Britain (like "fanny," which meant something very different in the UK than it did here), or a replacement swearword like "darn" or "shoot." In any case, I'd found myself using it on occasions when "dang" wasn't quite strong enough—like finding cookware in bathrooms.

I thought I was good to go when I found the baking pans. But when I opened the cupboard where there should have been ten bags of chocolate chips, there were only six. I searched the kitchen and came up with another one (open and half-gone) in the top cupboard behind the spaghetti noodles, which made six and a half, leaner than I liked for a double-quadruple batch, but it would do.

What would not do was no eggs. And there were no eggs.

I scrounged through the fridge for the second time, checking out the back corners and behind the milk, where things liked to hide. But even though I'd gotten four dozen eggs two days ago, there was not an egg to be had.

There were perils in living in the de facto clubhouse of a werewolf pack. Thawing roasts in the fridge required the concealment skills of a World War II French Underground spy working in Nazi headquarters. I hadn't hidden the eggs because, since they were neither sweet nor bleeding, I'd thought they were safe. I'd been wrong.

The majority of the egg-and-roast-stealing werewolf pack was currently downstairs, enthralled in games of piracy on the high seas of the computer screen. There was irony in how much they loved the pirate computer game—werewolves are too dense to swim. Coyotes, even coyote shifters like me, can swim just fine—except, apparently, in The Dread Pirate's Booty scenarios, because I'd drowned four times this month.

I hadn't drowned this time, though. This time, I'd died with my stepdaughter's knife in my back. Barbary Belle was highly skilled with knives.

"I'm headed to the Stop and Rob," I called downstairs. "Does anyone need anything?"

The store wasn't really called that, of course; it had a perfectly normal name that I couldn't remember. "Stop and Rob" was more of a general term for a twenty-four-hour gas station and convenience store, a sobriquet earned in the days when the night-shift clerk had been left on his or her own with a till full of thousands of dollars. Technology—cameras, quick-drop safes that didn't open until daylight, and silent alarms—had made working the night shift safer, but they'd always be Stop and Robs to me.

"Ahrrrr." My husband Adam's voice traveled up the stairs. "Gold and women and grog!" He didn't play often, but when he did, he played full throttle and immersed.

"Gold and women and grog!" echoed a chorus of men's voices.

"Would you listen to them?" said Mary Jo scornfully. "Give me a man who knows what to do with what the good Lord gave him instead of these clueless scallywags who run at the first sight of a real woman."

"Ahrrrr," agreed Auriele, while Jesse giggled.

"Swab the decks, ye lubbers, lest you slide in the blood and crack your four-pounders," I called. "And whate'er ye do, don't trust Barbary Belle at your back."

There was a roar of general agreement, and Jesse giggled again.

"And, *Captain Larson*," I said, addressing Adam—my mate had taken the name from Jack London's *The Sea-Wolf*—"you can have gold, and you can have grog. You go after another woman, and you'll be pulling back a stub."

There was a little silence.

"Argh," said Adam with renewed enthusiasm. "I got me a woman. What do I need with more? The women are for my men!"

"Argh!" roared his men. "Bring us gold, grog, and women!"

"Men!" said Auriele, sweet-voiced. "Bring us a few good men."

"Stupidheads," growled Honey. *"Die!"*

There was a general outcry because, apparently, several some-ones did.

I laughed my way out the door.

After a moment's thought, I took Adam's SUV. I was going to have to figure out what to do for a daily driver. My beloved Vanagon Syncro was getting far too many miles put on her, and her transmission was rare and more precious than gold on the secondary market. I'd been driving her ever since my poor Rabbit had been totaled, and the van was starting to need more and more repairs. I'd looked at an '87 Jetta with a blown engine a few days ago. They wanted too much for it, but maybe I'd just have to pony up.

The SUV growled the couple of miles to the convenience store that was ten miles closer to home than any other store open at this hour of the night. The clerk was restocking cigarettes and didn't look up as I passed him.

I picked up two dozen overpriced eggs and three equally over-priced bags of chocolate chips and set them on the counter. The clerk turned away from the cigarettes, looked at me, and froze. He swallowed hard and looked away—scanning the bar codes on the eggs with a hand that shook so much that he might save me the effort of cracking the shells myself.

"You must be new?" I suggested, running my ATM card in the reader.

He knew who I was without knowing the important things, I thought.

I found the limelight disconcerting, but I was slowly getting used to it. My husband was Alpha of the local pack; he'd been a household name in the Tri-Cities since the werewolves first revealed their existence a few years ago. When we'd married, I'd gotten a little of his reflected glory, but after helping to fight a troll on the Cable Bridge a couple of months ago, I had become at least as well-known as Adam. People reacted differently to the reality of werewolves in the world. Sensible people stayed a certain length back. Others were stupidly friendly or not-so-stupidly afraid. The new guy obviously belonged to the latter group.

"Started last week," the clerk muttered as he bagged the chocolate chips and eggs as if they might bite him.

"I'm not a werewolf," I told him. "You don't have anything to fear from me. And my husband has put a moratorium on killing gas-station clerks this week."

The clerk blinked at me.

"None of the pack will hurt you," I clarified, reminding myself not to try to be funny around people who were too scared to know I was joking. "If you have any trouble with a werewolf or something like that, you can call us"—I found the card holder in my purse and gave him one of the pack's cards, printed on off-white card stock—"at this number. We'll take care of it if we can."

We all carried the cards now that we'd (my fault) taken on the task of policing the supernatural community of the Tri-Cities, protecting the human citizens from things that go bump in the night. We'd also been called in to find lost children, dogs, and, once, two calves and their guard llama. Zack had composed a song for that one. I hadn't even known he could play guitar.

Sometimes the job of protecting the Tri-Cities was more glamorous than others. The livestock call, in addition to being musically commemorated, had actually been something of a PR coup: photos of werewolves herding small lost calves back home had gone viral on Facebook.

The clerk took the card as if it were going to bite him. "Okay," he lied.

I couldn't do any better than that, so I left with my cookie-making ingredients. I hopped into the SUV and set the bag on the passenger seat as I backed out of the parking space. Frowning, I wondered if his strong reaction might be due to something that had happened to him—a personal incident. I looked both ways before heading out onto the road. Maybe I should go talk to him again.

I was still worrying about the clerk when there was a loud noise that stole my breath. The bag with the eggs in it flew off the seat, and something hit me with a loud bang and a foul smell—and then there was a sharp pain, followed by . . . nothing.

I THINK I WOKE UP SEVERAL TIMES, FOR NO MORE THAN a few minutes that ended abruptly when I moved. I heard people talking, mostly the voices of unfamiliar men, but I couldn't understand what they were saying. Magic shimmered and itched. Then a warm breath of spring air drifted through the pain and took it all away. I slept, more tired than I ever remembered being.

When I finally roused, awake and aware for real, I couldn't see anything. I might not have been a werewolf, but a shapeshifting coyote could still see okay in very dim light. Either I was blind, or wherever I was had no light at all.

My head hurt, my nose hurt, and my left shoulder felt bruised. My mouth was dry and tasted bad, as if I'd gone for a week without brushing my teeth. It felt like I'd just been hit by a troll—though the left-shoulder pain was more of a seat-belt-in-a-car thing. But I couldn't remember . . . even as that thought started to trigger some panic, memories came trickling back.

I'd been taking a run to our local Stop and Rob—the same all-night gas station slash convenience store where I'd first met lone and gay werewolf Warren all those years ago. Warren had worked out rather well for the pack . . . I gathered my wandering thoughts and herded them down a track that might do some good. The difficulty I had doing that—and the nasty headache—made me think I might have a concussion.

I considered the loud bang and the eggs and realized that it hadn't been the eggs that had exploded and smelled bad, but the SUV's air bags. I was a mechanic. I knew what blown air bags smelled like. I didn't know what odd effect of shock made me think it might have been the eggs. The suddenness of the accident had combined the related events of the groceries' hitting me and the air bag's hitting me into a cause and effect that didn't exist.

As my thoughts slowly achieved clarity, I realized that the SUV had been struck from the side, struck at speed to have activated the air bags.

With that information, I reevaluated my situation without moving. My face was sore—a separate and lesser pain than the headache—and I diagnosed the situation as my having been hit with an air bag or two that hadn't quite saved me from a concussion or its near cousin. The sore left shoulder wasn't serious, nor was the general ache and horrible weariness.

Probably all of my pain was from the accident . . . car wreck, I supposed, because I was pretty sure it hadn't been an accident. The vehicle that hit me hadn't had its headlights on—I would have remembered headlights. And if it had been a real accident, I'd be in the hospital instead of wherever I was. Under the circumstances, I wasn't too badly damaged . . . but that wasn't right.

I had a sudden flash of seeing my own rib—but though I was sore, my chest rose and fell without complication. I pushed that memory back, something to be dealt with after I figured out where I was and why.

My body was convinced that my current location was in a room-sized space despite the pitch-darkness. The floor was . . . odd. Cool—almost cold—and smooth under my cheek. The coolness felt good on my sore face, but it was robbing my body of warmth. Metal. It didn't smell familiar—didn't smell strongly of anything or anybody, as if it had been a long time since it was put to use, or it was new.

A door popped open. A light clicked on, making all of my speculations moot, because illumination was suddenly effortless. I was in a room that looked for all the world like a walk-in freezer—all shiny, silvery surfaces. I'd jerked when the door opened, so it was no good trying to pretend to be unconscious. The next-best thing would be facing whoever it was on my own two feet.

I rolled over in preparation for doing that very thing, but before I could do more, I had a sudden and unexpected bout of dry heaves that did my head no good at all. When I lifted my head and wiped my mouth with the back of my hand, I noted that there were two men standing in the doorway, frowning at me. Neither had made any move to help or—at least that I noticed—reacted at all.

I dry-heaved a couple of extra times to give myself a chance to examine the invaders of my walk-in-freezer cell.

The nearest man was tuxedo-model beautiful, with dark, curling hair, liquid-brown eyes, and a thousand-dollar suit that managed to show off the muscles beneath without doing anything so crass as being tight anywhere. There was something predatory in his gaze, and he had that spark that made one man more dominant than another without a word being said.

I'd been raised by werewolves. I knew an Alpha personality when I was in its presence.

The other man was at least fifty pounds heavier and three inches taller, with the face of a boxer or a dockworker. His nose had been broken a few times, and over his left eye was the sort of scar that you got when someone punched you in the eye and the skin around the socket split.

The pretty man radiated power, but this one . . . this one gave me nothing at all.

His eyes were brown, too, but they were ordinary eyes except for the expression in them. Something very cold and hungry looked out at me. He wore worn jeans and a tight-fitting Henley-style shirt.

Visually, I could have been dropped into a scene in some Italian gangster movie. There was no mistaking the Mediterranean origins of either one.

My nose told me the real story. Vampires.

I was on my hands and knees, but standing up wasn't going to help me fight off a pair of vampires, so I stayed where I was for a moment.

I was wearing my own clothes, but they were torn and stiff with my own dried blood—and that blood smelled like it was at least a day old. An unfamiliar, plain gold cuff around my wrist covered a nagging ache I hadn't noticed before I moved. I reached up to make sure of what I was already pretty sure of—there was no necklace there. That meant I was missing my wedding ring, Adam's dog tag, and my lamb—my symbol of faith that helped protect me from vampires.

I was missing something else. Something that mattered a lot more.

"She doesn't need this in here," said the vampire with the broken nose. He reached out and did something that released the cuff on my wrist. The skin all the way around my wrist was marked with puffy red dots, as if a mosquito had bitten me in even increments.

I very carefully didn't move.

"You'll have to forgive us," said the beautiful vampire as he crouched down in front of me. The British crispness of his voice was only a little softened by his Italian accent. "We were told you were the most dangerous person in the Tri-Cities and gave you the courtesy of treating you as such." And he kept nattering on about injuries and a healer and blah blah blah.

I tried to reach out to Adam through our mate bond and touched . . . emptiness. Silence had fallen between us, not the electric, expectant kind. This silence was the emptiness that falls in the dead of night in the middle of a Montana winter when the world is encased in snow and icy cold, a silence that engulfed my soul and left me alone.

"—find you," he was saying. "The witch's bracelet blocked your inconvenient tie with your pack and mate until we could get you into our room here, where no magic can pass. If we had real-ized how fragile you were, steps would have been taken to devise a gentler method of extraction."

I only cared about the "no magic can pass" part. If it was some sort of barricade magic or a circle, then this . . . silence was tem-porary, brought on by the cuff and continued by some effect of this location. Until I got out of this room, or possibly out of some outer enclosure, I wouldn't be able to contact Adam using our bond. The imperative and hope I held on to firmly was "out."

I was alive, I thought as I fought down the panic of the blank-ness where my mate should have been. Alive was a very good thing. If they had wanted me dead, I'd have been dead, and there was nothing I could have done about it.

I considered the word I'd heard earlier—"healer"—and the image of my own rib out where it had no business being and had a moment of wow. The only healer I'd ever seen who could do something like that was Baba Yaga.

Very good. I was alive. I narrowed my eyes at the two vampires.

They were the ones who had gone to a lot of trouble (apparently—judging by all the talking the pretty vampire was doing) to get me here. They could tell me what they wanted, then I could figure out how to get out and reestablish contact with Adam.

I gave a momentary thought to what Adam would have done when our link went dark. I had to trust he had dealt with it.

It was more than time to start making some plans. If I had been sure my legs would hold me, I'd have stood up then, but whatever they'd given me, the healing, or the accident, or some combination of the three had left me pretty wobbly.

Trying to stand up and falling on my rump would leave me in

a worse negotiating position than simply staying where I was. So I sat, grateful that I hadn't actually thrown up, which wouldn't have done my dignity any more good.

I was all poised to wait for them to speak when something else the pretty vampire had said right at the first hit me.

"What idiot told you *I* was the most dangerous person in the Tri-Cities?" I said incredulously. "There are *goblins* who could take me without working up much of a sweat."

That was maybe a little bit of an exaggeration, but not much. Goblins were a lot tougher than they were credited with by those who knew them. They were in the habit of running first, second, and third, and only fighting when there was no way out. That running thing had garnered them a reputation as supernatural wimps, a reputation they actively cultivated. When they were cornered, they were vicious and deadly. We had only recently started working with them, and I'd developed a new respect for their abilities.

"Perhaps he didn't mean 'powerful' and 'dangerous' in the usual way," suggested the thuggish vampire mildly. Like Pretty Vampire, his speech had a touch of British enunciation, colored with Italian that was more of a hint than a real accent. Despite the fact that it was my question he addressed, he wasn't talking to me. His attention was on Pretty Vampire. "Wulfe is subtle, and he often gives correct answers that lead to the wrong conclusions. Someone should have broken him of that habit a long time ago."

Wulfe. Wulfe, I knew. He was the right-hand vampire of Marsilia, who ruled the vampire seethe in the Tri-Cities. He was the scariest vampire I've ever met—and by now I'd met a few real contestants for that honor—but Wulfe could work magic, was crazy powerful, and unpredictable. Like just now, for instance. What in the world had I done to him to make him paint a target on my back and send Thug Vampire and Pretty Vampire after me?

Unlike his cohort, Pretty Vampire spoke directly to me. "You are the mate of the Alpha of the Tri-Cities werewolf pack, who just negotiated a deal with the fae that turned your little conglomerate town of the Tri-Cities in the *retroterra* of eastern Washington State into a safe zone for dealing with the fae," said Pretty Vampire.

"We like the term 'neutral zone' better than 'safe zone,'" I told him. "It sounds less judgmental and more businesslike." Also more *Star Trek*–ish.

My stepdaughter called it a freak zone, which I thought the most accurate description. A number of the fae who had returned to or who visited the Tri-Cities did so without glamour now— they'd quit trying to pretend to be human. Our summer tourist season, usually driven by the wineries, was looking to be the largest in anyone's memory.

I hadn't missed the little bit of Italian that Pretty Vampire had thrown out. A lot of vampires had accents, especially the old ones. Vampires, like werewolves, had their origins in Europe. Among the vampires, being American was a confession of youth and weakness—so none of them was too eager to lose their accent.

I was starting to get a really bad feeling about these two vampires. Okay, being kidnapped had already given me a really bad feeling, but this was worse. If these guys were actually from Italy— recently from Italy—well, I knew of one Italian vampire that was really, *really* bad news. I wondered if Marsilia knew that there were strange vampires from her homeland trespassing in her territory. I was very much afraid that the answer was no.

It had become the job of the pack to investigate supernatural visitors, but I knew darn well that Marsilia kept herself apprised of everyone's comings and goings, too. If she hadn't notified the pack before the Italian vampires trashed Adam's SUV (and me), she probably hadn't known about them.

"You are the mate," said Pretty Vampire again, pulling me away from my racing thoughts. "You aren't a werewolf, as we had assumed. Werewolves bounce back from a little thing like a car wreck a lot faster than you did. Happily, our people on the street acted quickly when they realized you were dying, or we wouldn't be having this pleasant conversation."

"Happily," I agreed blandly.

"So why does Wulfe think you are so powerful?" he asked, an edge in his voice.

I widened my eyes at him and did my best to look helpless. "I have no idea. I'm a VW mechanic," I told him. And I showed him my hands as proof. I tried to wear gloves, when I thought about it, but dirty oil was ingrained into every crack and crevice, and my knuckles were scarred pretty good. "I'm the first one to admit that fixing old cars is a superpower, but it's only important if you have a bus or bug you want to get fixed."

He hit me. One moment he stood just inside the door of the walk-in freezer, six feet away from me. Then he moved so fast I hadn't seen his hand move, just felt the effects on my jaw. It laid me out on my side.

I'm pretty sure I blacked out for a moment because I dropped right into an argument that seemed to have been going on for a while. I couldn't tell what they were arguing about because they did it in Italian.

I half opened my eyes to watch their body language and was

pleased to find I was right. No matter how dominant Pretty Vampire was, it was Thug Vampire who was running the show. Radiating nothing in the presence of power is a sign of even more power. Thug Vampire pushed Pretty Vampire all the way out of the room without touching him. Pretty Vampire bowed and kowtowed apologetically as he backed up.

Thug Vampire returned alone and knelt beside me. His hand was warmer than the metal floor as he slid it under my shoulder and up against my face. He lifted me off the floor, my face carefully cradled against the front of his shirt.

I could have done without his picking me up. Vampires are evil. They are scary, and I don't like being carried around by them when I'm half-conscious. I sucked in air and tried really hard to stay conscious when dizziness threatened to make me totally helpless. Again.

He walked toward the door, then paused.

"Almost," he murmured, "I would take you out where you could be made comfortable. But you and I should negotiate before your so-famously-volatile mate figures out where you are, eh?"

He called out something in Italian, and there was the sound of scurrying, then two unfamiliar vampires carried a Victorian-style sofa, complete with purple velvet upholstery, into the room. They looked like normal people—but I could smell what they were.

He must have had them waiting. He'd had no more intention of taking me out of the cell than he had of running naked into the dawn to be turned to ash. He'd pretended he was going to take me outside, that outside would reduce his ability to negotiate with me. Why? Vampires think sideways. Old vampires think upside down with a widdershins spin.

"That is better," he said, setting me down on the sofa in a sitting position. He held out his hand, and one of the furniture-carrying vampires gave him an emergency cold pack, the chemical kind. He shook it, then put it into my hand and indicated that I should hold it against my cheek.

"Guccio forgot that you are not a trespasser or miscreant we are interrogating," he told me. "He doesn't have much experience with politics, so perhaps I expected too much from him. Who are you, Mercedes Athena Thompson Hauptman, and why did Wulfe tell me that you were the power we should contact to begin negotiations in the Tri-Cities?"

"Contact," I said, holding the bag to my face, still trying desperately not to pass out. My ears were ringing, and my vision was spotty, so I was proud of the steadiness of my voice. "Contact. Hmm. Full-body contact makes for an interesting negotiating technique. Diplomatic, even, like the discussions that the CIA's well-known negotiation and waterboarding team conducts." My voice was steady, but I was babbling. I shut up as soon as I noticed.

"My apologies," he said sincerely, without meaning the words in the least. "As Guccio told you, misled by Wulfe's information, we did not expect you to be so fragile."

It was still my head that hurt the most, but my jaw was now a close second. The whole slap thing and argument had been for show, I decided. If Pretty Vampire—Guccio—had been as out of control as they were pretending, I'd have had a broken neck or, at the very least, jaw. So what . . .

Horrified, I realized that they were playing good vampire/bad vampire. Bad Vampire had been sent away, and I was supposed to feel like Good Vampire was my friend. Just how dumb did they think I was?

Good Vampire, formerly known as Thug Vampire, made a soft, sympathetic sound and sat down next to me, his body turned toward mine in an intimate, sheltering way. "It looks like it hurts, poor *piccola*. That's all you needed, one more bruise."

I straightened, scooted away from him, and dealt with the resulting dizziness. I needed to be sharp, and I was anything but.

Vampires weren't fae, who always had to tell the truth. I could tell when a human was telling a lie—but, in general, the older the creature, the better liar they were. If he wanted to negotiate with my pack, any kind of negotiate, kidnapping me had been the wrong move. If he was who I thought he was, doing it wrong was highly unlikely. So maybe negotiation wasn't what he was after.

Wulfe had told them I was powerful. Wulfe knew them better than I. So why would Wulfe have picked me out?

And all the while I tried to figure out the vampires, some part of me was frantically beating at the silence in my head where the pack should have been. Where *Adam* was supposed to be.

"*Piccola*," said Good Vampire, his voice soft and chiding. Apparently he thought that I should have leaned against him and let him take care of me instead.

Why had Wulfe told him I was the most powerful person in the Tri-Cities? Vampires lied all the time—but Wulfe was more like the fae. It amused him to always tell the truth and make people believe it was a lie until it was too late.

Most powerful person in the Tri-Cities . . . hmm. Well, maybe so, if your perspective was skewed enough—and "skewed" was a good word for Wulfe. I decided it was also the kind of power that would keep me alive for a while longer and so should be shared with Good Vampire. Staying alive was the first task of any hostage.

"I am Adam Hauptman's mate," I told the vampire. I didn't

meet his eyes. My coyote shapeshifting was accompanied by an unpredictable resistance to some kinds of magic. Vampire magic especially had a hard time with me—but it wasn't anything as reliable or useful as immunity.

Good Vampire made an encouraging noise, but said, "We know that."

"Right. But it gives me power. There is this also: I was raised in the Marrok's pack, and his oldest son is a very close friend. Siebold Adelbertsmiter counts me as his family—and even the Gray Lords treat that old one with respect." They had, last I heard, finally found part of one of the fae who had trespassed against Zee. It had showed up on someone's dinner plate. "You might know him as the Dark Smith of Drontheim."

The vampire beside me didn't move a lot, but I caught it. He knew who Zee was all right, and, for the first time, was surprised and maybe a little impressed.

"I'm also a liaison of sorts," I continued as if I hadn't noticed. "The local police department turns to me when they need help with the supernatural elements in our territory. I may be fragile, but I stand on the shoulders of giants—which is, I expect, why Wulfe named me to you. Political power, not intrinsic power."

People would care if he hurt me was the subtext of my speech. I was pretty sure he heard it, but on the other hand, sometimes subtle wasn't as effective as shoving it in front of his face.

"The Marrok treats me as a daughter," I said, to that end. "My fae friend has killed to protect me. And my mate . . ." I tried to put it into words that were not a direct threat. "He would be very unhappy if I were hurt."

"The Marrok broke all ties with you and your pack," the vampire said.

I shrugged because that still hurt. "Yes. But that does not mean he would be indifferent if you hurt me. And Elizaveta Arkadyevna works for our pack." Elizaveta was powerful enough that her reputation should have drifted to the far corners of the earth. His lack of expression told me that he, at least, knew who she was. "So do the goblins." That last bit was probably not as impressive as it should have been, but it was true.

The vampire was quiet for a moment, then said, "You do not mention the vampire."

"Vampire?" I asked, clueless.

"The one who has you blood-bound to her," he said. "I tried to break the binding while you slept."

And suddenly I wasn't too busy to be terrified. I reached up and touched my neck with fingers that tried to shake. There were two puncture wounds in my neck.

I hate vampires . . . I hate vampires . . . I hate them.

This was the reason that vampires would never, ever be able to let the humans know about them. If a powerful enough vampire bit someone, especially more than once, that vampire could control them. They called it the Kiss. It was what allowed the Mistress or Master of a seethe to control the fledgling vampires who could not maintain sentience without feeding from a more powerful vampire. It is what allowed the maker to control his fledglings. A human who had been given the Kiss was a pet.

Thug Vampire had tried to make me his pet when I was unconscious and unable to defend myself.

"I could have done it anyway," he said. "But it would have killed the one you are bound to, and I'm not sure I want her dead." He smiled, reached up, and stroked my cheek.

I held myself where I was and didn't jump up and scream.

Mostly because I was certain that, dizzy as I still was, I'd land on my butt. But also because I thought that he was trying to work a bit of magic on me, and I wasn't sure I wanted him to know it wasn't effective. Tomorrow, his power might work just fine—but for right now, my quirky resistance to his magic was resisting for all it was worth.

"Love," the vampire said thoughtfully after a moment, "is the most powerful force in the world. You are loved by many. Wulfe is right, that is power. The vampire's hold on you was something you accepted, something you wanted. I could have broken it—but if I had, she would have died."

She? It dawned on me that he'd been using the wrong pronoun. The vampire I was tied to was Stefan.

This vampire thought . . . that I was tied to Marsilia. Who else would the mate of the pack Alpha be tied to but the Mistress of the seethe? He hadn't broken the bond because he wanted her alive. I was right. I was right. I knew who he was.

I knew who he was—and I was in real trouble. I could hear the blood pound in my ears frantically. Never a good thing when you are sitting next to a vampire.

"You are fond of her," he murmured. "You love her. You asked her for the bond, and that is why it is so strong."

There was something in the position of his body that told me that I didn't want him to talk about Marsilia to me. Something weird in his posture that spoke of jealousy.

I raised an eyebrow at him and answered him in an effort to change the topic. "Right now, I'm not too fond of you . . . Mr. Bonarata."

Iacopo Bonarata, the Lord of Night, head of the Milan, Italy, seethe, once lover of Marsilia, was the de facto leader of the

European vampires—and probably anywhere else he chose to travel. He wasn't the Marrok, who ruled because that was the best way to protect his people. He was just a scary bastard that none of the other vampires chose to challenge. He'd been unchallenged by anyone, as far as I could find out, at least since the Renaissance, when he rose to power as a very young and ambitious monster.

And *he* was jealous of my imaginary relationship with the Queen of the Damned, Marsilia.

Fortunately, my attempt to change the direction of the conversation seemed to have worked, and when I named him, the vampire threw back his head and laughed, a great booming laugh that invited me to join him.

For all that he wasn't pretty, he exuded a sexual bonhomie that was very powerful. The only thing I'd felt that was anything like it was when the fae tavern owner, Uncle Mike, turned on the charm. For Uncle Mike it was magic, and it had nothing to do with sex. The Lord of Night was all about sex and earthy things— but it was also magic.

He'd been using it on me subtly from the moment Pretty Vampire had left my cell, but when he laughed, the magic simply boiled out of him like an invisible fog.

I caught the shadow of its effect, intended or not. This magic should have enhanced the sexual pull of the Lord of Night. It brushed over me without affecting me overly much.

The vampire's sexual appeal was powerful even without magic—but, to me, he wasn't Adam. That meant that I could have appreciated him without temptation. He was also a vampire, and that doubled my resistance to his magic.

The Lord of Night sat next to me, waiting for me to start drooling over him.

For my part, I sat stiff and sore—and very worried about what he would do if he realized his magic had no effect on me. Would he attribute it to my tie with another vampire, or my tie to Adam and our pack, or would he figure out what I really was?

The vampires from my neck of the woods hated and feared what I was. The walkers, the children of the ancient ones, hunted down a lot of vampires in the American frontier during the eighteenth and nineteenth centuries. They ultimately failed, and the vampires exterminated most of my kind.

I didn't know if Bonarata, who'd been in Italy for the whole time, felt the same way. If he even knew about what my kind could do. If he did, he might kill me out of hand rather than . . . whatever else he had planned for me.

But I could not make myself relax into him. There were some things I could not do—and pretending to be attracted to Bonarata was one of those things.

I didn't want him to know what I was. I didn't want him to know that the blood bond—created, ironically enough, to keep me safe from another vampire—tied me to my friend Stefan and not Marsilia, because I wasn't sure how he'd react.

"So," the vampire was saying while I thought furiously about the dangers of unpredictable, psychotic, obsessed, immortal vampires. "You know who I am. That is good. You may call me Jacob. Iacopo is difficult for my American friends, so I have recently changed my name to the English version."

Apparently he was choosing to ignore the way I wasn't reacting to his magic. That didn't mean he backed it off.

"This was supposed to be a simple meeting." His voice was seductive. Not beautiful, but deeply, richly masculine in a way that owed nothing to magic. "I desire to have a place where others would be comfortable meeting with me. When you created such a space, it seemed that some useful agreement could be made between your pack and my people. We meant to take you somewhere that we could talk, but your condition meant we had to take you for longer than we meant to. Somehow, I think that your Alpha will not react well to this." Nearly every word out of his mouth was a lie. He must have thought that since I wasn't a werewolf, I wouldn't be able to tell. Either that, or maybe that I would be too far under his influence to notice.

He smiled a charming smile. "You know him best. How do *you* think I should proceed?"

"You should let me go," I told him instantly. "And never come back to the Tri-Cities."

His smile widened, but his eyes remained cool. "Try again."

I shrugged. "I don't know what you want. I fix cars. For hammering out interspecies treaties, your tools are better than mine."

"You make a very good hostage," he said. I was pretty sure he was noticing that I wasn't panting after him as I should have been because there was a hint of irritation in his voice. Hopefully he'd credit my bond to another vampire; sometimes, Stefan had told me, such a bond could work that way. "Don't you think that your mate will bargain to get you back?"

"Werewolves have a long memory," I told him. I didn't want to answer the question because the answer was yes, so I skirted it, like a politician up for election. "And they are regrettably straightforward. The wolves are not fae to hold to bargains they view as forced. Holding me hostage is not going to help you in the long run." Flattery was usually a good tactic with old creatures. It never had worked on the Marrok, but he was more honest with himself about what he was than most people are. "But you already know that," I told the vampire. "I suspect you already have something planned."

He smiled again. It was supposed to be sexy, and it was. But he smelled like a vampire to me—and I had Adam.

"I could kill you and try again," he offered gently.

And like turning a valve, he shut off the magic he'd been using to influence me.

Maybe I should have pretended to be interested in him, but vampires have better-than-human noses. Most people who are attracted to someone don't stink of terror and stress. I wasn't a bad actor, but I could not have disguised my reaction to sitting this close to the Lord of Night. If I'd tried, I'd probably have thrown up on him.

He pursed his lips. "You aren't doing this right," he informed me. "You need to convince me that leaving you alive is in my best interests. What can you do for me? What information can you provide to me to advance my goals?"

I rolled my eyes. "I think you screwed the pooch when you hit my car and kidnapped me. You'll have to figure your own way out of this one or wait until my head doesn't hurt."

He leaned into me. His body was warm—and all I could think about was how much blood he'd had to consume to raise his body temperature to a few degrees warmer than human.

"Poor little one," he crooned, cupping my face. "It was not my intention to hurt you."

I really wasn't myself. I am generally very good about accommodating megalomaniacal egomaniacs and waiting until it was safe to torment them. I had grown up doing that. But my head hurt, and he was creeping me out.

"Epic failure," I told him. "I'll have you know that I expect my archenemies to be competent."

He laughed, and I forgot to breathe because he was so scary. All that joyous sound and the empty eyes. The seduction had failed—the terrifying, not so much. It wasn't magic. It was just him.

"I do want a deal with Hauptman's pack," he said. "It is good for you that I don't think he'd forgive me for killing you. Werewolves are sentimental that way. But it would be easy enough to kill you—and kill him. His second might be grateful."

I met his gaze steadily and said, "I don't think he would."

Vampires cannot tell truth from lies the way werewolves (and I) can. But the older ones can usually sort it out anyway. Darryl would not deal with someone who killed Adam. I was certain of it, and I let the vampire know.

He smiled faintly. There was the sound of a polite knock on the door.

"Come," he said.

The werewolf who entered was a surprise, and she shouldn't have been. I knew that he had exiled Marsilia for feeding from his werewolf mistress. He and Marsilia were still lovers at the time—and that probably had made for added complications. I had the impression that Marsilia's feeding from the werewolf had some deeper vampire meaning, like maybe she'd been trying to claim the werewolf for herself. I'd been told once that the whole event had to do with Marsilia disapproving of Bonarata keeping a werewolf. Werewolf blood was apparently more enticing than human, and the implication I'd gotten was that the Lord of Night was addicted.

The woman who entered the room was beautiful. Strong features were arranged symmetrically, but there was no extra flesh on her face at all, so the total effect was fragile. Her hair was dark and formally arranged in something that was far too elaborate to be called a bun. The hair artfully left loose showed signs of being naturally curly.

She wore a white silk dress that made it clear that she was naked beneath it—and that she was too thin. The white fabric contrasted with the honey gold of her complexion and brought out the scars, small white blemishes that might have been pock-marks . . . or the reminders of where fangs had broken her skin.

She wore a silver collar, but it couldn't have been real silver because the only scars on her neck were from fangs.

"Lenka," said the vampire, and she flinched and glanced up.

Her eyes were werewolf gold—a sign that she was quite, quite lost to her wolf.

She started to speak. I thought it was Italian, but I don't know it, so it could have been Romanian or some other Latin language that wasn't Spanish or French.

He made a chiding noise. "Be polite," he said. "Our guest speaks only English."

She glanced at me with those wild eyes. "He is mine," she said, her voice as clear and precise as if she'd been born in London.

"Lenka," the Lord of Night purred, "do I have to punish you?"

Her eyes dropped to the ground, and she shivered, smelling of fear and arousal at the same time. I wondered if he knew that there was nothing human left to her, and the only thing that made us safe from her was that her wolf was utterly broken.

"You have a phone call," she said, her voice subdued.

"Ah," he said, "I've been expecting this call. You'll have to excuse me." He wrapped his hand around the werewolf's upper arm and escorted her out. He paused and looked back at me. "I will leave Lenka to guard the door. I assume that you, mate to an Alpha werewolf, understand that without me present, she will be quite unable to stop herself from attacking and killing you. As a favor to me, who values her, I ask that you not make me put her down for spoiling my plans."

He shut the door behind him and did not lock it.

I knew only two things for certain. First, Bonarata had lied about a lot of what he told me. Second, he very much wanted me to run through that carefully unlocked door.

I stared at the door thoughtfully and glanced around.

I generally don't give megalomaniacal monsters what they want. But that unlocked door was an opportunity I could not pass up. I smiled grimly, ignoring the burn the expression caused in the muscles of my much-abused face. Then I stood and started stripping off my bloodstained clothes in preparation to run for my life.

2

ADAM

For Adam, it began during that game of The Dread
Pirate's Booty. You can decide for yourself if he handled
my unexpected involuntary absence well or not.

ADAM FELT A FLASH OF PAIN THAT HAD HIM STAGGER-
ing to his feet, heedless of the monitor that crashed to the ground,
because it wasn't his pain—it was Mercy's. As the echo of that
flash hit the pack bonds a breath later than it had hit his mating
bond, he sensed the readiness that shivered through the pack as
they also rose, alarmed, alert, and awaiting his orders.

"What happened? Is it an accident?" Darryl asked. "Is she okay?"

His Mercy was fragile in body if not in spirit. Fragile by werewolf standards, anyway. The whole pack was aware of her vul-
nerability and driven to protect her to a degree that would infuriate
his wife if she knew about it.

"Not good," Adam said decisively, used to covering terror with logic and action. He started for the stairs. "I'll—"

Then silence fell in place of the pain.

The next thing he knew, Adam's shoulder hit the front door, knocking the sturdy (and expensive) steel door out of its frame and sending it flying out of his way. The wolf wouldn't allow him to stop for a car, instinctively knowing that he'd be faster on his own feet.

Adam braced himself to fight off the change—because that, too, would slow him down until he was finished shifting completely. But the wolf didn't try to do anything but give his feet more speed as he sprinted down the driveway and onto the road toward the last place they'd felt Mercy. Dimly, he sensed the pack running flat out behind him, heard the sound of engines—some of the more practical-minded figuring that a car or two might come in handy.

Cold sweat that had nothing to do with the effort of his muscles and everything to do with the way his mate bond ended in nothingness slid down his back as he pushed his body for another ounce of swiftness. His heart beat so hard that he could barely hear the footsteps of his pack.

He smelled the accident before he could see it. Diesel fuel, air bag, her blood—

There was a moment of time that was forever blank after he smelled her blood.

He came to himself standing on the hood of the remains of his SUV, staring into the empty cab. A semi tractor had entwined itself in the glossy black body of the SUV. The glass of the SUV was shattered, and something very strong had torn out the steering wheel to get to Mercy. Her seat belt was cut, and there was too much blood in the seat. Blood, broken eggs, and chocolate chips.

His human half fumbled a second, wondering if the person

who had freed Mercy had been him, because he couldn't remember. But Mercy was gone, and his wolf knew better.

Someone had been here ahead of them.

Someone had hit Mercy with a semitruck, then stolen her away from them.

They had left her purse, small and tidy because Mercy didn't like to be weighed down by anything big. It lay unopened on the passenger seat.

Adam leaned forward until his head was through the broken window and inhaled deeply. Along with the scent of Mercy's blood, raw eggs, and himself, he found the scents of four vampires. Vampires. Three of them were strangers. The fourth . . .

He turned his attention to the semi that had T-boned the SUV Mercy had been driving. He jumped easily from the SUV to the semi-tractor door, finding hand- and footholds in the damaged metal side that allowed him to open the door to examine the interior. When the door proved too bent to open, he simply drove his fist through the glass, gripped the door, and ripped it off. The sting of pain as the glass sliced his hand was oddly seductive—so much less painful than what was going on in his heart and his head at the moment.

His first find was that the tractor was new despite a very bad paint job. He took a better look at the outside and saw that someone had painted the whole tractor matte black, including surfaces that had probably originally been chromed and shiny. This vehicle had been painted so that it could be used to take Mercy totally by surprise. She might have heard the engine—though since she was driving his own diesel SUV, maybe not.

He could smell the vampire who'd driven the tractor over the leather and the new-car scent. That vampire had been hurt in the crash; there was a bit of blood somewhere. But he had not been killed or seriously injured. There was no smell of stress—fear, anger, excitement. Even vampires left the scents of their emotions behind. Most of them. That meant that this vampire had done such things before.

A professional. A vampire who specialized in accidents for assassinations or kidnapping. He fought the eagerness with which he wanted to embrace the idea of a kidnapping. He had to keep to the facts—and the amount of blood in the SUV meant that unless she had gotten immediate and professional emergency care, Mercy was in serious trouble.

He snarled, his lips pulling back from his teeth in helpless fury. She could be dying, and his mate bond could not tell him where she was or how she was. The only thing that kept him from surrendering to the wolf who needed something to kill, to destroy, was that he had not felt her die. She was just gone. He would assume that she was alive and needed him until there was proof that said otherwise.

"Adam," called Darryl's strained voice. "You should come here."

Adam looked through the driver's-side window and saw the pack gathered around something on the ground on the side of the road. He opened the driver's-side door and hopped to the ground. As he approached, the wolves—most of them midchange thanks to his wild flare of emotion—backed away from him, and he got a good look at the body on the ground.

He bent his knees and examined Stefan—the single vampire whose scent he'd recognized. The wolf fought to kill their rival, but Adam reined that part of himself in with cold truth. Like him, Stefan had a bond with Mercy. Likely that was what had drawn him here. Maybe Stefan could find Mercy when Adam could not.

And Mercy, not jealousy or rivalry, is what is important.

At that firm reminder, the raging violent spirit inside of him

settled. The wolf was a hunter; he understood patience. And even
the wolf could not doubt that his Mercy was *his*. Jealousy had no
place between them. Terror for her safety, yes. But not jealousy.

Stefan's eyes opened and, for a moment, they were empty of
personality, the eyes of a dead man. Then his face filled with
expression, and Adam saw the mirror of his own rage and fear.
The vampire exploded to his feet, turning in a circle to take in the
wolves who surrounded him.

Adam rose more slowly. Stefan wasn't going to hurt him, and
it would do no harm under the circumstances to keep his own
movements under control. The wolf wasn't fighting him, but the
beast was a cunning enemy, and if he had misread the wolf, Adam
didn't want Stefan paying the price.

Not when he could be the key to finding Mercy.

"Mercy?" Stefan asked Adam.

"Gone," Adam said, fighting down despair. It wasn't time for that
yet. But if Stefan had to ask the question, then his blood bond with
Mercy was doing him no more good than Adam's own mating bond.

He gave the vampire the information he had. "They hit her car
and took her. It looks well planned and professional at this point.
They are vampires—and not Marsilia's vampires." He paused.
"I've never heard of a professional team of kidnappers or assassins
who were vampires."

"There are some, but they keep a low profile." Stefan rubbed
his face with brisk hands, more as if something about it troubled
him than a simple gesture of weariness.

"I felt the wreck," he told Adam. "I imagine you did, too?" He
didn't wait for an answer. "I came to this place immediately and
found them already working to get her out of the SUV."

Stefan could teleport—a quirk of the magic that allowed a dead man to live. The Marrok's son Charles kept a database of vampires and their abilities. He'd told Adam that teleportation was rare. That both Stefan and Marsilia could do it might indicate that they were Made by the same vampire or vampires of the same lineage. Or not.

The vampire continued to speak. "I was focused on Mercy, or else I might have thought to look for more of the enemy. I jumped in to defend her, and someone caught me from behind with a jumped-up Taser, I think, given the results." He rubbed his face again.

"Can you tell where she is?" Adam asked tersely, though he was pretty sure of the answer. If Adam could teleport, and he had a clear signal to where Mercy was, he wouldn't be hanging around talking. He expected that Stefan felt the same.

The vampire raised his chin and closed his eyes, a sign of the trust he had that the wolves would not attack while he left himself vulnerable—or that he thought he could defend himself without watching his foe. Maybe some combination of the two. Though he didn't need to, the vampire took a deep breath.

When he opened his eyes, he met Adam's gaze with a bleak expression. "No," he said. "I can't feel her at all."

"Do you know who took her?" Adam asked.

Stefan shook his head. "Vampires, but they weren't anyone I've seen before. Not local."

"What kind of vehicle did they drive?" asked Darryl.

"They had a helicopter," Stefan said.

The wolf remembered hearing a helicopter, though Adam hadn't paid much attention at the time. Helicopters had become less notable the past few months because the cherry farmers employed them during and after rainstorms to help dry the cherries before the rain caused the fruit to swell and split. Cherry season was just over, and in a month or two, he'd have noticed a helicopter.

"I heard it," said Warren, who had taken his own look around the wreck. "But I only caught a glimpse of it while I was running here. They were flying without lights, boss. They were headed south, but they didn't land before the sound of the helicopter was too faint for me to hear."

No telling where the helicopter had been going, then. It could be five miles away or a hundred. The semi was probably stolen, but a helicopter and a team of professionals meant that someone had paid a lot of money to take his mate.

A wolf howled from the twenty-acre field on the other side of a wall of desiccated arborvitae.

"Sent them out looking for where the chopper was waiting," Darryl said.

Ben ran up, breathless and in his human form. There were maybe four or five of Adam's pack who hadn't shifted to wolf.

"Looks like it had taken up a f—" Ben glanced behind Adam to Jesse and Aiden, who were huddled quietly where they weren't in the way but could still hear everything, and cleaned up his language. "—a freaking home base. There's a low spot behind a rise that would have kept anyone from seeing it. That chopper has been parked there often enough to leave a bare spot. More than a day or two. They've been waiting for a chance at Mercy for a while."

"Might have used magic to keep people away," Darryl suggested.

"A *look-away* would have done it," said Stefan. "Most of us can cast something like that."

"We can follow up on the semi," said Darryl. "And I have a friend who flies out of the Richland airport. He might know something about a strange helicopter."

It would take hours if not days to run down Mercy's kidnappers that way. The wolf was very unhappy with hours—and Adam wasn't cheery about it, either.

"She went to the store," Adam said abruptly. He hopped back on his SUV and stepped through the broken windshield to pull the receipt off the seat.

He saw Mercy's lamb first. The leather seat under the little gold lamb was scorched as if the charm had been hot when it landed there. Her necklace, broken, was on the floorboard, his dog tag from his time in 'Nam still on the chain. He found Mercy's wedding ring eventually, hidden under the open carton of broken eggs.

He climbed out of the cab with the receipt in one hand and Mercy's necklace components in the other.

Warren stood in front of the SUV, one hand on the hood. The old cowboy's eyes were yellow—he saw what Adam's other hand held. If not for his eyes, someone who didn't know him would have thought he was relaxed.

"Stands to reason they wouldn't let her keep that," he said, his voice thick with wolf and Texas. "Mercy's right deadly to vampires with that little lamb of hers. Better'n most people with crosses. If you give me the receipt, I'll go see what it tells us."

Adam decided that he himself should not be dealing with fragile humans who might hold some clue to who had taken Mercy just now. He frowned at Warren because he wasn't sure Warren should be doing it, either.

"I know the owner of the store," Warren said. "I promise I won't kill nobody who don't need killing, boss." Warren only lost his grammar when he was really, really upset.

Adam handed the paper scrap over without a word. Warren glanced at the printing and held it to his nose. He nodded at Ben.

Together, Ben and Warren jogged to one of the cars—Ben's. Warren slid into the passenger seat, leaving Ben to drive.

"Is it my fault?" asked a small voice.

Adam, still on the hood of the SUV, looked down at the newest member of his family. Aiden appeared as though he should be in elementary school, but he was centuries older than Adam himself. Jesse, who treated Aiden like a little brother, had her hand on his shoulder. One of the cars parked nearby was Jesse's.

"No," said Adam's daughter in a firm voice despite the stark fear in her eyes. "Even if they came looking for you, it's not your fault. And Mercy will be okay. You remember 'The Ransom of Red Chief' we read a few months ago? Anyone who kidnaps Mercy will regret it thoroughly before she's done with them." She sighed theatrically, acting nonchalant for Aiden, when Adam could feel her distress. "I suppose that Dad is too straightforward to demand payment to take her back, though I bet we could get enough money to pay for my college that way."

She was worried, but he could hear the confidence in her voice. She was still young enough to believe her father could fix anything.

Adam didn't tell Jesse what the pack knew. His daughter was human and couldn't smell the blood. He knew that Mercy would tell him that he wasn't accomplishing anything by trying to protect Jesse from the full truth. But Mercy would be wrong, because, like Aiden, he needed Jesse's optimism. Even if it was a false optimism.

"Mercy will make them pay," he told them, his throat tight. He looked at Aiden. "It wasn't your fault, Aiden. We claimed this city . . . these cities, and put them under the pack's protection because they are our home. You were the catalyst. You *and Mercy* were the catalyst that pushed us where we should already have been. If that was what *inspired*—" And he'd given that last word teeth, hadn't he? He took a breath and tried again. "If that was what inspired someone to take Mercy, it still is not your fault."

"I will burn them," Aiden said, and the wolf in Adam loosened its jaws in approval and recognition of another predator, one possibly more dangerous than he.

"If there is anything left after Mercy gets done with them," Jesse said coolly, "I might help you with that, Sprout." She looked at Adam. "Is there anything I can do?"

He started to shake his head, then stopped. There was no hiding the accident. It was very late, but in a half hour or so, the people who had to head to work in the wee small hours would start driving past.

"Call Tony and tell him about this." Adam was afraid that he wouldn't be able to keep his temper long enough to stay coherent. But Tony knew Jesse well enough to listen to her. "Tell him I'll give him the whole story as I discover it—but that it is supernatural and probably treading into too-dangerous-for-humans-to-know territory."

Tony was a cop, the unofficial liaison between the police and the werewolf pack. There was an official liaison who was pretty competent. But Tony knew more than was safe for a human already. If he hadn't been under pack protection, the vampires or the witches would have killed Tony by now. Adam intended to keep the official liaison safely ignorant of vampires.

Tony was trusted enough by his department that they took his word when he told them it was too dangerous to know but matters had been handled. That was satisfactory to everyone involved.

"Can do."

Jesse dug into the small purse that went everywhere with her. A cell phone rang as she did so, but it wasn't hers. Adam glanced in the direction of the noise.

Stefan reached into his pocket, pulled out the phone. Without looking at it, he threw it. It landed against the side of the broken SUV, denting the already battered metal. The phone exploded into powder.

The wolf thought that it was an interesting reaction in a man who appeared so calm. But then he suspected that his own aspect looked cool and controlled because soldiers learn early to hide intense emotion when among enemies—even enemies who are people you like. He and Stefan had both been soldiers.

Adam's phone rang, and he pulled it out, half-surprised it was still in its holder. He glanced at the number and almost refused the call but stopped himself.

Vampires, he thought. *They weren't hers, but they had been vampires.*

"Hello, Marsilia," he said in a basso growl that he couldn't stop.

There was a pause. "Either you are missing someone or I am," she said. "I have contacted everyone who belongs to me except Stefan. You should contact your people, too."

"Stefan is here," he ground out. "Mercy has been taken."

"I see," she said, and if she'd been there, he'd have torn her throat out for the calm in her voice. "I just received an e-mail from an ex-lover of mine indicating that he has taken someone from us. From our cooperative."

"Cooperative?" he asked softly. "What cooperative?"

If it was an ex-lover of Marsilia's, Mercy had probably been taken because of Marsilia. Not because of the pack. The guilt he bore vanished and left him unbalanced before a rush of anger filled the empty space guilt had left behind. For a moment, the emotional wave was too wild for him to listen to her or anyone else. Wolf stepped in where the human faltered.

"This isn't her fault," said Stefan's cool voice. "This is old business, and she didn't start it, werewolf. Listen to her if you want to save Mercy."

Adam realized he must have blanked out again because he was no longer on the hood of the SUV—and other than the vampire, there was a very large space all around him. Adam couldn't find it in himself to care that the werewolf had taken over to the point that he could not remember what he'd done. That he didn't care was a worse sign than losing that much control in the first place.

Stefan said, "If your people have to put you down because you choose not to control your beast, then Mercy will have one less person looking for her."

The vampire's words had been uttered in a cold voice, but Stefan's eyes were hot. For some reason, that rage allowed Adam to catch his balance a little.

Adam swept his hand toward the cab of the SUV and said what his heart had been screaming since he'd first seen the damage to the cab. "Mercy is wounded," he ground out. "Bleeding out. Vampires aren't going to keep her alive. That's not what they do."

"Dad?" Jesse said in a small voice, and part of him wished he'd guarded his tongue, because he'd been trying to protect her from that knowledge. But it was mostly the wolf speaking now, even if it did it in Adam's voice, and the wolf was an honest monster incapable of human subterfuge, even when the lie was to save his own child from pain.

"Mercy is a hostage," said Stefan, speaking slowly, as if Adam were hard of hearing—or as if he were speaking to a creature who didn't pay a lot of attention to mere words. "Like it or not, our two people, werewolves and vampires, are bound together here, in this place, as we must be for our mutual survival. Others have noticed this. If they wanted to leave a dead body behind, they would have already done it. This means our enemies will target you, and your enemies will target us. Murder would have been a lot easier. Vampires are pretty good at keeping humans alive." The vampire looked a little sick as he spoke that last sentence, so it wasn't as reassuring as he probably meant it to be.

"Why does he listen to Stefan, when none of the rest of us could get through?" Adam heard Auriele ask someone quietly.

"Because the vampire smells a little of Mercy," Darryl replied.

Adam snarled because it was true, then took a deep breath to draw in the scent again. If the vampire still smelled of Mercy, Adam decided, it was because Mercy was still alive. Mercy was alive, and he would believe that until presented with absolute proof that she was not.

Adam bowed his head, reasserted his, the human's, ownership of his own damned mouth, and looked at Stefan. "What does he want, this ex-lover of your Mistress?"

"Not my Mistress anymore," said Stefan, but with more sorrow than heat. "I don't know." He looked around to the pack, now mostly wolves, until his gaze landed near Darryl. "Any of you have a cell phone I can use?"

And that was when Adam noticed that his phone was crushed in his hand. Some of the glass was sticking into the flesh, which had healed over the top. He busied himself picking it out with his pocketknife while Stefan used Darryl's phone to call Marsilia.

The negotiations, conducted with Stefan as an intermediary, made Adam dangerously impatient.

Marsilia thought that inviting Adam to her house was not a good idea. Adam concurred with a grunt.

Entering the vampire's seethe meant confusing the immediate

issue with outdated manners and games that he was in no mood to play. There was no time. Dawn would arrive soon, and the vampires would retire to slumber or whatever they did during the day, taking the knowledge of who had Mercy with them.

As a compromise, Marsilia proposed Uncle Mike's Tavern, a traditional place for hostile or nearly hostile negotiations until it closed when the fae had retreated to their reservations because they thought that Underhill had reopened to them. When she proved less welcoming than they expected, they had backed down from their initial silence and began arrangements to make peace . . . or at least not war with the humans. As part of that trend, Uncle Mike's had reopened a few weeks ago.

Adam had no desire to involve the fae in pack business that was already ass deep in vampires, and he told them so.

"So where?" asked Stefan impatiently.

"Not my house," Adam said. "I have no intention of inviting Marsilia over my threshold. Once you invite a vampire into your house, it is very difficult to uninvite them. Easier to kill them."

Stefan, who had an open invitation to Adam's house, rolled his eyes. "Could you, please, for Mercy's sake, come up with somewhere acceptable? I might remind you that Marsilia doesn't share our fondness for your wife. She just doesn't like losing a chess piece, so she is cooperating. And our time is limited."

Marsilia would shoot Mercy as soon as look at her. Adam reined his wolf in and took over.

"My backyard," he said. Mercy had littered the backyard with picnic tables and various seating arrangements that were annoying when he mowed but otherwise aesthetically pleasing and useful.

Mercy was alive. Marsilia was offering to help. Marsilia had not hurt or taken Mercy. This was not her fault. It was time to use prudence and not rage. There was no sense in angering his allies.

To that end, he took a deep breath and prepared to be diplomatic. "While I cannot in good conscience invite Marsilia into the house, I don't believe she means harm to me, to my family, or to the pack. I also intend no harm for her. Ex-lovers," he said heavily, "are something I'm familiar with. I cannot blame Marsilia for the actions of hers, no matter how seductive that idea is. I do not believe this is her fault."

"I intended no harm to your wife or any who are yours," said Marsilia. No conversation on cell phones was private around a werewolf pack—or a vampire seethe. "We will meet in your backyard, and I will tell you what I know. It will take us twenty minutes."

TONY CAME WITH ANOTHER SOLEMN POLICE OFFICER and met the wrecker who pulled the cars off the road and took photos and made a vague report Adam could turn in to his car insurance. As if he cared. The important thing was that the vague report would keep the police safe.

Tony looked worried at all the blood and glanced at Adam. Then he asked Jesse, quietly, "Mercy?"

She shook her head. "We don't know. I'll tell you as soon as we do."

Warren and Ben pulled in just as the pack was leaving the scene to the police. Adam slid into the backseat and directed them home.

"The store was empty and unlocked when we got there," Ben said grimly. "Warren called the owner. He must live pretty close because he was there in just a couple of minutes."

"The clerk was new," Warren said. "Hired last week. The

address and ID he used were both fake—owner wasn't looking closely because he was shorthanded. Didn't smell like vampires in there. But vampires don't have any trouble getting humans to do their dirty work."

"I'd appreciate it if you keep after the clerk angle," Adam said. "Might lead somewhere."

"Sure thing, boss," Warren said.

The vampires beat Adam and the pack to his house. When Ben stopped the car and he got out, he could smell them.

His wolf wasn't happy with vampires just now, but Adam subdued the monster and walked around the house to the backyard.

Marsilia, Wulfe, and Stefan awaited him, seated in three chairs they'd pulled away from a table. Someone—probably Stefan—had moved three more chairs to face them.

Marsilia had elected to bring only those two out into the open with her, though doubtless she had other vampires scattered about. Adam lifted his head and scented the air.

Or maybe not.

He waved a hand and sent those pack members who'd come to the backyard with him into the house. Everyone obeyed except for Darryl.

Adam raised an eyebrow at the big black man who was his second. Someday in the not-too-distant future, Darryl was going to move on. He was ready for his own pack and was beginning to chafe under orders.

Adam wondered how they would manage to find a pack for Darryl when his pack had no more ties to the Marrok, who ruled the wolves. Traditional methods tended to leave bodies behind. It was a momentary thought, though, brought about because of Darryl's disobedience.

Adam's wolf wasn't worried. The future was what the future was, and for now, Darryl was still *his*. Darryl was smart; he would have a reason.

"We can agree on Stefan as neutral," Darryl said when he was within conversational distance. "We think that you should meet as equals, though. So you need a second with you."

He was right. Good to have a second who could think things through when all Adam really wanted to do was hunt down the vampires who had taken Mercy and obliterate them. Killing was too clean.

Impatiently, Adam nodded his agreement and took the seat opposite Marsilia. Darryl sat at his right, and the chair at his left stayed empty.

Marsilia was a real bombshell. Blond-haired Italians were never common, and he knew that the color was natural, because Stefan had commented upon it. But her beauty wasn't a thing of color only; it was bone- and muscle-deep.

Beautiful people, mostly, lived like everyone else. Extraordinarily beautiful people, however, usually paid dearly for their beauty. Adam was pretty sure that had been no less true in fifteenth-century Italy than it was now.

Intelligent brown eyes examined him—maybe for weapons, maybe for weaknesses. He didn't mind because he was doing the same. Though for both of them, what they were made them pretty efficient weapons all by themselves.

She was wearing slacks and some sort of silk top that left her arms and shoulders bare, covering her adequately otherwise while leaving no doubt that she wore no bra. She could have appeared on a news program or a Hollywood premiere in her outfit without attracting comment. She wore it like a woman who habitually used her body as a weapon rather than someone aiming a weapon at him personally. To her left sat Wulfe, who'd succeeded Stefan as her second-in-command when Stefan had left her seethe. Wulfe looked like a sulky punk rocker from the eighties, though maybe that look was back. Without Jesse's prodding, Adam tended to lose track.

Wulfe's pale hair stuck out in chick-soft-looking tufts about an inch long, whose ends were dyed pink. Wulfe was, in Adam's estimation, more dangerous than Marsilia if only because he was unpredictable.

Stefan, interestingly, sat on her right. Wolves pay attention to body language, and Stefan's body language was protective and worried.

"First," she said, "I have to apologize for the way in which my past has rained down upon you. It is no secret that Mercedes and I are not friends, but I value the role that she plays in our community, and I do not think that anyone else could balance the werewolves, the fae, and the vampires as well as she does."

"Differently," murmured Wulfe. "More interestingly even, but not as peacefully."

"Are you finished?" Marsilia inquired politely.

"Excuse me, Mistress," Wulfe said diffidently. "I was just enlarging upon what you said."

"Who took her?" asked Adam. He wasn't interested in apologies that she didn't mean.

"He did not sign his e-mail," Marsilia said. "But I recognize the wording. It was Iacopo Bonarata, the Lord of Night. He who rules the European vampires."

As soon as she had told him it was her ex-lover, Bonarata had been Adam's pick. First, Adam didn't know of any other ex-lovers of hers. He suspected that if she had other ex-lovers, they either served her or they were dead. Marsilia was as pragmatic a creature as any he'd ever met.

"Why?" Adam asked. "What does he want?" *How do we get my Mercy back alive?* He didn't say it because they all knew what he was asking.

"His e-mail did not say," Marsilia told him. "Knowing him, it could be any of a dozen reasons. He could be reacting to our killing of Frost, which he might see as an elevation of my power. He sent me here to rot, not to rise up through the ranks and rule North America."

"He knows you well enough, he should have thought of that as a possibility," Stefan told Marsilia.

"Not his business what anyone does here," said Adam. "He rules Europe."

Wulfe laughed. "Innocent," he told Adam. "I find it so droll that you are such an innocent." Then the silly affectations left his body, and he was softly menacing as he said, "Iacopo Bonarata has spider silk throughout the world. He owns corporations based in New York and Texas as well as Buenos Aires and Hong Kong. He has owned four of the last six presidents, though they did not know it. Any other vampire rising to power is a threat, and he does not deal well with threats."

"He is a Renaissance prince," said Marsilia, almost apologetically. "The last of his house, the rest of whom died during the Black Death. Control everything or die: it is how he was raised, how he thinks. I do not know that he understands words like 'content' or 'enough.'"

"He threw away something of great value," said Stefan. "Something he viewed as a work of art—and he knows it. He regrets it."

Marsilia turned her great dark eyes on Stefan. "Don't be ridiculous."

"He told me, the night we left for the New World, that if I became your lover, he would hunt me to the ends of the earth," Stefan said.

"If Iacopo were a dog in a manger," Wulfe said, "he would urinate and defecate in the hay. And before he would allow anyone to spread the hay on the ground to at least get use of it as fertilizer, Iacopo would light the hay on fire. And then he would sing about how wonderful the hay was and how tragic its loss."

"You carry that analogy a little too far," said Marsilia.

"It is accurate," Wulfe defended himself. "The song was in a minor key—and the painting he did, I am told, was nearly as stunning as you actually are."

"So why did he take Mercy?" Adam asked Marsilia. If someone didn't distract Wulfe, he was likely to lead the conversation all around the mulberry bush until there was no time left.

"Because I told him that she was the most powerful person in the supernatural community of the Tri-Cities," said Wulfe. "I think."

Adam's wolf lunged forward without warning, and he would have killed the vampire if Darryl and Stefan hadn't pulled him back. No one had grabbed for Marsilia.

"Oh, don't hold him back," Marsilia hissed. She had, Adam noted, lost her usual composure. She was out of her chair and had Wulfe's throat in one hand. "Much easier to explain why the werewolf killed him than if I did it."

Wulfe dangled from her hand, though he was taller than she was. He managed it by bending his knees. He had a wide, sappy grin on his face until Marsilia looked at him, then his grin fell away, and he watched her soberly, apparently not discomforted by his position at all.

"Why did you talk to Iacopo without telling me?" she asked.

"I talk to him all the time," Wulfe replied, his voice strained. "You know that. That's why he let me go with you."

Adam saw from her face that Wulfe was right. He took a step backward and shook Darryl off. Stefan let go more slowly. Marsilia would get more out of Wulfe than he could—and she might be able to restrain herself from killing him in the process. Adam wasn't sure he could manage it.

"What did he want when he asked you who the strongest of us was?" she asked.

"I don't know," Wulfe said. "Not exactly. I answer his questions; he doesn't answer mine."

"You *Made* him," she said.

Wulfe snorted. "I haven't been his Master for a very, very long time. Any more than he is yours."

"Why did you put Mercy forth as the most powerful of us?" asked Adam tersely.

Wulfe's silly grin returned. "Because it was funny." He sobered. "Because it was true." He looked at Marsilia. "Because if I'd answered the question the way he meant it, he'd have taken Adam. And he would have killed Adam, he couldn't have helped himself. Mercy . . . he won't see the threat Mercy is until she has his head on a pike. He doesn't understand that kind of strength. He cannot use his most powerful weapons on her because of what she is, and he has no experience to understand what she is."

Marsilia looked at Adam. "Are you satisfied? Is there anything else you'd like to know?"

It could, Adam knew, all be a play for his benefit, but he didn't read it that way. Wulfe was as twisty as a carousel pole, but Marsilia was scared. She was also brave and smart, so she was facing the situation head-on, but she was scared of Iacopo Bonarata.

"You didn't warn any of us," Adam said softly, addressing Wulfe.

"Where would the fun be in that?" Wulfe answered. But then he said soberly, "You don't know Iacopo the way I know Iacopo. If I had warned you . . ."

"The Lord of Night," said Stefan reluctantly, "is the reason Wulfe is the way he is, Adam. He wasn't always . . ."

"Crazy?" suggested Darryl.

"No," said Marsilia with a sigh, letting go of Wulfe. He settled semigracefully onto the grass at her feet. "He was always strange. But he didn't used to enjoy pulling wings off butterflies."

"He wasn't sadistic," clarified Stefan. "Bonarata inspires loyalty by using various methods, and some of them are damaging."

Marsilia opened her mouth, glanced down at Wulfe, then closed it again.

"Especially to those of us who loved him," said Stefan insistently.

Darryl looked at Adam for permission and got it. He said, "Not that we don't appreciate learning more about our enemy. But what we need to know is how are we to get Mercy back? Where did he take her? Why he took her matters only in that it will allow us to use that knowledge to get her back."

As Darryl took the lead, Adam fought his wolf to a brutal standstill. He had to think. He had to think in order to see and plan the best way to help Mercy, to get her back. And in order to do that, his wolf spirit was going to have to . . . He had been trying to restrain the wolf, and it had put them at odds.

"I don't know where he took her," Marsilia answered Darryl. "He has homes in New York, Florida, and Arizona as well as South America. I don't know why he took her—other than to catch our attention."

We have to hunt, Adam whispered to the wild spirit who shared his body, the wild spirit he both despised and gloried in. *We have to hunt, find Mercy, and destroy the one who took her from us. And teach them that Mercy is ours.*

Inside him, the wolf paused, considering Adam's argument. After a moment, the beast agreed.

Freed of that battle, though he remained wary, aware that the wolf was only biding his time, Adam turned to the more important situation. First, to make certain his allies would shoot his enemies before they would shoot him.

"Compared to Bonarata," said Adam slowly, "Mercy matters not at all to you, Marsilia. So why did you approach us?"

She raised her chin. "I did not know it was one of yours he took at first. But even so, let us be honest, yes? Had he taken one of mine, I still would have come to you for help. I am myself a power in the vampire hierarchy. But when I was exiled . . . I quit trying. I existed, but for all intents and purposes, I did not direct my seethe other than to see to it that my people were safe and behaved themselves in such a manner as not to attract human attention. The result of my inattention is that outside of me and Wulfe, my seethe holds no individually powerful vampire. Wulfe . . ." She glanced down at the vampire, who, still sitting on the grass, had leaned his head against her knee. "I cannot in all fairness ask Wulfe to face Bonarata in person again."

"She is kind," murmured Wulfe. He smiled a hard, cruel smile directed at her. "But the reality is that she doesn't know whom I serve, her or my scion who re-created me as he pleased for his own purposes before he sent me with her. To bring me under such a circumstance would be stupid."

"Even so," she said evenly. "My seethe is stronger than it has been in years. We have had some new-made vampires and some who have come here, drawn by your declaration. It is not only the fae who are tired of fighting. But there are only three Master Vampires—those of us who do not need to obey our maker or the Mistress of the seethe. I am the first. Stefan is the second. And Wulfe is third. I know Iacopo."

"Jacob," murmured Wulfe. "He goes mostly by Jacob now."

"Jacob," she said. "I don't know why he took Mercy, or where he took her. But he will send us another e-mail or have a minion call and issue an invitation to come fetch our missing one. My strength is all in numbers right now, and he will not allow me to use that. I will need you and your wolves."

"To get Mercy back," Adam said.

"To keep Bonarata from coming here," she said, "and taking over my people and yours. Do not doubt that he could. He stole the mate of an old and dominant werewolf and made her his mindless slave. When her mate tried to save her, he destroyed the whole pack except for the Alpha. I have heard that Iacopo keeps that one alive still."

"Jacob," said Wulfe. "You keep forgetting. And the old Alpha is dead. Jacob lost his witch and doesn't know where to find her. Without her, he couldn't keep the old wolf around, so he killed him. It. Actually. I think the wolf was an it when it died."

Adam ignored Wulfe. Instead, he looked at Stefan. "You think Bonarata will call us to come to him?"

Mercy's vampire nodded. "It fits Bonarata's pattern. He will call us to come and make nice. He'll explain this all as a misunderstanding, and if he is satisfied with what we are—neither too strong to challenge him nor so weak that we are easy prey—he is likely to return Mercy with no more than a demand for some concessions that will be within our power." Stefan shrugged.

Marsilia smiled wearily. "It is his weakness, you see," she told Adam. "He loves adulation, to be admired. He is man enough to understand that if that sentiment is only the result of his magic, it means less."

"Assuming that you are right in your assumptions about why he took Mercy," Adam growled.

"Assuming that," she agreed. "And assuming anything about Iacopo Bonarata is dangerous. Even so, if we go meet his strength with strength, be charming and be charmed—it will not be difficult to be charmed. It is strongly possible that we will return with Mercy and a reasonable assurance that the Lord of Night will stay safely on the other side of the ocean and leave us be until we attract his attention again."

"Go where?" asked Darryl.

"Wherever he took Mercy, I imagine," she said. "I'll let you know when he contacts me."

3

~~~

MERCY

And here I am, standing naked before
the unlocked freezer door.

TO GIVE MYSELF ANOTHER CHANCE TO THINK, I FOLDED
the nasty rags that a day ago had been comfortable schlepping-
around-in-the-house-and-playing-pirate clothes. Now they could have
been costuming for a zombie movie—or, I supposed, a particularly
bloody pirate adventure. I tucked my underwear inside the shirt.

I took another look at my ribs, but there wasn't so much as a
scar left behind. That was some healer Bonarata had. He'd used
her on me when he'd thought I was powerful, that he might turn
me into an ally. I wouldn't let his earlier care delude me into believing that he didn't, now, think that it would be more convenient to
have me dead.

I was achy and sore but nothing too bad. My wrist, where the
cuff, the witch's bracelet, had poked little holes in my skin, was

itchy, but the dots were smaller than they had been. When I touched my toes, when I jogged in place, nothing hurt enough to interfere with my movement. Even the shaky, light-headed feeling had mostly subsided. Maybe it had been the lingering effects from being unconscious for so long, or maybe it was a side effect of the cuff's magic. I was good to go.

Part of me wanted to wait. I knew what I faced, more or less. In many ways, my whole childhood and adolescence had consisted of pitting my wits and thirty-five-pound coyote self against werewolves, some of which weighed north of three hundred pounds. All that experience told me that my chances were pretty much even against Bonarata's werewolf. Even odds weren't really very good odds against death-by-werewolf.

But most of one summer, the Marrok's terrifying son Charles had taken me on as a student, though I hadn't realized that was what he'd done until many years later. At the time, I'd thought it was a punishment for wrapping the Marrok's new car around a tree.

Right now, Charles's voice rang in my ears, as if it had curled up into some corner of my mind until I needed it.

"If you are taken by your enemies," he said, "don't wait to escape. The hour you are taken is when you will be at your strongest. Time gives them the opportunity to starve you, to torture you, to break you and make you weak. You have to escape as soon as you can."

Pretty intense stuff to say to a teenager you were teaching to do oil changes and rotate tires, but Charles was like that. It was part of what made him so scary.

Standing in front of the metallic door, I wondered if he'd had some prescience, some vision of me in my present circumstance—or if he'd just been passing on advice because everyone should know what to do if they were kidnapped. With Charles, it was hard to tell. His advice was good; now was the time to attempt to escape.

Even, I added to myself as I touched the invitingly unsecured door, if they expect you to try it. Even if they have set it up so they could kill you without accepting blame.

Another thing that Charles would say was that standing around staring at the door wasn't accomplishing anything useful except giving me time to scare myself.

Unencumbered by clothes, I opened the heavy freezer door and emerged into a moonlit garden. A light breeze, just this side of chilly, caressed my bare skin and brought a host of unfamiliar scents. I stepped over the doorway—and truthfully, despite the play Bonarata had made that there was something important about that space—I didn't expect to feel anything.

But my ears popped as if I'd just dropped a thousand feet, and magic shivered across my skin, scratching like spider legs. I froze for a heartbeat, but when that was all that happened, I took a cautious step forward.

There was packed gravel under my feet and a roof over my head, held up by huge old timbers. At first I thought it was some sort of porch around the building I'd just left, but the covered part was bigger than the building. It was more carport-sized, with two adjacent sides open. The building was the long, closed side, and the end of the building met a yellow, stuccoed wall.

The freezer end of the building tucked into the corner next to the wall and took up about a third of the building. The other two-thirds looked like long-abandoned horse stalls.

The building, roofed area, and wall were all set in a large walled garden that held rows of grapes and fruit trees. Ivy climbed the ten-foot walls.

On the opposite corner of the garden was a huge house in the shape of an "L" that appeared as hoary as the building at my back. The whole place looked as though someone had tried very hard, with better-than-average luck, to re-create the set of a movie that had taken place in Italy. I assumed it was to make Bonarata feel at home in a strange land.

I couldn't get any sense of what lay outside the walls—there were no towering mountains, but it didn't feel like the Tri-Cities, either. The air smelled different; it was cooler, and the air was damp.

Maybe I was in Yakima or Walla Walla. I hadn't spent a lot of time in Yakima, but Walla Walla's air wasn't as dry as the Tri-Cities', and it was cooler.

I took another step away from the doorway, and I quit worrying about where I was when I felt . . . something. Someone.

Heart pounding with hope, I looked back at the open doorway. I let my eyes become unfocused, then I could see it—a ring of magic that stretched along the edge of the building and disappeared around the open edge and, on the side with the wall, slipped under the stones like an electric cable made of magic, or a circle of magic.

Bonarata hadn't lied. I was a better prisoner inside that circle than I was outside it. Because outside it, the bonds that tied me to Adam—and to the pack—were functioning again. Sort of, anyway.

I reached out with my soul, down the familiar path that had so recently been blocked by silence. I reached for Adam.

It didn't quite work. Not the way it should have.

I could feel him at the edge of my awareness, but that was it. Maybe the wreck had done something—or the drugs or magic that had kept me quiet until they got me here. Maybe it was some kind of witchcraft or magic I wasn't resistant to right now, or that the circle was still affecting me. Maybe there was another circle around the whole property.

But I could tell that Adam was alive. Hopefully he could do the same. I'd examine the bonds more carefully later. Right now, I had to work on survival, because I could smell the distinctively musky mint of the werewolf's scent.

"You might as well come out," I said to Lenka the werewolf. That way I'd know where she was, and I could head for the garden wall in a direction that gave me a head start. "I know you're there."

She'd meant for me to scent her. She wanted me afraid. A low growl filled the air—soft enough not to be heard in the house. I think it was supposed to be scary, too—which it was, but not because I was afraid of the sound of her voice.

I remembered her crazy eyes and was scared. Fear was good. Fear would make my feet faster.

"I live with werewolves," I reminded her. "Hiding doesn't make you more frightening."

The wolf who rounded the corner of the walled side of the roofed area was too thin, and her fur coat was patchy. But her movement was easy, and the fangs she showed me as she snarled were plenty long.

I'd grown up hearing the old wolves talk about how much more satisfying it was to eat something while its heart pumped frantically from terror. Some of the old wolves who came to live out their last years in the Marrok's pack were not kind.

"Hi, there," I told her casually—and then I bolted for the wall surrounding the yard.

I smell mostly human to a werewolf's nose, especially if I haven't recently been running around on coyote feet. Human is a smell with enough variability that unless they know what I am, werewolves mostly chalk up the bit of odd in my smell to that. Vampires, I don't know as well.

I was betting that the vampires here didn't know what I was. That they thought I was human. I'd very carefully left it out of the mini biography I'd given Bonarata, and it wasn't widely known. My best-case scenario was that she would think I was a human woman trying to run for her life, penned inside the yard because, outside of a few martial artists and acrobats, the walls were enough to keep most people in.

I don't get super strength or scary points. But speed is my friend, and I caught her flat-footed because she thought one thing was happening when it was really something else. She thought I was running from her—and I was just trying to get up some speed.

I ran for the wall. I don't know what she thought I was doing, but she chased me hard for most of the distance. But as I approached the giant stone wall that surrounded the grounds, she slowed, anticipating that I would be stopped by it.

A few months ago, a bunch of the pack had been at Warren's house watching a Jackie Chan movie—I don't remember which one because we were having a marathon—and Jackie just ran up a wall like magic. Warren had a wall around his backyard. Someone stopped the movie, and we'd all gone out and tried it. A lot.

The werewolves had gotten moderately proficient, but my light weight and speed had made me the grand champion. The trick is to find a corner and have enough speed to make it to the top.

Instead of stopping at the wall, I Jackie-Channed it up the stone surfaces and leaped over. I caught the werewolf totally by surprise.

I don't expect Bonarata and she watched old martial arts movies together. It didn't seem like that kind of relationship.

Her pause meant that the wolf, who could have caught me

because as agile as I'd learned to be imitating Jackie Chan, going up was still slower than going forward, had missed her chance. I didn't intend to give her another.

I changed to coyote as I came off the top of the wall. I'm not a were-anything. It takes them time to change from human to wolf. I could do it—well, in this case I could do it in the time it took me to drop off the wall.

I landed on four feet, running as fast as I could down a narrow road that was walled on both sides. I had no idea where I was, but out was a good direction, and I didn't hesitate as I headed one way. Nor did I slow or look behind me.

I didn't need to. My ears told me when she landed on the outside of the wall. I could hear her running behind me, her claws giving her better purchase on the ground than mine did. Werewolves had huge freaking claws, and she was using them to give herself traction like the big cats do.

Experience had taught me that I was faster than most werewolves. Most, but not all. It was my bad luck that she wasn't one of the slower ones. She was closing in on me by inches.

I watched for a cross street, a change of some sort that would allow me to use my small size to my advantage, but there were only stone walls and stucco walls and cement walls and tall, solid gates. So I ran as fast as I could and hoped that I had more endurance, that her sprint would slow faster than mine.

I don't know how long we ran through the night streets. On a moon hunt, the pack would run for four or five hours at a time, for the sheer joy of it—so, outside of a few lingering aches from the wreck, I was in good shape. Better than she was, half-starved as she appeared.

Certainly in better shape than I would have been after being

Bonarata's guest for weeks. I'd have to thank Charles if I made it out of this alive.

Eventually, condition counted. I started to pull away from her, very, very slowly. About that time, the walls on either side of the road fell away, and I found myself running along a country lane with vineyards rising on gentle hills on both sides. There were still fences, but that was okay, I could deal with fences—vineyards were a godsend. There are vineyards all over the Tri-Cities. I know about vineyards and werewolves and coyotes.

I slipped through the bars of an ornate steel gate and ran along the length of the first row of grapes. I think she knew what I was planning—maybe she'd hunted smaller prey in this very vineyard before—because she sped up and closed the distance I'd opened between us. But, once again, she was too late.

I would have hated to face her if she'd been in top condition, if she hadn't been half-crazy. But if she hadn't been Bonarata's pet . . . mistress . . . something, she wouldn't be trying to kill me.

Grapes are grown in rows. The path between rows is kept clear, and it is easy to run through the vineyard from that direction. But the grapevines are trained to spread tidily on a wire or rope fence, so running through the vines themselves is difficult—unless you are a coyote. The fence the vines are grown along leaves plenty of space for a coyote to slip through between strands.

I turned into the vineyard.

After the second row, I got a feeling for the spacing and didn't have to slow or shorten my stride as I ran through the gracefully draped vines.

The werewolf was a lot bigger than I was. She had to jump every row. It wasn't the additional effort that won the race for me—it was just that every time she jumped was that much time she wasn't propelling herself forward. It slowed her down, and it required more energy.

She was moving roughly ten times as much mass as I was, which hopefully would tire her out faster, though that didn't seem to be happening with any appreciable speed, even given her poor condition. I kept waiting for her to break down the row and run on the road beside the vineyard instead, where her speed would be less hampered than mine was. But she just kept following me as if she was incapable of more tactical thinking.

By the time I reached a road again, ducking beneath the tall hedge-and-fence that the werewolf would have to vault over, I'd gained nearly forty yards. This road traveled straight uphill for about a half mile, then, from the sign on the verge, intersected with another road.

The last steep bit I managed by ignoring my tiredness and occupying myself with the very important decision of whether to continue straight or turn left or right. My life hung in the balance, but I had nothing to draw upon to make the decision an informed one. The high hedge lined both sides of the road I was traveling on, and I could not even see the new road.

I hesitated a moment . . . one second and two, right at the intersection. I glanced over my shoulder and saw the satisfaction in her eyes. My indecision had given her the hunt. She was still stronger than I was, and the long uphill stretch had eaten most of the lead that the vineyard had given me.

She was so busy seeing me as her prize, she didn't pay attention to anything else. So when I bolted across the intersection, she did, too—and the bus that I'd waited for hit her and rolled over the top of her with both sets of wheels.

I turned right, the direction the bus had come from, and kept going. Behind me, I heard the bus slow and stop. I hoped that she was dead—or dead enough to leave the bus driver and the people riding in it safe.

After a while, I heard the engine sound change as the bus pulled out again and headed away on its original course. I dropped from a sprint to a jog. She might still be alive, but she wasn't going to be chasing me again until she'd had time to heal. Without a pack, it was going to take her a few hours at least.

It was still dark, though, and there was the possibility that the vampire hadn't left his—what? lover? food?—to kill me on her own. I needed to find a safe place. I needed to contact Adam. I needed to eat something. Not necessarily in that order. Water, the most immediate need, I found in a trough set out for some cows. They watched me curiously, but I didn't alarm them.

I thought about cutting through their pasture and into more vineyards, but I wanted to go home. Following the road until I found a familiar setting seemed to be a better choice. The road I followed was, other than the small cow pasture, bordered on either side by vineyards until civilization crept very slowly back in, but not in any useful fashion.

I traveled for another hour or four, until the first rays of the next day dawned, without finding anyplace that seemed safe. I think if I hadn't been so tired, I might have done something smart, like changing into a human and going looking for help. Though maybe not. Bonarata would not be kind to any human who thwarted his will and helped me—that was his reputation, anyway. Instead of looking for help, I found railroad tracks and followed them for a while, exhaustion leaving me very focused on putting more miles between me and the vampires. On getting away safely. A train seemed like a very good idea.

In the end, I didn't take a train. I found the station, right on the edge of where village turned into tight-packed city. As I was trying to figure out just how to jump on a train without anyone's seeing me—pack magic could make people not pay attention to me only as long as I didn't do anything too interesting—I realized that there was an easier ride to be had.

The small train station shared space with a bus terminal. There was, not ten feet from where I'd emerged from the tidy bushes surrounding the whole space, a bus with the luggage doors open on both sides. Even as I noticed it, attendants closed the doors on the far side.

I jumped in the near side and scrambled over bags and suitcases before dropping into an empty space and stillness. I lay there panting as quietly as I could until the doors closed. Five minutes later, the bus lumbered forward in a wave of diesel fumes, and I took a deep breath.

Safe.

Relief washed over me, and I put my head down. I slept.

I DREAMED OF ADAM.

I sprawled awkwardly over a chair shaped for a person in my coyote body, my muzzle on Adam's lap. His strong hand rested on my back. I moved so I could see his face: he looked tired. I think we were on an airplane—which made no sense at all. But it was only an impression. Everything except for Adam was pretty vague in the way that dreams sometimes are.

"There you are," he said. "What in . . . what did you get yourself into this time?"

Coyotes can't talk.

"Mercy," he said.

Sometimes I have been known to use the not-talk thing to my

advantage. He sounded like he was mad at me. I was tired. The pads on the bottom of my feet, tough enough to run over the desert, had not fared so well running over blacktop all night. My shoulder hurt, my jaw hurt, my heart hurt. I was stuck in a luggage compartment without food. My stomach was pretty sure my throat had been cut.

I put my muzzle back on his lap and closed my eyes.

He was very still for a moment.

"Not doing so good, huh?" he said softly, running his hands over my sides gently before he touched both sides of my face in a caress that was both soothing and possessive. "Sorry. I've been fuc . . . very worried." Adam doesn't swear in front of women or children if he can help it—a product of a childhood in the fifties or abnormally good manners, take your pick.

He bent over me, put his head down on top of mine, and I heard him inhale as if he were breathing me in. "Are you okay?"

I wiggled a little closer to him, but I didn't open my eyes.

Apparently that was enough of an answer, because he exhaled and relaxed. "All right, then," he said. "I'll tell you what I know."

He sat up, but his hands stayed on me. "You just disappeared, sweetheart. We found the SUV and the stolen semi that hit it. Found your blood on the seat—that was rough, because, Mercy, it was a lot of blood. But we couldn't find you. The gas station was deserted. We think the clerk belonged to the vampires. That they had been waiting for you to go there by yourself. It was so close to home, you'd feel safe—and that would give them a chance to act.

"We might have been at a dead end, but things really got interesting when we talked to Marsilia."

I raised my head and looked at him, but he was staring at something I couldn't see.

"She'd gotten an e-mail," he told me. "Implying that you were being held to persuade her to present herself before the . . ." He stopped here. "I am informed that speaking his name or title might allow him to eavesdrop because we are speaking via a witch's spell rather than our bond. Do you know who I mean?"

I nodded, disconcerted by the idea of a witch spell. Adam's hands tightened painfully.

"Does he have you?" Adam asked urgently, and I shook my head.

"You got away? Where are you? Are you all right? Are you safe?" he asked.

I would have said something then. But I was in coyote form—and I didn't have the faintest idea how to answer any of his questions.

His nostrils flared, and he frowned at me. "I smell diesel. I thought it was just you . . . but, Mercy, are you on a bus?" he asked.

But he was gone before I could answer, the quiet dream blown to bits by the abrupt sound of hissing brakes. The noise and rough jolting brought me back to the dark underbelly of the luggage compartment, which was a cold substitute for Adam's lap. I stood up. My legs had trouble compensating for the wallow as the bus rolled over speed bumps, curbs, bodies, or something that lifted up one side, then the other a couple of times.

I didn't know how long I'd been asleep. Not very long, I thought. I would have been stiffer if it had been more than a half hour or so—not long enough to be safe from the Lord of Night. I waited, and when the bus stopped, I readied myself.

When the luggage doors opened, I dashed out as quickly as I could. The bus attendant cried out as I ran by him, but this was a huge station, and I quickly lost myself among the buses and passengers towing luggage.

A man reading a book crossed my path, and I slowed down, walking at his heel for a dozen yards until the pack magic settled lightly around me and I became less interesting. I could feel the lessened pressure at the back of my neck as people quit looking at me. Pack magic would help, but I'd have to do my best to blend in because it was weak.

We moved past a bright yellow bus just as a woman reached up to close the cargo area but paused as something caught her attention. It was too good a chance to miss. I broke smoothly away from the man I'd been trailing and slipped unseen into the luggage compartment. I found a pair of big beige duffel bags and stretched out between them, just another beige lump to human eyes. The luggage-bay doors closed.

I stayed still until the bus was moving, then stayed still some more as it turned a corner and picked up speed. I had to stay still, or I was afraid I would lose my battle with panic.

I'd assumed that the Lord of Night had taken me to Yakima or Walla Walla. Both were within a reasonable travel distance of the Tri-Cities, and both had gently rolling hills and vineyards. When I'd been running my hardest to stay ahead of the werewolf, I hadn't been paying attention to much beyond generalities.

But the voices at the bus station hadn't been speaking English. They'd been speaking Italian.

I wasn't in Yakima or Walla Walla; I wasn't in Washington or even in the US. The Lord of Night had taken me to Italy, and that was the reason I couldn't reach Adam or the pack through the various bonds I had to them as soon as I was free of Bonarata's magic circle.

I wasn't sure how far Italy was from my home, but my liberal arts education told me that the world was roughly twenty-five thousand miles around and that Italy was about a quarter of the world away. I called it six thousand miles, give or take a thousand miles.

I was in the belly of a bus in Italy, alone, naked, and penniless. Also without a passport.

In a place that a coyote was likely to be noticed because coyotes aren't exactly native to Europe.

I thought a little more and added "can't speak the language" to my woes. I'd never traveled out of the country—except that summer road trip to Mexico with Char, my college roommate. Char spoke fluent Spanish, so my bits and pieces hadn't made me completely helpless. I put my head down and felt sorry for myself for a long while.

Then I pulled on my big-girl pants (which were figurative at this point) and started dealing with the situation as it stood. In front of me and behind me was the solution to my nakedness problem, and I had no room to be squeamish.

I shifted back to my human self and started opening luggage.

It took me a while to find someone who was reasonably close to me in size. I didn't want to strand her with not enough clothes, so I took the bare minimum. I'd found a notebook and pen in someone else's duffel bag and left a note and the address and phone number of Adam's business as well as a detailed list of what I'd taken from the suitcase—a copy of which I kept. I found a pair of tennis shoes that fit in another suitcase, along with twenty euros. There had been maybe two hundred euros in the suitcase, but my conscience, already pushed to the brink, could only deal with twenty. I left a note for her, too.

I had no idea how long this bus ride was going to be—though the luggage suggested that most people weren't planning on a short trip. Even so, I hurried, so that I wouldn't be caught in the middle of my theft.

I found an empty backpack—not a sturdy can-hold-all-your-college-textbooks kind of pack, more of an I-don't-want-to-carry-a-purse-and-think-pink-lace-and-flowers-are-pretty pack. I thought it was pretty, too—if not really appropriate to anyone over the age of seven. But my coyote self could carry it, and it would hold the fruits of my heist job, so I took it.

Stealing was quick. Writing all the notes took a lot longer. I was tucking the last note in when I noticed an e-reader sticking out of a compartment in the suitcase I'd taken the shoes from.

I was pretty sure most e-readers had Internet capability, even old ones like this one. I added it to the list of things I owed the nice woman who was going to be short a pair of tennis shoes, too, when she arrived at her destination. I was sorry for it, but I'd make it up to her as soon as I could. If I could.

If I couldn't, if I didn't get myself out of this, Adam would know I would want these people compensated for the things I took.

I packed everything in the flowery backpack and pulled it into the far corner of the bus. Then I changed back into the coyote and curled up in the corner, the metal of the bus's walls on either side of me.

I'd grown used to feeling safe again, ever since Adam and I had become a couple. Okay, vampires, trolls, and a host of other villains that ranged from terrifying to scary had tried to kill me on a fairly regular basis, but Adam had my back. I hadn't realized how much I craved it until it was gone. Again.

I'd thought I was safe before. I'd left most of the supernatural behind me when I'd left the Marrok's pack at sixteen. I'd gone to college, had decided that being a mechanic suited me better than teaching. For nearly ten years, I had lived in my trailer, had gone to work every day, and no one had tried to kill me. I'd felt like I didn't need anyone at my back. Not even when my world had started to fill with the affairs of the supernatural community had I lost my ability to find a place of safety—a home.

But no one is really safe. Not ever. Afterward, after I picked up the pieces and glued them back together with a bit of hope and trust and fairy dust, I'd found another place to be home and safe.

I paused in momentary horror. Had I married Adam just so I could feel safe? The panic lasted only for a moment, because I knew better. I'd had hours and hours of counseling with a pretty awesome counselor. Part of it was to address some bad things that had happened, but part of it was so that I could choose Adam— because I chose him and not because I knew that anything that came after me would have to go through him.

But still . . . I had thought I was safe.

The Lord of Night had come to my home ground and taken me there, then hauled me to Italy as if the pack, as if all of my allies, were no obstacle at all. He'd extracted me as cleanly as if I'd hopped on his airplane—because no way had he brought me here on a commercial plane—of my own volition.

I'd had some time to think while I ran. My current version of why Bonarata had brought me here went like this: he'd wanted to bring me here, thinking that I was Marsilia's, because the thought that Adam and the pack could be cooperating without her being in charge just never occurred to him. I was a piece on a chessboard he'd decided Marsilia was the queen of. He'd taken me, who Wulfe had told him was the most powerful of Marsilia's associates, to show her how powerless she was. I don't know what he'd have done if I were the werewolf he'd originally thought me. But his little pet werewolf was enough to make me wary. She'd smelled off, smelled sick—the kind of sick that made my coyote decide something wasn't good to eat.

I had other versions of why Bonarata had stolen me—but none of them made sense, including that one. Bonarata was smarter than that; he had to be to have lived as long as he had.

I really was certain that Marsilia was involved somehow. There had been something about the way he'd looked at me when he told me he hadn't wanted to kill Marsilia, so he hadn't broken the bond I shared (supposedly) with her.

I shivered, though the bus wasn't particularly cold and my summer fur coat could have protected me in the heaviest blizzard likely to fall in Lombardy.

He'd thought that I was bound to Marsilia.

I hated that the word for what the vampires did to their victims was the same word that described what was between Adam and me, between the pack and me.

My understanding, from the things I'd learned since Adam and I were bound as mates, was that all magical bonds are formed from the same sort of magic. Humans have those kinds of bonds, too—but theirs are softer and more fragile. Breakable.

Like most things, pack bonds and mate bonds could be twisted, but by their nature, they encouraged empathy because they are emotional links. They were bonds between equals—even the bond between the pack and its Alpha. The Alpha had a job to do, but it didn't make him more important than the most submissive of the wolves in the pack. Adam was of the opinion that he was less important. We agreed to disagree.

The bond between a vampire and his victim (I say his because the vampire who owned me—and that was exactly the right word—was a him) put the vampire in the driver's seat. The vampire could, if he so chose, make his pet do anything, feel anything. Whenever the vampire decided to, he could take away his victim's free will—and the victim might not even know.

The Kiss doesn't always work. Stefan told me that it was almost impossible to take a werewolf the way they could take humans because of the pack bonds. That Bonarata had succeeded in doing so had added to his legend. There were people who were difficult to break. But given time, a strong vampire could control most any human he wanted to.

Stefan told me he didn't know if that was true between us—but that he would not test it. I trusted Stefan.

Even so, Stefan owned me. He had saved my life by claiming me, and I'd agreed to it. But I'd thought it was broken, gone. Thought my ties to Adam and the pack had erased it, because Stefan had wanted me to believe it.

Apparently, because I'd taken the bond willingly, it wasn't something Stefan could break even if he wanted to. Knowing Stefan as I did, I was willing to believe that.

The Lord of Night had tried to break it and failed. Or so he said.

My heartbeat picked up, and my mouth dried as I opened it and panted in fear. Of course he would lie. He lied a lot. I couldn't remember now if I'd been watching for lies while he spoke of the bond I shared with a vampire. I'd been paying attention to the jealousy he'd displayed. Had he lied? Was he, even now, in my head, waiting to give me orders?

To take me from Marsilia would have been a better lesson than to have his wolf kill me trying to escape. I had only his word that he hadn't done it.

Hadn't I done what he wanted when I escaped? I'd known he wanted me to try it. What if he hadn't wanted me to die at the fangs of his pet werewolf as I'd first thought? What—what if *this* was his plan? That I'd escape, think I was free, get back to the pack—and destroy them because I belonged to Bonarata. That story, unfortunately, made better sense than some sort of unrequited jealousy as a motivation.

Had Bonarata broken the tie between Stefan and me? Had he been able to do something that Stefan couldn't? Was I a slave of the Lord of Night?

Since learning it still existed, I had never tested the bond between Stefan and me. Just the thought of that tie made me wake up in a cold-blooded sweat, understanding exactly how a trapped wolf could chew off a paw to escape.

The bus continued to rumble at a consistent speed, unimpressed by my panic. I needed to find the bond between Stefan and me and make sure Bonarata hadn't done something to it—something that would turn me into his creature.

I didn't even really know how to look. But even as I thought that—I knew I had a stepping-off place. After Adam brought me into the pack bonds, I'd had a bad incident because a couple of the members of the pack were able to manipulate me through them. After that, Adam taught me how to deal with pack magic and the bonds. Part of that process was learning to "see" the bonds in my head.

I closed my eyes and, after a fairly tough and lengthy struggle, calmed down enough to find the light meditative state Adam had taught me to help me negotiate the pack bonds—as well as the mate bond between him and me.

Eventually, I stood on the battered stage of my old high school—the one in Portland. The floor was lit by a single spotlight, the one just over the control booth that sat in the middle of the balcony seats. I knew it was there, but, caught in the spotlight's glare, I couldn't see it.

The boards under my feet had been polished at one time, but years of student productions, of rolling the risers and the piano in and out, had left the old floor scarred and rough under my bare feet. Though I was wearing my coyote shape in real life, here in my mind, I was looking for human things, so I was in my human shape, naked, because naked made me feel vulnerable, and I couldn't seem to find the safe space I needed to allow me to go clothed.

Darkness gathered at the edges of the stage and covered the auditorium in shadows that my eyes couldn't penetrate. But I wasn't here to explore my memory of high school.

I looked down at myself and patted the tattoo on my belly for a minute. There was nothing magical about the tattoo. It was just a paw print—a *coyote* paw print no matter what Adam said. But it centered me—it was at the center of me, a symbol of the coyote within. My fingers came down for the hundredth or two hundredth time—and hit a thick rope that wrapped all the way around me.

It was a rope that should have been too big to tie around me, but, as my perceptions of it changed, clarified, I could see that it wove around my upper torso like a bulletproof vest, if bulletproof vests were made of silk rope. I could not feel its weight, but here in that place between waking and sleep, it was warm and comforting—and it stretched into a gray mist that had somehow gathered in the darkness surrounding me.

I bent my head and pulled the rope to my nose. It smelled like Adam, and I touched it to my cheek. Under my hand, it felt alive and well—I could, faintly, feel Adam's resolve, his stress and his fear. Gently, I let the rope fall away from my hands. I was not looking for my mate bond.

The pack bonds were woven through my vest, the warp to Adam's weave; fluffier than the silk that was my bond with Adam, my pack bonds came in the shape of colorful Christmas garlands. Far lighter than the bond between Adam and me, they sparkled and shimmered as I moved. They stretched out from me in a braided cable about half as big as the mate bond. Like that bond, the pack bonds disappeared in the mist of distance. When I touched them, I could feel, very faintly, the lives of the wolves on the other end.

But I wasn't looking for the pack, either. I stood in as neutral a position as I could: feet apart, knees bent, arms at my sides, closed my dream-self's eyes, and thought, *Stefan*. I pictured him in my head, a moderately tall man with dark hair and eyes, very Italian, I'd always thought him. His smile was warm, and his posture varied—when he paid attention, he slumped a little and stomped a little. When he didn't, he had the same sort of ramrod-straight posture that Adam had—they'd both been soldiers as young men. He was a dangerous man who was able to put it aside and joke and laugh as he helped me repair his van. A powerful vampire who knew ASL and unself-consciously watched *Scooby-Doo*.

When I was done, I opened my eyes, and he stood in front of me—a statue without life.

I walked all the way around him, looking for something, anything, that tied us together. A sparkle teased at my senses, but I couldn't find it—and was afraid I was making it up.

I closed my eyes again and ran my hands over my neck. After a few minutes, my fingers tangled in a necklace. It was gossamer fine and cool against my fingers. I searched for a clasp and found, instead, a small circle of metal that gathered the strands of necklace together, and attached to it was another chain.

I opened my eyes as my fingers followed the chain out far enough from under my chin that I could see it. A fine silver chain lay in my hands—and once I saw it, I could see that it led to the hands of the version of Stefan I had on my stage.

It looked so fragile—I tried to break it, but it wouldn't break or bend, not with anything I could bring to bear on it in my mind.

I fought and fought, pulling frantically on the necklace collar around my neck until blood stained the chain, running down it from my neck and from my fingers.

Shhh, said a cool voice. *Shhh, you're breaking my heart,* cara.

I froze, then looked up from the now-heavy chain to my image of Stefan, which crouched next to me on the stage.

I promised, he told me. *I promised not to tug on the leash. I promised. Don't hurt yourself so. I keep my promises, Mercy.*

His voice flowed over me—a friend's voice. I was so alone. His voice was like a warm blanket over my nakedness. It gave me strength to allow my fingers to release the chain. I sat up.

My intention was to find the bond, I remembered, not to fight it. I took my terror, the atavistic fear of a trapped animal, and stuffed it back so I could think.

I'd been looking for it to make sure that it tied me to the right vampire.

"Who are you?" I asked him. "I need to be certain. The—" I remembered that Adam hadn't used his name, so I switched it up a little. "Marsilia's Master took me. I need to make sure that this"—I indicated the leash between us that now resembled a rusty lumber chain instead of fine jewelry—"is between you and me. That he didn't break this bond and replace it with one of his own."

Stefan sat back on his heels and tilted his head. "Fair question," he said. "If he held your bonds, he could . . ." He frowned, then pulled a knife out of a pocket and sliced his palm. He pressed it against the chain he held, and the red drops landed on the metal. There were only five or six drops, but gradually the whole chain turned rust red. When those red links came close to me, I touched them—and the faded, cartoonish figure of Stefan solidified into the vampire himself.

His gaze traveled around at my stage and the fog, at the two cords that disappeared into the mist, and smiled at me. "Good to see you. This won't last long, but while it does I have some things to tell you. Adam told us that you got away—keep running. Don't trust anyone. We'll find you, all right? We're on our way to Italy. Once we are there, your ties to Adam should start working again, at least well enough for him to find you. He says that without the pack nearby, you should expect your ties to him and to the pack to remain weak until he is quite close. We can beat *him*, I think, Marsilia's old Master, but only if you stay free. And don't contact me this way again. *He* can't, *probably* can't, listen in, but he might be able to feel our conversation and follow the thread of it to you."

He was still Bonarata; I knew that without Stefan's using his name.

Stefan looked at the chain and said, "Really? This looks like something you'd find in a dungeon."

I opened my mouth to explain about the necklace but changed my mind at the last moment and shrugged instead. "Scooby-Doo would be impressed."

He smiled—and I was alone again, holding the fine chain that now disappeared into the mists.

I took two deep breaths and returned to the belly of the diesel beast that was carrying me to some unknown destination. We'd been traveling for a while. From the angle of the floor and the swaying as we turned one way, then the other, we were traveling through mountains. It was unlikely that I was going to find myself in Milan when the bus stopped. The farther I could manage to travel, the better off I'd be.

I was still tied to Stefan and not the Lord of Night.

Stefan was a vampire. He killed people to survive. It was true that he tried his best to keep them alive. It was true that he was funny and honorable. It was true that I liked him. But he was a vampire, and he owned me. The thought of that was enough for me to have to open my mouth and pant out my fear.

But at least it was still Stefan and not Bonarata, not the Lord of Night.

Stefan's bond had saved me again. Had I been free, I would probably belong to the other vampire right now. He could have used me to get whatever it was that he wanted from our pack and Marsilia. I could have been his Trojan horse.

As the bus rattled on, I continued to play with various people's motivations as best I could. It wasn't really a waste of time—the exercise made me feel like I was doing something.

Bonarata had taken me because Wulfe told him I was the most powerful person in the Tri-Cities.

Why had Wulfe done that? Maybe as a joke—but I didn't think so. It was probable, Stefan had told me not too long ago, that Wulfe was in Marsilia's seethe as a spy.

"But," he'd told me with a wry smile, "I doubt that Bonarata would approve of Wulfe's methods. In his own way, Wulfe is more devoted to Marsilia than any of her seethe, more devoted to her than to the Lord of Night. Wulfe is old and strange; who knows how his mind works?"

I had to agree about the strange, but I had some experience dealing with old and strange people. And I thought that Stefan might be well on target about how Wulfe served Marsilia and let Bonarata think Wulfe served him instead.

So Wulfe had thrown me under the bus in order to do what?

The first thing I thought of was that by taking me instead of, say, Stefan or one of Marsilia's other vampires, all of the werewolves would be fighting to get me back. If Wulfe had given them Adam . . . I thought of Bonarata trying to get Adam and was pretty sure that it would not have gone smoothly. Someone would have died, maybe many someones. But me? Blindsided by a kidnapping done by vampires? I would not stand a chance. Not of avoiding capture—but I was good at surviving, wasn't I?

And if I'd died—it wouldn't mean much to Wulfe or Marsilia, either. Not as long as Adam never found out that Wulfe had set me up, anyway. Even so—Adam would take out Bonarata before looking to Wulfe.

That felt right. Felt like a move Wulfe might make. Once he knew that Bonarata was moving against Marsilia at last, he'd want to consolidate her power, to put the werewolves firmly at her back.

Wulfe knew that I was tied to Stefan. Would he know that Bonarata would have trouble breaking that tie? *Yes,* I thought. James Blackwood, the one the vampires called the Monster, had tried to break our bond and failed. If I came back from visiting Bonarata unharmed, Wulfe could set up some sort of test to discover if I were unwillingly working for Bonarata. Probably would do so if I managed to escape cleanly.

Somehow that made me feel better. Wulfe would have figured out if I had been made Bonarata's pet.

So Bonarata, operating on Wulfe's very Wulfe-like information, had found himself holding a weak female instead of Marsilia's most powerful supporter. My tie to Stefan—that Bonarata thought was to Marsilia—meant he couldn't use me as a puppet. So Bonarata was left with a useless hostage. If he killed me outright, Bran Cornick, the Marrok, would declare war. To Bran and to the world, I was one of those he'd sworn to protect. If he didn't avenge me, he'd lose face.

But an accident—that would simplify things greatly. He forgot to lock the door, and his half-crazed werewolf pet had torn me to bits. So sad. Tragic, even. I bet he would look very apologetic.

His story would have worked to keep Bran off his back. Not that Bran would believe him—but without proof, Bran could not attack Bonarata with impunity. Bran couldn't go after Bonarata without starting a war with the other vampires. Such a war invited complications and disasters that might make World War I look like the "jolly little war" the British thought they were marching to.

My death wouldn't endear him to Adam, though. But neither would my kidnapping have. If he wanted to use our neutral zone, then my kidnapping didn't make sense at all—but, I remembered, he'd been lying to me when he'd told me he was interested in a place where supernatural creatures and humans could interact safely.

The bus braked hard, then started up again, in a low gear that vibrated nastily in the luggage compartment, and I momentarily lost my train of thought. It wasn't like I enjoyed picking apart the plans of supervillainous vampires. But the bus had been traveling for a long, long time, and it wasn't like there was anything else going on. And there was the minor, inconsequential motivation that my life was in the balance.

No. Bran wouldn't go after Bonarata without proof that left him clearly in the right. Adam might—but he didn't have Bran's resources. Bonarata wouldn't be worried about Adam. He didn't know Adam like I did.

For the moment, we had the upper hand. He'd underestimated me by a hairsbreadth, because that's how close that chase with the werewolf had been. I'd escaped.

But he couldn't allow me to stay free. He had to retake me to save face.

No.

He still needed me to die in order to save face—and to come out on top. He wouldn't underestimate me again. I couldn't afford to underestimate him, either.

I knew more about vampires than I'd ever wanted to. The old vampires operated like spiders—with webs strung all over their territory. A vampire like Bonarata probably had people all over Europe. It wouldn't be hard to find me here. There weren't a lot of coyotes in Europe, probably none outside a zoo. He'd have people looking for my coyote self.

I had to disappear.

I put my head down on my paws and tried to ignore the diesel fumes.

4

~~~

MERCY

*Still somewhere in Europe, stuck in the luggage
compartment of a bus. I'm just lucky I'm not
prone to car sickness.*

THE BUS CONTINUED MOVING FOR A VERY LONG TIME.
Twice it stopped without opening the luggage doors—presumably
to let people eat and take care of business. That I didn't have to
figure out how to get out to take care of business probably meant
that I was dehydrated—I was certainly hungry—but it was convenient, and my coyote body was better at dealing with less regular food and drink than my human one.

When it stopped for a third time, I was ready to get out. Fortunately,
this time the doors to my compartment opened with a screech of
hinges. I pulled on pack magic, which answered my call sluggishly, but
it was enough for me to scoot out of the luggage compartment and
into the shadows of the twilight surrounding a tourist-friendly hotel.

The bus had traveled all day. That meant I was approximately five hundred miles from wherever in Italy I'd been to start with, give or take a couple of hundred miles. I could smell a freshwater river nearby but not an ocean. There were no large mountains, but there seemed to be some rise and fall to the land.

I found a place behind a pair of giant potted plants near the corner of the hotel that left me a dark shadow to hide in. With the pack magic to help, I didn't think anyone would see me as long as I wasn't moving. I took some time to examine my surroundings.

Buildings rose all around me. Not skyscrapers, but four- or five-story buildings, most of which dated back a few centuries. I saw a street sign and it had a few marks above the letters no Romance language had—but it wasn't Cyrillic, either, at least not any version of Cyrillic I was familiar with.

After a few minutes of observation didn't help me figure out where I was, I took a tighter hold of the threads of pack magic, faint because my pack was a very long way away, and ventured out into the growing darkness.

As I traveled through the city, heading for the origin of the scent of the river, the buildings got older—a lot older by centuries—and the streets turned to cobblestones. There were distinctive red-tile roofs and artwork on the outside of buildings. Probably not frescoes, though that's what they looked like. My liberal arts education had given me enough of a basis in architecture that I could tell the difference between Gothic and Romanesque with about 70 percent accuracy. It did not tell me what it was called when there were designs all over the outer surface of a building.

The overall effect was an exuberant, almost boisterous, eclectically historical architecture. Here and there, aggressively plain buildings squatted between the beautiful, centuries-old masterpieces like defiant toads set between swans, hinting that this city had spent some time behind the Iron Curtain.

I had my suspicions about where I was. But it wasn't until an hour later, when I'd found the river and looked down it to see the most famous and unmistakable of its many famous landmarks, the grand old medieval Charles Bridge, that I knew for certain where I was: Prague, the heart of Bohemia.

I knew a little bit about Prague. The first thing that came to mind was that Prague citizens had a habit of throwing powerful officials out of windows—the Second Defenestration of Prague began the Thirty Years War in 1618. There wasn't another capital city with a First Defenestration that I knew of, let alone a second one. Prague was full of my kind of people.

By leaping a few low stone fences, I found a chunk of ground next to the riverbank (I couldn't remember the name of the river except that it began with a V and that the Germans called it something else that reminded me of mold) tucked next to and around the edge of a restaurant that was hidden from the view of street, restaurant, and boats on the river. It was not particularly clean or lovely, but it was hidden—and that's all I would ask for tonight.

And I lay there in the hard-packed dirt for maybe an hour next to the river. After ten minutes or so, I remembered it was the Vltava. Three unlikely consonants in a row. I still couldn't remember the name the Germans called it. It was full dark, but there were lights all over the city that gave the river's graceful flow a surreal beauty.

I knew that Stefan had given me good advice. I should just lie low and wait to be found. But I'd slept most of the day cramped up in the belly of the bus, and I was now too restless to sleep.

There were werewolves in Prague. I knew that. The mad and

powerful Beast of Gévaudan, who'd ruled most of Europe for centuries, had seen to it that the packs were few and far between, as he did not brook competition. In Spain, where Asil the Moor had ruled, the Beast had left them alone. But he had stayed away from certain other places, too. Milan, where the Lord of Night reigned supreme, had been one of them. I was pretty sure that Prague had been another.

There was something about the werewolves in Prague I couldn't remember. Something that urged me to caution. I hadn't expected to find myself in Europe . . . well, ever, really. So I hadn't paid much attention to them.

The werewolf who ruled here was very, very old—like Marrok or Asil old, I could remember that much. For some reason, I had the picture of a very hairy man in a medieval kitchen with his hirsute arms folded on the top of a rough-hewn wooden table in my head—it made me want to smile. Likely someone had been talking about him when I was a child, and I'd formed an idea of what he looked like. To have been Alpha enough to keep Gévaudan at bay, he was doubtless a scary man. But I'd grown up with werewolves, and being a werewolf was an insufficient reason to be frightened of him.

Even so, running around Prague was probably a bad idea until I could remember what I had heard about the local Alpha that had worried me. I should stay where I was.

I'd lived more than half my life essentially alone. Sometimes in the past few years, I had *longed* to be alone, just for an hour or two. And here I was. Alone. Sometimes getting your wish really sucks.

I still could not feel the pack bonds unless I was in a trance. My bond with Adam was faint, like a memory of the strong line of communication—or noncommunication, during its contrary moments. I tried not to notice the bond between Stefan and me, and since it, too, was faint, was mostly successful.

Adam had traveled to Washington, D.C., several times during our marriage, and our mating bond had been strong and true—or as strong and true as ever, because it was eccentric. Given the current evidence, the pack magic must have provided the power to keep our bond going over the distance.

Those dreams I'd had in the bus, I refused to believe they were only dreams. The first one . . . might have been, I admitted reluctantly. Though it had felt more real than most of my dreams. But the second one, the one with Stefan—that one was real. And if both Adam and Stefan said that they were on their way to Italy, I had to believe that was what was happening. To face Bonarata.

The Lord of Night had taken me from my mate, and now Adam was going to visit him. There was no way that was not going to be a disaster. Not at all.

What was everyone thinking to have allowed that to happen? Okay, granted that Adam made his own decisions. But Stefan had sounded so confident that as long as I remained at large, *diplomacy* could happen.

My husband was not overly diplomatic under the best of circumstances.

I had escaped the plans the Lord of Night had made for me. Neither he nor Adam was going to be in a good mood. I didn't see how this was going to work out without one of them dead, no matter what Stefan said. I knew very well that my friend Stefan could lie like a carny on a bally stage. I wasn't certain he couldn't lie to me, too, in order to spare me from worry. My internal lie detector was very good but not infallible.

I popped up to my feet. I could not—*could not*—sit around all night with nothing for company but my thoughts, kept there by some vague worry about the Alpha of Prague and the probability that I was, at this very moment, the subject of a deadly hunt by the most powerful vampire in . . . well, anywhere, I supposed.

I left the backpack where it was because my nose told me that people didn't come to that tiny forgotten corner of the restaurant grounds very often. My little bit of pack magic would have an easier time hiding me if I wasn't doing something remarkable, like carrying a backpack around.

On four feet, I retraced my way back to the street and set out to explore nighttime Prague with the faint concealment that the remnants of pack magic wrapped around me. I was in Prague, in the Czech Republic, and I'd never traveled out of the country before—except for that one crazy trip to Mexico with Char, during which we had avoided jail by the hair of our chinny-chin-chins because of Char's exquisitely horrible taste in men. So what if an old vampire was going to murder my husband, I was . . .

If I wasn't going to let myself be distracted, I might as well go curl up in a miserable ball and wait for Adam (or maybe Bonarata or Whateverhisname the Alpha of Prague) to find me. Wait to be rescued, Stefan had told me—not very flattering in retrospect. I don't follow orders, even kindly given, and I wasn't going to wait around to be rescued like some helpless princess when there was exploring to do.

Just then, I passed a restaurant or pub or something that had a sign in the window that said FREE WI-FI in about ten languages. It would open at 11. I made note of it because my stolen e-reader and I needed free Wi-Fi. But it was a long time until 11 A.M., so I kept going.

Eventually, I found myself in the famous Old Town Square, with its fabulous clock tower that looked as though it had been transplanted from the Middle Ages. The rest of the buildings were, even to my relatively uneducated eyes, a mishmash of eras—that seemed to blend together in a . . . well, a *Bohemian* style. My favorite was a glorious old church or cathedral with Gothic (I think) towers whose spiky tops reached for the heavens—and promised impalement to any angel who happened to fall down upon them.

There were still a few people meandering about the open-air restaurants, though the actual commerce seemed to be finishing up. I moved slowly and stuck to the shadows, and no one stood up and pointed at the coyote in the middle of the city, so I was pretty sure that the "see what you expect to see and don't be alarmed" part of the pack spell was working okay.

Narrow cobblestone streets led off from the square in a higgledy-piggledy fashion that had nothing to do with convenience and everything to do with their medieval origin. Charmed, I started down one at random.

Like the square, the street was cobblestone, the "road" barely wide enough to accommodate a single car or small delivery van. My feet, still sore from running from the werewolf, would have preferred a nice grassy verge to the granite cobbles. But the rest of me? The only thing that would have made my first exposure to medieval Prague better would have been if Adam were by my side.

I was in *Prague*, walking down cobblestones through a street that probably looked a lot like this a *thousand* years ago. Granted, it wouldn't have *smelled* like this. Medieval cities had to cope with the waste of horses, cattle, sheep, and geese, not to mention people, and mostly, by modern standards, they failed. I was most content with this version of the Middle Ages. My tongue lolled out in pleasure not even sore feet or being hunted by vampires could impact.

Cobblestones had been necessary in the Middle Ages—a huge upgrade from dirt/waste/mud. Cobbles could be washed clean and swept. They didn't get the nasty ruts that could deepen until they trapped any cart with the misfortune to fall into them.

I trotted past closed tourist shops filled with an unlikely mix of chandeliers and alcohol and T-shirts situated next to antique shops—*Good heavens, was that an absinthe shop?*—and jewelry stores that specialized in amber and garnets. The absinthe shop had a neon-green T-shirt in the window that read ABSINTHE MAKETH THE HEART GROW FONDER, which was a little too close to my situation to be comfortable. There was a lot of English around, from the T-shirt to the signs in the windows.

There was a lot of graffiti, too, which surprised me for some stupid reason. In the Tri-Cities, we fight the good fight against graffiti. Most of it is gang-related, but some is just teenagers striving to make their mark in an indifferent world. I guess graffiti seemed like it was exclusively a New World problem—which was a stupid assumption. I *knew* that there was graffiti that dated back to the Romans and said largely the same kinds of things that our modern graffiti does: your sister sleeps with gladiators, I was here, Flavius is hot—that kind of thing.

Maybe the narrowness of the street had to do with defense. You wouldn't have to do much to block such a narrow lane and keep armies trapped in small spaces, where hot grease or tar and arrows or rocks could be flung on their heads with very little work.

And right in the middle of envisioning medieval battles, I caught the scent of werewolf in the air, musk and mint and . . . yeast, which wasn't a usual werewolf scent. I turned and trotted as silently as I could back down the street, but I wasn't silent enough.

Someone trotted after me, a fit, young-looking man in baggy pants and a skintight muscle shirt. I was suddenly glad the pack magic that kept people from noticing me was as thin as it was, because though most werewolves can't actually feel the magic that makes their lives so much easier, if I'd been covered with it as I might have been in the Tri-Cities, he probably would have noticed.

As it was, he saw me plenty clearly. I hadn't seen a single stray dog since I'd started my adventure tonight, though I could smell that there were a lot of dogs around. I think that's what he thought I was. He was being a good citizen and helping the poor stray dog, nice werewolf that he was.

He sped up, and I didn't dare do so. Never run from were-wolves; it only makes them hungry. He said something soothing. It might have been in Czech or Slovak, but "Here, puppy" is a phrase that needs no translation.

A four-board-wide fence spanned a rare space between two buildings. I'd paid little attention to it when I'd passed it the first time except to note the dark green splatter of graffiti that was no more legible for being in Czech than the graffiti was at home. Now I was happy to note that the fence was level, top and bottom, but the ground had a little swell on one side. So there was a space just big enough for a coyote to slide underneath with enough panache that it looked like I'd done it before.

See? I am a dog going home, not the foreign mate of a foreign Alpha running away from a nice werewolf.

I found myself in a garden that was much bigger than the four-board fence had made it appear, because the garden extended along the space between the two buildings and into a back area that was pretty and green.

There was a dog in the garden—a very big dog who couldn't have squeezed out the hole I'd squeezed in through. The large female mastiff came around the corner of the building just as my follower grabbed the top of the fence and chinned himself up to look over the fence.

The werewolf probably thought I smelled weird. It is hard to smell yourself—but I'd been in an accident, been hauled to Italy, smuggled myself aboard a diesel bus, then traveled halfway across Europe. "Interesting" was probably a light word for what I smelled like. Maybe he'd caught a whiff of pack, but since I could hardly feel them, I didn't think so.

The mastiff, bless her, welcomed me into her yard like a golden retriever welcoming a burglar into his home—that is to say, with a wagging tail and licks of affection. That is not my usual experience with mastiffs, but I wasn't going to complain. The werewolf in human form laughed, dropped off the fence, and patted it. He said something cheerful and quiet—and he left.

I snuggled against the lonely mastiff for maybe a half hour before getting up from her side and sliding back under the fence. She didn't notice my going. Her quiet snores made me feel guilty, like a lover who sneaks away in the night. I was comforted by her sleek, well-groomed body; someone loved her.

I checked the fence from habit—and yes, I'd left some fur behind, but that couldn't be helped short of changing back to human and cleaning the bottom of the boards—naked. So I ignored it and walked off thoughtfully (and painfully—I was becoming less pleased with the cobblestones with every step).

I probably would have returned to my camping spot, but I didn't want to go straight back to where my purloined backpack was. I was being paranoid, but paranoia was a good thing. The Lord of Night was after me.

The circuitous route back to the restaurant took me through the old Jewish Quarter—I knew that because there were lots of signs for lost English-speaking tourists like me to follow. And because of the Old-New Synagogue.

The Old-New Synagogue was about six hundred years old or so, which made it the oldest operating synagogue in Europe. I only remembered all of that because I thought the name was funny. I'd wondered about the Old-*Old* Synagogue, but I guess the name was a translation error and there wasn't one. Still, it was an awesome name—and the building was interesting-looking.

Six hundred years old. I stared at it and tried to imagine how it would feel to be Bran or the Moor and look at such things and remember *before* they were built. To look around the city and realize that the oldest thing in this old city was probably you.

Adam would be there someday, assuming nothing killed him before then. I don't know about me. I don't think anyone does. My half brother, who is also Coyote's child, says that sometimes we live a long time, half-mortal and half-avatar or manitou or whatever Coyote and his kindred spirits are. Coyote told me I was too caught up in naming things—which is an excuse to not understand them. I had a few names for Coyote that I was too polite to use.

I was trotting down a very narrow backstreet, this one less touristy than the first few I'd found, when, between one step and the next, every hair on my body rose.

I shrank down against the wall I'd been walking by, trying to hide myself between a step and a garbage can. Magic swept through the street and paused by me. Magic and something that called to my supernatural nature in a way I'd never felt before.

My hiding place had not worked, so I stepped out to face . . . a ghost.

I have an affinity for ghosts, something I inherited from my father in addition to being able to change into a coyote. I see them when other people don't. I used to think I knew a lot about ghosts, but I'd started to believe that no one did. I generally tried not to pay attention to the ghosts because it made them pay attention back.

This one waited with the same utter stillness I'd seen in Stefan and a few other vampires. But it wasn't the ghost of a vampire—yes, there are such things. It wasn't anything I'd ever seen before. I'd never seen a ghost that could hold as much magic as this one did.

Darkness gathered around it, giving it size without form. Ten feet at least, maybe a little more. There was a heaviness about it—it felt dense. The weight of the magic it held, a weave of magic filled, in part, with a kind of power I'd never felt before, made it difficult to breathe.

Some of the energy felt very familiar, but I couldn't place it. It wasn't fae magic or witchcraft. Maybe if it hadn't been entwined with the totally alien feel of the other magic, I could have placed where I'd felt it before.

I took another step, and the mist of magic touched my feet, washing over me with a strange, clean warmth. It should have scared me, that feeling. Whenever any magic feels good—that's the time to worry.

But, alone in a strange city, with the monsters hunting me, I closed my eyes, and the shadow pulled away the weariness, the pain, and the fear that I'd been battling since I woke up in the house of the Lord of Night. It fed me comfort and energy and light—and it fed from me, too. At the time, caught in its magic, I didn't care. I felt the magic brush the bonds I shared with Adam and the pack and hesitate on that other bond.

Impulsively, I took my human shape and stood before the ghost of Prague's past with my hands open and outstretched. "I mean no harm to you or yours," I told it—it did not feel male or female to me. To my human eyes, it was even less clearly defined.

There was no reason to suppose that it spoke English. But the words had come to my tongue by instinct—as a coyote shapeshifter,

I trusted my instincts more than most people did. Ghosts generally could understand me no matter what language I spoke.

It contemplated me for a moment more, then cried out hoarsely, a sound of rage and frustration and loneliness that should have shook the windows in the nearby buildings but didn't. No one came to see what caused the noise.

Runnels of magic slid down my face, as if it had taken a swipe at me with claws. The sensation dug into my bones like hot metal—almost as shocking as the wrenching twist from warm delight to fear. Then the whole thing, magic and all, slowly dissipated. For one instant, I glimpsed something glowing on the center of its forehead, letters that disappeared before the last of the magic. Not letters in any alphabet I knew, though they resembled two oddly written "n"s and an "x." It could have been Arabic or Russian, but I was pretty sure it was Hebrew and that the three letters together spelled *emet*, truth.

Because I had just met the Golem of Prague—or what was left of him, anyway.

What other giant ghost would be wandering the streets of Prague in the Jewish Quarter in the middle of the night radiating magic, but the most famous local legend?

In the sixteenth century, a revered and learned rabbi named Judah Loew ben Bezalel, disturbed by a series of attacks on the people living in the Jewish Quarter, created a golem, a giant creature made of clay. On the creature's forehead he inscribed the word for truth. In so much all of the accounts agreed. The end of the story was another matter.

In some versions, the rabbi lost control of the golem and was forced to destroy it. In another, the creature fell in love—and nothing good ever comes (in stories) from a monster's falling in love. In yet another variation, when the rabbi died, the golem retreated to the attic of the Old-New Synagogue and lay down to wait for his master to return. A lot of the stories end with the golem's clay body remaining in the attic of the Old-New Synagogue, a room reachable only from the outside of the building. I thought it unlikely that it was still there (if it ever had been). Prague had been occupied by the Nazis, after all. Hitler, who had been obsessed with all things magical, must have looked for it there.

I stared into the night and shivered. I was very glad that I had not been in this city when the golem wandered the streets in its physical form.

IT WAS AS NEAR TO NOON AS I COULD RECKON BY THE sun when I strolled into the restaurant that had offered free Wi-Fi. I'd brushed my hair and braided it, securing it with the band I'd stolen from the person I'd taken the money from. I walked directly to the doors marked WC, having read just enough British mysteries to know that WC stood for water closet, which is a bathroom. The women's restroom door had a doe-eyed woman in a pink dress painted on it by someone who was better than an amateur.

The bathroom was clean and bright and had plenty of soap and paper towels. I looked in the mirror and saw that I had a large bruise down my face on the opposite side from my scar. My eyes were shadowed, and my cheeks were hollow. Coyote me had helped herself to the mastiff's food and a couple of rodents of unusual shape, but that was all I'd eaten since the vampires had taken me. I had no idea how long I'd been unconscious.

I looked like the victim of domestic abuse. I smiled experimentally— and to my surprise, that helped a lot.

IN PRAGUE, APPARENTLY, THEY DO NOT USE EUROS. They use something called koruna. Also in Prague—or at least in the little Wi-Fi restaurant in Prague—people are kind.

There were ten people in the restaurant, including the staff: five Czech women, three Czech men, and two Russian tourists, both women. We spoke roughly a dozen languages between us, though I might have missed one or two, but no one spoke English.

One of the Russians spoke a little German. She didn't have quite as much as I did, though to be fair, my German tends to be Zee German—what is not centered around cars and things mechanical is closer to the language spoken in Iceland (which hasn't changed in the last thousand years) than anything spoken in modern Berlin. So maybe her German was fine, and mine was the problem.

I think she understood that I had gotten separated from my tour—which is the story I made up on the spot. My bus, I explained, had gone on to Milan with my luggage and things. I was going to use my e-reader to get on the Internet and call home. Home would then relay information for me.

It was actually useful that none of them could speak to me, because it reduced the number of lies I had to tell them. And also made it harder for them to offer me a place to stay—which is what I think one of the Czech men was offering. No one appeared worried, so I don't think he was offering me what it looked like he was trying to.

They (collectively, it felt like) took my twenty-euro note and, after consulting a cell phone for the current exchange rate, carefully counted out 550 koruna in various bills and coins. The waitress brought me out a soft drink and a thick sandwich, waving away my attempts to pay her.

I pulled out my e-reader (stolen) and turned it on. There had been no charging cable, or I'd have taken it, and the power bar on the screen told me I'd have to be fast—which was interesting with an e-reader that probably had less than half the computing power of Adam's watch. Setting up a generic e-mail account at one of the big anonymous servers—CoyoteGirl was taken, as were several variants—took up too much time. I needed something that would cue the pack without attracting attention. I didn't have to just worry about the vampire; I was pretty sure that various government agencies were doing their best to keep track of our correspondences. 1COYOTELOST worked.

I wrote a short e-mail that said:

Dear People,

Prague is lovely this time of year. You should visit.

M

And then I sent it to everyone in the pack (and a few out of it, like Zee's son Tad and Tony) whose e-mail addresses I remembered. Then I turned the e-reader off to conserve its battery. I ate the sandwich and drank the soda.

Just before I turned it off, the e-reader had told me it had 20 percent power and I should plug it in or it might shut itself off. I knew I should leave the café, wait a few hours, and come back. That's what I'd planned to do.

But the lure of contacting home was too strong.

I told myself I needed to know about the Prague werewolves. If I could round up some support from them, it could be useful. If not, then I could hop a bus for somewhere else and try again.

Waiting until later might not be practical, I reasoned. I'd run across the scent of three different werewolves on the way here. In a city the size of Prague, with only one pack, that either meant that the pack was centered in Old Town or that they were hunting me.

Even if they didn't know about me, the kidnapped by the Lord of Night but subsequently escaped mate of the Columbia Basin Pack Alpha, coyotes don't smell like dogs—not quite. Eventually, if I kept running around on four feet, they'd get interested and track me down. I had gotten lucky last night, and I didn't like to rely on luck. I needed to know if the Prague werewolves were tied to the Lord of Night right this minute.

Really.

I turned on the e-reader and checked my e-mail.

I had one response from Benjamin.Shaw@IT.PNNL.gov. It said:

> OMF**KING G*D*MN Flyingf**kingmonkeys. WHERE? Are you safe? How did you get away? DID you get a f**king way?

The asterisks were his; apparently his work had had a discussion about swearwords in professional e-mails with him. Being Ben, he'd actually increased the swearwords, but added asterisks. It made me laugh even as my eyes watered with relief.

Of course Ben would be checking his e-mail—computers were his job.

> Prague. As ever. As usual. Yes. What can you tell me about our coworkers in Prague? Considering dropping in for consult.

Ben was from Great Britain originally, so he might actually have more insight into the werewolves here than I did.

Hairyb*ttbunnies, girl. Good for you. Prague boss is dangerous bast*rd. Has a real h**don for the boss at your first job. No one but the two of them knows why that I ever heard—and there has been a lot of discussion about it. So someone is suppressing information. It wasn't helped when we came out of the closet— something our colleague in Prague was very unhappy about. Can you avoid?

Okay, so there was bad blood between the Alpha here and . . . the boss at my first job. If I called the werewolves coworkers, then my first job would be the werewolf pack I grew up in. So Bran. Well, that could explain why I thought there was an issue with the Alpha here. I might have overheard a conversation sometime. It wouldn't have been important to me at the time, but I'd filed some alert concerning the Prague Alpha.

Is he working with the Italians?

E-mailing back and forth wasn't as good as texting. The anonymous e-mail server took its own sweet time downloading.

No. But the next closest company, in Brno, is. They were a part of Gévaudan and are now running scared of Prague. Am on phone with Sam's brother right now. Sam's brother says that Prague CEO, Libor, might get a kick out of helping you as a One-Upmanship move on Sam's father—and because he hates Italians more than anyone. He owns bakery in Old Town. Don't know address. My boss is headed to Italy. Does he know you are visiting Prague?

Ben was on the phone to Charles, the Marrok's son who was, among a lot of other things, an information guru. If he said Libor was a good bet, I'd take it.

He knows I'm on my own, and he can find me via GPS if he needs to find me.

He'd know that GPS was our mate bond because that was one thing it was pretty consistently good at. The e-reader gave me another warning.

Out of battery on borrowed e-reader, sorry.

I sent the e-mail, then the e-reader died. I wasn't sure if it had had time to upload my last message or not. I slipped the device back into my backpack. As I got ready to go, one of the men—I think he was the restaurant manager—brought a bag of food to the table and gave it to me.

He was an older man with kind eyes and a rumbly voice, and he smelled of cigars and coffee. He said something solemnly as if he were making a vow, reaching out and gently brushing my bruised cheek. Behind him, the older woman who had brought out my free lunch wiped away a tear.

I had no idea what he said, but my nose could smell the memory of his sorrow and his sincerity now. I felt like a fraud for a moment, deluding these people into believing I needed help. And then I remembered that I'd been violently kidnapped and hauled to Italy, and was now wandering Prague with one stolen set of clothes, 550 koruna, which translated to a little more than twenty dollars, and a defunct e-reader. Maybe I did need their help.

I stood on my tiptoes and kissed his cheek. The whole place burst into applause.

People are pretty cool.

———

SOME PRETTY COOL PERSON PICKED MY POCKET while I was wandering around Old Town trying to find a bakery where there were lots of werewolves.

I'd found one bakery that a werewolf had gone into sometime that day, but the scent was no stronger in the building than it had been outside. Somewhere between that bakery and Wenceslas Square—a more modern city square than Old Town Square, where I found a McDonald's—someone stole all the money I had in one of my pockets.

It was embarrassing.

My only excuse is that there were a lot of people wandering about, and most of them didn't pay attention to personal space the way Americans do. It could have been any of twenty people who bumped into me.

If the person who'd stolen my money had been nervous about it, likely I could have caught them because I'd have smelled it. He or she had made off with roughly ten dollars, hardly worth their effort even if it was half of my resources. At least I'd been smart enough to split my money between pockets.

I hastily checked my mostly empty backpack, but they hadn't

gotten the food or the dead e-reader. I bought a small soda with my diminished funds and sat down on one side of a bench next to a statue of a horseman and ate the food before it was stolen, too.

The woman breast-feeding her baby on the other end of the bench paid me no attention. A man with two children in tow brought the young mother a sausage baked in a bun and an orange juice bottle.

I licked the last of my food from my fingers, gave the happy little family a grin, and wandered off. The sausage smelled good; it made me . . . I slowed my steps . . . made me think of home.

"Excuse me," I said to the family. "Do any of you speak English?"

The oldest of the children, a boy of twelve, did. And he was able to tell me where they'd bought his mother's lunch, a lunch that smelled, very faintly, of werewolf.

THE BAKERY WAS DOWN ONE OF THE NARROW STREETS in a building that looked like it had grown there beginning sometime in the first century. I don't suppose it was that old—not even Prague, I think, was that old—but it had been there a long time. It had taken over the buildings to either side of the original one, growing like China had, taking over previous civilizations and replacing them with its own. The smell of yeast and wheat was warm and welcoming as I stepped through the old door to stand in line.

The bakery played up the age of the building to the tourist trade—though a lot of the people in line (from the scents they carried) seemed to be locals. I wasn't any older than I looked, a well-preserved midthirties. My history-degree emphasis was skewed more to people and politics than it was to fashion and living conditions. All that meant I didn't know for sure, but I thought that the bakery rocked a very sanitized medieval feel with all of its warm-yeast-smelling heart rather than looking as a bakery would have during the actual Middle Ages.

The people hustling behind the counter and carrying trays to tables all wore clothing that looked like something a set director had decided people wore in Prague when the building had been built. There was a costume feel that made them representative rather than authentic. They weren't uniform, in the sense that no two outfits were exactly the same, but the color scheme and general style made it clear that anyone wearing the costumes worked there.

A hand-painted sign that hung on the wall behind the bar told English-speaking visitors that there had been a bakery here, in that spot, for over 450 years. The sign in German said the same thing, and I expected the four other signs that hung around the bakery followed suit in various other languages. Prague was a city that catered to visitors, and this bakery was no exception.

When it was my turn, a young-faced man in dark trousers and a white shirt with blousy sleeves sporting heavily embroidered ribbons greeted me warmly.

"Do you speak English?" I asked.

"Of course," he said with a strong British accent. "What can I get for you? We have today cherry, apple, and peach kolache fresh this morning. If you are interested in lunch—"

"Moon Called," I said very quietly, underneath his practiced patter. He would hear me just fine, but I didn't need everyone in the busy bakery to overhear. I addressed him with that appellation because my nose told me he was a werewolf and because my words would tell him that I knew what he was. "I need to speak to Libor on business."

The smile froze on his face, and he stopped midsentence.

"I'm from the United States, the Columbia Basin Pack," I added.

His nostrils flared.

"Just tell him," I said impatiently. "I can't explain things properly here."

He put a hand on the counter and easily hopped over it. It was a move within the abilities of a young human man of physical prowess—which is what he looked to be.

"Come with me," he said. The words were peremptory, but his tone and manner were not. He led me through a narrow archway into a room filled with tables and chairs set up for people who wanted to eat their treats or lunches inside, and most of the tables were full.

He waded gracefully between the tables, and I followed him to a door in the back of the room. It led out to a garden area. Like the yard where the mastiff had lived, it was the center of the block surrounded by buildings, but open to the air. There were tables here, too, but none of them was occupied.

"You aren't a werewolf," said my guide.

"My mate is," I told him.

"If you would be so kind as to wait here," the werewolf told me, "I will let Libor know you want to see him."

"He'll not have a choice," I told him, and he stiffened. "Curiosity, at the very least, will bring him out. Tell him I'm the mate of the Alpha of the Columbia Basin Pack and I'm on the run from the Lord of Night, who kidnapped me."

"Bonarata?" exclaimed the werewolf, then he held up a hand when I started to explain further. "No need to talk to me. I'll let Libor know. It might be a while." He left.

A while was right. It soon became evident that if Libor wanted to see me, it wasn't a priority. I waited on my feet for ten or fifteen minutes until one of the human waitstaff—and not one who spoke English—produced a tray with one of those baked-bread-wrapped sausages that had brought me here, three pastries that looked like a bagel filled with various fruit fillings, and a tall glass of lemonade.

The harried woman looked pointedly at her tray, then at the tables. I picked one with a comfortable-looking seat that backed up to one of the surrounding walls and sat so she could put the tray down. She smiled, then said something in a happy voice before whisking herself out of the garden and back into the bakery.

I was left alone to eat in the late-afternoon sun. Even though I'd just eaten a fairly large meal, I had no trouble eating a second one. I finished both food and drink and set the tray aside.

The sun warmed my back and birds sang in trees and my eyelids, stupid things, decided that the warmth, the gentle sounds, and the smell of werewolves meant that it was safe to sleep. I stood up and walked the little area, trying to stay awake.

I hadn't gotten any sleep last night.

I knew, without acknowledging it, that when I started to talk to dead things, other ghosts seemed to sense it. A few months ago, after a rather violent encounter with a ghost, I'd spent days with ghosts following me.

Ghosts are mostly bits and pieces of people, of emotions, left behind—so it was like being followed by zombies. They want me to do something for them, but there isn't enough of them left to communicate exactly what that is.

Mostly, when I did find out what they needed, it wasn't anything I could do. I couldn't fix the life they lived, the people they failed. I couldn't give them their life back.

Anyway, I didn't know exactly what the golem had been, except that it was complicated. But he had evidently powered up my ghost-attraction circuit to stun. Judging from the results, my meeting with the golem had lit me up like a target for any ghost in the area. The lingering effects made certain that my safe little corner next to the river had been invaded all night by ghosts. A city as old as Prague collects a lot of ghosts along the way. The worst of them had been a drowning victim.

I'd done my best to ignore it; however, it was true that drowned ghosts smell like the body of water they drown in. The Vltava smelled like any other river from the top, but evidently having been occupied by humans for better than a millennium meant that the bottom was full of rotting things. And I'd learned something new last night, too. Apparently some drowned ghosts were just like the stories—they could drip real water. Being dripped on by a foul-smelling ghost all night had not been conducive to sleep.

Though there'd been a few ghosts as I'd followed the werewolf through the bakery, they hadn't been drippy or smelly, just faded remembrances of people who'd once worked or lived in the build-ings. They'd drifted past me and through the visitors. And what-ever the golem had called up in me had faded enough that they had taken no notice of me at all. I'd returned the favor.

There were currently no ghosts in the little sunlit garden where I was. The sounds of the tourist-filled streets were muted. What-ever was going to happen to me, I wasn't going to be attacked, robbed, or arrested in this little garden until the Alpha of Prague came to see me.

I sat back down at the table I'd claimed for my own. I put my head down and closed my eyes, letting the sweet scents of fruit filling and sugar frosting linger in my senses as I fell asleep.

5

ADAM

While I traveled by bus, Adam made do with a
luxurious private jet. That is kind of how my life goes.

"YOU CONTACTED HER?" ASKED ELIZAVETA IN RUSSIAN
as she put Mercy's repaired necklace into Adam's hand.

Elizaveta usually spoke to him in Russian, and mostly that was
fine. Adam's mother had spoken Russian in their home throughout
his childhood, leaving him almost as fluent in it as he was in
English.

But leaving Mercy behind when he'd just found her was painful.
And whatever the old witch had done to allow him to contact
Mercy, now that their brief conversation was over, it had left the
werewolf magic, both his pack ties and his mate bond, in a state
of outrage—a painful state. The combination of loss and pain left
him unable to speak in Russian or English.

He closed his fingers around the necklace and drew a deep

breath. When that wasn't enough, he shut his eyes and rested his head against the back of the airplane seat. His wolf was fighting for control in a way it hadn't since he'd been very new—and had been pretty much since Mercy had gone missing.

He'd forgotten how tiring it was to fight the beast to a standstill. He'd had decades to become complacent, to believe that he had a handle on just how bad things could get. As the hours had passed, and Mercy was no closer than she had been, the wolf had fought and fought and fought.

When his mating bond had found Mercy again, faint though the signal had been, just after he'd gotten on the plane, he'd thought he would be back to normal. But once the wolf figured out just how far away Mercy was, how poorly the bond was functioning . . . He'd found a quiet corner in the plane designed to please the kinds of people who rented private jets as a matter of course and had been trying to meditate to keep his beast under control when Elizaveta found him.

She'd sat down on the floor next to him with an ease a woman of her age shouldn't have had and handed him a small bottle of Russian vodka.

He'd handed it back. "Thank you, but not right now."

She took the bottle and took a long drink before capping it and tucking it away somewhere in the layers of her clothing.

"To break a werewolf's mating bond," Elizaveta said, "this is something very difficult—but to block it?" She laughed gently and patted his cheek. "Such a thing is child's play to such as I. Witches like me and werewolves like you have existed in the same places for centuries. Much werewolf lore has been passed down in my family and others."

She spoke in Russian, and the wolf quieted as he let himself be comforted by the way it brought back childhood memories of his mother sitting beside him and explaining how the world worked to him in much the same voice.

"I have a book written by my great-grandmother," she said. "It is all about werewolves. A whole section of it deals with mating bonds and pack bonds—which are different aspects of the same magic. I am sure that many witch families have copies of this book—or one like it. She tells us that a specific kind of circle of warding, one that does not let magic pass in or out, will block the bond. With a day to work, I could put together something that could do it for a few hours. Give me a week and the right ingredients, and I could block it for longer."

"So the fact that I can feel her now is only a sign that whatever they have been using to block our mating bond has burned out?" he asked.

"A sign that something has changed," Elizaveta said. She pursed her lips and nodded to herself. "Perhaps we could ask her."

"I've tried," Adam told her. "I think that our bond is working fine, but we are just too far away. Without the pack for me to draw upon for power, we might have to be in the same city to make real contact."

Elizaveta snorted. "Adya, you underestimate me. If you have something of Mercy's, I can use your bond to give you a few minutes to talk."

In that moment, he'd have given her his heart, dug it out of his chest in order to hear Mercy's voice. But that would have been dumb, and in the end, all Elizaveta had needed had been Mercy's necklace.

He wasn't stupid, so he made her work her magic in the biggest of the rooms in that huge plane so that the vampires and Honey would be there if something went wrong and he lost control.

Elizaveta had come through for him again, as she always had. So now he knew that Mercy was alive.

Eyes closed, heart pounding, Adam pressed his body back into the leather chair. Mercy had even rescued herself from the monsters. But now she was lost and alone somewhere in Europe. Both he and his wolf found that unacceptable—but much, much better than knowing that she was bleeding and taken by vampires, which was all he'd had before.

The monster inside him didn't want to fly to Italy and treat with a vampire. It wanted to go to Italy and kill all the vampires. All of them everywhere. Then find Mercy, take her home, and barricade her in their home so that no one else could take her from them. Part of Adam's trouble in bringing the wolf under control was that he pretty much felt the same way. Only his intellect could see how disastrous that might be. Still, his heart fought on the side of the monster.

Elizaveta—he knew because he could smell the faint whiff of her scent, a blend of tea-tree oil and herbs—kissed his forehead. Then she stood up and said, "I am an old woman, and this has tired me."

"And hurt you," he said, opening his eyes to look up at her.

Witchcraft was powered by pain, the witch's or someone else's. She had dug a knife into her scarred forearm and cut a slice of skin. When she'd burned it in the incense, she'd had to grit her teeth—as if burning her flesh had done even more damage to her.

"I'm sorry," he told her.

"Don't fret, Adya," she said. "A little pain, and it is gone. Pain and I are old friends. I am going to go use one of the back rooms and sleep on the couch."

Mercy was scared of the old witch—as she should be. Elizaveta was dangerous. Her own family was terrified of her. But she reminded Adam of his mother—her accent, the way she smelled, her turns of phrase—and he couldn't be afraid of her.

"Sweet dreams," he said, and she smiled at him with her eyes.

No one spoke until she left the room.

"So what did you learn?" Stefan asked.

"Has Bonarata harmed Mercy?" asked Marsilia.

Adam realized that he didn't know—and that set the wolf off again. He gritted his teeth and fought for control. If Bonarata had done something to Mercy, he would have known it. She was all right. Tired. Sad. But defiant—even toward him—and funny. She was all right.

"Adam?" asked Marsilia.

"Leave him be," growled Honey. "He needs a moment."

HONEY HAD NOT BEEN HAPPY THAT ADAM HAD CHO-sen her to travel with vampires. She didn't have much experience with them—and that's how she'd preferred it.

He'd explained that he needed her because the Lord of Night was addicted to werewolf blood—and preferred females to a degree that was pretty rare in a creature as old as he was. Most predators became quite practical about their food after a few centuries. Adam intended to use Honey, if he could, to distract Bonarata. He trusted her to be able to defend herself from the Lord of Night if everything went sideways.

To prove that no matter how old Adam got he would never understand women, telling Honey he was using her as bait for the nastiest vampire on the planet made her happier with his decision.

"It really isn't just Mercy," she'd said.

"What isn't just Mercy?"

"The reason that my status in the pack has risen," she said. "I thought it was just Mercy who was behind the shake-up in the pack organization."

"No, Honey," he'd told her. "It is you. It always has been you."

"Bonarata has a pet werewolf," Honey said.

"I know." He waited for her to elaborate, because Honey didn't do much casual talk.

"Lenka," she said. "I didn't know her very well, but she and Peter were lovers before I met him. His first, as human or werewolf. They weren't in love, either of them, but he liked her, even after she picked her Alpha instead of Peter. It sent him wandering, though, until he found my pack. And me. I always figured I owed her for that."

Adam put a hand on her shoulder. Werewolves need contact more than humans do. It had taken him a long time to understand how important touch was, but he didn't forget it now.

"She was strong," Honey said in a low voice. "Strong and brave and true. She had a moral compass that always pointed north. She was like Mercy in that, but without the sense of humor—Lenka took herself and the world very seriously."

Honey closed her eyes and rested her cheek against his hand. "When Bonarata took her, we were in Russia. Peter was restless, and he liked to travel."

Submissive wolves—and their mates—were welcome in any pack they chose to honor with their presence. Alpha werewolves practically needed a treaty drawn up to move around. Only Mercy's kidnapping meant he didn't have to bother with the politics that were usually a basic part of any travel plans he made.

"We didn't hear about it for almost a decade," Honey said. "How Bonarata killed the whole pack—Peter's first pack. Most of the pack, anyway. He didn't kill Zanobi or Lenka, and we heard how that was a lot worse. Peter was wild." Her breathing was labored, as if it hurt to draw in air and let it out.

But she didn't say anything about why Peter hadn't done

something—or if he'd tried and what had happened. Knowing Peter as he had, Adam couldn't believe that Peter hadn't tried *something*.

"Will Bonarata know you?" Adam asked.

"No," she said. "We never met."

Honey had pulled away from his touch then. She wiped her eyes with her thumbs, and he pretended not to see. She looked away for a moment, then met his eyes. "You think I can do this? I don't know anything about vampires."

"I think," said Adam slowly, "that you've never let anyone down in your life. You won't fail for any reason other than that old vampire is just too powerful or too smart—or because the rest of us fail you. I honestly believe that you are our best hope for winning."

After a moment, she nodded. "Okay. I'll do my best."

Bonarata had sent the second e-mail by then, the one Marsilia had predicted. It had come very early in the morning, just before the vampires retired for the day. The e-mail had been . . . a real piece of fiction.

Bonarata had been coming to visit Marsilia when he'd happened upon a terrible wreck. The mate of the oh-so-famous Adam Hauptman was dying from a tragic car accident. He had scooped her up and taken her to his home, where the healer in his employ had fixed her up. Having done so, he was concerned lest more harm come her way—as her rescuer he felt some responsibility for her continued safety. He therefore invited both Marsilia and Adam to come to Milan and convince him that Mercedes would be safe in their care. He allowed them two people each as well as the pilot and copilot of the airplane.

Wasn't that just swell of him? The problem was, the Lord of Night really was powerful enough that it was necessary to play his game as long as he was willing to avoid outright attack. Adam hadn't just taken Marsilia's word about that—he'd called Charles. And information wasn't the only thing he'd called Charles for.

"I need a pilot," Adam told the Marrok's son, after absorbing everything that Charles knew about the Master of Milan. They both knew he was asking if Charles would be that pilot.

"Da says I can't do it." The edge in his voice told Adam that Charles wasn't happy about that. Adam didn't even ask how Bran had found out about Mercy. Adam's pack knew, and someone would have called the Marrok to keep him informed. The Columbia Basin Pack might no longer be affiliated with the Marrok—but habit was a difficult thing.

Charles continued speaking. "He is keeping his distance from you to save us all, he said. Too many people know me. He is right about that. He said that it's likely Bonarata expects me to be your pilot; otherwise, he wouldn't have made such a direct reference to the flight crew. People like him don't pay any attention to the staff."

Of course. Adam had missed that. He'd been distracted.

"He's right," Adam said. "Of course he is right. And if you are not a surprise, then you become . . ."

"Da called it a 'complicated hostage,'" Charles said dryly. "I told him that I could protect myself, and I got a lecture on diplomacy. Apparently that wasn't the point. If I go, I become a thread that leads to my father. Which makes me very interesting—too interesting for the delicate balance of manners and power that Marsilia is organizing in the hopes of getting everyone, including Mercy, home safely. He might be willing to throw everyone else away for a chance to take Da down, so I have to stay here. I might chance it anyway, but as it happens, I've had a run-in or three with Bonarata; he knows my face." Charles cleared his throat.

"Da told me to tell you that he very much expects and trusts that you will get Mercy home safely."

At that point, Adam hadn't slept since the vampires had taken Mercy, and it was beginning to affect him. But he was still sane enough to trust Bran's judgment. "If he says you wouldn't be an asset, he's probably right." Where did that leave him? Oh, yes. "So do you know of a plane we can hire to take us to Italy? Someone who won't be surprised or worried about carrying vampires and werewolves?"

Adam's firm had two or three charter companies that they used. But the vampires added a serious problem to the whole thing—no one could afford for humanity to find out about vampires. Vietnam would be a kindergarten tea party compared to what would happen if people discovered there were vampires feeding on them and playing games with their minds.

"That I can help with," Charles said, and he gave Adam a phone number. "It's a small firm but big enough for this. The pilot and owner of the company, Harris, is a goblin, so you won't have to hide anything from him. He flies out of Northern California." His voice gentled. "He's a good pilot. He'll get you where you are going. Then you can go fetch our Mercy home before she destroys the Lord of Night's holdings and causes a war."

Adam couldn't help but laugh. She would, too, if she could. But even if she thought she was indestructible, he knew better.

"Thanks," Adam said, his voice ragged. "I needed the reminder. Mercy is pretty good at survival."

"It's a Coyote thing, survival," Charles said. And Adam suddenly realized that Charles, too, was under no illusions as to the identity of Mercy's real father. "Get some sleep, Adam. You're getting foggy, and you can't afford to be anything less than your best."

———————

HE'D FOLLOWED CHARLES'S ADVICE ABOUT THE PLANE and about the sleep. He'd decided on Honey. Then he'd made the difficult decision of who his second person would be. Aiden was right out—he was a target for the fae. Adam didn't have the resources to protect the boy and retrieve Mercy at the same time, no matter how useful the fire-touched Aiden would be. Joel was out because without Aiden to help him control the tibicena fire spirit he held, he was too likely to be a liability.

Another time, Adam would feel pretty good about taking Warren or Darryl and leaving the pack with only one of his top two people. But right now there were too many balls in the air.

Aiden's status as most wanted by the fae was the biggest issue. Though the Gray Lords had agreed to leave him alone, recent events had lessened Adam's faith that they had absolute control, even of their fellow Gray Lords.

Aiden represented too much possible power, and the absence of both Adam and Mercy would be a tempting time for some independent fae to make a play. Especially since Mercy had been kidnapped, which made them appear weak. Like the werewolves, the fae were predators, and weakness would be an almost irresistible draw.

And the pack's resources were strained trying to make their territory safe from supernatural predators. It was a delicate balance that would need both Warren and Darryl to keep a lid on troubles at home when Adam left.

But the attack had not been aimed at the werewolves alone, no matter how personal it was. It had been aimed at the coalition of supernatural powers that Bonarata seemed to believe existed in the Tri-Cities, a belief that Marsilia had been encouraging for a long time.

So they should travel with a fair representation from the membership of their imaginary support group, right? Adam appreciated the irony that Bonarata's attack was making real the alliance whose imaginary existence was, probably, the catalyst for the Master of Milan's kidnapping of Mercy. So he'd contacted Marsilia and suggested that instead of three vampires and three werewolves, maybe they should find a couple of other people to bring.

Marsilia hadn't been difficult to convince. As she'd said, there were only two other Master Vampires in the Tri-Cities. One was crazy and his loyalty was doubtful—and she didn't want to bring him into contact with Bonarata. Stefan had agreed to go, but she would still have had to bring at least one underling vampire, which would be a tacit admission of weakness.

They settled on a representative from the goblins. Adam hadn't known who the leader of the goblins in the Tri-Cities was, but Marsilia did, and he'd agreed to come. They weren't a long-lived race, as fae went, but they were clever and more powerful than most people gave them credit for. Adam liked that they were often underestimated. Marsilia liked that they were old allies of hers. They were, Adam had found, more reliable and oddly honorable for one of the fae folk.

As for Adam, his first pick for the empty slot was Zee. The old fae had grumbled and grumped—because he badly wanted to come—but finally told Adam that he would not be an asset. Like Aiden, he was too likely to draw attacks from outside interests who would otherwise stay out of matters that did not concern them. Moreover, he and Bonarata had had interaction in the past. One in which the vampire had not come out on top. If they were going to try to negotiate—and Marsilia and Charles (coming to the conclusion separately) believed that was the best way to get Mercy out alive—then Zee could not come. Adam hadn't asked Tad. Like Aiden, Tad was too likely to be a target for European fae looking for power. Equally possible was that he would draw fire aimed at Zee.

Adam didn't trust any other fae enough to bring them into this. So he had asked Elizaveta Arkadyevna Vyshnevetskaya, and the old Russian witch had been very pleased to accept.

Very pleased.

He was glad that she'd agreed to come, too.

His beast, his heart, and the abused pack magic all subsided eventually. He opened his eyes to see that, outside of the witch, they were all still gathered in the smaller of the airplane's little sitting areas.

Honey sat on his left, Stefan on his right. Marsilia and Honey were in the facing seats, Elizaveta's empty one in the middle. The goblin sat on his heels in the walkway and looked perfectly comfortable doing so.

With the shades pulled, the quiet rumble of the engines was the only real indication that they were in an airplane. This plane had been built to shepherd captains of industry, sheiks, and princes. The floor was carpeted, and the seats were creamy leather and polished walnut.

"Adam," said Marsilia after a moment, her voice oddly gentle. She asked, "Are you all right? Did you speak with her?"

He rubbed his face and moved to the edge of his seat. "I did." He gave his comrades a genuine smile. "You know Mercy. She escaped and is now traveling somewhere in the luggage compartment of a bus. How does that change our game?"

"He will be furious," said Marsilia. She smiled, a surprisingly sweet expression on such a dangerous woman. "Somehow, when she is destroying other people's carefully laid plans, she is not so annoying."

"Fabulous," said the goblin. "Such a clever coyote is your Mercy."

Mercy had seemed frayed, but Adam would never admit that in the present company. "Never admit weakness before your enemies" had been his mantra long before he'd been Changed, and he wouldn't betray Mercy's, either. He'd just met the goblin—and Marsilia was not a fan of his wife.

"Do we continue to Milan?" Adam asked. "Or divert to another country and try to find Mercy before he finds her?"

"Milan," said Stefan. "This isn't an isolated incident—something he can only do once. Next time, he might make a more lethal move."

"What if the fae threw in with us?" Honey asked. "Would that be enough to back him off?"

The goblin, who went by the human name of Larry Sethaway, shook his head. "Never happen," he said. "The fae would rather watch the battle, then pick at the corpses like the carrion crows they are." He grinned briefly, fully aware that in the supernatural world, it was the goblins who were looked upon as scavengers. "Can't hardly get them all pointed in one direction if they were all dying of thirst and there was only one place to get water. I don't mind them as noncombatants, but I'd just as soon keep them off the field. You don't know who they'll decide to kill first, your enemies or you."

The goblins didn't consider themselves fae, though the reverse wasn't true. Most of the fae looked upon the goblins as sort of lowborn, weak, stupid cousins. Some of the fae looked upon them as food—and the goblins never forgot that.

Larry could pass for human, though some of his kind could not. When he'd met them at the airport, he'd been wearing dark glasses to cover his yellow-green eyes, and leather driving gloves to hide his four-fingered hands. Here in the plane, he'd left off both.

"I agree," said Marsilia. "Both with Larry and with Stefan."

She smiled a little, a cat's smile. "Let's not tell him we know she's gone. Let's see what he chooses to do now that he's lost her."

"Will he believe we don't know?" asked Honey. "She's Adam's mate."

"The only reason we know she escaped is because Elizaveta was able to use their bond to work her own magic," Marsilia answered.

Stefan nodded. "And Wulfe told him that your mate bond is erratic. If you act as if you don't know, he'll probably believe it."

"He might just tell us that she escaped," Marsilia said. "But I don't think he will. It betrays a weakness, a mistake. He doesn't like admitting to real mistakes, only pretend ones."

"Like if he killed her," murmured Stefan. "Oops. I accidentally killed your wife, poor thing. I hope you didn't care for her too much. I just don't know my own strength."

"Would he have done that?" asked Honey. "If she hadn't gotten away?"

Stefan glanced at Marsilia, who glanced surreptitiously at Adam.

"I am very glad Mercy managed to get away," Marsilia said finally. Adam knew diplomacy when he heard it.

"What would you have done with me," said Adam very quietly, "if he had killed her while you were trapped in here with me?"

She met his gaze with her own. "Died with everyone else if you lost control or destroyed this plane," she said. "But you wouldn't have given Iacopo—Jacob," she corrected herself with a cool smile. "You wouldn't have allowed him such an easy victory as that. I know you too well. But Mercy is not dead."

She leaned forward. "I have not lied to you about the danger we face. I do think that we may come out of here with nothing worse than an unplanned trip to Europe. But there is an equal chance that he will start killing—and if he does, all of us will die."

Larry leaned his head in the direction of the cockpit. "Including our pilot and copilot? Such a shame. He is quite beautiful for one of our kind." The pilot, he meant. The copilot was a werewolf, though not Charles.

Marsilia smiled at the goblin, and Adam realized, somewhat to his surprise, that she genuinely liked Larry. He wasn't used to associating Marsilia with such a . . . gentle emotion as that.

"No flirting until we are back home and your wife can't blame me," she said.

Larry shrugged. "No harm in looking, is there?"

Stefan stiffened. He looked at Adam. "Mercy is trying to get my attention. Do you have any message for her?"

"Tell her to stay safe," Adam said. "See if she knows where she is yet."

He made note that Stefan's bonds with Mercy were able to function at a greater distance than the mating bond. He didn't like it, but he made note of it.

Stefan smiled compassionately. "It is a simpler thing," he told Adam, "the tie between vampire and prey, than the one between mates—as the bond between master and slave is simpler than a marriage. And Mercy is bleeding." He held up a reassuring hand. "From a few small wounds only. But the blood feeds her call."

He took out a pocketknife and cut a shallow wound on his thumb. He put the bleeding digit in his mouth, then froze.

Adam was determined not to be jealous. He was too worried about Mercy to be jealous. If she could contact the vampire, then they had two ways to find her.

Two was better than one. If Adam died here, Stefan could still get Mercy to safety.

Even the wolf thought so.

―――――――

IT WAS NIGHT AGAIN WHEN THEY LANDED AT THE PRI-
vate airport Bonarata had specified. There would be no trouble
from customs; Adam's pilot (and the owner of the company) had
assured him that all of the paperwork had been taken care of. His
pilot had also timed the flight so they landed on the morning side
of midnight. Adam was pretty sure that Bonarata didn't own the
airstrip, but he wouldn't need to. Being the Lord of Night meant
he would have lots and lots of minions.

Bonarata's people met them as they exited the plane. There
were six of them, all male, all vampires, all dressed in the exact
same very expensive suit. Dark hair cut into the same style—like
Ken dolls but not so handsome.

One of them stepped forward and spoke in British-accented
English. "My Master bids you welcome to Italy. He would have
met you himself, but business matters kept him away. No need to
see to your luggage; it is my honor to see that it makes it to your
rooms with all haste."

He signaled, and three of the vampires headed to Adam's left
toward the plane.

One of them smelled familiar.

This one had been among those who stole Mercy from him.
Adam noted his face very carefully. There was nothing remarkable
about his face—but Adam would remember it for a very long time.
The vampire caught him at it and involuntarily met his eyes.

Adam let the wolf surface for a moment, let the vampire know
that he'd been recognized.

The secret weakness of all vampires—and it was a big one—
was that they all feared death. The only way any vampire was

Made was because they feared the ending of life enough to give up everything in order to survive. Everything, including the person they had been.

Adam saw fear rise into the vampire's eyes, and he was momentarily satisfied.

"Adam?" Honey said, and there was a note in her voice that told him he'd missed something important.

He turned his attention to the matters at hand.

"It was not made clear," the vampire repeated, "what your preferred sleeping arrangements were?" He was so carefully not looking at Marsilia that Adam turned and raised an eyebrow at her.

"I wasn't certain what would please you," she said apologetically.

She intended to play second to his first. Adam wasn't alone in his determination to use weapons that weren't purely physical against Bonarata. He thought of how he would feel if he saw Mercy playing devoted follower to another man and had to fight back an inappropriate growl.

Marsilia smiled at him, and it was an intimate smile, a lover's smile—a little deferential still. And Bonarata's vampire saw it for what it was.

If Mercy were playing a man like that, Adam would know she was about to stab that man in the back. His wolf settled. Mercy wasn't above playing roles and fighting dirty when the odds weren't in her favor. As long as she felt she stood on the side of the angels, she wasn't particular about how her enemies fell.

Marsilia was no more ethical in that way than Mercy—and far more vindictive. Bonarata had chosen his addiction over her, and she had not forgotten nor forgiven it. Bonarata would eat glass at the sight of her catering to what he thought were Adam's . . . what? Needs? Ego? Distracting Bonarata would be to their advantage. Hadn't Adam told Honey that he was going to use her to do that? Marsilia could play that game, too.

He did wish that Marsilia had discussed this aspect of her plans with him—but even as he thought it, he knew why she hadn't. Marsilia knew that he wouldn't have agreed to play ball. He didn't cheat on Mercy, not even mild flirtation for appearances.

What were his choices now? Expose Marsilia? Reject her? He thought about that one. He could do that without making her lie apparent—but the whole point was that Bonarata saw them as a united front, not to leave Marsilia exposed as a target.

Honey, he trusted, could protect herself from anyone but herself. Marsilia . . . she was strong as hell, but she was vulnerable to Bonarata.

"Adam?" Marsilia asked again, this time touching his shoulder. He didn't back away from her touch, though he wanted to.

Adam glanced at Honey and Larry, then shrugged. In for a penny, in for a pound—Mercy might, on a very bad day, have a moment of weakness that would let her believe that Adam would cheat on her with Marsilia. But—

"Give us a suite that will sleep six," he told the vampire. She would never believe that he'd also sleep with Stefan, Honey, some goblin he'd never met before, and—holy cow—Elizaveta. She'd know that this was the easiest way for him to make sure all of his people were safe. And to really stick a bug in Bonarata's peace of mind while he did so.

Adam looked at his people and said, "We might as well share space as spend the night running down hallways." He turned back to Bonarata's head minion and let the thought that they were going to be in a vampire's lair—a consideration, not a cause for alarm—come and leave his eyes. Then he said casually, "Or days, I guess."

"Mercy might object to Larry," murmured Stefan. He was going to play along.

"Larry might object to Mercy," said Larry in the exact same tone.

"You should be so lucky as to have Mercy pick you," said Stefan shortly and, Adam's wolf noticed with sudden sharp interest, totally honestly.

Adam shrugged again. "Mercy can organize us as she sees fit when we get her back."

"It will be like a vacation," said Honey in sultry tones, because Honey was sharp as a tack and a fine actress. "We haven't had one of those in a long time."

Honey sold the lie with her body language and her voice—and gave it just enough to be believable. Most of the other supernatural folk kind of thought that the werewolves, who touched a lot more than was a comfortably human norm, all probably slept with their pack mates anyway. And those stories were fed by the now-vanishingly-rare Alpha who felt like that was the only way he could dominate his pack. Come to think of it, those would probably still be fairly common in Europe, where there was no Marrok to deal with them.

"That is not your reputation," said Bonarata's minion, sounding a little . . . shocked. Which he shouldn't be, given the stories Adam had heard about Bonarata's parties. The minion was looking at Marsilia, and Adam wondered abruptly if the vampire was old enough that he'd known Marsilia before she left.

"A suite," said Marsilia shortly, but her body leaned into Adam. Her heart was racing—unusual for a vampire, but she'd been very stressed since this had begun. Adam could relate, but he gave her a reason for her racing heart by caressing her face lightly.

He let his wolf rise just a bit—rage and lust smelled very similar. In his experience, vampires weren't good at sorting through emotions, though they could smell them very nearly as well as a wolf. But the vampires' emotions were skewed, they were selfish creatures by definition, and it left them in trouble when it came to sorting someone else's out.

"We have a suite with three bedrooms," said one of the vampires. "We can house your pilot and copilot in servants' quarters."

"My pilot and copilot?" Adam said. "They will stay with the plane."

"I'm afraid that won't be possible," said the head minion. "My Master made a special request that they, too, accept accommodations with us." He smiled slyly. "We could bring trundle beds if you want them in your rooms, too."

Adam looked over his shoulder to see that the two men were climbing out of the plane with the small bags they carried with them. The pilot was as good-looking as Larry had said, tall for a goblin, with sandy-gold hair and robin's-egg-blue eyes. He watched the vampire escorting him warily, temper in the set of his shoulders. But Austin Harris was smart enough not to argue with Bonarata's people.

Harris reached out to steady his copilot without looking at him when he wobbled on the ramp, too busy watching the vampire to watch his feet. The copilot was medium height and average-faced, and so intimidated by the vampires that he very nearly clung to the side of Harris. The copilot was a werewolf. The way he sought protection from Harris told Adam—and anyone else who was watching—that he was submissive. It was dangerous to be that submissive when surrounded by vampires.

Bonarata's head minion cleared his throat. Right, he wanted an answer to his question.

If Adam pulled the pilot and copilot into the suite, it would look like they were afraid. Which they were. But it would also look like an insult, making clear that they did not expect Bonarata to keep guesting laws.

Adam raised his eyebrows in surprise. "Does Bonarata sleep with every damn person he hires? Give them their own rooms."

He glanced over his shoulder at the pilot and the werewolf again. Harris met his eyes with a worried gaze and then glanced at his copilot. "One room would be better," he said.

"Better give them one room with two beds, I suppose," Adam said. "Someone as scared as he looks to be isn't going to sleep well alone in a vampire seethe. If we can't make him comfortable, the pilot is going to have to fly us home all by himself while his copilot sleeps."

"That can be arranged," said the minion, who was watching Harris with interested eyes. Predatory eyes.

"I trust in the honor of the Lord of Night that those two will be safe from the seethe," Adam said softly.

The minion started, looked at Adam, and flushed when he realized that Adam had seen his hunger. The minion closed his eyes and went very still.

"They will be our guests," he said after maybe half a minute of blank face and quiet body. "My Master's word on it."

So Bonarata could get and give information through his minions—at least through *this* minion. Adam would remember that.

Adam glanced at Harris and the wolf again. Putting a handsome man and a vulnerable one in the middle of a seethe . . . if Bonarata didn't have iron control of his vampires, there might be trouble.

Then he thought of Marsilia's assertion that Bonarata didn't like making mistakes—though he didn't mind hiding behind an apology and the claim of a mistake that wasn't really a mistake.

Bonarata's vampires probably wouldn't attack Harris and his man by accident. But if it was in the Lord of Night's best interests to have them trapped here without a pilot . . .

Adam sighed audibly and said, "Oh, put them somewhere near us. At least that way if someone starts screaming, there's a good chance we will hear them."

The vampire drew himself up. "Do you doubt my Master's honor?"

"No," Adam said. "But I won't trust the self-control of vampires I don't know when presented with prey that looks like this." He waved a hand at Harris, who raised a good-looking eyebrow.

"Sorry," he apologized. "This is really what I look like. I don't have enough magic to keep up glamour."

When things might get dangerous and I might need every ounce of power I've got, the goblin pilot didn't say. Probably the vampires wouldn't hear the unspoken message—and if they did, likely they'd understand the reasoning behind it.

Harris frowned suddenly at Adam. "And you have no room to talk."

"Yes," Elizaveta said venomously. "We are all beautiful here. Can we get going? Or do I need to get the makeup mirror out of my purse so you two can admire yourselves a little longer?" She looked at the vampire. "I hope there are sufficient bathrooms in the suite. I don't like to share"—she glanced at Adam, laughter in her eyes—"bathrooms."

Bonarata's minion nodded, but he wasn't really paying attention to Elizaveta, which was a mistake he might regret. It didn't do to forget that she was a power who could make even the Gray Lords of the fae back down. Instead of paying attention to someone who could make him wish she was only killing him, he was staring at Harris's copilot, who had been doing a pretty good job of being unnoticeable.

"That one is a werewolf," he said abruptly, as if he'd just figured it out.

Harris frowned irritably. "I was told that this involved vampires. I have five people who can fly this bird from the US to Europe, excluding me. Four of them are humans, so I brought the werewolf. He doesn't belong to Hauptman's pack. I cleared it with Hauptman." He turned his frown to Adam.

"I was told a pilot and copilot were acceptable," said Adam coolly. "What race or species they belonged to was not specified."

The vampire was doing its mind-out-of-body thing again. When he came back, the vampire's body language changed entirely, and the beast who lived in Adam's heart suddenly took notice. Adam didn't know who was looking out of the head minion's eyes, though he had a good guess. One thing Adam *knew* was that it certainly wasn't the vampire he'd just been talking to.

"Are you Charles Cornick?" the vampire asked the man standing just behind Harris.

The werewolf's jaw dropped. "Oh, hell no, sir," he said in a shaky voice, his shoulder bumping into Harris's.

He might as well have screamed "I'm a victim" to the biggest predator in Europe. Adam could see the urge to attack slide into the bodies of all the vampires in the area—including Marsilia and Stefan.

Adam pinched his nose and closed his eyes briefly as the weight of responsibility fell on his shoulders. He had to keep all of these people safe—and they were going to be doing their best to get themselves killed. Some of them because he had asked it of them. The only shining thread in this whole mess was that Mercy had managed to extract herself: Bonarata did not have Mercy.

Harris's copilot continued to babble, the smell of his panic filling the air. "Have you ever seen Charles? He's about twenty feet tall, and he's Native American. Do I look Native American to you?"

"Leave him alone, Bonarata," said Adam. "He's not your food. He is . . ." Adam surveyed the trembling wolf without affection, but sighed. "He is under my protection."

"I thought you said he wasn't one of yours," the vampire observed.

"He doesn't belong to my pack," Adam said. "But for the purposes of this trip, he put his neck on the line for me. That means he is mine to protect."

Bonarata's puppet turned to Adam. "My apologies," Bonarata said through his puppet's mouth. "But you pricked my temper, because I am most disappointed. I was sure you'd bring the boogeyman of the werewolves. I've been looking forward to meeting him."

"I did ask," said Adam coolly. "But the Marrok forbade it. Charles is very good at ending people . . . monsters, let's say, and the Marrok apparently thinks that bringing him here, where there are so many monsters to be slain, would be a bad idea. Maybe he believes that. Maybe he believes this is my problem, not his—and he doesn't want to risk losing Charles. Or maybe he is reluctant to deal with the headache of the power vacuum that your death at Charles's hands would leave in Europe. It would be nearly as large a mess as the death of Jean Chastel, the Beast of Gévaudan, left."

"Charles didn't kill the Beast," said Bonarata. The vampire's voice wasn't as certain as it would have been if he knew what he said was a fact.

Adam shrugged. "I wasn't there when Chastel died."

Charles had been, though, and rumor persisted in laying the old villain's death at Charles's feet—as if Charles's reputation needed any help from killings he hadn't performed. Whether it had been at Charles's hand or not wasn't the point. Adam was just reminding Bonarata that even powerful old monsters could die.

"Master," said a soft voice. It belonged to the vampire who had been on the crew that had taken Mercy. "You asked me to remind you when you were close to harming one of your own."

Bonarata, still possessing his minion, nodded. "*Grazie*, Ignatio. Hauptman, I look forward to meeting you and yours in person. My people will escort you to my home." Then the vampire staggered, dropped to his knees, and shivered in a fit very like a grand mal seizure.

Ignatio—and Adam stored his name for future reference—waved, and a couple of the vampires picked up their fallen companion.

Ignatio bowed. "If you would be so kind as to follow me?"

As they moved toward the waiting vehicles just off the runway, Adam walked behind Ignatio and to his right. "Your scent was on my wife's car seat along with her blood," he murmured, though everyone in their group would hear him. Quiet, he had found, could be a lot more menacing than loud.

The wolf wanted to kill him, but Adam understood about being a soldier and taking orders. Still . . .

Adam said, "I will remember."

"Pack remembers," Honey added.

6

MERCY

So from now on, the timing between my part of the
story and Adam's gets tricky, and you'll have to pay
attention. This chapter begins late afternoon, the day
after Adam and his people land in Milan. I'm asleep
with my face plastered against the top of a metal table.
Being sophisticated like this just comes naturally
to me—what can I say?

I WOKE UP. MY CHEEK WAS HALF-GLUED TO THE TABLE-
top from drying sweat and (probably) drool. But I didn't pry it loose
because there was a werewolf watching me, and I was still caught up
in dreams that had me riding a troll over the Cable Bridge, jousting
with the Golem of Prague while the drowned ghosts of a thousand
werewolves climbed up the side of the bridge asking for jelly beans.

I needed a moment before I could deal with the real live

werewolf. The troll I got, and the golem, of course, but I couldn't figure out why the wolves wanted jelly beans.

"I know you are awake, Mercedes Hauptman," growled a soft tenor voice with the seductively thick vowels that the Slavic languages are famous for. Czech was different from the Russian accents that I was more familiar with, throatier and deeper. Not so much less musical as *bassier* musical.

I sighed, sat up, and rolled my head, then my shoulders to ease my muscles. "Now I'll never find out why it was jelly beans," I said.

"Jelly beans?" he asked.

I drew a deep breath. "Just a dream," I told him, and took a good look at Libor of Prague, the Alpha who had some sort of secret grudge against the Marrok.

He smelled of werewolf, of butter and yeast and wheat and eggs. And a little of the same fruit filling I'd eaten in the pastries he'd fed me earlier. The smell was sweet and rich: like jelly beans.

Libor looked nothing like I imagined him—at least not as I'd imagined him when I was a child. Probably that was a good thing for him.

His hair was medium brown and cut almost brutally short. His face was clean-shaven but, like Adam tended to, he already had a shadow of a beard making itself felt this late in the afternoon.

Libor, the Alpha of Prague, was a big man, not so much tall as massive. There was something more leonine than lupine about him. His features were of average attractiveness. He was neither beautiful nor ugly. It was a strong face and intelligent. He reminded me, superficially, of Bonarata, in that people would look at him and expect brutality and risk missing the intelligence altogether.

But Bonarata had been cold all the way to the bone. Any

warmth I'd seen in him was an illusion created by a master manipulator.

Libor, my coyote informed me, was many things, but cold was not one of them. He smiled as I met his eyes and held them. His smile expected me to turn my gaze away and leave him in charge. His problem was that I had just had a few very bad days and was done with being vulnerable and lost. A minute passed. Two.

"You tread upon dangerous ground, Little Wolf," he said softly.

"My apologies," I said insincerely, without dropping my eyes. One of the cool things about my coyote is that dominance battles aren't usually a problem for me. I could stare down just about anyone except for the Marrok himself. Libor wasn't my Alpha, and I was just not going to give in.

After a moment, my brain kicked in. Staring down a werewolf was dumb. I'd spent my life trying not to be any dumber than I had to be.

After a few more heartbeats, during which time I acknowledged to myself that I was antagonizing someone I hoped to elicit help from, and being dumb with no end in sight, I said, "I'm trying for strong enough to pay attention to but polite enough not to cause a real fight. How am I doing?"

He lost his smile, which was good because it had become sharp around the edges, and he narrowed his eyes until I could feel his power beating at me angrily.

"As I said," he told me, his voice as casual as his eyes were not, "dangerous. You should probably consider how . . . thrilled? Yes, that is the word. How thrilled I am to have the daughter of Bran's heart here in my territory. It is something that gives me great pleasure."

He didn't look like a man who was pleased. He looked like a

starving wolf who'd caught a glimpse of a wounded deer. "Pleased" was such a bland word for that emotion.

I tried to figure out how to answer him.

Death threats—and he had just issued one, if obliquely—are to be gotten through as lightly as possible. I'd noticed that if I paid too much attention to them, matters tended to proceed from bad to worse.

I was tired, and I'd hesitated too long to deny that Bran had treated me like a daughter, before he'd abandoned me and the pack for political reasons. Our pack was the only pack in North America not affiliated with the Marrok. We stuck out like a big sore thumb, and someday soon, someone was going to give in to curiosity and see what happened when they hit us—as they would not dare do to one of the packs under the Marrok.

I took a breath. Had I misread Bonarata? Had that been what he was doing? Did his kidnapping of me have nothing to do with Marsilia at all?

But Bonarata was in Italy, and I was sitting across the table from a werewolf I needed to pay attention to instead of playing my I-wonder-why-the-big-bad-vampire-took-me game.

I had missed my chance to claim that Bran didn't care about me. Likely, Libor wouldn't have believed my disclaimer anyway because I only mostly believed it. Bran hadn't abandoned us because he didn't love me anymore; he'd abandoned us because he had a Greater Cause, the survival of the werewolves, that he loved more.

So. Death threat.

It was likely that Libor didn't intend to kill me unless I pushed him into it. First, Charles had sent me here. Though Charles maintained that he wasn't good with people—which was true enough—it didn't keep him from reading people pretty well. Second, and even more telling, I wasn't already dead. Alpha werewolves don't tend to be the kind of people who dither.

I realized I was watching my fingers tap on the table. At some time during my thinking process, I'd dropped my eyes to the table. It hadn't been because I'd been intimidated, or at least I didn't think so. But if I was going to get into a staring contest with a dominant wolf, I probably should have been paying more attention.

"I had heard that you and Bran weren't on speaking terms," I said. "So . . . you'd have killed me already, but you don't want me to die before I satisfy your curiosity?" I hazarded lightly. Not afraid of the Big Bad Wolf—no, sir, not me. "You want to know what I'm doing, alone, in your territory and why I mentioned the Lord of Night?" I shrugged. "Otherwise, I'd probably be dead instead of fed good food and left to sleep in safety."

He leaned back comfortably in his chair (it creaked alarmingly) and said nothing.

"I am here because of Bonarata," I said blandly. "He kidnapped me about a mile from my home in the US. Apparently he was under the impression that I was the most powerful supernatural entity in the territory of his discarded mistress and One True Love. I think he'd forgotten all about her until recent events put the Tri-Cities of Washington—state of—USA into national and international news. Reminded of his love, he chose to go after her by kidnapping me." That was my current favorite theory. Or maybe it was a hit directed at Bran—or the pack. But I'd go with my first instinct. So I nodded as if he'd said something, and continued, "I know. It struck me as stupid, too. But I'm not an ageless vampire, so I'll cut him some slack."

"Are you?" Libor asked.

"Am I what?"

"The most powerful supernatural entity in the Tri-whatsit city?"

"I change into a coyote," I countered. "That's my superpower. What do you think?"

He'd been sarcastic with his question, but at my answer, he straightened ever so slightly and looked . . . intrigued.

"I had forgotten that about you," he said slowly. "And I do not think that you have answered my question. Which I find very interesting. *Are* you the most powerful supernatural creature in your territory?"

I shrugged uncomfortably because I couldn't lie to him. "Maybe," I said. "Possibly. But not because of what I am. More because of who I know. I was raised in the Marrok's pack. I'm mated to Adam Hauptman, who is Alpha of our pack, and not least among Alphas in the other packs. I have a friend who is fae—and he is someone even the Gray Lords don't mess with." They were looking for more pieces of one of the Gray Lords who had ticked Zee off. My informant (Tad) was pretty sure that they would find them all. Eventually.

"I have a friend in the human police department and another in the local vampire seethe." I shrugged again. "Anyway, Bonarata was disappointed because he'd expected someone . . ." I tried to decide how to explain it.

"More powerful," Libor supplied.

I shook my head. "Whose power wasn't all in the people she knows. Intrinsic power." I waved a hand vaguely down myself. "Stronger, at least. Anyway, he decided to engineer my failed escape during which I would conveniently die, and he could blame it on me—and humiliate my mate for failing to take care of me. Instead, I really did escape, hopped on a bus, and ended up here. Penniless. Friendless. And passportless."

"Pathetic, in fact," he said dryly.

I widened my eyes and nodded, answering the humor in his eyes with my own sincerity. "On the way here, I got pickpocketed. They stole half of my money. I have about two hundred koruna left." That I had stolen first. Borrowed, really, since I intended to pay it back with interest, but borrowed without consent was, strictly speaking, theft.

"I'm about as pathetic as it gets," I told him honestly.

He folded his arms. "Peanut butter," he said.

"Excuse me?" I tried to sound blank. That stupid story had made it all the way here? Jeepers creepers. If I'd known how long I'd have to live with that, I'd have figured out some other way to get back at Bran.

"You," he said, "are Bran's little coyote girl who made him sit in peanut butter because he made your mama cry." Foster mother, actually, but I wasn't about to correct him. Not until I knew him better, or it was over something more important.

He gave me a wolfish smile. "You wrapped his new and very expensive car around a tree. People still talk about the chocolate Easter bunny incident with awe. And *still* Bran did not kill you. You escaped from the Lord of Night, Master of Milan. And you want me to think you pathetic?"

He leaned forward. "I know a little more about you, Ms. Hauptman, than that old vampire did. I do not think you would find it so easy to get away from me."

"But you haven't taken me prisoner," I reminded him, and carefully didn't say "yet." "So I don't have any reason to run away. Charles told me that I should throw myself on your mercy—and ask you to help me stay alive and out of Bonarata's clutches until Adam can get to me here."

"*Charles* said that," he said neutrally.

"Well." I tried to stick to the absolute truth. "It was through a third party, and our communication was necessarily brief—but I can read between the lines. I would *rather* you come with me to storm the seethe of the Master of Milan so that we could extract my husband and the small number of people he took with him to broker my release, which brokering is now unnecessary."

"No," he said.

I gave him a look. "Do I look stupid to you? Tired. Pathetic. Yes. Stupid—not usually. I'm not going to ask you to face down any vampire in his den for me, let alone the Lord of Night. I request, respectfully, sanctuary for three days. Charles seemed to think it would allow you to count coup on Bran if you protected me when he couldn't."

"You are the mate of another Alpha," he said, his eyes half-lidded with menace. "Intruding on my territory without prior arrangements. I could have you killed for that alone."

I'd kind of thought we were past the death threats. But apparently I was wrong.

"Yes," I agreed. "But it wasn't on purpose—and killing me would make you look like a real jerk."

He laughed. "You think I mind looking like a *real jerk*"—he tasted those two words as if they were something he hadn't said before—"do you?" But his whole body had relaxed. Once they laugh, they are mine. Mostly.

"If you were going to kill me," I said, "you'd have done it already."

"You," he said evenly. "You are a threat to my people. If I grant you sanctuary and you die, the Marrok will come here and kill my people while I watch. If Bonarata comes after you, he will do his best to kill my people, and he will never let it drop."

"Libor," said a small voice chidingly, "you are being mean to the nice lady. Stop it."

I looked. I couldn't help it. I hadn't heard anyone come in, hadn't smelled anyone approach, and as wound up as I felt, I should have.

I'd expected a child, but instead there was a woman with bright blue eyes and curly hair several shades lighter than Libor's, a medium brown. She was wearing a folk costume, a more authentic version of what the man at the counter had been wearing: a simple white blouse with a string neck covered partially by a laced-up, heavily embroidered bodice. She wore a multitude of lightweight, bright-colored skirts of various lengths. Her face was cheerful and rounded, like her body.

She met my gaze and grinned. "My Libor, he has grown cranky. He needs a good meal and his wife to cheer him up."

"Don't look at me," I told her. "I'm not that young, and I'm very much married."

About that time, I realized several things. The first was that her English was awfully good, complete with an American accent that came straight out of the Pacific Northwest. The second was that she was about four feet from me, and I still didn't smell her. The third was that Libor, after a quick glance behind him that didn't land on the woman whose hand was on his shoulder, stared at me intently, his eyes going gold with the presence of his wolf.

"Damn it," I said with feeling. I was good at this. I was very good at spotting the ghosts. The days of my randomly addressing people and only realizing later that no one else could see them were long gone. Or so I'd thought.

The golem's odd effect on my ability with ghosts was still making my life difficult.

"I had heard this," Libor said, frowning, "that the Marrok's little coyote could see ghosts."

The ghost behind him smiled at me and brushed at Libor's hair as if there were something out of place, though his hair wasn't long enough to be obstreperous. She leaned back and angled her face as if checking to make sure she'd managed everything correctly, and I suddenly knew, without a doubt, what it was that Libor held against the Marrok.

Zack.

If this woman were male and had been starved for six months, then she'd be a dead ringer for our pack's sole submissive wolf, Zack. It wasn't just a passing resemblance. I'd seen twins who didn't share as many similarities.

Zack had come to us a restless wanderer who showed signs of abuse. He'd gradually settled into the pack, losing most of the wariness he'd arrived with.

But Zack still thought he was going to take off again for someplace else someday real soon, but that "real soon" had changed in emphasis as if it were gradually lengthening from "probably tomorrow" to "next week" and finally a vague time receding into the future.

He was rooming with Warren and his human partner, Kyle, another temporary situation that was sliding into a permanent one. Warren's presence kept the pack happy with the safety of our submissive wolf (something that preoccupied the wolves in a way I'd never understood until Adam had made me part of the pack's magical ties), and Warren was never obvious with his protectiveness. Unlike almost any other old wolf I've ever met (and Zack had once told me he'd been a werewolf for over a century), Zack was not homophobic and seemed content with the place he'd made for himself in Warren and Kyle's home.

The whole pack was trying to make a home for Zack with us, and we were all holding our breath, hoping he wouldn't notice until it was too late and he already belonged to us. A submissive wolf was a gift to any pack. They tended to cut down the petty bickering that was part and parcel of having a roomful of dominant personalities, and they settled the pack, made it feel, for everyone, as if pack was more than a necessity, that it was a good thing to be a part of. A submissive made the survival of all the wolves in the pack more likely.

I don't know how Zack had become a bone of contention between Libor and Bran—but I would bet all the money I didn't have at the moment that he was at the bottom of their feud. Because there was no way that lady could look so much like Zack and not be closely related to him.

"There's a ghost here," said Libor.

I looked at him and sighed. "I try not to pay attention to them," I told him. "There's no good to be had from it."

"Who is it?" he asked.

"Don't tell him," said the ghost, still sounding like she'd grown up in Aspen Creek, Montana, like I had. Some of the stronger spirits did that—they communicated so forcefully that I heard them without any distortion, as if death granted them a universal language, a quick conduit to my brain without language at all, maybe. I found it very disturbing when they did that. "It would hurt him to know that I watch over him still."

But she didn't, not really. This wasn't truly the woman she resembled, just a skin of personality shed when she'd died however long ago and her soul had gone to wherever souls go. I didn't know why some ghosts stayed fresh and strong while most others faded—though sometimes it was because the living paid too much attention to the dead. But that didn't make the ghosts into the person whose face they wore; it just made them stronger ghosts. I'd seen souls tied to their ghosts once, and I'd never again made the mistake of thinking of a normal ghost as a real person. This woman's soul had gone on a long, long time ago.

I was coming to believe that ghosts were something, though, something that could think and plan and do. Not living, precisely, but not inert, either. It was a belief that went against everything I've ever heard about ghosts—but I interact with them more than most people.

Still, even though she was not the person who had been Libor's wife, she had once been part of her. She knew Libor, and I chose to follow her advice.

"I don't know, and I'm not going to talk about it long enough to give it more power," I told Libor. "Look, ghosts are like discarded clothing left behind when a person dies." Of so much I was still sure. "I'm sorry to distract you from the matter at hand. I wouldn't have if I weren't tired."

"Is it my wife?" he asked softly. "She was a tiny thing, but rounded where a woman should be rounded. Her eyes were blue as a Viking's."

"I don't talk about ghosts I see," I told him. "No good comes of it."

The ghost of his wife smiled at me. "He doesn't like it when people don't do what he says. I'd watch my step if I were you."

Another ghost had found its way out to the courtyard, attracted by the attention I was trying not to pay to Libor's dead wife. This one wasn't anything anyone would have called pretty. Werewolf killed, I'd guess from the damage. If I were a normal human, I'd probably have been more appalled. But my other self is a coyote. I might not take down humans (or any other large prey), but I've eaten a lot of field mice and rabbits. I let my gaze pass over that ghost.

"Is it my wife?" Libor asked intently, and this time there was a bit of growl in his voice.

"I don't talk about ghosts," I told him. "I don't describe them. I don't name them. I don't look at them if I can help it."

We had ourselves a little bit of a stare-down again. Three more ghosts, one of those I'd seen in the main room of the bakery, drifted in. I was busy staring at Libor, and it weirded me out that I still knew they'd come in. Usually I have to use my eyes (or ears or nose or some normal thing) to know when they are around. Evidently not today. Stupid golem.

"Look," I said. "It isn't safe to pay too much attention to ghosts. They start to linger, and they pull you in the wrong direction." My half brother had told me that it was less safe for someone of our lineage to pay attention to the dead than it was for regular people. Too much attention tended to strengthen ghosts and anchor them in the world of the living. Attention from one of our kind was apparently even more energizing.

"I am very old, little girl," Libor told me. "If ghosts were going to get me killed, they would have done it a long time ago." He frowned at me with consideration. "You will tell me what I want to know—and I will give you your three days."

"You want me to describe the ghost I see here?" I asked him. "Though I have clearly stated that it is a bad idea. But after I do this, you will grant me sanctuary for three days."

"Yes," he said, sounding half-irritated, half-amused. "Talk for two minutes, a description and maybe a little conversation. Then I and my pack will protect you for three days. I give you the better end of the bargain."

He was going to get the bad end of the bargain, that was for certain. Fine. I'd warned him, and it was on his head. He was so certain he wanted me to do this—I was going to do it right for him. I closed my eyes and tried to draw upon the power that I'd only touched a time or two on purpose.

There were a lot of ghosts here in the courtyard of Libor's bakery. More than I'd sensed before. When I reached out to them, it felt as though I were breathing them—bits of pain and fear and terror, most so faint that they'd lost any touch of personality or coherence.

I opened my eyes and looked around. I might have been a little ticked with Libor for not listening to me when I told him it was a bad idea, but I was also concerned about adding any power to the woman who was still petting him. If she could get into my head enough to talk to me without an accent, then she was powerful enough to affect things in the real world. And if I gave her more power while he was still here loving her, I might never be able to get rid of her.

She was tied to Libor already. People tied too closely to ghosts tended to do things like drive their cars into trees, shoot themselves, or drink themselves to death. The dead want to be closer to the living.

So I picked someone else.

"He looks as though he was attacked by your pack," I told Libor with not-really-faked reluctance. This guy wasn't someone I'd want to be haunted by. "The suit he is wearing looks like it is from the 1950s, and it looks like he was wearing it when he was killed, because it is shredded and covered with blood."

Dan, whispered the ghost painfully, though the bottom half of his face was gone. *Dan.* Under my attention, the misty edges of the transparent body drew together, condensing and solidifying at the same time.

"His name is Dan . . ."

Danek. The ghost's voice was suddenly stronger, as if my voice on his name was giving him energy.

"Danek," I said at the same time Libor did.

As soon as I spoke his name, the ghost was as solid as any person I've ever seen in my life. I could smell him, could smell his anguish and his sweat. I could see the weave of his blood-soaked silk tie. If I'd seen him on the street, I'd have called 911 for him.

What had that golem done to me? And how?

"Danek is a ghost?" asked Libor, who evidently wasn't getting the same sensory load as I was, because, though he looked over his shoulder, he wasn't looking in the right direction.

"Apparently," I told him.

The old wolf laughed without amusement. "Of course he is. Danek never knew which way to go without someone's telling him first when he was alive. It makes sense that he'd be the same dead."

I almost gave my speech about how ghosts are not really the people who died, again, but Libor was one of those people who liked to tell others how the world worked and not listen to anyone who thought differently. I kept my mouth closed.

Libor smiled sourly. "Danek worked for the resistance here, such as it was, during World War II. His resistance group contained some of my pack and was supported by the rest of us. We only found out later, after the war was over, that he'd been working for both sides. He told the Nazis that the people who planned the assassination of Reinhard Heydrich came from the village of Lidice. It wasn't true, the Nazis even knew it wasn't true, but they paid him. Do you know what they did to Lidice?"

I did, actually. I'd written a term paper on the assassination of Reinhard Heydrich in Prague in May of 1942. Heydrich had survived the initial attempt, and if he hadn't been adamant that only German surgeons work on him, he might have lived through it. Then again, maybe he'd been right to be afraid. If I'd been a Czech surgeon, I'd have made sure Heydrich didn't survive. Heydrich made Hitler look like he should win the Humanitarian of the Twentieth Century award. Nasty piece of work. In any case, Heydrich died. And so had Lidice.

"The Nazis killed all the men over fifteen right off the bat," Libor told me, without waiting for my reply. "They picked out a handful of very young children who looked German and sent those off to be raised as good little Nazis. Then they shipped the women and the rest of the children to concentration camps. They killed all the livestock and all the pets in the village. They looted the village, down to digging up the cemetery, hunting for gold teeth or jewelry. When they were done, they burned the buildings. When that wasn't complete enough for them, they blew it up. They covered the whole thing with topsoil and planted it. The roads that led in and out of town were rerouted, as was a stream. When they finished, there was no sign that Lidice had ever existed there."

Delenda est Carthago, said the ghost, just before Libor said the same thing.

"When the Romans destroyed Carthage, they leveled it so not one stone stood upon another," Libor continued. "Lidice was a multilevel message from the Nazis. The first message was to those under their rule, that any assassination would be punished, and punishment would not just fall on the conspirators but on their families. Second, to the German people, that Heydrich was properly avenged and that it was Czech rebels, not Hitler, who engineered his death. Heydrich was being groomed or grooming himself, accounts vary, to take over the Third Reich from Hitler. Heydrich, unlike Hitler, was tall, blond, athletic, and smart. The German ideal, in fact—which Hitler himself was not."

Had we killed Heydrich? They asked me, said Danek's ghost. *How could I tell the Nazis that? They would have killed me, too, even though I was working for them. They would have asked why I had not warned them. If I told them nothing, they would have suspected me. So I gave them something else. A rumor, I said, that the assassins came from a little village. They didn't need the real assassins if they had a village to punish. Lidice didn't die for a lie. For my lie. Not really. It died so we could go on fighting the Nazis. We won. We beat them. I did the right thing. For Prague. For the resistance.*

The other ghosts, including the woman who must, from his description and her behavior, have been Libor's wife, were backing away from Danek, as if something about him was repellent to other ghosts. They drifted, almost casually, through the walls until, by the end of Danek's self-justification speech, the only ghost in the garden was Danek's.

I was working really hard at keeping a calm facade. I'd never done anything like this. I was pretty sure that I should have kept on following my brother's advice instead of giving in to my temper when Libor pushed me.

"We killed Danek when we found out what he had done," Libor said. "He *knew* what the Nazis would do, and he gave them a random target that was away from him. A village small enough to destroy—because that's what Hitler wanted."

Monsters, said Danek in my ear. I might have jumped a little because he hadn't been anywhere close to me when he said it. *I'd been working with monsters, and I didn't know it. I thought the Nazis were the monsters, and I was so afraid of them. I was wrong.*

"He was so afraid of the Nazis," said Libor, "that he betrayed that little village to them. Oh, he took money, too. But mostly it was to save his own skin. We'd never have known it, but he started dating one of my pack—and he lied to her about it."

Libor's commentary and the ghost's were so close to the same topic that I wondered if the ghost was somehow influencing Libor even though he couldn't hear what the dead man said.

"The village of Lidice wasn't the only thing he'd given to the Nazis," said the Alpha werewolf. "He sold them some of our group, too. One of the ones he sold was a boy who ran messages for us. He was ten."

No one important, said Danek. *Just a few, so the Nazis would know that I was cooperating fully. So they wouldn't kill me. But I was afraid of the wrong monsters.*

"He was a coward," said Libor. "And he feared the wrong monsters."

The war was over, Danek said. *We won. My side won, then they killed me. I died anyway. It wasn't fair. They didn't even allow me a funeral. No marker for my grave. No mourners.*

"He died too easily," Libor said. "But the war was over, and time enough had passed that we couldn't just leave his body. So we buried it here." He nodded toward a corner of the garden. "Under the cobblestones beneath that green table."

"I see," I said. The effect of the two-sided narration was really eerie.

"Danek is the only ghost here?" asked Libor.

I made a production of looking around carefully. "Yes. He is the only one here in the garden with us."

Danek reached out and touched the back of the chair that sat at the green table. Frost followed his fingertips but melted away quickly. It left no moisture behind, so maybe it hadn't been frost at all but some sort of residue. I'd never seen a ghost do that.

"Then I will give you the sanctuary I offered," Libor said briskly.

"Thank you," I said, my eyes still on the ghost. "And when you are tired of Danek, let me know. I'll come back and see if I can fix this."

"Fix what?" Libor asked.

"I told you," I said. "It isn't smart to pay too much attention to the dead. It is especially not smart for *me* to pay too much attention to the dead."

The chair Danek had touched fell over on its side. Libor jumped and stared at it.

"I don't think," I said, "that Danek is going to be the sweet kind of ghost who finds lost things and contents himself shutting doors a little too hard. We can give him a few weeks, to see if he fades on his own. But if that doesn't work, I'll see what I can do."

Hopefully I'd be home in a couple of weeks. That would mean I would have to fly back. I could fly back with Adam and see Prague properly. As long as we all survived.

HOT WATER AND SWEET-SMELLING SOAP DID A LOT for my spirits. I was still stuck in Prague without papers or money, but at least I was clean and had a change of clothes I hadn't had to steal. I had a bed and a safe place to sleep.

The clothing they had found me was typical of spare werewolf-pack clothes (apparently) the world over: running pants and a tank top—a little closer fitting than what our pack used, but still stretchy enough to fit a wide variety of body types, male or female.

I had a small room at the top of the stairs, a little isolated from the rest of the living space over the bakery. It was still daylight, I was surrounded by strangers—one of whom was pretty unhappy with me even if he did acknowledge that I had told him over and over that what he wanted was not a good idea. Even so, I think I was asleep before my body hit the mattress.

I woke in darkness, and someone was stroking my cheek gently. I rolled away from the touch and buried my head in the blankets.

"Leave me alone," I said with force.

Then I realized that I was alone in the room—and had been while those fingers had been touching my cheek.

I hoped sincerely that it was still a residual effect of meeting the golem that left me such a magnet for the ghosts of Prague. I hoped even more fervently that whatever it was that had caused this would go away soon.

I also felt guilty.

I try not to give orders to the dead unless it's important because they can't refuse me, not if I focus my will strongly enough. I wouldn't have done it except that I had been mostly asleep. But I had ordered the ghost to go away—and it had gone.

I think it had been trying to warn me because, a few minutes later, my door popped open.

I was up on my feet beside the bed, with my right hand still trying to close around a gun that wasn't there, before I was aware enough to remember where I was.

"Wake up, woman," said a gruff voice that belonged to a man I hadn't seen before.

He was slender and compact, like a gymnast. If you saw him

in a suit, you would never know how much muscle he carried. In the tight tank shirt and jeans, he emphasized it. He looked a little like the man who had followed me until I'd taken refuge in the garden of the friendly mastiff. Maybe they were related. He was one of those men who would look like a teenager until his hair started graying, but since he was a werewolf, that would never happen. I wondered if he'd learned to turn that into a strength yet.

I'd been raised in the Marrok's pack. I never judged the strength of a person by their outward appearance. The Marrok didn't look like a man who held the reins of thousands of werewolves who would die for him. He looked like a pizza delivery boy or a gas-station attendant—right up until he didn't.

"What do you need?" I asked.

"Libor says to tell you that there are vampires here, looking for you and being forceful about it. We need to move you. Gather your things, and I'll take you." His voice was British-pure, though that wasn't a guarantee that he was from the UK. Most English speakers in Europe, I was discovering, had learned to speak British English rather than the American version.

I turned on the table lamp and realized that my other set of clothing was in the wash. I put the borrowed shoes on without socks and took the pack that contained a very little money and a dead e-reader.

"Ready," I said.

Danek met us at the base of the stairs and pointed in the opposite direction the werewolf was trying to take me. That left me in a quandary. Ghosts, like the fae, don't lie. They are so literal, you have to be careful about believing anything they say. He might have been pointing us toward the bad guys instead of away.

Before I could ask him anything, Libor's dead wife appeared and pointed the same way.

Tell him to take the way through the kitchens, she said. *The vampires have the usual exits surrounded.*

"The ghosts say that there are vampires at the usual exits," I told the werewolf. "We need to use the way through the kitchens."

He froze.

"I only get weirder the longer you know me," I told him, quoting one of the T-shirts I'd gotten for my last birthday.

His nostrils flared, and he looked around a little wildly, trying to see the ghosts, I think. Danek brushed against a table, making it scrape across the floor, and the werewolf jumped.

I rolled my eyes (a gesture I'd caught from my teenage stepdaughter). Sometimes it was the only thing that properly expressed my opinion. Seriously? The werewolf was afraid of ghosts?

Ignoring him, I started down the route Libor's dead wife was still indicating, across the room and down a dark hallway.

"I thought ghosts were just bits and pieces of the person who died," said the werewolf very quietly as he passed me.

He seemed to suddenly know where we were going and led the way at a brisk pace.

"Yes," I said. "No. Sometimes." His words were close enough to what I'd said to Libor that I was pretty sure Libor had been talking to his wolves. And well he should, because though his wife had been relatively benign, I was pretty sure Danek was going to be a problem.

"Then why are they warning us about something happening right now?" he asked.

The hall floor suddenly dropped about three inches and took a jag to the right. A few paces farther on, there were three shallow stairs that took us up about a foot altogether. The wolf had continued speaking quietly as he held my arm to make sure I didn't stumble up the steps. "If they are just bits and pieces, don't you think they should be moaning here and tossing things about rather than giving warnings about vampires?"

"Some of them retain a lot of their predecessor's personality," I told him, though I'd wondered about the nature of ghosts for exactly the same kinds of reasons. All well and good to dismiss them as . . . as nothings when one of them wasn't leaving you drawings or another one wasn't trying to help you survive. But I gave him the only answer I had. "The ones who bear grudges or are extremely attached to someone who is still living seem to be the most independent of thought."

The kitchens were huge, and there were two of them. The front half was modern and filled with ovens, various kinds of cooking surfaces, and giant mixing machines taller than I was, with bowls that sat on the ground. Everything was immaculate.

There was a half wall and a wider than the usual doorway opening that led into a room that looked as though it had been pulled directly from the Middle Ages. The far wall had a giant fireplace with a spit. Beside it was a stack of metal pots that looked as though they should have a witch throwing eyes of newts and snail tails or something in them. One of the long walls was covered by a giant brick oven with rows and columns of regularly spaced openings that were about two feet square.

My werewolf guide trotted right up to the farthest opening and climbed through. I did the same and found that the inside of the oven was a room in its own right. Against one of the inner walls was a narrow metal ladder, up which my guide was already climbing. I followed him up a couple of stories and out to the roof of the building.

The werewolf had quit talking and was making an effort to be silent, so I followed suit. We weaved our way between chimneys on the roof of the bakery. When we reached the end of the bakery, there was a narrow hop, and we kept going on the roof of the next building. We probably made a quarter of a mile before we jumped to the ground.

The werewolf, still quiet, didn't speed up from the easy jog we'd begun on the rooftops, and he took us into a more residential and modern section of the town. In total, we ran maybe six miles, long enough for me to regret my lack of socks. He took me to a garage under an apartment building built in the last hundred years and stopped by a motorcycle. He started to get on it, then stopped.

"We'll attract too much attention without helmets," he said. "Wait here, I'll be right back."

He was as good as his word, returning with a pair of helmets. He tossed me one and put on the other himself.

Mine wasn't a perfect fit—and I didn't like the way it restricted my vision—but I didn't complain. When he mounted the bike, I climbed on behind him and held on.

The last time I'd ridden behind someone on a motorcycle I'd been in college. Char, my roommate, had had a Harley. We'd taken it out and gone camping now and then, just to get away from school.

This bike was about half the size of Char's and much quieter, but being a passenger behind the werewolf wasn't much different than being a passenger behind Char had been.

7

_____

ADAM

Bonarata's villa in Milan, in the wee small hours of
the first night I spent in Prague. At this moment I was
huddled next to the Vltava while a ghost dripped water
on my head. So this chapter begins before the previous
chapter started. I told you it was going to get tricksy.

THEY WERE GIVEN A LARGE SUITE WITH THREE BED-
rooms, each equipped with a king-sized bed and a bathroom. They
looked pristine and newly remodeled, but this was a very old
building, and it had seen a lot of violence. Adam could smell the
faint musk of fear and the rotten iron of old blood as if it, like the
stone, wood, and paint, was part of the material that made up
the structure.

Their luggage had been piled tidily inside the main door of the
suite when they got there. Adam figured that they'd been driven
from the airfield the long way to allow the luggage to beat them.

"Dress for dinner, he says?" said Larry as soon as their escorting vampire guide had left. "It's four in the morning Milan time."

"You can hardly expect vampires to eat in the day," said Marsilia.

"Or to eat at all," offered Honey. "Are we going to *be* dinner?"

"They always have last meal at 5 A.M. here," answered Stefan. "'Dinner' is a word used for guests—think of it as a very early breakfast if you'd like. There are usually guests who aren't vampires. Bonarata uses it as a gathering for the seethe. There will be fresh blood for all the vampires and good food for everyone else."

Elizaveta had paced around the room muttering to herself. She entered the first bedroom, and Larry moved to follow her.

"Leave her be," said Stefan. "She's checking for magic. Bonarata has a few witches in his employ, had a very good witch at one time, and, according to rumor, a fae half-blood. There are a lot of things a witch could do to us without breaking guesting laws. I don't have to tell you to clean your hairbrushes and burn the stray hairs, do I?"

"Standard stuff," grumbled Larry amiably. "Trimmed toenails get eaten, I know."

Honey made a sound, and the goblin flashed a grin at her. "Of course, you can flush them if you'd like. I prefer to be certain. Witches are bitches and they'll burn your britches sure as kittens have itches if you give 'em half a chance."

Elizaveta was in one of the bedrooms. She might not have heard Larry. But Honey was standing right next to him.

"I'm a bitch," said Honey in a smooth voice.

The goblin laughed. "That you are, dearie. Don't take offense where none is meant." He wasn't dumb, thought Adam. This was about establishing boundaries. He was telling the room that he was sure enough of his ability to protect himself that he wasn't afraid of offending anyone in the room.

Good to know. Adam was sure he'd appreciate the information at some other time. Just as he was sure that another time he'd have been pleased and impressed with the suite they'd been given.

"Just keeping things out in the open," said Honey, but she wasn't really paying attention to the goblin. She was watching Adam out of the corner of her eye.

The noise of their getting-to-know-you bickering rubbed like sandpaper on Adam's skin. Adam was sure before this was over he'd be wishing for a hotel room by himself. Or with Mercy. He checked, like a man with a toothache, and their bond was still there. He wasn't getting much from it. He knew it was because she was no longer here and that without more of the pack, he couldn't reach her more clearly.

His control was fraying. His wolf . . . no, to be honest, it wasn't just his wolf who wanted to rip out Bonarata's throat. Having his pack back home was not making his wolf any more comfortable, any safer for the people around him.

Honey knew it. She wasn't exactly avoiding him, but she was being very careful not to meet his eyes and to give him plenty of space. If he let this continue, he'd either kill Bonarata or Bonarata would kill him—and that's what they had come here to prevent, right?

Part of him, the biggest part of him and not just the monster, wondered why he was standing in the vampire's stronghold and not over the vampire's dead body or out hunting down Mercy.

He abruptly turned to Marsilia, interrupting a quiet-voiced conversation she was having with Stefan about sleeping arrangements.

"Tell me that leaving Bonarata animate another hour is the right thing to do," he said. "And make me believe it." If he couldn't figure it out, maybe someone else could. If not . . .

Adam didn't know what was in his face, but Marsilia looked at him and stilled. But it was Stefan who answered him.

"Iacopo Bonarata is a monster," Stefan said. "He does terrible things, then lies to himself about it because he doesn't want to believe that he is any different from the Renaissance prince he once was."

"I agree," Marsilia said a little sadly. "He was never a hero like you were, Stefan—no matter what either of us tried to believe."

Stefan didn't look at her, just continued to speak. "Iacopo Bonarata is an addict who glories in his addiction because it brings him more power. He broke the werewolf he feeds upon so that no one will ever believe that the addiction he won't admit to is a weakness or a problem to anyone except the poor damned wolf."

Everyone, including Elizaveta, had stopped doing whatever they'd been doing to pay attention to Stefan.

"He is a monster," said Stefan. "But he is good at it. Good at survival—and that makes him good for the rest of the monsters who have to live, seen or unseen, with the human population, who have grown a lot more deadly since they virtually wiped out the witch population in Europe."

"It was a civil war among the witch families that did the most damage," said Elizaveta. "But the Inquisition was thorough about sniffing out the remainders."

Stefan nodded carefully in Elizaveta's direction, giving her the point. Then he continued, "Bonarata is smart, savvy, and incredibly wealthy, and he uses it to ensure his own survival. But because he sees his survival as depending upon how the supernatural predators interact with humans, he is a very strong force for stability."

Marsilia put her hand out and touched Stefan, who fell silent.

"Killing him," Marsilia said, "will cause the death of thousands—not just vampires, but all of the people who will fall victim to their power plays." She hesitated briefly. "Mercy doesn't need you, Adam—she doesn't need us—to rescue her or avenge her. She rescued herself. By doing so, she gave us the opportunity to build bridges, to keep all the monsters"—here she curtsied with an ironic lift of her brow—"behaving themselves."

It was a good answer. Adam didn't know that it would be enough of a good answer to keep him from going for Bonarata's throat at the first opportunity. Mercy's rescuing herself didn't mean that Bonarata deserved to be excused for taking her in the first place. He remembered the blood and glass all over the SUV, all of *Mercy's* blood staining the leather seat, the necklace he kept tucked safely in his pocket.

"He nearly killed my wife," Adam said.

Stefan said, "But he failed."

"Not good enough," Adam said. "Not a good enough reason."

There was a small silence, then Larry spoke.

"You aren't used to dealing with bad guys who are this much more powerful than you are," he said. "No offense meant. One-on-one, if you and Bonarata got into it, the betting would be pretty even. But Bonarata isn't just an old vampire. He's the head of a collective of vampires—just as your Marrok is the head of a collective of werewolves. And it is the collective that is most important to the choice you are making tonight."

Adam looked at the goblin, and Larry dropped his eyes, without otherwise changing his body language. Larry wasn't afraid of him. He was just doing his best not to cause a fight.

"Go on," he said, because Larry seemed to be waiting for him to respond in some way.

The goblin nodded. "Bonarata has not named an heir for a very long time."

"The ones he picked kept getting ambitions," murmured Marsilia. "He got tired of killing his favorites. What he has now is a collection of lieutenants, powerful in their own ways, but not a second. He has no Darryl."

Larry said, "So what happens to the collective when Bonarata dies is this. Every Master Vampire in Europe and a fair number of them back home think that they should step into Bonarata's place. Most of 'em because of ambition, because vampires, present company excepted, I'm sure, are ambitions. But there will be some of them who are interested because they don't want to be bowing and scraping to a vampire who might be stupider or more horrid than Bonarata."

"You have a point?" Adam said.

"So how do you think that they will make their first bid to step under Bonarata's empty crown, eh?"

"Kill the dumb werewolf who assassinated the king," Adam said slowly.

"And failing that—or even if someone gets you, Adam—someone else will go after your people and your family, too, in an effort to build a name for themselves. Killing Bonarata won't keep Mercy safe. If you kill him, his successors will go after you, after Mercy, after your daughter, Jesse, your whole pack, Marsilia's seethe, and any supernatural or human who has been associated with you. The best way to keep your people safe is to make Bonarata believe that it is in his best interests that your wife and daughter—as well as everyone in this room and their loved ones—stay alive."

And that rang true enough that the beast inside of Adam considered it.

"Talking with Bonarata is best," said Honey. "But if you want to kill him, I'll help."

"And I," said Elizaveta, "would enjoy it, Adya."

And with all the reasons for leaving the vampire walking that he'd been presented with, it was the voices of murderous support that allowed him to take his first deep breath since he'd gotten off the plane.

"Thank you," he told them with real gratitude. "But Larry is right. Without the Marrok to shield us with his reputation, our people would be targets."

As good as it would feel to kill Bonarata, he didn't want to loose a horde of vampires on his people. Larry had also been right that Adam had gotten used to dealing from the position of strength provided by the Marrok's support. It had been so much a part of being a werewolf Alpha that he hadn't even thought about it. He was going to have to fix his thinking.

Everyone was still watching him intently, so he waved them off and changed the subject back to an earlier one, saying, "Elizaveta gets a bedroom. Marsilia gets a bedroom. Stefan, you and Larry can fight over the third bedroom—loser gets the couch out here. Honey and I can sleep in wolf form out here, too."

"Adam, if you want to continue our ruse, you should put your luggage in my bedroom," suggested Marsilia. "Larry, you should take the third bedroom. Stefan and I can share a bed."

"I will have the gold room," said Elizaveta coolly before he could answer the vampire. "Marsilia, the rose room is the biggest. If you share it with Stefan, then your purported threesome will have the largest room. The blue room should be adequate for the goblin king."

"We don't call ourselves that," said Larry dryly. "That was just that one movie. I mean, 'Larry the Goblin King' just doesn't have the right ring to it. The blue will do fine, I'm sure."

The gold room was, Adam noticed, the only bedroom that

didn't share a wall with the interior of the house. If Bonarata sent someone through the wall after them, they would either break into the main room, the rose room, or the blue room. Perhaps Elizaveta hadn't noticed that, but he wouldn't bet on it. The witch was very good at looking out for herself.

INSTEAD OF A DINING ROOM, THEY WERE TAKEN TO A large room that had once been a library. Adam could still smell the old glue and leather that had been used to manufacture books—as well as the complex musty smell libraries accumulated over time because paper absorbed odors.

Their entrance was more dramatic than he'd have willingly participated in, but he hadn't noticed until much too late to do anything about it. Truthfully, he wasn't entirely certain how or when the theatrical element had been instituted, though he had a very good guess about who was responsible.

As they'd exited their suite en masse, Marsilia had taken his arm—evidently deciding that, since he hadn't spoken, Adam would be willing to continue the farce that he and Marsilia were lovers. Only then did he realize that their entire party—including Elizaveta—had somehow managed to be color-coordinated.

Adam's gray suit was Mercy's favorite of the suits she had picked out for him, claiming that his choices of business wear were deliberate attempts to downplay his looks. He'd worn it this evening for Mercy, with a black shirt and his brown-and-silver tie. She wouldn't know, of course, but he did. He would have sworn that no one except he himself had known which suits he'd packed, or which one he was going to wear until he had it on.

Even so, Marsilia's semiformal dress was silver with brown

trim. Stefan's suit was a pale brown, and he wore it with a gray shirt and a silver-and-black tie. Larry's suit was black and silver with a silvery waistcoat, and his shirt and tie were brown. Honey wore a dark brown dress trimmed in black that wasn't as formal as Marsilia's even though it covered less.

Contrary to type, Elizaveta had chosen to dress all in black. She usually dressed like a fantasy-novel version of a Russian grandmother who'd been raised by the Roma, complete with multiple skirts, scarves, and jewelry in bright colors.

Mercy had told him once that she thought that Elizaveta had once been a beautiful woman, not just attractive, but world-class beautiful. Tonight, he understood exactly what she meant.

Adam wasn't interested in fashion as an art form, but he understood how he could use it as a weapon in the business world against men and women who used wealth to judge power. That meant he knew men's fashions, but also that he didn't pay any attention to women's clothing except to note whether it looked good on Mercy or not—which put him one up on Mercy, who didn't pay attention to fashion at all.

Not that women didn't use clothing like a weapon in the business world, too, but because he never judged people by the richness of their clothing, he was free to ignore the fashionable weapons of the opposite sex. But that indifference left him without words to label the outfit Elizaveta wore.

It was silk—he knew fabric, and silk had a recognizable smell and a sound as it slid over itself. It was black, and it was form-fitting, and Elizaveta wore it with style, whatever it was, because it didn't fit neatly into the categories he knew: dress, pants, suit.

It began with a long, tailored shirt that hung down to her knees while it sprouted embroidery that was black but also iridescent.

Beneath the shirt, her skirt was narrow and slitted up to midthigh on each side to allow for movement. She went barefoot for reasons of her own—probably related to magic. Her feet were lovely, with manicured and polished (in sparkling silver) nails.

She was old—nearly, he thought, as old as he was, and unlike werewolves, witches aged just like regular humans. But she had muscle and not an extra ounce of anything else on her frame. He'd always known she was strong because he watched the way people moved. He hadn't known that her body was beautiful. She'd toned down the makeup from pancake to ballroom, and it suited her. She did not dress to minimize her age—she didn't dress to minimize anything. She didn't need to. She looked exactly like what she was: beautiful and deadly.

The only two of his people left out of the fashion show were his pilot and copilot, who trailed behind the rest of them. They were still wearing the semi-uniform business garb they'd flown in—black slacks, white dress shirt, and green tie—though for all Adam knew it was a second set of identical clothing. Still, they didn't match everyone else, so that was something.

Their guide to dinner—a female vampire clad in a tuxedo—had been under the impression that "the help" would be dining in the kitchen with the rest of the human staff. Adam had put the kibosh on that.

Harris had put his neck out a lot farther than Adam or he had planned when the vampires insisted that they leave the plane. Adam wasn't about to let Harris or his copilot run around loose in Bonarata's seethe without protection. They would eat with his party in reasonable safety.

They had waited while the vampire had texted someone. As soon as the return text came, she'd agreed to the "additions to dinner"—a phrase that made Larry grin and mock-snap his teeth behind the vampire's back.

The arrangements for dinner had distracted Adam, so he hadn't noticed the black, silver, and brown theme until they were following their guide through the halls. Far too late to run back and change into his blue suit.

Adam wasn't entirely certain that the color coordination wasn't an accident. But instincts (and a hint of guilt in Honey's face) told him that this whole performance had been planned behind his back—up to and including the way that Marsilia clung to his arm.

All this drama was in keeping with the vampires and with Marsilia, anyway. Adam was an old soldier who, like good boots, could be polished up and given a shine—but in the end he was happier being a weapon than an art piece.

This was the second time Marsilia had changed their approach without checking with him. If that was how she wanted to play this, he'd feel free to do the same.

In any case, the entrance was wasted because the room was empty. With a murmured encouragement for them to await Bonarata here, their guide executed a quick bow and left.

Adam surveyed his people rather grimly.

Stefan broke first—probably because he was enjoying himself. "I told you the color thing was a bad idea," he told Marsilia.

"Not here," Adam said, though their guide was gone. His ire was appeased, not by Stefan's apology. With Bonarata apparently claiming the right of making a grand entrance, the whole drama had been mostly a wasted effort. Punishment enough to suit the crime, he thought.

Since they were stuck here, Adam did a little recon.

Sometime in the last ten years, the room had been gutted, fitted with modern electricity, and put back together with drywall and engineered hardwoods. There were only two windows—the light would have damaged the books when it had been a library, he supposed.

A good designer had done his best to make the room look as though it had last been decorated a couple of hundred years ago despite the modern lighting, air vents, and energy-efficient windows. The central area was mostly empty, with chairs lining the walls and a small writing desk in the corner.

Art was the true focus of the room. Oil paintings of eclectic sizes from various eras covered the walls three layers high. They were all originals, and mostly, to Adam's averagely educated eye, very well done. One or two were spectacular. There were no signatures, and he did not recognize any of them, which surprised him a little. He'd have thought a vampire of Bonarata's reputation would put out famous artists to establish his status.

Then Adam realized that he knew the subject of the painting he'd paused by. Marsilia, her eyes in shadow, crouched gracefully on a rock on the edge of a stream. Her hair, longer than he'd ever seen it, did nothing to cover her naked body. Clasped loosely in one hand was a dagger.

Seeing that famous-in-certain-circles painting, Adam realized that the vampire had been establishing his status all right. All of the paintings had been done by Bonarata himself.

A door opened—not the one they'd entered the room through—and Bonarata strolled in.

Adam had never met Bonarata in the flesh, but he'd seen a few sketches, and there was one painting (perhaps also painted by

Bonarata) in Marsilia's seethe. That was enough to allow him to recognize the Lord of Night on sight even if he probably couldn't have picked him out of a crowd.

Like the rest of the men, excepting Adam's pilot and copilot, Bonarata wore a suit. The biggest difference between his suit and Adam's was that Bonarata's suit only emphasized the vampire's brutally stamped features. It wasn't that the suit looked wrong; it was that it looked like it was designed to showcase a warrior, a dangerous man.

Adam's suit, which made him look very civilized, was a disguise. Adam preferred it that way.

The Master Vampire gave Adam a half bow. "I am Bonarata. I have met you through the eyes of my servant, but you have not met me."

Adam introduced his people gravely, including Marsilia and Stefan. Both of whom Bonarata greeted mutely with that quick, polite nod, as if they were strangers. For their own protection, Adam stuck his pilot and copilot in the middle of the introductions, to make it absolutely clear that Adam felt they fell into the category of his people. He did not introduce them by name—as an added protection for them. Including them in the middle also mixed up the whole color theme, which he appreciated.

All the while, he and Bonarata sized each other up.

"Your wife is no longer in my care," Bonarata said, apparently deciding to be straightforwardly honest.

Adam waited politely. On the outside, he was sure his face was polite anyway.

"She misunderstood my intentions, I think," said the vampire, with a small smile on his face. "Otherwise, she would not have run from here. I did not get the chance to let her know you were coming."

Or maybe not so honest.

"Did she?" Adam asked. "So she misunderstood that you hit her car with a semi, almost killed her, then compounded the incident by kidnapping her?"

"Adam," Marsilia said, her grip on his arm tightening to painful levels.

When she spoke, there was an instant during which something passed across the Lord of Night's face. Marsilia saw it, Adam felt her fingers clench, but he couldn't see her face.

"We know that Mercy isn't here," he told Bonarata, and by the vampire's careful lack of expression, Adam knew that Bonarata had thought to surprise them. He didn't want Bonarata to have an opening to ask how they knew Mercy was gone. Not while Mercy was still out on her own. So he continued briskly, "Recovering my wife is no longer our purpose here. I think we should talk about why you decided to take her in the first place."

"I had hoped to talk business after last meal," said Bonarata.

"Had you," said Adam neutrally. Not a question, just an acknowledgment of Bonarata's plans.

It was a good thing that Larry had talked sense before they'd come down to eat, because Adam's temper flared hotly, and he knew that his eyes were wolf-yellow.

He took a deep breath.

"It is something civilized people would do," Bonarata said mildly.

"Which neither of you is," Marsilia said archly.

Bonarata looked at her sharply, his eyes lingering on the way her hand stayed on Adam's shoulder.

This time Adam recognized the flare that broke through Bonarata's semicivilized expression as jealousy.

"Why did you take my wife?" he asked.

The vampire's eyes met his, and Adam felt the draw of the vampire's gaze even as he cursed himself for allowing it to happen. He *knew* better. He prepared to fight his way out of it, drawing on his bond to Honey—and to Mercy.

And the vampire's gaze slid right off Adam without effect.

"Why"—Adam let his voice soften with the rage that simmered around the image of his SUV after the semi had hit it—"did you take my mate?"

Silence rang loudly in the room as no one moved or spoke.

"Iacopo," murmured Marsilia, letting her hands slide off Adam's arm.

"Jacob," the vampire said coolly.

"Jacob," she corrected without apology. "You did not set out to kill Adam's mate. That would be stupid and wasteful, and the man I knew for centuries is too smart for either."

"Or to respond to flattery," he said.

She threw up both hands high, then let them drop to her sides as she spoke. "It is not flattery if it is true. You did not intend her death—so why did you take her?"

"You are in the wrong," murmured Stefan. "Everyone in this room understands this—including you, Jacob. To pretend otherwise is unproductive."

"And heaven keep us from being unproductive," growled Bonarata. But he turned to Adam. "I went to Wulfe for information, as you know. This was my mistake, and I apologize for it. I have known Wulfe a long time, I know that he enjoys causing trouble, but I thought I had taught him better than to cause *me* trouble. I will see to it that it does not happen again."

Marsilia reached out and grasped Adam's arm, digging her nails in deeply. But he didn't need her request.

He shook his head at Bonarata. "Wulfe lives in my territory. He is under my protection; moreover, he did not lie to you. My mate is the single most powerful person in our territory." He waved his hand to include the rest of his people in the room. "Witness the quality of the people willing to put their necks out for her—and I turned down a lot of help." He decided not to give Bonarata an excuse to react to Adam's defense of Wulfe—a defense that Bonarata had been expecting, if Adam was reading the vampire aright. So he kept talking. "Why did you kidnap someone you expected to be the most powerful person in the Tri-Cities?"

Bonarata veiled his eyes. "Your territorial grab is a very interesting thing, Mr. Hauptman. A place where we could deal with the humans and each other in safety is very valuable. But to say that is what you have—and to actually be able to keep people safe—is another thing entirely."

"I agree," said Adam.

Bonarata turned and walked to a dry bar and poured himself a drink of something that smelled like port to Adam. "Would you like some? It doesn't affect me, of course, any more than it would affect you. But I like the taste."

Adam let his eyes become half-lidded, and Marsilia petted his arm soothingly. Adam watched Bonarata notice her hand. Watched the vampire throw the alcohol back. It wasn't true that it didn't affect either of them. Alcohol would give a werewolf a momentary jolt, then the effects dissipated.

Sherwood Post, one of the last werewolves Bran had sent to join Adam's pack, said he'd discovered that even a werewolf could get drunk by drinking Everclear, the 190-proof version, fast enough. He'd stayed that way by drinking steadily for two days before Bran took away his alcohol and told him to grow up.

"No," Adam said. "I never acquired the taste before I Changed, and I see no reason to start now. You were going to tell me why you took my wife."

Bonarata set his empty glass down. "Yes. Where did I leave off?"

"You had decided to see if we could protect our own," said Marsilia softly. "You asked Wulfe who the most powerful among us was, and he told you—for reasons that make sense only to Wulfe, for all that he explained them to us—he told you that person was Adam's mate, Mercedes. So you broadsided her car with a semitruck and hurt her mortally—and then kidnapped her."

"She is alive," Adam said, and despite his best effort, his voice emerged as more of a growl than a human voice. "Despite your best efforts."

"Ah, yes," Bonarata said, "the famous mating bond of song and story." He smiled tightly at Adam. "She was dying," he said, "because Wulfe misled me. If you wish for him not to have consequences for that, I suppose I am not the one to suffer the most from his games. My people called me to report the issue, and I almost left her there. Her death would have told me what I wanted to know, after all. That you cannot protect your own."

Adam didn't say anything, just watched Bonarata with patience. His wolf was pretty convinced that Bonarata was not going to survive long, no matter what the overarching consequences might be. Bonarata kept setting himself in front of them and making himself a target. Eventually, Adam's control would fail, and the wolf would feast.

Bonarata tried to outstare Adam. Marsilia let out a huff of air and walked between them, breaking their stare-down with her body. For the first time, Adam realized that the heels she wore made her taller than either of them. "But you didn't leave her to die," she told Bonarata.

"No," he said, his face and body language softening as he spoke to Marsilia. "Because ultimately, my aim wasn't to destroy what you had built but to use it. Her death was not my intent. So I had my team fly her to Portland, where I have a witch on retainer. She kept Mercedes alive until she could be brought here, and my own healer could bring her out of danger."

Adam was pretty sure that the pause that Bonarata followed his speech with was intended as an opportunity for Adam to say thank you, which he wasn't going to do.

"I have a witch on retainer also," Adam murmured instead. "A very powerful witch." Elizaveta made a pleased sound. "It would, perhaps, have been better for Mercy to stay in the Tri-Cities when she was so badly hurt—rather than carting her halfway around the world."

A chime sounded.

"Ah," Bonarata said. "That would be dinner. I'm afraid my chef insists that we not dine late. I've had to increase his salary twice this year after such incidents. We will have to hold this conversation after we sit and you eat. Yes?"

Adam nodded politely and let Marsilia and Stefan follow Bonarata through yet another door, while he lingered to take the rear. Elizaveta kissed his cheek as she passed—probably because of the compliment he'd thrown her way.

Larry and Harris, the goblins, were deep in discussion in a language he didn't know, but it sounded vaguely Germanic. Norwegian or Norn, or Old Icelandic for all he could tell. Harris's copilot trailed behind them, apparently following the conversation. Honey, who had taken it upon herself to play guard for the copilot, fell in beside Adam.

"What *is* his name?" Adam asked, tilting his head toward Harris's man. He'd been given it when he met the two pilots at the airport, but he'd been struggling with the wolf, and it had gone in one ear and out the other—something not usual for him. But if the copilot was going to be among the people Adam was responsible for, Adam needed a name.

"Matthew Smith," said the man himself in a meek voice, though he didn't turn back. "You can call me Matt, sir." Then he gave Honey and Adam both a shy smile over his shoulder. "I've heard all the jokes. I preferred Tom Baker, anyway."

Honey looked at Adam, puzzled by the reference.

"*Doctor Who*," Adam told her. "Matt Smith played the Eleventh Doctor. Tom Baker was the Fifth or Sixth."

"Fourth," said Harris with a grin. "He's the guy with the scarf."

"*Doctor Who*," said Honey slowly, because the whole pack knew that Adam didn't like TV much.

"Mercy makes me watch it," Adam said defensively. "She says it's for my own good." Matt the copilot huffed a little laugh under his breath, and Adam caught himself smiling a little. "I'm not sure what that means. But I'm enjoying it." *Doctor Who* had been unexpectedly good, but he'd have watched reality TV or even a soap opera in order to sit around for an hour with Mercy cuddled beside him.

He checked his bond—and Mercy was there, too distant to communicate with, but she was there. Just as she'd been the last hundred times he checked for her.

———

DINNER WAS THROUGH A DOUBLE DOOR AND INTO A well-lit, high-ceilinged room that could have been the main seating area of any high-class restaurant. Instead of a single long table, there were a number of tables that sat from two to six people, spread with conscientious randomness around the room.

The whole room could have seated maybe a hundred people, but not so many were expected tonight. Numerous tables, each seating four, were decorated with pink linen tablecloths and blue-and-white place settings. There were deep-rose-colored place cards on each plate with names scribed on them. The first one that Adam glanced at proved that Bonarata had investigated Adam's people: it read MAT-THEW SMITH.

He rounded the table, reading the other names at the table—Stefan Uccello, Larry Sethaway, and Austin Harris.

"Matt, here's your seat," he said, keeping his voice kind because the other wolf didn't deserve the sharpness of the sudden, possessive bite of an Alpha wolf who feels like someone is trying to take his pack away from him. It wasn't just that Bonarata had known Matthew Smith's name—it was that he had surrounded the vulnerable wolf with the people Adam would have put around him: Stefan for strength, Harris for familiarity, and Larry because no one would expect him to be as dangerous as he was. He'd have weighed replacing Larry with Honey, but the two goblins would be more likely to fight well together.

Bonarata had done him a favor, and it drove his wolf wild because of the impertinence of it—presuming to make decisions that belonged to Adam. Protecting his people was his job. Or maybe he was overreacting because he didn't know where Mercy was. Probably he was overreacting.

The copilot sat down in the chair Adam had indicated for him. He put a hand on Adam's knee and asked, "Trouble?" in a low voice that wouldn't carry, even to the ears in the room.

This wolf was the only person besides Honey in the room whom Adam's wolf did not view as prey or possible threat. The touch on his knee steadied him as nothing else could have in that moment. Adam had a job to do—and that job did not include playing stupid games with an ancient vampire.

He took a breath and nodded to the other wolf. "Thank you," he said.

The copilot dropped his eyes and bowed his shoulders to look smaller than he was—and he wasn't a big man. "Glad to be of use," he told Adam.

Feeling more in control—though he supposed he wouldn't be back to normal until he had Mercy back safe—Adam patted the wolf on the shoulder in thanks, and when Harris found his way to his seat, he left him in good hands.

He checked on Elizaveta and Honey, both of whom were sitting surrounded by vampires. Elizaveta was flirting gently in Russian with a vampire who looked like he'd rather be anywhere else.

Honey ignored her table companions, who were not only vampires but also women. Instead, she kept watch on the table where Matthew Smith and Harris were. It would have been rude, but the other occupants of her table were busy ignoring her pointedly, too. He just bet Honey's tender feelings were hurt—he hid his inner smile. Honey was as tough-minded as any werewolf he knew.

There were, by his count, sixty people in the room, not including the waitstaff. Adam's small pack was vastly outnumbered. That was probably not an accident. Some of the guests were human. A few were *other*, people who were magical but fit poorly into established categories.

Adam was mostly intrigued by the people he *didn't* see. Bonarata had Lenka, the werewolf he had enslaved. But she wasn't the only nonvampire Bonarata had in his arsenal. He'd had a powerful witch at one time, though she seemed to be missing—but there were others in his hire now. The only werewolves in the room were in Adam's party—and Elizaveta was the only witch.

By the time Adam made his way to his table (he aimed for Bonarata, assuming that would be where he'd be eating) the others were seated. The Lord of Night had placed himself across from Adam. Marsilia was seated on Adam's right (Bonarata's left), and a strange vampire had the seat to Adam's left.

"You like the room?" asked Bonarata pointedly. "You took your time examining it."

"I take care of my people," Adam said with a peacefulness won from a hand on his knee and watching Honey ignore the people ignoring her—and the solid connection of his mate bond. He decided that he could also be gracious. "The room is elegant—and interesting."

"You were going to explain what happened to Mercy after you brought her here," said Marsilia.

Bonarata sighed. "Not knowing anything about her, except that Wulfe had told me she was powerful—not strong, I grant you, but powerful—I put her up in a safe room outside this house, where I could keep her protected from my people and keep my people safe from her. She woke up, and we had a polite discussion. I thought all was well when I was called away to deal with other issues. I left my own werewolf to guard her. At this point, I was more concerned with my people hurting her rather than the other way around."

"*Concerned,*" thought Adam, *could be a very unspecific word.*

"You left your bloodbitch to guard Adam's mate," said Marsilia, real anger in her voice. She looked at Adam. "He stole the wolf female from the Milan Alpha because he could. When the Alpha objected, Iacopo had him brought here and tortured him until he'd broken them both. But Iacopo—"

"Jacob," corrected Bonarata softly. "Jacob is easier for my American contacts."

"—Jacob," continued Marsilia without a change in her voice, "doesn't feed from males. So he had the Alpha killed but kept his mate. She was quite mad when I left here. I cannot think that a few centuries will have helped her."

All of which Marsilia knew that Adam knew, which meant that she was bringing it up to get a reaction from Bonarata. It wasn't working.

"If Mercedes had not run, the wolf would not have chased her," Bonarata said easily. He didn't address or acknowledge Marsilia's charge except for that correction over his first name. "She would not have disobeyed me. Mercedes was safe until she tried to run."

Adam understood what he was hearing. Mercy had not been what Bonarata was prepared to deal with, so he'd set her up to die. A very practical thing, really. If there was only one person telling the story, there could be no debate about what had happened.

Food was served at just that moment. Adam held his tongue and watched as a very rare steak was set out for him while he fought the beast inside him to a standstill. As soon as all of those eating food were served, vampire waiters brought out trays with golden goblets that they placed before the vampires. The last person served was Bonarata.

He held up his goblet and said, "Eat and drink, my friends. Tonight is a glorious night, and tomorrow will be better." Then he said something in Italian. Adam was pretty sure the vampire was just repeating his words.

He sipped his drink, and Adam did, too, because there was nothing wrong with drinking to tomorrow. As soon as Bonarata set his goblet down, people started to eat.

Most of the place settings were silver. Adam's was gold. He glanced at Honey and saw that her tableware was gold as well. He'd assume that Smith received the same courtesy. Adam cut into his steak and took a bite and chewed with what he hoped looked like thoughtfulness instead of restrained rage. If Mercy had not managed to escape, she'd have been dead when they arrived.

"So," he said softly, "where is your pet werewolf whose job it was . . . to keep Mercy here, I think you said?"

There was a pause, then the beautiful male vampire to his left said, a hint of amusement in his voice, "She was hit by a bus and is currently recovering."

And just that easily, Adam's equanimity was restored.

Adam nodded. "People who stand in the way of my mate's ability to get herself out of trouble often feel like they were hit by buses. I think this might be the first time it is literally true, though." He looked at the second vampire. "We weren't introduced."

"This is Guccio," Bonarata said. "He is responsible for the night-to-night running of the seethe. My apologies for not introducing him earlier."

"*Don* Hauptman," said the pretty vampire, "I have heard many things about you."

Adam opened his mouth to tell him that his name wasn't Don, when Bonarata spoke. "*Signore* Hauptman is a young wolf, not even a century old." He looked at Adam. "'*Don*' is an old term of respect; Guccio meant it so."

The explanation—though necessary—had been given with a hint of patronization.

"A bus," murmured Marsilia. "At least she never hit one of mine with a bus. I wonder if it was a mark of respect—or the opposite. It doesn't do to underestimate Mercedes, *Jacob*, something that I had to learn, too. Did she give you the spiel she likes to bring out now and again about how she's mostly no more powerful than the average human? It is a most effective speech, because I think she actually believes it."

Bonarata frowned at Marsilia. "She is weak," he said. "She is easily broken, easily killed." He frowned at Adam. "You cannot afford a weak mate if you seek out power. A plaything can be weak, because such a one is disposable. But a mate must be an asset."

Mercy, weak? Adam thought. "And yet," he said coolly, "Mercy is not here. And the werewolf you sent after her is still recovering."

"I have news for you, *Jacob*." Marsilia placed a little more emphasis than necessary on the vampire's name. "There have been a lot of people, monsters, and other things who have tried to kill Mercedes Thompson Hauptman, and most of them died in the attempt. She is not helpless, nor is she weak."

"I didn't try to kill her," said Bonarata.

Adam stared at the vampire, hearing the lie clearly. Did the vampire not know he could hear the lie? Adam couldn't trust himself to speak.

"I never said you did," Marsilia said diplomatically. "Nor have I. But I have seen her at work. Your wolf is lucky it was only a bus."

"Do you know where she is?" asked Adam. "I trust you have been looking."

On the plane, Marsilia had told Adam that Bonarata would not rest until he found Mercy. She had made him look incompetent, and his ego would not allow him to let her escape without consequences.

Bonarata spread his hands, sighed, and said, "I have my people looking for her. It appears that she has left Italy entirely, probably by bus. We tracked her to a bus stop in Austria, where she either traded buses or changed her mode of transportation. I have some information that makes it apparent that she has made her way to either Prague or Berlin or possibly Munich."

"Who did you send after her?" asked Marsilia.

"You would not know them," Bonarata told her. "But they are good hunters. They will find her and bring her back."

Adam said slowly, "You were given misleading information that inspired you to take my wife. I think it is only fair to give you information that will keep you from making a bigger mistake."

"Yes?" Bonarata said.

"Bran raised Mercy."

"She was raised in his pack," said Bonarata. "Foster parents, of which one was a wolf." He smiled. "You are correct, I started with too little information. I have made up for it."

"Very good," Adam said. "You already know that if my wife dies, I will not rest until you are no longer walking the earth. You don't fear that, though you should. But what you don't know is that Bran feels the same—and only an idiot would not fear Bran."

"Bran has cut his ties to your pack," said Bonarata.

Adam nodded. "See? I thought you'd gotten the wrong information. That part is true enough. But that is politics—family is different. Bran could not love Mercy more if she were his own daughter. He's funny about family. His own mother tried to hurt one of his children, and that tale is still told. You do know the story of Beowulf?"

And, from the vampire's carefully blank face, he was fully aware of how Bran's descent into madness, when his witchborn mother had tried to force Bran to hurt Samuel, Bran's son, was tied to the myth of Beowulf.

"Bran is very practical," Adam said. "He is a zealot whose cause is the survival of the werewolves. He will sacrifice almost anything to that cause. He believes that he would sacrifice either or both of his sons—and they believe it, too. But whenever that seems to be a necessity, somehow matters work out differently. And Bran is nowhere near as protective of his sons as he is of Mercy. You need to listen to me as I tell you the absolute truth." He ate another piece of steak and resisted the need to meet the vampire's gaze, because Mercy's magic had rescued him once, and even for Mercy, that only worked some of the time. "If Mercy dies because of you, there is not a hole deep enough for you to hide from him."

"If Bran behaves aggressively toward me without cause, he will force a war between the vampires and the werewolves," Bonarata said.

"He won't care," Adam said, his voice sure and certain. Not all vampires could tell the difference between the truth and a lie when they heard it. But he was willing to bet that a vampire of Bonarata's age could. "He might care afterward. He might care that you didn't intend her death. But that will be afterward. Please don't push him into it."

8

MERCY

Running from vampires, again. Still. Go me!

I DIDN'T HAVE A WRISTWATCH, AND, SINCE IT WAS nighttime, there was no sun to help tell the time. It felt like we'd been riding the motorcycle less than an hour, but I had no way to be sure. We sped our way out of Prague proper and into a more rural area, where the road seemed to weave in and out of one tiny village after another.

We turned off the main road onto a blue-railed modern bridge that crossed a river and into the labyrinthian streets of yet another village. We drove past a castle—because it was the Czech Republic, and apparently castles were required by all the best villages.

The Tri-Cities had no castles. I'd never felt the lack before.

My guardian-angel werewolf slowed, and we puttered very quietly through a sleepy residential area. If we'd been in the US, I'd have said it was a bedroom community for Prague. But, remembering that there was a castle, I was hesitant to apply New World labels to Old World places.

Some of the houses looked very Bohemian. Some of them were very modern. We passed a couple of apartment complexes, took a hard right just past the second one, and found ourselves in an area where, on one side of the road, houses had gardens, huge yards, and trees. On the other side of the road was open land. It was too dark to be sure, but I thought they might be growing hay. Though it could just as easily have been some other grassy plant. It was dark, and I wasn't a farmer.

We pulled into the driveway of a mansion-sized house that could have been a well-preserved three or four hundred years old—or a run-down twenty years old. It was hard to tell in the darkness.

My werewolf driver barely slowed down as we passed the ornate building, a swimming pool, and a stable, to park next to a much smaller house that might once have been a carriage house. Unlike the big building, where all the lights were on the outside and the interior was dark, the smaller house had no exterior lights on. There were fixtures beside both of the doors I could see, but the bulbs had been removed.

The purr of the engine stopped, and my werewolf guard removed his helmet and braced his feet. I was wise to the invitation, and I hopped off and took my own helmet off, giving it to him when he held out his hands for it.

I could smell and hear horses nearby—the swish of a lazy tail and an occasional snort. Horses are prey, and they don't sleep in long stretches.

In the pen nearest the house, someone was in the middle of planting a garden in a pen that had been set up for livestock. They weren't there now, of course, but the area had been expertly scythed. The cut hay was piled to the side, presumably to feed to the horses I'd sensed. Turf had been cut and was partially rolled, exposing rich, dark soil. Packets of seeds and a couple of mesh bags of bulbs sat in a cardboard box for planting.

I only knew it had been scythed because the implement was leaning against a fence post. I knew it was expert because I'd scythed a very small pasture once—a punishment for the Easter bunny incident, I think. My field had looked nothing like the neatly trimmed grass in the pen.

While I'd been getting the lay of the land, my companion knocked at the door softly.

It popped open after a bit. A woman clothed in a man's white shirt and nothing else said something in Czech that was both quiet and irritated. Her hair was dark and cut in an asymmetrical bob that flattered her cheekbones.

My escort responded in a voice that was conciliatory without being submissive. The woman was a werewolf, too, a pack mate from their body language. Near equal in status, too, if I was reading it right.

She turned from him to me. "You are English?" she asked.

"American," I told her.

"So what are you doing here, and why are the vampires after you?" Her English was very good—smooth, as if she spoke it often. Her vowels were thick, though, and the consonants muted.

I rubbed my face wearily. "I got in the way of a murky vampire plot," I told her.

She threw her hands up impatiently. "Vampire plots are always murky. What kind of murky?"

I said, "The Lord of Night hit me with a car and kidnapped me from Washington—the state—in the US and brought me to

Milan. I escaped with nothing but my skin and hitched a ride on a couple of random buses and ended up in Prague. Is that murky enough?"

"You are not a werewolf," she said suspiciously, "and still Libor helps you?"

The man who'd brought me here spoke, and whatever he said made her frown. Frown harder, anyway.

"Stop that" was what she said. "You are being rude, Martin. Speak English." To me she said, "Why are we helping you?"

Martin was evidently my rescuer's name.

"I'm the mate of the Alpha of the Columbia Basin Pack," I said.

She stared at me for a moment, then said, a little incredulously, "*You* are Bran Cornick's foster daughter?"

I nodded carefully, keeping my eyes up because her reaction was a little off. "Expecting someone better-looking?" I tried. "Smarter? Taller?"

The wind came up, rustling in the grassy fields and blowing her scent to me. In addition to the werewolf, I could tell she was the person who had most recently used the helmet I'd worn here, and, from the scent of rich earth and broken grass, she was the person responsible for the project of turning a horse run into a garden.

"Well," she said after a silence that lingered a little too long to be comfortable, "you must be the Mercedes who goes by Mercy, then. I'm Jitka—" and she told me her last name, but the sounds in it had little to do with English, and I'm not sure I caught it all.

I looked at the man, who gave a little laugh. "Yes," he agreed, "matters were a little fraught for introductions. I'm Martin Zajíc, Libor's second. Jitka is—"

"A lowly woman," she said with a little growl in her voice.

"But after the Great War, Libor said that for me to be last because I would not take a mate was stupid. Clearly, I was more fierce than most of the pack and more clever than any. He set me third behind Martin. It was acceptable—and I buried the ones who objected with my own hands."

Martin grinned and said, "Pavel didn't die."

"Or I seduced them," she agreed placidly. She wasn't exactly beautiful, though she wasn't exactly not beautiful, either. But she looked soft, warm, and strong. Sexy. She looked like someone who could give comfort when you needed it—or a belt in the jaw if that was more appropriate. "Pavel is a good man who needed to rethink a few things. There were several like Pavel."

She looked at Martin. "I am going to get dressed. Then you two may come in, and we will discuss what has happened and what is to be done."

She left us abruptly and went back inside the little house.

Martin started to speak, stopped, then laughed. "I was going to give you my standard warning—how you should not underestimate our Jitka, who has been outwitting men since the day she was born—but I imagine that you know better."

"Not being a man?" I asked.

"Being a person used to having people underestimate her," he said. "Libor feels that you bested him. We've been . . . pack mates for a very long time. He doesn't pout like a child on the outside. But when he does not get what he expects, then he pouts on the inside. Anyone who can get one over on Libor is—"

"Lucky?" I guessed.

He smiled again. "Maybe luck would work once. Against Libor or against Iacopo Bonarata. But not against both, one after another."

"You aren't afraid to say his name?" I asked. I was pretty sure that Marsilia was—there was an edge of defiance in her voice whenever she said his full name. "And you missed the memo. I guess he's in the process of turning from Iacopo to Jacob."

Most of the immortals changed their names as time passed. I used to think it was to protect themselves from the humans discovering how old they were. But I'd changed my hypothesis lately. I think after a long time, some people grew tired of themselves. A new name gave them a chance to reinvent who they were, to become someone else, some other kind of person. Or sometimes, as in Iacopo Bonarata's case apparently, they decide to pick a name easier for their soon-to-be minions to say.

"Jacob," Martin said thoughtfully. "I had not heard." He shrugged. "I am not a vampire to fear Bonarata's power. He will not lightly take on Libor or the Vltava Pack. That is not to say that someday there might not be war between us. But it won't be over something as small as my saying his name." He smiled, and it lit his eyes. "It might take something like you. Or not."

Jitka's door opened. "Okay," she said. "You—"

And that's when the vampire dropped off the roof and on top of Jitka like a piano falling on Roger Rabbit.

Vampires are hard to detect because when they are still, they really don't make any noise at all. I don't know what they had done to disguise their smell, but I'd seen too many vampires move to mistake them for anything else. And once the one landed on Jitka, there were suddenly more of them.

My whole life, I've heard people trying to compare vampires and werewolves. Vampires are faster and werewolves stronger. Or werewolves are faster, and vampires are stronger. I've now seen them both in combat enough to form my own opinion: the one thing that really matters is that both werewolves *and* vampires are stronger than I am. The only thing I have going to match them is speed—which is why I broke and ran.

I didn't run to the road—there were innocent civilians in that direction. I didn't run to the woods. I didn't know the lay of the land, I didn't like being lost with vampires chasing me, and my coyote didn't blend in with the local fauna.

Because I also didn't believe in letting other people fight my battles while I watched, I ran to the fenced paddock, rolled over the rail fence, and grabbed the scythe. I especially didn't run from a fight when there was such a handy weapon lying around.

Properly armed, I turned to see what had happened while I'd been running. There were four vampires swarming Martin and Jitka—presumably having gone through the same basic evaluation that I'd just done. The werewolves were more of a threat than I was.

Assuming they came from Bonarata, the only thing they knew about me was that I'd run from Bonarata and I was weaker than a werewolf. In the fields and the woodlands beyond the fields, it would take me a long time to run far enough that the vampires couldn't find me. So they'd ignored me and attacked the werewolves.

Fights usually happen really fast, especially fights between supernatural creatures. I'd seen one or two that lasted longer because the combatants were just that tough, but even then, seconds counted.

I stood behind the fence, waiting for what seemed like ten minutes and was probably closer to thirty or forty seconds. I thought I was going to have to try something else because the fight stayed too far away.

But then Jitka threw one of her attackers like a shot put. She—the vampire, not Jitka—hit a post and staggered. She grabbed the fence for support, her eyes on Jitka.

I hooked the scythe between the top two rails of the fence and around the vampire's neck, just under her jaw.

I never, ever thought that mowing that field with a scythe would be useful to me. Who uses a scythe in the era of lawn mowers and tractors? To make that exact point, Bran had parked a new, wide-swath, riding lawn mower just outside the field. He wanted to rub in the fact that all the sweaty, backbreaking work I was doing could have been done in an hour on the riding lawn mower. By the time I'd finished, I'd had blisters, muscles in my arms and back in places I didn't know I had muscles—and I'd learned a lot about how a scythe worked.

The first rule of cutting grass with a medieval farm implement is that the blade has to be sharp, or when it hits the grass, it will bend it over instead of cutting it. The sharp side of the blade is on the side nearest the scytheman, so he hooks the grass and pulls it with a smooth motion that uses his whole body, like a golfer. I think. I don't golf, but the motion a golfer makes when hitting the ball looks a lot like the one I developed by trial and error to cut waist-high grass.

The same motion I used on the vampire. I caught her totally by surprise because her attention was on the werewolves.

Evidently, Jitka knew about keeping her scythe sharp, because it slid through flesh like a hot knife through butter. It was easy, only a little hesitation as the blade hit the bone, and it was done. Expecting a more difficult task, I used too much force and over-balanced myself, put a foot on the edge where the sod had been cut, and rolled and fell on my butt in the dirt.

I was too worried about cutting myself with the scythe to try to roll, but I scrambled to my feet as quickly as I could. Or almost as quickly as I could, because I found a little more speed when I realized that the head had landed right next to me.

Pretty much anything that is decapitated dies and stays that way, even the kinds of things that are otherwise immortal. Vampires' bodies turn to ash when they are dead, mostly—though I've learned over the past few years that isn't always true. There are apparently some strains of vampirism that don't do that at all. Younger vampires tend to have bodies just like real people. But vampirism is magic-fueled, and magic doesn't follow the rules all the time like science does.

What that means is this: if I decapitate Wulfe someday, he will probably turn to ash because he is very old. If he doesn't turn to ash, I'll burn his body and his head. Either way, I will take his ashes and scatter them in both the Atlantic and Pacific Oceans— salt being a pretty effective deterrent to magic. I don't know of anything that decapitation followed by burning doesn't kill, but with Wulfe, I wouldn't take any chances.

I was comfortable that the vampire I'd scythed was dead. The eyes staring at me were blank and fogged. I didn't know her well enough to know if I should have been as scared of her as I was of Wulfe, so I assumed not.

While beheading the vampire had only taken seconds, the fight had gone on without us. I didn't think anyone had noticed what I'd done—the vampire hadn't made much noise, and the other combatants were fully engaged in their own battles. Moving fast requires a lot of focus. It takes a Charles or an Adam to pay attention to anything more than the fight in front of him.

Jitka had a knife in one hand and something I couldn't see too well in the other. Maybe it was a screwdriver. The vampire she was fighting had a short sword. Jitka hadn't been exaggerating her competence. Despite the inequality in weaponry, the battle was not going in the vampire's favor.

Martin had incapacitated one of his opponents. The big male vampire wasn't going anywhere with his back broken and his body spasming helplessly under the randomized signals his nervous system sent out.

Short swords must have been the weapon of choice, because Martin had one that he was using to engage the short sword his second vampire opponent had. The wolf must have taken the sword from the disabled vampire, because he hadn't been carrying it with him on the motorcycle. I'd have noticed.

The vampire jumped back out of the way of Martin's strike and staggered. I hopped on the top rail of the fence and brought the point of the scythe over his shoulder and into his abdomen. The blade stuck—maybe it caught on a belt buckle. I tried to throw myself backward off the fence to use the weight of my body to force the blade deeper. Had the vampire panicked or frozen, I'd have eviscerated him. But he grabbed the shaft of the scythe, and I had to let go or risk his pulling me somewhere I didn't want to go. I could not afford to let him get a shot at me.

When I hit the dirt this time, I rolled to my feet and took a quick step back before I figured out that the vampire wasn't going to be coming after me—or anyone—again. Martin had taken advantage of the vampire's distraction and used his sword to do what I hadn't managed. He'd broken the blade doing it, but he'd cut the vampire—pretty messily—in half from belly through collarbone and out the top of the shoulder. The end of the sword had lodged in a rib and broken off. Martin brought the broken blade down on the vampire's neck and decapitated him.

Jitka's final opponent went boneless and dropped to the ground, a screwdriver sticking out of one eye. Face grim, the werewolf took the sword the vampire had been using and struck off his head as if she'd worked for years decapitating vampires on an assembly line—the stroke was that precise and emotionless. The dead vampire crumbled to ash in a flash of heat that ate the clothes he was wearing but left the shoes untouched. About that time, the female I'd killed just sort of faded into dust—a lot less dramatic than her comrade.

Jitka took the sword and looked around, her body language relaxed. She walked to the spasming vampire, looked closely at his face with a frown, then beheaded him. Without a guillotine or, evidently, a scythe, beheading someone isn't as easy as the werewolves made it look, which is why most human-strength people are better off hammering a wooden stake into a sleeping vampire's heart.

Martin and I were both watching Jitka, so we jumped when the vampire who was wearing the scythe burst into flame, scorching the grass, the fence, and the scythe, but not quite getting Martin, who'd been standing too close.

The scythe fell to the ground, a third of its blade blackened.

Jitka looked at me. "Do you know how long it's going to take to sharpen that blade after this?"

I touched it with my toe, and the blade broke in half. "Huh," I said. "When a job can't be done, does that mean it will take forever—or no time at all?"

She laughed. "You fight good," she said. "And smart, which is rarer."

Martin said, "I think we might have a problem."

She turned to look at him.

"Did you recognize any of them?"

She snorted and nodded at the vampire Martin had disabled and she had killed. That one had done the creepy thing where one moment it was a body and the next the body had become ash, which blew away.

"I would know that idiot," she said, "if I were blindfolded. Someone should have rid the world of him fifty years ago. Ivan Novák."

"What if I told you that the vampires who attacked the bakery were from Kocourek's seethe?"

It certainly told her something more than it told me, because she stiffened and grunted. "Let's get this mess cleaned up and go inside before someone looks out of the big house and wonders what we are doing."

JITKA'S HOUSE WAS MORE OF A STUDIO APARTMENT than a house. The bedroom, kitchen, and living room were all one space. She sat on the bed, and Martin and I each took one of the kitchen chairs. There wasn't any more furniture in the room than that. Jitka was not a cluttered person—except for the wall of plants that were set about two feet from the north-facing windows.

"So what do you think, Martin?" she asked. "Are the two seethes working together?"

"Excuse me," I said. "You think that the vampires who attacked the bakery and the ones who attacked us here are two different groups of vampires?"

"Yes," said Jitka.

"We know they are," said Martin. "The thing is, having them fighting on the same team is like . . ."

"Bosnians and Serbs," suggested Jitka helpfully. "Russians and Germans—or cowboys and Indians."

"I get it," I said. "Would they both follow orders from Bonarata? Cooperate by mistake because they are doing what Bonarata tells them to do?"

Both shook their heads, and Martin added, "No."

"Kocourek is the Master of Praha," said Martin.

"Prague," said Jitka. "Americans call her Prague."

"Prague," agreed Martin. "Yes. He is the Master of Prague, and like all the Master Vampires in Europe, he obeys Bonarata. Otherwise, he is destroyed."

"Not like the Marrok," Jitka said disapprovingly. "Bonarata protects no one. He just dictates, and they do or they die. Kocourek has been Master here for longer than I have been alive. Only Libor is older than Kocourek. Kocourek would not dream of disobeying Bonarata. Kocourek is a survivor. Vampires who defy Bonarata die."

"Ivan belongs to the other seethe in Prague," Martin said. "The woman who rules it calls herself Mary." He said the name with a decided English twist. "She's been gathering the scum of the vampires to her for the last four or five decades. As best we can figure it, she must have come in at the close of World War II. But we only noticed her in the middle of the fifties, when Kocourek blew up an old factory trying to find her and kill her and her people. He's been trying to run her down ever since."

"Someone is helping her," said Jitka.

"Yes, I know," Martin returned in an exasperated tone. This, it seemed, was an old argument. "But we have no clue as to who it is, right?"

"So what do we do now?" I asked. "I could go find a hotel—a hostel, something. I honestly didn't expect to run into trouble here. Prague is a long way from Milan. I figured that I could hit up Libor—your pack—for room and board for a couple of nights. I didn't intend to get anyone killed."

"No one's been killed," said Jitka.

"Four vampires here," I retorted, "who would have been running around free and clear if I hadn't come to Prague."

"Didn't sound like you had much choice," said Martin.

"That lot isn't worth anyone's time mourning," said Jitka at the same time. "Mary's vampires go out and harvest food wherever. They take more than they need because they have to replenish the vampires Kocourek's people have destroyed. They are somehow tied up with the drug trade here, too. Most of their vampires are young, see. They haven't accumulated wealth, and so they are going in some nasty directions to get it." She looked at Martin.

He sighed and shrugged. "I've told you before—Libor is letting the vampires feed on each other. Eventually, either Kocourek will find them all and eradicate them, or they'll weaken his seethe, and Libor will finish them both off."

"Lots of folk dying and hurting in the meantime," Jitka said.

Martin nodded. "But Libor is old and slow to act when it is something outside of pack that is wrong. He doesn't view humans as people, much. Like as not he's right to sit this out. If Kocourek can't find Mary's people, there's nothing saying we could, either. Let Kocourek do the work."

"He cared about people during the war," she said. "During World War II."

"No," Martin disagreed, his voice soft. "He just hated the Germans. Hated to see Prague under German control. It was when his wife died and Radim, his son, left."

Radim, I thought. *Zack's real name is Radim.*

"Look," I said. "All this is well and good. But it appears that at least two groups of vampires are after me, here, in Prague. They are attacking your pack. I need to leave before someone else gets killed."

They both looked at me as though I was being ridiculous.

Martin said, "Kocourek attacked the pack stronghold, Mercy. Whether you are here or in Germany, there will be more blood

spilled between Kocourek and our pack. As for Mary's seethe . . ."
He shrugged. "They have been launching offensives at us ever
since one of them seduced Pavel and tried to turn him into her
servant. We think that somebody decided that the reason Bonarata
was so scary was because he drinks werewolf blood."

Jitka shivered. "Bonarata is scary because he is scary. The
werewolf thing . . . that he could do that to an Alpha and his mate
is scary. But—" She looked at Martin.

"It is also a weakness," he said in a low voice. "I remember
when no one thought he had any weaknesses. When the Lord of
Night had his Blade and the Soldier and the Wizard . . . it was like
the *Avengers*—except they were bad."

Vampires did the one-name thing before Madonna and Prince.
The Soldier, I knew, was Stefan. The Wizard was Wulfe. The Blade
had to be Marsilia.

"I'm not that old," said Jitka. "They left a hundred years before
I was born. But I know that anyone who has an addiction as strong
as Bonarata's must have more weaknesses."

"At any rate," Martin said briskly, "an idiot is born every
minute, and someone in Mary's seethe—possibly Mary herself—
decided that werewolf blood would make vampires stronger. So
they got a pretty little thing to seduce Pavel."

"Not difficult," said Jitka. "He's a good man, but"—she smiled
wryly—"he has a weakness for women."

"What happened?" I asked.

"Libor happened," said Jitka at the same time as Martin said,
"Libor killed her and forbade sexual congress with vampires."
They spoke over the top of each other without really noticing it,
so it must have been habitual.

"And how does he enforce that?" I asked.

They both looked at me incredulously. "He can tell through the pack bonds."

I blinked. "Libor knows if his wolves have sex with a vampire through the pack bonds?"

Martin nodded. "It's part of being the Alpha. And it's not just sex—it's anything very intense. Grief, joy, horror—he gets it."

I was pretty sure that Adam wasn't that connected with his pack. Almost sure. Because . . . ick. Invasion of privacy didn't even begin to cover it. Maybe he just hadn't told me because he knew how I'd react.

I was tired, and they must have been, too, because we kept wandering away from the point.

"What do I do to keep your pack as safe as I can?" I asked.

Jitka snorted. "Not your job, by my reckoning. Libor gave you three days of pack protection. Your job is to let us keep you safe."

Martin grinned at me. "But if you want to behead a few vampires with a scythe, that's okay, too."

"It was only the one," I said.

But he was looking at Jitka. "She got one and a half. I got two halves, and you got one and a half."

Jitka shook her head. "No. I got one—I just finished off the one you'd already done."

"So one and a half vampires for the poor weakling who matched or beat the scorecard for the werewolves." Martin gave me a look. "All luck, was it? Luck didn't kill those vampires, did it?"

"Martin," Jitka said mildly. "We need to find all of us someplace safe to rest." To me she said, "We didn't think any of the vampires knew about this place. I only just moved out here, and Dobrichovice is pretty far out of their usual haunting ground."

"We need to find a safe place for Mercy to sleep the rest of the night," Martin said.

I don't know why it bothered me so much. I mean, that's what I'd been doing since I got to Prague, right? Finding a safe place to wait for Adam.

But we'd just killed four vampires. I wasn't helpless. Helpless people get hurt.

And just for a moment, I flashed back to the time when I had been rendered helpless by a fae artifact and a creep named Tim . . .

"Mercy?" Jitka asked.

I realized I was sitting on the floor in the corner of her room. Martin was as far from me as he could get, watching me with a concerned look. Jitka was crouching about three feet from me, careful to give me space.

I met her eyes and said, "I hate PTSD, you know?" I remembered I was talking to a werewolf and turned my gaze to the floor. It was less humiliating talking to the floor, anyway. "It's been years—and I killed that bastard. And it's not like I was really hurt, right? I've been sent to the hospital by a volcano god, and that didn't do anything but give my *husband* nightmares."

Jitka nodded like all this was making sense. "Hurt comes in all forms. I wake up at least once a year to a memory that makes me shake for hours—something that happened 122 years ago. I have seen and done so much worse since that thing, and it wasn't even something that happened to me. And still."

She didn't say what it was she dreamed of, and I didn't ask. The whole room smelled like fear. My fear.

I didn't do this hardly at all anymore. Maybe once or twice a month as opposed to the three or four times a day it used to be. Most of the panic attacks weren't this bad. I hadn't had a real episode for a couple of months.

And it had turned the respect in Martin's face into compassion, into worry, into pity.

I stood up. Went into the little bathroom and closed the door behind me. I washed my face and looked at myself in Jitka's mirror. The big bruise on my left cheek had spread since I looked at it this morning. There were dark circles under my eyes from lack of sleep.

I looked like a victim.

I was done, really done, with being a victim.

I opened the bathroom door and sat down where I'd started. "We cannot stay here because the vampires know where we are, right?" I knew, I knew that I shouldn't do this. But the image of the victim remained in my mind.

I was dog-tired, and when I moved again, I was going to be stiff from hitting the ground and from bruises I didn't remember getting: this wasn't my first fight. I knew all about the aftermath. I should go and let Libor's pack pay for a hotel room for me until we could pay them back. I should wait for Adam.

"Yes," said Jitka.

I didn't want to get anyone into trouble. So I said, "At this point, even if I ship off to Port-au-Prince or Timbuktu, the violence is going to continue between your pack and the vampires."

Jitka said, "This attack and the one on our pack home make it quite clear that battle with the vampires is coming. It no longer matters if you are here or in China, Libor will not let this rest."

"Yes," said Martin at the same time. Jitka was just talking, but Martin watched me. His shoulders tightened. Maybe it wasn't just me who needed to do something.

"And you would love to rid Prague of Mary's seethe . . ." I said.

"Yes," said Jitka, frowning at me. "But we cannot find it. We track them, and the trails just fade into vampire magic."

"Okay, then," I said. "I think I might be able to help you with that. What do you think the chances are that the vampires came here in a car with GPS?"

In the US, the chances would be pretty good. GPS or a cell phone with GPS, which would be harder.

Martin shrugged. "Maybe, maybe not. The vampires tend to have expensive things—especially Mary's people, who are trying to establish themselves with humans."

"If you can get me to the place the vampires got in their car in Prague, assuming they walked from their seethe, then I can find it," I told them.

Martin gave me a pitying look. "We have tried that many times, and we are werewolves."

"Vampire magic doesn't work right on me," I told him. "Sometimes not at all."

"Why not?" Jitka asked.

"I have no idea," I told her honestly. "But I can see ghosts, too. Maybe one has something to do with the other." I didn't say that I could do other things with the dead. If no one knew, then no one could force me to do something I didn't want to.

"What are you?" Martin asked.

"Not a werewolf," I said. "Would it be useful to know where Mary's seethe is?"

"We could go kill them," said Jitka. She was all but vibrating with eagerness. "Kill them again, I mean, so they stay dead this time. Destroy Mary and her filthy followers in one shot."

Martin's eyes brightened. "Yes," he said.

It wasn't as stupid as it sounded. If Mary had been strong, she'd have already battled the Master of Prague. Instead, she'd been reduced to rebuilding her vampires, which was a slow and troublesome process, with failure rates higher than the werewolf Change. Most seethes, as I understood it, had a bare handful of strong vampires, then maybe as many as a dozen lesser vampires who depended upon their Master to sustain them.

We'd just killed four of Mary's seethe. All of them had been vampires for a long time or their bodies wouldn't have gone to dust. That didn't mean that they weren't still lesser vampires, because that usually required a century at least and often more. But I bet she didn't have a whole lot more at that level. Not if her seethe was only sixty or seventy years old.

And, presumably, Jitka and Martin meant to gather the rest of their pack to destroy the seethe.

But they didn't know how many vampires they were facing. I'd been raised by a master strategist who taught me that you never go to battle with an unknown enemy.

The werewolves probably knew that, too. Either they knew more about Mary's seethe than it sounded like, or, more likely, the frustration of hunting her for so long was driving them into recklessness. Apparently it was going to be my job to be the cooler head.

Adam would think that was pretty funny, but I was not a rash person. I did think things through—and then I tried to do the right thing. Just because the right thing and the safest or easiest thing weren't usually the same didn't make me rash.

We planned and talked for maybe an hour. When Jitka couldn't get through to Libor—something that didn't seem to be unusual—we came up with an alternate plan to frontal assault, which, though satisfying to talk about, was (we decided) unlikely to result in anything useful, especially if we had to do it without help.

It required a lot of tact for me to steer the wolves, since I wasn't a member of their pack or a werewolf. Only because I was the one they were counting on being able to find the vampires did they listen to me at all.

Martin suggested that we take a page out of Bonarata's playbook and extract a single vampire. We'd question that one, then turn them over to Libor for further questioning.

That made me pretty queasy. Killing an attacker is an entirely different thing than turning one over for torture. Happily, Jitka batted that one back, so I didn't have to.

"That is foolish," she said. "We have tried that. They do not talk. After the third one, Libor said it was enough. That if they were not talking after what he did to them, it was because they could not, not because they would not. There are some witchcraft spells that will do that. Maybe there is vampire magic that stopped their tongues."

I tried not to think beyond the surface of her words.

Torture was a lot further than I was prepared to go just to find out why they'd decided to work with the other Prague seethe. Maybe I'd feel differently if I lived in Prague, though I didn't think so. There were probably circumstances that would make me reconsider, but this wasn't one of those. Probably I should feel badly that Jitka and Martin seemed quite convinced that the endgame would be to destroy the seethe—but vampires are evil. I might like one or two on a personal level—but they kill people in order to keep living.

"So let's just go find the seethe," I said, "get what information we can get from watching them, then go back to Libor with that."

Safe enough, I thought. I'd already proved I could get away from the biggest, baddest vampire in Europe. This shouldn't be so bad. And I would be going out and *doing* something.

WE STARTED BY BACKTRACKING THE FOUR WHO HAD attacked us to their car, parked a couple of miles away. Actually, I started by sifting through vampire ashes looking for a car key or fob or something. Jitka and Martin put together a pack of things they were sure would allow us to extract a single vampire and restrain it with minimum chances of having it break free and kill us all. Just in case, they said when I objected that we were only going in to observe and report back.

The car was an expensive new model with a correspondingly expensive new guidance system on board. Jitka and Martin complained about how well financed Mary seemed to be getting. They seemed to take the luxury car as a personal insult, and I was reminded that not so long ago by the standards of long-lived creatures, the Czech Republic had been part of the Soviet bloc. Under the communist regime, personal wealth had been viewed as a moral failure.

I wasn't sure that wasn't correct.

We got lucky with the car key I'd found on the third ash pile I'd gone through. It was one of the keyless fobs and half-melted, but apparently the right half was undamaged, because the car unlocked when Martin held it next to the door.

I did know how to start a car without a key—even a modern car—but I needed a few more supplies than I had at hand. It was a good thing the key had survived.

Still commenting—presumably, because they'd switched back to Czech to continue their complaints—Martin started the car, switched on the nav system, and found, in the saved locations, one that was helpfully labeled with the "home" icon.

If their car hadn't had GPS, Martin knew of a few places

where one of the dead vampires had been spotted a couple of days ago. I could have tried picking up his trail and following it. But, probably, we would have given the whole thing up and gotten a hotel room for the rest of the night. The GPS was a big break.

"If they weren't living like rich people," said Jitka in satisfied tones, "then we would have had to give up. This is what living too well does. It makes you weak."

We piled in, and Martin drove the car sedately back through the streets of Dobrichovice, past the castle, and back on the highway. *Home* got us to a parking garage in a section of Prague filled with older apartment complexes. In the Tri-Cities, older would mean fifty or sixty years; here, older was two or three hundred years.

There were two spaces empty, and we pulled the car into one and parked. The smell of cars and city and lots and lots of people filled the garage. It was pretty easy to tell we'd hit gold because the cars on either side of the car we'd come in smelled of vampire, too.

Less happily, Jitka, who'd begun calling as soon as we started back toward the city, hadn't been able to get through to Libor. She put her phone in her pocket.

"I left a message for him this time," she said. "He does not text. I told him we were in Josefov, and we have a way to find where Mary and her vampires are. I told him we would go looking and call him if we find something."

Martin nodded. "Can you trail anyone in this?" He waved his hands around to indicate the complex muddle of scents.

She took a deep breath, then shook her head. "I can smell vampire, but to track, I will need to be wolf."

Martin nodded agreement. "Me as well. I have not changed for three days. I could do it as long as I could stay in wolf form for four or five hours."

"Hold it," I said. "We probably want both of you in human skins, assuming we can keep this from being an outright battle. Why don't you let me do this?"

"What are you?" Jitka asked with an edge to her voice, as if she had already been anticipating the beginning of her change.

I stripped off my borrowed clothes and looked around helplessly for a moment. In any other circumstances, I'd have thrown them in the nearest garbage can, but I'd started to feel possessive of my meager wardrobe.

I rolled the shirt and pants into a bundle as quickly as I could manage—it wasn't likely that there would be visitors to the garage this late at night. Still, I preferred not to moon people who didn't deserve it.

I gave my clothes to Jitka because that was slightly less embarrassing than handing them over to Martin.

"You aren't a werewolf," said Jitka positively, and not for the first time.

"There are supposed to be other kinds of shapeshifters." Martin's voice was hushed. "I've read stories. Weretigers. Dragons. That sort of thing."

"If you are expecting a dragon, you're going to be disappointed," I told him.

And I changed into my coyote shape. When I was a teenager, I changed back and forth in front of a mirror, trying to see what it looked like. But one of the things that changes dramatically for me while shifting is my vision, so things get blurry. I've never seen much, but Adam told me there isn't a lot to see—one moment I'm human, the next a coyote.

I might not get to see myself change, but I'd seen a lot of werewolf changes, and I'm very glad that mine is both quick and painless.

Martin's jaw dropped open.

"What *are* you?" Jitka asked. "Some sort of dog?"

I flattened my ears at her and gave an impatient yip.

"You aren't a wolf," said Martin. "Something native to the US?"

"Coyote?" Jitka said. "Like in the cartoons with the Road Runner."

I let my ears pop back up and smiled at them both.

"Well." Jitka dragged the word out as she inspected me. "I thought coyotes were bigger."

"Maybe roadrunners are smaller," speculated Martin. "I guess the question is, how is your sense of smell?"

I yipped once, put my nose to the ground, and began casting about.

Scent trails are something that training makes better. The real trouble I've always had is that the information my canine nose gives me is overwhelming. When I was a teenager, Charles spent a lot of time and effort teaching me how to sort things out. I'd gotten a good sniff of our attackers, but the scent of the woman I'd killed with the scythe was strongest in my memory, so I focused on her.

I caught her scent right away, but I didn't start following immediately. I let my mind relax and walked back and forth for a while until I was sure that I'd found the freshest scent. It was the one with a hint of absinthe, as though she'd been intimate with someone who was drinking or maybe someone spilled some on her. Maybe she'd been drinking it herself, though that was fairly unusual for vampires.

In any case, the absinthe edge distinguished that trail from all the others. It was the trail that contained the most nuanced complex of odors, which meant it was freshest, because those fade with time.

She had used the steps instead of the elevator. I focused on my prey and let the werewolves take care of keeping up with me.

MERCY

*I seemed to be spending a lot of time wandering the
streets of Prague at night. Not the best way to see
Prague, but at least we weren't running into
very many tourists.*

THE APARTMENT BUILDINGS THAT LINED THE STREETS
were probably not old by Prague standards, since they certainly
didn't date back to the Middle Ages. But they weren't built in this
century, either. They were stacked six or seven floors high and
shoulder to shoulder, leaving no room for a mouse to squeeze
through between them.

They also looked vaguely familiar. We were close enough to
Old Town that the streets and sidewalks were cobbled, so at first
I assumed that it was because I'd passed this way when I had
traveled the streets alone last night, and that was sort of true.

I looked down a cross street and suddenly got it. Someone, a century or more ago, had been trying to make this neighborhood look like Paris—which is why all the buildings had appeared so familiar. I hadn't been to Paris, either, or I'd have figured it out sooner.

The cobbles were very picturesque, but my feet were looking forward to going home, where I could run in the fields. Even the cheatgrass and the tackweed didn't seem so bad in retrospect, because I could avoid them. The cobbles were everywhere, hard and sharp-edged, and they dug into the pads of my feet.

When we passed by the Old-New Synagogue, I realized we were in the Jewish Quarter, near where I'd had my run-in with the golem—so that probably had added to the feeling of familiarity. Jitka had said we were in Josefov, and that name had thrown me. I'd heard it called Josefstadt, which would be German for Josef's city. Presumably, Josefov meant the same in Czech.

This seemed awfully . . . in the middle of things, for a seethe that had been evading the Master of Prague for half a century or more. I'd expected someplace less densely populated with a few more hidden places and a thousand or so fewer people.

But scents generally don't lie, and the female vampire's scent was definitely leading me through the Jewish Quarter. I was starting to pick up more of her trails, too, as if she'd passed this way many, many times. And she wasn't the only vampire who'd been down this sidewalk, either.

The scents of vampires gradually coalesced into something much worse. Someone wasn't good at housekeeping, either, because the smell of blood and rot and old death wafted thickly around my nose. It was so obvious that I glanced at the werewolves, but both of them were paying attention to me rather than looking around for the building housing a couple of dozen vampires.

Given the stench of vampire, I thought the werewolves' focus on me was weird, but I couldn't ask them about it. I rounded a corner, and there it was, just across the street.

There was a huge park. Any open land I had seen in Prague was covered in lush green, whether tended park or wild riverbank. It wasn't as overwhelming as the greenery in Seattle or Portland, where they fight a losing battle against the blackberry bushes that threaten to take over any spot with more than an inch of exposed soil. But it was very green.

This one reminded me of Howard Amon Park at home. Huge old trees shaded graceful paths and lots and lots of grass—most of the parks I'd seen here had more flower gardens. The whole park was carefully tended until it wasn't. As if there were an invisible fence, a sharp line marked where lawn mowers stopped, and beyond that line was a jungle of overgrown grass and brush.

In the center of the overgrown area was one of the ubiquitous off-white apartment buildings I'd been walking past. This building wouldn't look at home in Paris, any more than it looked at home in the neat and tidy (with graffiti) streets of Prague: it was in terrible shape.

I stopped, standing on the tidy side of the demarcation line. I'd spent the better part of the hour with the coyote in charge of the human because the trail had not been an easy one. I was puzzled by the situation with the grass and a little uneasy, and that started to bring my human side out. I didn't think that I was as dual-natured as the werewolves, but when I operated on instinct for a while—it sometimes took me a moment to think like a person again.

In the center of the wilder area, the ruined building was, as far as I could tell, something that should have been used for a horror film about vampires in Prague. And no one had checked here to see if, maybe, possibly, there were vampires tucked in here? And not just any vampires—these were filthy, degenerate vampires.

Marsilia's seethe was clean enough that I'd feel comfortable eating off the floor. Even the freezer (serving as a jail cell) at Bonarata's had been pristine. This place smelled like those photographs of people who were found to have two hundred dogs and forty-five cats living in their house in itty-bitty cages that no one ever cleaned. And Libor's pack had no idea it was here?

I didn't know if Prague had been bombed during World War II, but the building in the heart of the wild looked as though it had been bombed—and then simply left where it stood, including the broken bits of the apartment buildings whose walls it had once shared. Unbelievable that it had just been left here among the meticulously maintained streets of the Jewish Quarter. Maybe it was a war memorial, or something like, a memorial filled with vampires. Somehow, it didn't seem likely.

I was just getting ready to change to human so I could ask Jitka and Martin what was wrong with the collective noses of their pack when something moved inside the building. It was just a glimpse, but it was enough to tip the balance back. The coyote had been hunting or hunted by vampires all night, and she stuffed my human reasoning aside because she could see our prey.

I crossed the invisible border from tended lawn to wilderness, instinctively trying to blend in, though the coyote's coat, a mix of beiges and grays that served me well in the dry scrublands of the Tri-Cities, wasn't as useful in the lush green of Prague.

I crouched low and wiggled my way into the underbrush, leaving the trail of the female vampire entirely. I had the sense that we weren't very far from the parking garage where we'd started, though her trail had led all over Josefov.

Hidden in the greenery, I stared at the building, but the figure that had caught the coyote's attention was gone. About that time, I realized that I was alone in the middle of vampire territory. Impossible that I'd lost two werewolves while I was doing nothing more taxing than following a trail at walking speed or a little less. Impossible that they hadn't known about the seethe. Impossible, unless . . .

A cold chill slid across my spine as I realized what had happened and how much trouble I was in right now. Stupid, imprudent coyote had gotten me into the vampire seethe without backup.

I tried to be silent as I withdrew from the bushes I'd buried myself in. It took longer to get out than it had to get in, but as soon as I was out of the undergrowth, I spotted my werewolves. I'd traveled farther than I thought I had.

Martin and Jitka were pacing uneasily back and forth along the line that demarcated the change in territory from city park to vampire seethe, maybe half a football field away. I'd seen that sort of behavior, or something very like it, before, though the sheer power necessary was something I'd only seen from the fae lords, and the magic here reeked of vampire. And witchcraft. In fact, now that I was paying attention with my other senses instead of only my nose, there was a huge amount of witchcraft all around me.

I knew what this was.

Mary or one of her minions was a witch. I really hate it when the bad guys double up on powers. To my sure and certain knowledge, it was forbidden to turn anything other than a mundane human into a vampire. That witch had set up a barrier around the seethe that kept it safe from prying eyes, noses, and anything else. Martin and Jitka had not smelled the vampire seethe—or they hadn't known that they were smelling a vampire seethe.

That sounded more like it.

A spell that affected anyone in the area, that kept them from realizing they were sensing the vampires, was much less magic intensive than an actual barrier of the type the Gray Lords of the fae had placed around the Walla Walla reservation. Anyone who ventured into the area wouldn't sense vampires, wouldn't pay attention to anything the witch who set the spell didn't want them to notice. Passersby probably saw the battered apartment building—they just didn't *notice* it.

I'd heard about witchcraft spells like this.

When I was growing up in Bran's pack, he required the pack and their families to attend a regular musical night. We all participated.

I sometimes wondered at the control that it took for Bran, a musician born and bred, to listen to an unhappy eleven-year-old (me) fight the piano through a Beethoven piece that would not have been one of the great man's better melodies even had it been played well.

For two years, I played the same piece, as badly as I could manage without looking like that was what I was trying to do, at about half the speed it was meant to be played. I still hear it in my nightmares sometimes, and I imagine Bran does, too. Eventually, to my immense satisfaction, he quit calling upon me to play.

Usually Bran closed out those evenings by singing something himself, sometimes alone or with Charles or Samuel, his sons. But sometimes he'd tell us stories instead. His stories had the cadence of a fairy tale—something passed along and recited so often their words remained almost the same each time they were told. But most of his stories I'd never found anywhere else.

One of those stories that he'd told a couple of times talked about a castle bespelled by a wicked witch. Witches were always wicked in Bran's stories. This story's witch cast a spell that made people avoid looking at the castle, talking about it, or thinking about it until it was as well hidden in plain sight as it would have been surrounded by walls and a thicket of brambles. After a few generations, no one lived who knew there was a castle in the town though it sat upon the top of the hill in the center of town.

I wondered if Bran and this vampire had happened upon the same trove of stories and the vampire had found a witch to hire. No vampire who could do this, or who controlled a witch who could do this, was someone I wanted to trifle with. Especially not on a whim of curiosity. Whatever had caused Mary to take an interest in me was better discussed when I stood next to Adam in the center of the local werewolf den surrounded by werewolves. Or, better yet, over the phone, while I sat beside Adam in our own living room.

Being mostly unaffected by vampire magic had its upside and its downside. It meant that the mind tricks that most vampires could pull on their victims didn't work well on me. But it also meant that I'd walked into the middle of a vampire's stronghold by myself without meaning to.

I took another step, and something fell around my neck with brutal swiftness. In my misspent past, I've been picked up by a dog catcher or two, and I know what a catch pole feels like. I froze. *Why would a vampire seethe have a catch pole?*

A voice purred behind me in Czech. I had no idea what she was saying. She gave the pole a jerk, half strangling me, and I coughed.

Jitka and Martin were only fifty yards away, but they were on the other side of the barrier. They were no good to me at all. As I watched, they exchanged a few quiet words, shook their heads, and walked with brisk energy out of the park. The spell probably encouraged people to go away. That's what I would have done if I could set a spell like that.

I would have been better off, in retrospect, if Jitka had gotten her way and we had grabbed all the werewolves and charged the front door of Mary's home base. Assuming my coyote wouldn't have allowed herself to be separated from the pack the way she'd just done with Jitka and Martin.

I SHIVERED MISERABLY IN THE DOG CRATE IN THE BASE-ment of the apartment of the vampire seethe.

The basement, lit by two bare bulb fixtures in the high ceiling, had a dirt floor and rough-cast cement walls. The crate I was in sat next to the remains of an old furnace that was in the same state the rest of the building was in. It probably hadn't functioned for fifty years.

The dog crate answered why the vampires would have had a catch pole. It was made from welded metal mesh that was probably steel underneath its coat of silver and was riddled with magic. It had held werewolves—I could distinguish five or six different scents and some too faded to assess. No one I'd met. The silver affected me not at all, nor did the magic, but I was exhausted. The dead and rotting corpses I shared the basement with were not reassuring. Worse was the vampire chained to the wall, not too far from me. He was wearing jeans and a short-sleeved shirt over a tank top. None of them looked dirty enough to have been on his body for more than a day or two, proof that he had recently had enough control he could put on clothes. He watched me with hungry-mad eyes while he screamed in inchoate rage at irregular intervals.

I reached out to Adam. Though I couldn't actually communicate with him yet, I could feel the steady warmth of his presence. I clung to that as hard as I could.

And attracted the attention of something else.

PERHAPS AN HOUR LATER, MARY, THE MISTRESS OF the seethe, came down the stairs of the basement with the easy, definite movements and bearing of a career soldier. She didn't introduce herself, but she came striding boldly into the darkness with an I'm-in-charge air—who else could she have been?

If she'd been in Prague since the late 1940s, then I didn't see how she could have been a soldier. There are a lot of werewolves I'd known who'd served time in the military of one sort or another, though, so I'd seen a lot of soldiers. The posture was unmistakable. If she were German, she could have been one of the Hitler Mädchen, maybe. The Hitler Mädchen were sort of a paramilitary Girl Scouts trained to nark on their parents and neighbors.

Mary was not a lovely person. Her face was broad and flat, her eyes small, and her mouth wide but ungenerous. As a human, I thought she probably had tended toward heaviness. Her frame looked gaunt and wrong, with the model thinness that most vampires carried. Her hair was blond and pulled back into a bun, and even I could tell that was an unfortunate choice.

She trailed followers behind her as though she were a bride and they the attendants assigned the task of carrying her veil off the ground. The attendants closest to her were human, one pretty blank-faced man and a pretty blank-faced woman.

Both humans were naked and covered with bite marks on all of their pulse points and lots of other points, too. The girl had suntan lines, and some jokester had drawn along the bikini top with a black Sharpie. The boy was very dark-skinned, and in the shadows of the basement, he was harder to see.

I tried not to look at their faces, because it was unlikely I could do anything to protect them. Unlikely I could do anything to protect myself from what was coming tonight. They'd been here long enough that some of the bite marks were scars, so there might not be a lot left of them to save.

A vampire like Stefan, who took care of the humans he fed from, could keep them mostly unaffected by his bite for decades. But most vampires were too impatient for that. I was betting that Mary's seethe was full of vampires who didn't care about the humans they fed from. The Sharpie bikini was a dead giveaway.

The rest of Mary's attendants were vampires of both sexes and various appearances. None of them was the woman who had caught me and stuffed me down here. When they quit coming down the stairs, there were ten of them, not including the humans.

I wondered that she thought I was so dangerous. Surely she didn't always travel around her own home with twelve minions? Maybe she was trying to impress me. Maybe she was simply making a statement of some sort.

Or possibly she trailed minions wherever she went. Just as she trailed the stench of a black witch. What idiot vampire had decided it was a good idea to change a witch into a vampire? She must be able to hide her scent—or she never went out on her own—because any werewolf with a nose would otherwise understand immediately what she was. I supposed that a witch who could hide her seethe in the middle of Prague for over half a century could probably manage to hide what she was if she wanted to.

Libor's pack thought her a lesser vampire, but a vampire who could pull on the power of witchcraft was a contender for the scariest monster in town by any definition.

I clung to the contact I had with Adam, drawing courage and resolution in equal measure. I would not let this be the last place

I saw on this earth. I would not let the last time I saw Adam be the laughing face he'd given me as I died a dramatic death at the hands of his daughter. I would not let the last air I breathed be the fetid stench rising from the dirt of this abattoir.

I would survive this. Somehow.

"Mercedes Thompson Hauptman," Mary the vampire said. Her accent was heavy, definitely Eastern European, but I couldn't decide if it was actually Czech, Serbian, or even Russian. That put paid to my Hitler Mädchen guess. Hers was not the usual Czech accent, though.

I stared at her without meeting her eyes. Probably she couldn't have caught me with her gaze, but I'd met at least one who could. Being immune to most vampires sometimes seemed as useful as being immune to none.

She said something. I stared some more, and she made an impatient sound. One of the vampires came over, a male, and knelt beside her, facing me. She put her hand on his head and said something again.

The kneeling vampire said, his voice accented with the same upper-crust accent that Ben used, "How thou art fallen, daughter of the Werewolf King."

I continued staring at Mary. She knew who I was. Possibly she'd gotten word from Bonarata. Less likely was that she knew more about the werewolves in the States and our families than the rest of the supernatural community I'd run into here.

What did she intend with the misquote of the Bible? I couldn't see why she'd compare me to Lucifer, at whom the original quote had been aimed. I wondered if stealing and mutilating phrases from Isaiah was a kind of assumption of power—a dare of sorts. Though I knew that biblical readings did not affect vampires, not everyone (including some vampires I'd met) knew that.

Or maybe the translating vampire was taking a few liberties

with what she said. I kept myself from looking away from Mary to look at her translator by force of will. Mary was the threat.

"I have seen nature films of coyotes," Mary continued through her translator. "I expected that you would be bigger. More impressive. He told me that you had escaped the Lord of Night, so I should make sure of your captivity."

It must be hard, I thought, to give a proper villain speech when your victim couldn't say anything, and you could only speak through another person. It didn't seem to bother Mary much. Nor did she appear to be rattled by the clank, clank, clank of the vampire chained to the wall. He'd quit screaming but now jerked on his chains in a heavy-metal precise rhythm that pounded my ears.

Mary paid him no obvious attention, though the structure of her sentences started to follow the beat of that chain. As bad as the clank, clank, clank was, I still preferred it to the screams.

"I think, Mercy . . . that is what they call you, yes?" Mary smiled a little at me, as if she found me charming or something. I was betting on the or something. She waited a moment or two after the other vampire had translated for her. Presumably, she thought I might respond, but I made no move.

"A shortened version of your real name," she said. "*Mercy*, the weakest of all the virtues. I find your name ironically appropriate."

She reached out and ran her long fingernails musically over the welded metal mesh. I noted that she had a French manicure, though the nail on her little finger was broken raggedly.

She whispered, "Mercy has no place here, except that she is locked behind bars of steel and silver and magic."

As if no one had ever had clever things to say about my name before.

"I think," Mary told me, "that you should not anticipate

escaping from here. We have kept your greater cousins here for months at a time, and none have escaped us that we have not let go. We will keep you alive, because that is what he wants. You should remember that—that you owe him your life."

Him who? Bonarata? Oddly, I thought not. The other Master Vampire, Kocourek, had Bonarata's support. Bonarata, evil and rotten to the core though he might be, had a code of honor he followed. I knew the stories—and some of them were gruesome. It was the belief that Bonarata would keep his word that had allowed him to amass power for as long as he had. If he supported one seethe, he would not undermine that with another in the same hunting ground.

So whom did she mean?

I cocked an ear at her. And she got it.

Her eyes half-lidded, and she smiled secretly. "Guccio," she said.

It took me a moment to process his name. Pretty Vampire. Hadn't his name been Guccio? I'd been meeting a lot of people in the past day or two. But I was pretty sure that Pretty Vampire had been Guccio.

"I see you know of whom I speak. Though you met him only briefly, he leaves an impression most rare." She took a step forward and dropped to her heels, so her face and mine were even. "He said you were ugly and fat. He said he prefers me."

Yippee. She was welcome to him. Even if I wasn't married, I don't date the dead.

Mary's mouth was pursed unhappily as she examined me. "You do not look as though you are fat. You look puny and stupid, but not fat. I think he lied to me. And why would he lie unless he wanted you and he didn't want me to know it? Are you ugly?"

Heaven save me from jealous vampires. I'd always thought that vampires were cold-blooded, and, if they thought about another creature at all, it came with thoughts of food.

I didn't make the mistake of trying to answer her question. There was no right answer to a question like that. In my coyote shape, I had the perfect excuse to maintain my silence.

"You brought another witch with you," she said after a moment.

I had no idea what she was talking about. Had Bonarata had a witch travel with me from the US?

"He said"—she frowned unhappily—"he said he wasn't looking for another witch because he had me." Shrewd eyes examined me. "But I'm not stupid—I'm not as stupid as he thinks I am, anyway. He lied about you. If he weren't interested in the witch, he wouldn't have brought her up."

He wanted to keep her on edge, I judged. Keep her trying to please him. It was easier to control someone who understood that they were replaceable.

"He told me he thought about taking her, too, since I worked out so well for him. But she was old—and while vampires don't age, they don't get younger-looking, either." She leaned close to the cage and murmured sweetly, "And it looked as though she had her claws into your mate anyway. They are sleeping together."

My mate. Adam had made it to Milan, then, to speak with Bonarata. Had he brought Elizaveta? Why had he brought Elizaveta? That was a stupid question. Elizaveta was a very strong arrow in our quiver as long as she chose to aim herself in a useful direction. She liked Adam. I realized that I should have known he'd brought her—it must have been her magic that had allowed him to contact me while I was in the bus's luggage compartment.

Mary made a disappointed sound. I guess I was supposed to be jealous over the comment about Elizaveta and Adam sleeping together. If there was one constant in my life, it was my mate. Pyramids would roll down the desert before Adam would break his word or betray anyone, let alone me.

Finally, with a little unattractive pout, she said, "It is good for you that Guccio didn't like that witch. He said he didn't think she'd be cooperative, not useful to him as I have been. If he chose another to do for him what I do—I would not have liked that. You might have had an accident."

Elizaveta was well able to defend herself. I expected that if Guccio had tried to suborn Elizaveta, the vampire would have found himself overmatched. I didn't know much about him, but I knew quite a bit about Elizaveta.

"He'll be so pleased with me," she said, apparently to herself, because she got to her feet and turned her back to me, though the translating vampire kept translating.

Her gaze fell upon the chained vampire.

"Why is he still here?" she said. "I told you that experiment was a failure."

Someone said something.

"Not him?"

Apparently my translator was only translating Mary, so I was getting half the conversation.

She looked at the vampire on the wall and frowned. "This is Weis? He was doing well, I thought."

The translating vampire looked up and met my eyes and broke protocol while Mary's attention was elsewhere.

He spoke to me very quickly in a low tone. "She has been using witchcraft to try to make humans into vampires more quickly. Recently, she has been successful. That one took her two weeks to make, and he functioned for three months. But they devolve with suddenness and without warning." He paused. "If you escaped the Master of Milan, then perhaps you will survive this. Someone should know what she has done, so that they are prepared for the problems this will cause. They should destroy any vampire who belonged to her, so that news of this does not get out."

Two weeks to make a vampire, something that could take years by the standard manner. He was absolutely right. If the other vampires knew there was a way to make vampires so quickly, we'd be armpit deep in them before we knew what we were doing. Armpit deep in vampires who could switch to mindless monsters.

I nodded to show him I heard what he was saying.

Mary, meanwhile, walked up to the vampire chained to the wall. At her approach, he quieted. She held her wrist to him, and he lunged forward violently, digging his fangs into her as if he were afraid she would pull away.

But, though her body stiffened a little, she did not move away. The smell of witchcraft grew stronger, and I remembered that witches turned pain into power, even their own pain. She reached up with her free hand and petted his hair.

She said something to him, but my translator fell silent, so I don't know what it was. It sounded tender, something a mother would say to a sick child.

The feeding took a long time, and no one but Mary made a move of any kind. I don't think they were performing for me, so I upped my assessment of how scary Mary was, and she was already pretty far up there.

I put my head down and tried to look small and innocuous, and at the same time keep an eye on everyone. The only good thing about the cage, from my perspective, was that for any of them to touch me skin to skin, they'd have to open the cage door.

Murmuring softly, Mary pulled her ravaged wrist away from the feeding vampire. He stood for a moment in a daze, blinked, then looked around.

He said something.

"Why am I in this place?" translated my ally—if he was an ally. "Why am I here, Mistress? Did I displease you?"

Mary patted his cheek with her good hand while the human girl wrapped her wrist with a cleanish once-white cloth. She said something to him, and he smiled.

In a blink of an eye, his face changed and he lunged forward. This time he buried his fangs in the neck of the girl, whom Mary jerked in front of her as a shield against the attack. Mary stepped back out of range. She reached out, grabbed the girl's arm, and pulled her away from the crazed vampire without any care for how much more damage she was doing to her pet. The human girl stood where Mary had set her for a moment, her mouth open in pain or astonishment. Blood gushed out of her torn throat, a black arterial flow that covered her tan skin and slid downward. The girl brought her hand to her throat, then fell, face forward. She hit the dirt floor with a thump, dead, I judged, as she fell, though her body kept moving for a few moments more.

Mary turned her attention to the vampire, who was now hanging limply from his chains. She raised her hand toward him—a hand covered liberally with blood, both hers and the dead girl's and probably the other vampire's as well. And she began chanting.

Witchcraft.

For a moment, hers was the only voice in the room. I could feel the draw of it. It crawled over me like a wet mouth looking for something good to eat, but it slid off me, leaving only a residue of magic behind.

Just about then the vampire in the chains began screaming again, but it was a different kind of scream. His body jerked and shook as if he were hooked up to electric prods. After a few minutes, his voice broke under the strain—and still he screamed.

Witches feed on pain.

Eventually, he fell silent and I knew—because I could feel it through the residual bits of her magic—that he was gone. He didn't rot or turn to dust. He must have been very new, though, because he didn't even smell like a rotten corpse. He just smelled dead.

"So you see," said the English-speaking vampire very quietly. "Abomination."

This time Mary heard him. She turned to him, her eyes cool. She said something.

"Why are you whispering to her, Kocourek?" she asked, and he translated her words for me.

Kocourek. Kocourek was the Master of the primary seethe of Prague. So what was he doing on his knees in front of Mary? I wondered how long he'd been under her thumb.

Libor should have paid more attention to the vampires in his city.

Kocourek said something to her.

Mary considered the kneeling vampire. She looked around and said something to the rest of the room.

"Who else speaks English here?" she asked, and again he translated.

No one volunteered.

She said a word and closed her fingers briefly next to her mouth. He bowed his head and rose. When she walked up the old wooden stairs, he followed without looking back at me. Her train was a little lopsided, without the human girl, but no one seemed to notice except for me.

She stopped at the top of the landing. "*He* says that your mate convinced the Lord of Night that your death will cause a war between the Werewolf King and Bonarata's people. *He* asked me not to kill you just yet until he can check it out." She smiled, and this time it was the kind of joyous smile that made her plain face beautiful. "But he will let me know shortly. And in the meantime, I am welcome to enjoy myself. I am busy just now, but look for me in a few hours. I've never gotten to play with one of your kind before."

They left the two bodies where they were. They weren't the only dead in that basement. A city as old as Prague, a place as old as this building, has a lot of ghosts. And the dead of this part of Prague had witnessed Mary's visit. Now they, like me, turned their attention to the other monster who had waited while those who could not see the dead conducted their business.

———

ALMOST AN HOUR EARLIER, WHEN I'D REACHED FOR Adam, hoping that somehow our link would function as it should, that somehow I could find him, let him know that I needed him, that I loved him, that I was scared and alone . . . I'd felt something touch my bond with Adam and slide away, unable to penetrate, to get inside of me or my bond. Instead, whoever it was used our bond to slide through the witch's spells and into the basement where I was held.

It was different than it had been before. Its presence was even bigger. I could feel its magic, unfamiliar and familiar at the same time, and it flowed through me like an electric current as all around us, ghosts stirred. There were a lot of ghosts.

The vampire on the wall had drawn a breath to scream again,

but instead he fell silent, as if he could sense the golem's presence. He flattened against the wall and turned his face away from us.

The biggest difference between the first time I met the golem and this time was that it spoke to me.

Mercy, said the golem in my head. It didn't really use my name, not as such, but an identifier that was more who I was than my own name could convey.

Its magic felt like . . . I swallowed when I figured out why some of it felt familiar. It felt like Guayota, the volcano god who had almost killed me not so long ago. My ankle still ached before storms.

I'd lived with magic my whole life—and not in a happy Harry Potter sort of way, either. Sure, magic worked by rules, but those rules were flexible, and different kinds of magic worked differently, and there were lots of different kinds of people and creatures who could access certain aspects of it. So there was pack magic, vampire magic. Witch magic. Wizard magic. Fae magic. Sorcerer magic.

Me? I had a bare thread of magic. I could shift into a coyote. I was a walker, descendant of the avatars who represented the animals to the native peoples of the American continents. Among other things, our jobs—back before the European invasion and their attendant diseases nearly wiped the native peoples off the planet—had been to attend the spirits of the dead. For that reason, as best as I could piece it together, the magic of the dead did not affect me, and the influence worked the other way around.

But the dead golem's presence had amped my attraction for ghosts up to maximum, until I'd been swimming in ghosts. If there was any question that it had been my encounter with the spirit of the golem that had been responsible, the effect of its presence here answered that.

With it in the cellar, ghosts were flooding in despite the

presence of vampires. Ghosts didn't like vampires. I'd once thought it was because the vampires had killed them. But then I learned that there are some vampire gifts that allow vampires to command ghosts and other gifts that allow a vampire to consume them and use their substance for power.

Or it might be something as simple as the instinctive revulsion that cats (my own cat is an exception) feel for vampires.

The dead gathered around the golem and me like we were a campfire in a Montana winter. The air grew thick with that not-substance that seems to make up their immaterial bodies, and the feel of it vibrated my bones.

We are like, the golem said. *We guard against evil. You found what magic has hidden from me, a canker, a cancer, a rot at the heart of my territory and lit me the path here also. Can you destroy these demons?*

If we were going to have a conversation, I needed to be human. I supposed that we could converse without sound, as the golem was not really making sound. But I preferred to use real words, something I could shape with more sureness than the unruly babble that was my usual thought process.

The golem's presence initially stirred up some hope that I might make it out of this alive. But by the time I was back in my human skin, the hope had drifted away with the warmth of my vanished fur. The basement was a lot colder when I was kneeling naked in the cage, and the golem was a ghost.

At the very least it was a spirit without form—that it passed through the witch's wards was proof that it could not affect the material world any more than it could be affected by it.

I took a deep breath and felt the golem with other senses. It didn't feel quite like a ghost, not quite, which is why I kept trying to identify it as a spirit instead. A different word for the same thing, but not quite. What was left of Rabbi Loew's golem was very close kin to a ghost. I couldn't figure out if it was the rabbi's magic that made him feel so different, or if it was the magic that felt like Guayota's magic.

He—unlike the first time I'd encountered the golem, it felt like a him, so I went with that feeling—had no power because it had been taken from him by Rabbi Loew all those centuries ago when the rabbi had stolen back the life he had bestowed.

When I had thought of golems, which wasn't often because they are not common back in the Tri-Cities, I had conceived of them as magical robots, an animated bit of stone, obedient to the will of the man who had called them into being.

Our earlier meeting in the streets of the old Jewish Quarter had shaken that conviction. There had been an element of . . . self-determination and thought that had not belonged to a robot. And no robot ever had a spirit that traveled the streets long after the body was gone to dust.

Part of me had been working on the puzzle of the golem ever since I'd first met him.

I am no kind of skilled magic user. I didn't know anything at all about the kabbalistic magic the old rabbi had used to create the Golem of Prague. But I've been exposed to lots of other kinds of magic.

Whatever it was now, based on the feel of the magic that surrounded him, I was pretty sure that the golem had started out as a manitou.

Manitou, according to Coyote (yes, that Coyote), are the bits of the spirit of the earth. The whole earth has an enormous manitou, it can stir as one spirit, but it is too large to be concerned with minor things. Mostly the earth's manitou sleeps, and all of us should thank our lucky stars that is true.

Each dandelion or pebble has a bit of that manitou, a bit that is fully independent of the whole. But the manitou of a dandelion is very small and does not have much power to affect things around it. The mountains and lakes also have manitou; theirs are powerful and tend, like Mother Earth's greater manitou, to be dangerous when roused. Mostly, that doesn't happen a lot.

As he explained it, Coyote and his fellow avatars are very closely related to manitou—like a horse and a jackass. He'd flashed me a wicked grin as I lay in a hospital bed—put there by Guayota, who was, again according to Coyote, the manitou of a great volcano.

I might not be an expert on kabbalistic magic, but I was pretty sure that Rabbi Loew, who had created the golem, had found a manitou from something in between a mountain and a pebble. It had been strong enough to become the golem but small enough to be controlled by a man who worked kabbalistic magic. It had probably not been the manitou of the Vltava, which would be huge and powerful. Maybe it was from some long-buried stream or hill or something native to the earth of Josefov.

To me, such an act would have been evil. He had enslaved a living spirit. I doubted that a man European-born and -bred would have thought of the spirit as living. He would have considered it magical energy, maybe. That a manitou spirit was naturally territorial would only have helped the rabbi's magic along.

The rabbi was a good man in all the stories I ever heard. If he'd known what he'd done, I was sure he'd have been appalled. But most Judeo-Christian churches do not believe in manitou. He had, as I had previously, thought of the golem as a robot, an object without feelings or true life.

When the rabbi had, to go with the robot analogy, turned the golem off, he'd locked the manitou in an artificial and uncomfortable existence. Dead but not dead. Partially, I thought, by the way the off switch had worked.

Depending upon the story—probably because there were several ways to power a golem—Rabbi Loew had carved into the golem's forehead the word "emet," which is the Hebrew word for truth. When the rabbi deactivated the golem, he removed a letter and left the word "met," which is dead.

The problem with this, as I saw it, was that a manitou cannot die. It just is, like the sun and the rain. It can be changed or hidden, but it cannot be killed. But the rabbi's magic imbued the death command too strongly for the golem to ignore, so it could not live, either.

In my head and without real words, the golem had been following my thought process. I couldn't tell if he agreed with my assessment or not, or even if he understood it, but something made him speak.

Neither spirit nor golem nor ghost, he told me, *but at the same time all of them together, I kept watch over the streets of Prague. I was helpless to do anything against human evil or things like the vampires, those who could neither see nor sense me.*

But I was driven *to do this thing that I could not. Rabbi Loew gave me the task of keeping Josefov safe. So I drifted through the night streets of Prague, able neither to forsake my task nor accomplish it. And then I encountered you. Afterward, I frightened a thief away—I, who no one could perceive before. You did something to me, made me more real, real enough to rip a door off its hinges.*

His interaction with me had lit up my magic until I'd been swamped (almost literally) by ghosts anywhere near me. That was another reason I thought the golem had been created from a manitou. If we weren't as closely related as "a horse and a jackass," then he probably wouldn't have affected me that way. I hadn't considered what it had done to him.

The golem returned to his original question. *Can you destroy these demons?*

I gave a disbelieving laugh. "Does it look like I am in a position to do anything to the vampires?"

The cage was coated with silver, which mattered not a whit to me, but the metal-welded mesh was strong. The holes were too fine to allow me to stick more than a pair of fingers through it. If someone handed me the key to the padlock, I couldn't have unlocked it from inside.

I patted the cage door. "But even if I were out and free, I'd be no match for them. I'm not a power, golem."

The golem made a rumbling sound that made the vampire on the wall flinch. *You are one who walks the path of the dead,* he told me. *The dead must hear you and obey. These demons, these vampires, have swallowed death to stay on this earth. They are not exempt from your power.*

In one brief statement, the golem had clarified something that I'd been working through my whole life: that my kind had a purpose, a reason, for existence.

I stared at the golem and sucked in a breath of air. I reminded myself that my kind originated on another continent. The golem could not have encountered someone like me.

I know what you are, the golem said. *Mercy.* Again it wasn't my name; it was bigger than that. It fit better.

To him I said carefully, "My experience is that I might be able to make one vampire obey me, and only for a very short time. But there are a lot of vampires in this place." I could feel the weight of them.

The vampire on the wall screamed at me again, as he been doing off and on since the vampires who'd caught me had stuck me in the cage. This time it made me jump, because he'd been quiet awhile and I'd been paying attention to the golem.

I turned to him and, pulling on the authority I'd been learning use in the pack, said, "Quiet."

He screamed louder and with more feeling.

I said it again. As I did, the golem reached through the cage and touched my chest. Power flooded me, and the vampire shut his mouth.

"Quit looking at me," I whispered, pushed by the golem's wishes rather than my own, and the vampire turned his head away.

I clamped my mouth shut. It was wrong to do that, to have that kind of power over someone, even a vampire, and to use it as if they weren't a thinking being. To give them no choice but to listen to me.

A cold hand stroked my shoulder. One of the ghosts had crawled in beside me and touched me. I shivered, but I didn't give it any orders. Cooperation is one thing; enslavement is another. I knew better than Rabbi Loew, so there was no excuse for me when I did it.

Not that I had never forced a ghost to obey me. Ghosts weren't the humans whose death had birthed them. But I was increasingly uncomfortable with the assumption that that meant they weren't alive anymore. And that meant that other than for my own defense or in defense of someone else, I could not bind them to my will again.

If my whisper could influence the vampire as strongly as it had, no ghost had a chance of resisting me.

The vampire, not looking at me, began to jerk on his chains. Clank, clank, clank. He kept going with the steady reliability of a drum major. Clank. Clank. Clank.

233

"See?" I said to the golem. "He's working his way out of it. Imagine if I were trying to control a dozen of them. And he's crazy—I don't think that helps him resist me."

The golem looked back at me. He didn't have eyes—I saw him more with my other senses than I saw him with my eyes. But I could feel his regard.

I have a counterproposal, he said. *I have had a very long time to think about what I could manage. My master worked his magic in front of me and taught his students in front of me. I have knowledge but no power.*

"I can't help you there," I said. "I have no power to give you."

Do you not?

The golem turned his attention to the ghost beside me. She shrank away from him, huddled against my side as if she thought I might help her. I don't know how long she'd been a ghost, maybe a day, maybe a century. She could have been a victim of the vampires or the Nazis or one of the pogroms that had inspired Rabbi Loew to protect the Jewish Quarter with a golem.

I could see twenty or thirty ghosts clearly enough to see their faces. Another dozen were wisps of whatever substance ghosts are made of. But beyond them I could feel them filling the room. I realized I was paying attention to them because the golem wanted me to.

Don't you? asked the golem, again. *Feed them to me, and I can go remake myself. I know how to do it. So I can protect my territory again.*

"Feed them to you?" I asked.

Feed me the ghosts, he said, as if he thought I hadn't understood him the first time.

"No," I told him. "They don't belong to me." As if to disagree, the ghost who clung to my side put her face against my shoulder and wept silently. Her tears ran down my shoulder.

Feed them to me. I will clean this place of the vermin who prey upon my people. If you tell them, the ghosts, to let me eat them, they will give themselves to me. He paused. *I cannot get them to do that, though I have tried since you and I met, and I conceived of this possibility.*

I opened my mouth to answer, but at the top of the stairs, the doorknob turned. The ghosts left more quickly than they had come. I shifted to coyote and waited to meet Mary and discover just how bad a fix I was in.

———

I HAD BEEN VERY SURE OF MY ANSWER TO THE GOLEM before Mary's visitation, but Kocourek's information changed everything.

———

AS SOON AS MARY AND HER CADRE TOOK THEIR LEAVE, I changed back to human and looked at the golem, who'd observed the whole thing undetected.

I did not order the dead to give themselves up to the golem. Apparently he needed their consent, but he did not need their informed consent or even their willing consent.

But I did. Because unlike Rabbi Loew, I knew what I was doing. I knew the difference between good and evil, and I knew that the humans on this planet were not the only ones deserving of being treated under the "do unto others as you would have done unto you" clause of good behavior.

I called the ghosts to us, not just those who had come initially, drawn by the combination of our presence together. I called all the ghosts I could sense. When the golem touched me to reach farther, I accepted it. This was a horrible thing to do—and the only thing more horrible would be to take everything from those who had only a little existence left and have it not be enough to get the job done. They came, filling the basement impossibly deep, until I breathed shallowly in an attempt not to breathe them in with the air I needed to live.

"Listen," I told them. As with Libor's ghosts and the golem, there was no language barrier between me and the dead here. They fell silent, and I could feel their attention, like the sun on the back of my neck in the summer.

"I have an offer for you," I told them. "It will mean that you will cease to exist here. I do not know what that means, exactly, to you or for you."

I explained what we needed and why, ignoring the golem's impatience. I think about half of them understood me. The others were too fragmented to reason or communicate what they thought even if they could comprehend what I told them. Some of them were old, older than the apartment building. And they kept coming as I talked until the weight of their presence dropped the temperature in the basement, until I could see my breath and frost formed on the metal of the cage.

I explained everything twice. When I had finished, I waited. The weight of the dead was heavy on my chest.

Yes, they said as one. Those who could speak.

"Feed him," I said, and the golem's power gave my voice more authority somehow, both an order and a spellcrafting that was of the golem's making.

They came to him. There were ghosts so lifelike, I could have mistaken them for the living. There were others who were reduced to an emotion or a single moment of time. Still more I could only sense and not see, even with the augmentation the golem provided.

The golem's spirit surrounded them, sucked them into his darkness, until only one remained, the young woman who had stayed by my side through Mary's visit. She hid her face from the golem.

That one, too, he said.

No, she whispered in my ear, sending a chill across my skin that raised goose bumps.

"No," I told him. "Only those who were willing."

I need them all, he thundered in a voice that made my bones ache.

I didn't say anything more. Her tears were real enough now that I could feel them slide down the naked skin of my shoulder. The golem wasn't solid, not yet, but his presence thickened the air as he leaned his will against mine—and lost.

Eventually, he left.

I told myself that I would not have given the dead to the golem had I not found that Mary was doing something even worse than I'd believed possible. I told myself that the evil in Prague was my business, because if word of what Mary had managed got out, it would affect everyone. Every human, every vampire, and every person in between.

The vampires, long subdued because of the difficulty of making more of themselves, would jump at the chance to increase the speed and effectiveness of their procreation. They would recruit witches.

I tried to imagine Elizaveta as a vampire and stopped myself because I really needed to think and not rock back and forth in the corner of my cage.

The newly created vampires apparently had a shelf life with an explosion at the end. So it wouldn't be long before the humans noticed.

There would be war. I was old enough to remember the rampant paranoia about the fae when they came out. I remember mobs in small towns burning down the houses of their neighbors on suspicion that someone was fae. I remember people being torn apart. There was a reason that, when the fae proposed forming reservations, the government had no trouble making that happen. And the fae, especially the fae as they had represented themselves at the time, were not considered predators. They did not need to kill humans to live.

Vampires did.

Lots and lots of people, all kinds of people, would die if the human population decided to believe that vampires were real the way that the fae and the werewolves were real. I think one of the reasons that Bran had held out so long before allowing the werewolves to come out was that he knew that people who believed in werewolves would have less trouble believing in vampires.

So there was a very good reason to loose the golem on the vampires and hope he did not continue on to the unsuspecting inhabitants of Prague. Rabbi Loew had tried to kill the golem in the end. I remembered the rake of the golem's fingers across my face and the burning pain he'd left behind.

I was very much afraid that the real reason I had done as the golem asked was because I could not bear what would happen to Adam if I died here. My faith was strong enough to believe with confidence that death was not the end. Torture was nothing I looked forward to—we had a wolf in the pack who'd been tortured by witches—but there would be an end to it. But Adam . . .

Adam, I worried about. I had promised him once that I would

do everything I could do to live, to survive for his sake. I was still bound by that promise.

Yes, I would have asked the ghosts to sacrifice themselves, would have given the golem the means to remake himself, all for Adam's sake. That there were other, very good reasons for it only made it easier, but it didn't make me a better person.

Rats scurried around the edges of the cellar. Confused, I think, by me. They might not know what a coyote was, but they knew all about dogs—and I worried them despite the call of freshly bleeding corpses.

I put my muzzle down on my front paws and closed my eyes. After all the energy I'd expended, I was hungry. But behind the mesh of the cage, I wasn't going to go hunting rats, and they weren't going to be nibbling on me, either.

I waited for the golem and hoped. Hoped I'd done the right thing. Hoped that it worked as the golem expected it would. Hoped that, burdened with a physical body, he could still find his way through the witchcraft to find this place. Hoped that he would be a match for the vampires in this place. Hoped that something good would come of this.

But mostly? I worried.

10

ADAM

*Adam's story continues, at daybreak of the first morning
he spent in Milan. At about this time, I got to my feet, put
on my clothes, and went out to find the café that had
free Wi-Fi so I could try to contact someone. Adam and
his people have retreated to their assigned rooms.*

ADAM KNEW A DOZEN WAYS TO DEAL WITH A TIME-
zone shift, but mostly he'd found that staying up when he had to
stay up and sleeping whenever he could took care of fatigue eventually. He hoped not to be in Europe long enough to adjust.

Since their host was a vampire, that meant they went to bed at
dawn. The good news was that since his inner clock was already
screwed up from the time change to Europe, adding the whole switch
from functioning in the night rather than the day was just a blip.

He didn't like that their party was split up, but there had been
no way to include Harris and Smith without indicating that he

didn't trust Bonarata's ability to keep his people safe. Adam was pretty sure Bonarata could keep his vampires under control if he wanted to. He just didn't trust that Bonarata wanted to keep Adam's people safe.

He also wasn't sure that letting Bonarata think they were all one big traveling sex orgy was helping their cause. The meal they'd spent with the vampires made him suspicious that Marsilia's act was mostly because of matters between her and Bonarata and had nothing to do with consolidating the sleeping space for defensive reasons.

He was pretty sure that Bonarata—for all that he was as jealous as a cat whose owner had two dogs—knew they weren't sleeping together in any but the most mundane sense of the word. Any werewolf worth his salt could have figured it out. There was something about body language and scent that made such things obvious.

At least her machinations had reduced his patrol area to two. His two outliers were only down a short hall and up a staircase from them. Adam wasn't happy; it was too far for tactical safety. Smith's victim-like demeanor made him a target in this house of predators.

If something happened in Harris's room, Adam was pretty sure he'd hear the screams from the big suite. It didn't make the beast who lived in his heart content—or Adam, either—but it was the hand he had been dealt.

"Dawn is coming," said Marsilia as Stefan closed the door of the suite. The two vampires had volunteered to escort the pilots to their room. "There isn't much time."

"Rest well," Adam said, though he knew that it wasn't a rest at all—the vampires died with the rising of the sun.

Stefan, who had followed Marsilia as she walked rapidly toward their room, paused to give Adam a wry smile. "Stay safe," he said, then disappeared through the doorway behind Marsilia.

Larry rubbed his hands together thoughtfully, staring at the door that had just closed behind their vampires. But when he spoke, it wasn't—directly—about Marsilia or Stefan.

"I think that went about as well as could be expected," he said. Then he said what Adam had just been thinking. "I'm not sure anyone but a love-struck fool, which Bonarata isn't quite, would think there was anything between you and Marsilia. But the Lord of Night was plenty jealous anyway, for what it's worth. I heard you open Bonarata's eyes about the relationship between the Marrok and your wife. Is it true? Would the Marrok still go to war for her?"

If the goblin had heard all of that, he not only could hear as well as any werewolf Adam had ever met, he also had a larger capacity to sort through data than Adam had. The conversations in the dinner hall had blurred to incomprehensible for Adam.

He nodded in response to the goblin's question. "Bran would not be pleased if something happened to Mercy. *Very* not pleased."

Larry tilted his head in a way that was neither human nor quite wolflike. "Bran was Grendel?"

He thought about Larry the goblin king and how everyone underestimated goblins. He decided it would be a good thing if the goblin king knew something of what the Marrok was.

"Not quite," Adam said. "As I understand it, *Beowulf* was written down a long time after the events it purports to tell. The purpose of the story as it was recorded was to recite the final deeds of Beowulf, a great hero. Somewhere along the way, someone put him up against the scariest monsters they'd ever heard of instead of the terrible monsters who did kill him. That tale then blended back to the original."

On one remarkable night, not long after Adam had been Changed, the Marrok's son Samuel had sung (then translated) several versions of the tale of Beowulf.

"*Beowulf*," Adam told the goblin, "isn't any more accurate than any story told by mouth for centuries before it was written down, which is not very. Bran's story is that a long time ago, he was broken. It had something to do with protecting his son. For a very long time afterward—decades and maybe longer—Bran was a mindless monster who killed every living thing in his territory."

"When you were talking to Jacob, you said Bran's mother was a witch," said Elizaveta.

He hadn't. She was fishing. So he said, "Bran has never said so. I've heard the rumors, though. So has Bonarata."

Samuel had told him that Bran's mother was a witch, and Adam figured that, being Bran's son, Samuel had been in a position to know. But he didn't have to tell Elizaveta who his source was. If Bran had wanted it to be known that he was witchborn, he'd have told everyone himself. Since he hadn't, Adam wasn't going to do it for him. But everyone had heard the rumors, and *those* Bran encouraged. Adam just didn't need to confirm them.

"Interesting," she said thoughtfully. "It would explain some things if it were true." She smiled wickedly at Adam. "Some things that others have tried to do to Bran Cornick and failed miserably."

He didn't want to know, especially because she wanted to tell him. Elizaveta was one of his, but that didn't mean he didn't know what she was—*witch* and all that entailed. He wouldn't invite her to bring her brand of horror to their suite—and it did not matter to him in the slightest that it was only Larry and Honey here, and they could protect themselves.

"Be that as it may," Elizaveta said when it became clear he

wasn't going to question her. He could tell she was disappointed with him for spoiling her fun, though she knew him better than to have expected him to allow her to play her games here. "I am an old woman, and I've been up for far too long. I'm going to bed and going to sleep."

"Wait," he said impulsively. "Can you help me contact Mercy again?" It was maddening the way the faintness of their bond told him nothing except that she was alive.

Elizaveta sighed. "I can. But it is not easy, Adya. And I do not think that it is wise to do not-easy magic in the home of one such as Bonarata unless it is necessary. Especially since such an effort will weaken me in this place where we might need every bit of power all of us can muster. Is there something that makes you think this is necessary?"

He gave her a tight smile. "Nothing more than that she is on her own, without friends or money, alone in Europe."

"Your mate is good at finding friends wherever she goes," Elizaveta said with a little acid. Elizaveta was not herself a friend of his mate. "She escaped Bonarata. I expect she can look after herself for a day or two."

Looking after her is my job, he thought. But he said, "I expect you're right. But even so, I might ask it of you at a later time." If the wolf demanded it.

She nodded. "That is fine, so long as you know what you risk. I bid you all good night. Wake me, Adya, if anything interesting happens."

"I will if I can," he promised.

After Elizaveta's door closed, Larry gave Adam a measured look, then waved casually at Adam and Honey before he went into the room Elizaveta had picked for him. He closed his door, too, leaving Honey and Adam alone.

Adam considered staying in human guise. After daylight, it was unlikely that he'd run into trouble from the vampires. But vampires have allies—and this one had a werewolf under his thumb. His wolf form was the better one to face a true attack. Unlike less dominant wolves, he could shift back and forth several times in a day—though having the pack so far away would limit that a bit.

He began stripping out of his clothes. Honey made a sound as he pulled off his suit jacket, and he looked at her.

"Is it legal for you to carry that in Italy?" she asked. "And what did you do to the scent? I didn't smell it—still don't."

"Not legal, no," he said, taking off his shoulder holster and the HK P2000 that was his usual concealed carry. "But who is going to try to arrest me? If they do, they're going to be more worried about the werewolf than the gun."

"So they should," she conceded. She frowned. "Your shaving-lotion smell is different. Does that have something to do with my not picking up the gun scent?"

"Elizaveta," Adam said. "Not much magic, mostly just something that smells a little like gunpowder and oil that isn't."

Honey took a deep breath. She nodded and didn't say anything else. Honey was like that. She didn't mind quiet and only said what she had to say.

He stripped off the rest of his clothing, laying the suit across a chair for the night. Everything else he folded on the chair seat. When he was naked, he changed.

Honey followed his example without a word. When the whole painful business was over, he curled up on the rug in front of the fireplace, checked that somewhere Mercy was still tethered to him, and settled in to wait. Honey hopped on the couch and put her head on the arm with a deep sigh.

He drifted into the light doze that would leave the wolf on alert to any changes but still allow him to rest. It was something that he'd learned to do in Vietnam, when he had been a soldier and not a werewolf. The wolf just made it more effective.

It was late morning when his phone rang. Grumbling, he rose to his feet and stalked to the table where his satellite phone rested. He knocked it to the floor where it would be easier to see and looked at the display.

Ben.

The phone quit ringing, and a few moments later, a text message popped up. URGENT.

He checked his bond, and Mercy was still there. He could breathe again without his chest hurting. The URGENT didn't go away—it just became more manageable.

So he could breathe, but worry still hung on. A host of possibly urgent things popped into his mind. Maybe something had happened to the children. And when had Aiden become one of his children? Aiden, who was older than . . . well, probably older than Bran for all that he looked like he belonged in elementary school.

Speaking of Aiden, maybe he'd finally succeeded in burning the house down. It was bound to happen one of these days.

Change with speed, then, he decided. It hurt more when he forced it—especially without the pack to draw upon. Honey whined, and he realized that he was automatically pulling energy from her. He stopped that, and his change slowed. Growling, he redoubled his efforts, and in something under ten minutes by his phone's reckoning, he was in human form: naked, covered in sweat, shivering from pain and shock that made the warmish room feel chilly, but human.

He picked up the phone without bothering to dress and called Ben. "Yes?"

"Hey," Ben said cheerfully. "We are sodding and shagging in honey, Adam. Mercy stole an e-book reader from the Dark Ages and used it to contact me via Gmail. She's in the Czech Republic. I think they call it Czechia for short now. Prague."

And it took a moment for Adam to breathe again, but when he did, the air was sweet. He collected himself, aware of Ben waiting patiently on the other side of the phone connection.

"Prague?" He did a quick check of his mental map of Europe and blinked. "That's what, five hundred miles from here?" *That was some bus ride, Mercy.* No wonder his bond was so weak. Without the pack, he was surprised he could touch her at all.

"About that," agreed Ben blandly. "I contacted Charles, and he told me to put her in touch with Libor of the Vltava Pack. I haven't heard back from her, but the e-reader was out of juice, and she apparently didn't steal the charger when she took the reader."

Prague. Adam took a deep breath. He'd have to wait for Marsilia and Stefan to wake up; he couldn't abandon them in Bonarata's care. He took another breath and tried to subdue the wolf, who wanted to go right-the-hell-yesterday.

"She's okay?" he asked.

"She's okay," Ben assured him. "I told her you were hot on her ass to Europe. She'll hunker down with Libor for a couple of days."

Adam pinched his nose—a habit he'd gotten from watching Bran do it one too many times. "Tell me about Libor."

"Alpha of the Vltava Pack. Been around since the Middle fucking Ages. Apparently a *baker*—of all the sodding things for a fearsome Alpha to be. We are all glad we don't have to tell people our Alpha is a motherhumping baker."

Adam made an encouraging sound and waited for Ben to quit distracting himself. As the other wolf got back to matters at hand, Adam filtered out the expletives that were Ben's attempt to shrug off an upper-crust but hellish upbringing—Adam was able to assume from Ben's casual attitude that various people weren't really pedophiles nor did they do interesting and unlikely things with animals and/or machinery. When Ben was finished, he left Adam with something worth worrying about.

"Libor has a legendary grudge against Bran," Adam said slowly. "*Charles* doesn't know what it was about. Did you try Samuel?" Surely one of the two would have the story.

"Sorry," Ben said regretfully. "I did try. Since it was I sending Mercy into the mouth of the monster, I decided I was on the need-to-know list. Took an act of God to get in touch. Samuel doesn't know. Charles says he doesn't know what it was. All he has is a couple of comments Bran made once upon a time—and Bran won't say anything more. Apparently there was an oath involved, and you know how Bran is about that."

Adam cursed under his breath.

"How many years in the army, and that's all you've got?" Ben said. "I thought the army guys really know how to swear."

Despite everything, Adam grinned at the phone. "We didn't swear in my day," he lied. "We just killed people."

"There is that," said Ben. "What can I do? Samuel says he can head to Prague, but it will take him a couple of days to get there. Apparently he's in Africa."

"I thought he and Ariana were in the UK?" Adam said.

"He said he was doing a favor for an old friend," Ben said.

"Medical, I think, and not werewolf or fae business. They're not in a civilized area, and it will take a day to hike out."

Adam thought about that. "Tell Samuel no. It sounds like the crisis is mostly over. Does Charles have a way for me to contact Libor?" Trouble between the Prague Alpha and Bran or not, the vampires were a real threat. Though he, like Larry, thought he'd convinced Bonarata that killing Mercy would be a mistake. Still, he'd be happier to put Mercy with allies just in case.

"I can get that," Ben promised. "I'll text it to you in the next fifteen minutes. That work?"

"That works," he said.

He ended the call and paced restlessly, waiting for Ben's text message. Eventually, he put clothes on.

As soon as Ben sent over the information, Adam called the Alpha of the Vltava Pack, the Alpha of Prague. It took a few minutes to get Libor on the phone, which was only to be expected. Adam happened to pace by a mirror as he was waiting and stopped when he noticed that his eyes were bright gold.

It would be a mistake to let his wolf do the negotiations with another Alpha. He practiced the breathing exercises he'd learned to help his control. By the time Libor came to the phone, he was under control.

It took a while to negotiate a language to speak in. Libor pretended not to speak English because English was Adam's native tongue. They both spoke Russian, but Libor still held a grudge against the Russians. German was out of the question for the same reason—for which Adam was grateful because his German wasn't good enough for delicate negotiations.

Finally, Adam said, in English, "Look. I'm an American; you're lucky I have two languages I'm fluent in. We can do this in English or Russian, or I can find a translator. That will complicate things worse than they already are, especially since, where I am, the most likely translator I can find will be a vampire." He could do basic Vietnamese and Mandarin, but he bet that neither of those were in Libor's repertoire. And Adam hadn't used either language in several decades.

"Russian," conceded Libor without pause. He'd probably already come to the same conclusion Adam had voiced, but he'd waited for Adam to point out his inadequacies.

That was fair, because it was Adam who was going to ask for a favor.

Ben had said that Libor was a man of his word, but he was as slippery as a Gray Lord. Adam preferred to work with straightforward people, even if they were enemies, instead of subtle, slippery allies. But that wasn't his choice to make at this point. Bonarata and Mercy between them had brought him to this pass.

That didn't mean Adam needed to follow Libor's game. Instead of working up to what he wanted, he just said, "My mate is in Prague by herself on the run from Bonarata, with whom I am currently in negotiations. She needs a safe place to await help. I should be able to be there—"

An hour, said the wolf. *Probably two. We could fly to her in a couple of hours.*

Adam closed his eyes and forced himself to remember that two of his people were currently vulnerable until nightfall. That he *was* in negotiations with Bonarata, which were not going to benefit from a hasty departure. Those negotiations were necessary to keep his family and his people safe. Bonarata and Adam still hadn't come to any kind of agreement about the situation, whatever it really was, that had made Bonarata decide to take a shot over the bow at Mercy.

He wasn't going to see Mercy today. Not today.

"Early tomorrow morning at the latest," he said.

"You lost your mate?" said Libor in an amused voice.

Across the room, the mirror showed gold flooding Adam's eyes, and he bit back a growl.

"I know exactly where she is," Adam said carefully. "I will come for her shortly. It would be useful to have a quiet place for her to rest until I can come." There. He'd backed down from "need" to "it would be useful to."

"I need more detail than what you have given me," Libor said. "I have to protect my pack first."

So Adam went through the whole scenario from the moment the vampires had hit Mercy in his car right up to their current situation. Edited, but still most of the story.

"I see," said Libor, when Adam had finished. There was a long silence, presumably as Libor weighed what Adam had told him. Then he said, "You managed to let your mate get kidnapped by the most ruthless vampire on the planet, and now you need my help."

Yes. That "need" had been a mistake. Hard to judge words when he wasn't face-to-face with the other werewolf. If it had been Bran he'd been talking to, "need" would have been the key word. Bran didn't turn away werewolves who needed him.

Libor had just downgraded himself in Adam's book of evaluation. But Adam hadn't spent his formative years in the Army Rangers for nothing: he knew how to manipulate arrogant asses even better than he could manipulate competent commanders—the former having been much more common in his experience than the latter.

"If you are afraid of the vampires," Adam said, "I understand. Mercy can take care of herself just fine." He fiercely believed that.

It was the only reason he was still here, doing his duty and protecting those who'd trusted him enough to follow him into the den of the boogeyman of the vampires, instead of grabbing one of the pilots and making a beeline for Prague. "She got away from Bonarata with nothing more than her brains and determination. She won't have any trouble surviving your streets for a day. I'm not so sure if your streets will survive, though."

He thought of Marsilia's rubbing Mercy's escape in Bonarata's face and said, "My mate hit Bonarata's pet werewolf with a bus. I wonder what she'll do to your territory on her own?"

The other werewolf growled and bit out, "I do not fear the vampires. Bonarata was a child when I was an old, old wolf, and his territory is far from here. Very well, we will protect her from Bonarata's vampires until you come for her. Where shall I find your mate?"

"Mercy will find you," Adam said, satisfied at having goaded the other into defending himself. They were both aware that whatever the limits of Bonarata's territory, his fingers were in the business of every town in Europe. Libor's words were hollow, and they both knew it. Anyone within a thousand miles of Bonarata should feel a healthy amount of fear. But Adam chose to be conciliatory. "I appreciate your aid in this situation."

Libor disconnected without further words.

Adam stared at the phone. For two cents, he'd drop everything and go find Mercy. Now.

Mercy *could* take care of herself. She'd survived just fine before he'd married her. Afterward, both he and she had done all that they could to ensure that continued to be true. He could trust her to take care of herself. But when he started to make another call, he knew the wolf was in his eyes again. He didn't bother trying to calm down.

"David," he said as soon as the other side of the phone call was picked up. "I need to land a private jet in or very near Prague. Do you know somewhere I can do that?"

David Christiansen, the werewolf on the other side of the conversation, was a mercenary with contacts all over the world. He was also one of Adam's oldest friends.

"How are you, Adam?" David said with mock cheer. "It's good to talk to you. Even 'hi, hello, how's it going' would have been okay."

"Mercy's loose in Prague. I'm in Milan, and I need to get to Prague tomorrow morning. Very early. Money is no problem, but if the price is too high, we might need to wire some."

David wasn't stupid. He heard "Milan" and that Mercy and Adam were separated. He added those two together and came up with Bonarata because he said, "Messing in vampire business isn't for wusses. Try to look unimportant, Sarge; maybe they'll be low on ammo."

"Too late," Adam said with an involuntary grin. He hadn't heard that phrase since 'Nam, when officers were favorite targets of the enemy. "But there aren't any bullets flying right now." In the background, he could hear the scratch scratch as David wrote something on a piece of paper.

"What kind of plane?"

Adam gave him the specs, and David wrote those down, too.

"Give me a minute, my people are on it," David said. "If you kill that old bastard in Milan, I'll treat you to the biggest steak in Chicago. Or Seattle, if you don't want to come my way."

"Doesn't look like murdering vampires is in my near future," admitted Adam. "Much as I'd enjoy it."

David murmured something to someone else, then was back

on the phone. "Got it. Do you have something to write with or do you want me to text you?"

"Text me," said Adam. "Thanks."

"I still owe you, I figure," David responded. "Do you need some backup? I can be in Prague with a crew or two in about seventeen hours."

Adam considered it. But if the people he had with him weren't enough, he reckoned he'd need a nuclear strike and not more people to die trying to rescue him and Mercy.

"I think it's handled," he said. Though he'd have been happier if Libor had been the same kind of polite liar that Bonarata was— odd that he trusted the vampire further than his own kind. But he'd met Bonarata, and he figured he had his measure. No telling whether Libor was just being a pain for the sake of annoyance—or if he was a problem.

"Let me know if that changes," said David. "Keep your head down."

"You, too."

They disconnected, and Adam was left with a whole day to get through and nothing to do. Sleeping was out of the question.

Honey was awake and watching him. She'd have heard everything. She wagged her tail and smiled hopefully.

Adam ran his hands through his hair. "Right. This is good news. Mercy is safe. I'm pretty sure Bonarata believed me about Bran—and put a call out to his hunters before he went down for the day. He isn't interested in the kind of war Bran would bring him." The kind where everyone loses. He smiled at Honey, because he knew she'd understand. "It's just that now that I know where she is, I'm not sure I can find the patience to wait. And talk and talk and talk without killing someone."

Honey's ears flattened with amused agreement. She wasn't fond of talk and talk and talk, either.

"I'm going to go notify the pilots that we're flying to Prague before morning tomorrow," Adam said, because it would give him something to do besides pace restlessly. He'd wake them up when they should be getting sleep—but he was paying them enough money that he didn't feel too bad about that.

"Stay alert," he told Honey.

She put her nose down on the couch and watched as he put his shoulder holster back on and resettled his suit. He took a good look at himself in the mirror to check for wrinkles, lopsided tie, or the gun printing too obviously.

Satisfied that he was as put together as he was likely to get, he left the room. He couldn't lock it behind him without locking himself out—they hadn't been issued keys. He opened the door again and looked at Honey.

"Remember the door won't be locked until I get back. Keep an ear out," he said.

Then he left his chicks safe in her care. His mouth turned up as he thought about what any of the people in that suite would think of his considering them in need of his care. Except for Elizaveta, of course—she would accept his concern as her due, if only a small part of her considerable defenses.

Adam climbed briskly up the hardwood stairs, turned the corner, and knocked on the door. Movement exploded within.

"It's me," he told them low-voiced—which is probably what he should have done in the first place.

"A moment," said Harris tightly. "I've got some safeguards in place. Give me a moment."

Good, thought Adam.

The door opened, and Adam stepped inside, closing himself inside. It wasn't a suite, or even a good hotel room, but there was room for two twin beds, two chests of drawers, and a TV. It was clean, and there was a big window looking out on the same courtyard the main room of the suite did. From up here, he could see over the wall and out to the villa next door. Matt Smith was sitting cross-legged in his bed with his back to the wall. He looked interested but not particularly concerned.

"We've found Mercy," Adam told them.

Harris's eyebrows climbed. "How did you manage that? Bonarata's people are asleep now, surely."

Adam shook his head. "I should have said Mercy found us. She evidently stole an e-book reader with Wi-Fi, found a café with free Wi-Fi, and spent the next ten minutes in frantic conversation via e-mail with one of my wolves before the battery in the e-reader died. She's in Prague."

"Prague?" said Smith.

Adam nodded. "Since I was out of reach, Ben consulted the Marrok's son Charles, who told him to send her to the local Alpha for protection."

"Libor?" said Smith. "I've . . . heard things about Libor of the Vltava."

"Charles recommended him," said Adam.

"Oh, sorry," Smith said. "Probably okay, then, right? Charles doesn't make mistakes."

Harris looked back and forth between the two werewolves. "Trouble?"

"I called Libor and confirmed he'd provide safe space for Mercy until I could get there tomorrow morning," Adam said when Smith didn't say anything. "If that's dangerous, if you know something, Smith, this would be the time to let me know."

Smith shook his head. "No. Libor is a man of his word. If he told you she'd have safety with him, she will."

"We could be in Prague in an hour and a half," said Harris. "Maybe a little longer. Do you have a place I can set down there? If not, I have a place to land in Brno and another in Dresden, and it's only a couple of hours by car from either one to Prague. We could use the main airport, but that might be more public than we want to be."

"I have a place for you to land in Prague," Adam said.

"Not a good idea to offend Bonarata," suggested Smith quietly. "If you leave without clearing it with him, you are putting him in a corner in which he has no choice but to call you an enemy for breaking guesting custom."

Harris gave his copilot a sharp look.

Adam smiled at the goblin's surprise. "Remember that werewolves can live a long time, and just because one is submissive doesn't make them stupid. My experience has suggested the opposite. We have a saying, 'Listen when the soft ones speak.'"

Smith smiled with only a little irony. "Your mate has a reputation of her own," said Smith. "Do you think she needs your help? My feeling after the dinner was that Bonarata intends to diplomatically forget about Mercy."

"Did you overhear something?" Adam asked alertly.

Smith ran his hands though his hair. Glanced up at Adam and then away. "He told one of his vampires, the woman with red-and-gold hair, to call off the hunt. Unless he's found someone else to hunt, I suspect that's the hunt for your wife."

"I heard that, too," said Harris. "Didn't make the connection. He said the hunting had lost its joy this season—or something flowery like that. Decided to cancel the hunt. My Italian is pretty bare-bones."

"I should have said something," Smith said after a glance up at Adam's face.

Yes, but there hadn't been a very good time to do it. It wasn't anything that he hadn't expected—it was just a relief to hear.

"All right." Adam let out his breath. "Mercy should be fine until we can get her. We'll talk to Bonarata tonight—and then we'll go find my wife."

Smith said, "There are some stories you should know that I've heard about Prague."

"Like the stories about Libor?" asked Harris.

Smith shook his head. "Libor is difficult, but there's not an Alpha on the planet who isn't difficult one way or the other." He paused. "Present company excepted, I'm sure."

Adam snorted.

Smith continued, "At any rate, there are two vampire seethes in the heart of Prague."

Adam frowned. "They're even more territorial than we wolves. Is there room for two seethes in Prague?"

"Exactly," Smith said. "Nothing really wrong but . . . I think it would have been better if your mate had found her way to Munich or Paris. London, even."

"Up to you, Hauptman," Harris said. "We could fly to Prague, collect your mate, fly back. Depending upon how long it takes to find her, we might make it back before dark."

Adam considered it. But it would still mean abandoning Marsilia and Stefan—and that was wrong.

Smith said, in a low voice, "You'd be bringing your mate back into his clutches. He'd see your going as an insult or a challenge. It might make him do something interesting. If you leave her in Prague—and let him know you have her location—he'll know you respect her ability to take care of herself. It will leave you in a more powerful position in the end."

"Mercy *can* take care of herself," Adam growled, because it was his privilege to take care of her anyway. He took a deep breath and turned to Harris. "Be ready to leave anytime after nightfall tonight. I'll let Marsilia handle the negotiations. She knows how the bastard's mind works."

"No one knows how Bonarata's mind works," murmured Smith. "That's why he's still around."

"Get some sleep," said Adam. He was starting to feel the long day, too. He hadn't done anything more than catnap since Mercy had been taken. He had a course in front of him now, and even if the monster inside him wasn't happy with his decision, it was made.

He closed the door and started down the stairs but paused because someone was walking down the hallway from another wing of the villa. He couldn't see him, but he heard his footsteps. Inside him, Adam's wolf alerted, because the other was walking softly, like a trained fighter who doesn't want to be noticed.

He trotted back up the stairs he'd just come down. Unlike the other man, Adam made no sound. He timed his approach so that he stepped into the hallway about five feet in front of the other man.

In front of the vampire.

Guccio's pretty face broke into a pretty smile that didn't show his teeth. "Adam," he said. "I didn't expect to see you here."

Were they on a first-name basis? Adam's wolf said no, but Adam swallowed it because all he knew was the vampire's first name.

He managed a casual raised eyebrow when the wolf wanted to eliminate the threat to his people.

"Vampire," Adam said, tipping his head toward Guccio in something that the vampire was welcome to read as greeting. "Should you be out in the day?"

There were vampires who could move about in dusk or twilight, but Adam reckoned they were close upon midafternoon.

Even though the inner halls of the villa were windowless and lit by artificial lights, it was the sun that mattered. When the sun rose, a vampire's spirit or soul or whatever left their body and no longer animated it. The corpse left behind smelled and felt like a corpse. Vampires were dead every day; wolf noses don't lie.

Guccio's smile widened. "The Lord of Night once had a very powerful witch." He held up a hand-stitched cloth bag tied around his neck.

It appeared, to Adam's Southern-bred eyes and nose, like a *gris-gris* bag. He smelled a number of herbs, but the main scent was something organic decaying. Maybe Bonarata's witch followed voodoo or hoodoo practices. Or maybe she (because strong witches were mostly women) was African, which was where the practice of making *gris-gris* originated.

Adam had never heard of a witch who could let a vampire walk in the daytime. Maybe because there weren't any witches who would want to do so.

"It only allows me to walk when otherwise I would have to rest," Guccio said, letting the bag settle back against the hollow of his throat. "It cannot protect me from sunlight."

Adam wondered if Guccio knew how much longing was in his voice when he said "sunlight." The vampires called it "sun-sickness" when their kind became obsessed with the sun. Without intervention, vampires affected by sun-sickness died within a year or two—walking out into the dawn of their own volition. Suicide of sorts. If they hadn't already been dead.

Guccio was one of those people who liked hearing his own voice so much that he thought everyone felt the same way. He kept talking, but all Adam paid attention to was the threat he represented. Adam made answers that Guccio probably took as polite and wondered if he was going to have to kill Guccio before going to Prague.

And Adam waited at the top of the stairs until Guccio turned back the way he'd come and kept going, following the hall as it took a sharp turn. He had never said what he was doing over by Adam's pilots' room.

His wolf furiously disturbed, Adam knocked on Harris and Smith's door for a second time.

"Get your things," he said shortly when Harris finally opened the door. "There are vampires wandering around in the daytime here. I'm not leaving you here alone."

———————

HE GAVE THE PILOTS THE COUCHES. HE AND HONEY, both in wolf form, curled up on the throw rug in front of the cold fireplace. Honey slept, but Adam only managed to doze off and on, his wolf restless.

He found himself checking the bond with Mercy over and over. All he could tell was that she was there, but for a few minutes it would quiet the wolf. He hoped it was just the wolf's reaction to the meeting with Guccio and not something about Mercy that the wolf could feel and the man could not.

No one in the bedrooms stirred, not even to his wolf ears.

Smith slept like the dead. Harris . . . Harris snored. Just enough that it made Adam worry that it would cover a noise that might warn him of an attack.

People started stirring out in the hallways as the light outside bloomed into a glorious sunset. Adam shifted into his human shape, gathered his luggage, and went into the vampires' room to use their bathroom to shower, shave, and change.

By the time he was done, both vampires were awake. They didn't speak—maybe they couldn't. Adam could see their hunger—just as they could see his wolf.

They had better get things tied up here tonight, or Bonarata might not be the one they had to worry about. He hadn't thought about the vampires' need to feed. He didn't know much about it. It was a touchy subject for Stefan, though maybe not for all vampires. Should he have suggested that they bring one of their willing donors—what did Mercy call them?—one of their sheep with them?

But he didn't think he could have stood back and watched, not knowing that the human's willingness might not be anything more than a strange and strong addiction.

They were adults. More than adults, they were powers in their own right, he decided as he nodded to them and kept going out the door to the main room of the suite. He would do his best to keep them safe, but they could find their own food.

In the common room, Harris and Larry were up, dressed in keeping with their differing roles in this play. Elizaveta was wearing a slate-gray suit with a diamond brooch. She looked like someone's sweet and expensive grandmother. Soft. He wondered whom she was planning on blindsiding.

There were two people showering. By process of elimination, that would have to be Honey and Smith.

A polite knock sounded at the door.

Adam started to get it, but Harris waved him back.

"I believe that's my job, sir," he said deferentially, then flashed Adam a cheery grin.

He opened the door to a male and female vampire, each pushing a trolley.

"Good morning," said the woman with a friendly smile and downcast eyes. "With my Master's compliments, we have sustenance for your bloodborn. For the rest of your party, there is tea, coffee, and drinking chocolate. First meal will be served in an hour in the main dining room. It is generally less formal than last meal—no ties required. My Master requests that a half hour before the meal, you attend him again in the receiving room. If you would like a guide, one will be provided you."

"The receiving room is the old library?" Adam asked.

She gave him a surprised look before dropping her eyes. "Yes, sir."

"It still smells of books," Harris explained, touching his nose. "The wolves pay more attention to the scents of things than most people do. We won't need a guide."

The servants withdrew. Adam claimed the cart that held a tea service with a large, elaborately fashioned black-and-gold teapot that did not, according to his nose, hold anything like tea.

"I'll take it in to them," he said. He trusted that Marsilia and Stefan had enough control not to attack anyone even with their hunger riding them, but he wouldn't send anyone else in. Just in case.

He knocked once—they would have heard the exchange with Bonarata's servants—and went in. Marsilia was dressed and putting a diamond drop earring on. Stefan was buttoning his white silk shirt.

"Thank you," Marsilia said.

There was no trace of the Hunger in either of their faces, but Adam knew what he'd seen. He pushed the cart all the way into the room and turned to leave them to it.

Marsilia said, "Wait."

He stopped and looked at her.

"Please," she said. Then she nodded to Stefan, who closed the door.

As soon as the door shut, she approached him. "Did you meet with a vampire in this house between the time we retired and awakened?"

"Guccio," he said. "Mercy contacted Ben via e-mail using a stolen e-reader. She's alive in Prague and likely to stay that way until we get there. I went to talk to Harris to let him know we'd be wheels up tonight as soon as *you* figure out what a proper leave-taking of Bonarata consists of. Sooner rather than later if you can manage."

Marsilia absorbed all of that. While she did, Stefan said, "Guccio? In the day?"

"He had some sort of magical bag. Witchcraft. I want to ask Elizaveta about it."

Stefan considered that. Then he said, "Did he do anything odd?"

"No bite marks," Adam said. "I checked." And he had. He knew about vampire mind tricks—and his wolf was even more agitated than it had been when he found out about Mercy.

Stefan nodded slowly. "Okay. Okay. You should be okay, then. You just—" He glanced over at Marsilia, who sighed.

"Vampires have scent markers," she told him. "It's not quite a secret, but not something we tell everyone about. We leave them involuntarily when we feed off a human, but we can also do it deliberately—a touch, a brush of skin on skin. A way of marking someone as *ours*. As soon as you walked into the bedroom, Stefan and I could tell you'd been marked by someone. I didn't know Guccio well enough to remember how his scent marker smells."

Adam sniffed himself, but he couldn't detect anything different. It made him uneasy that the vampires could smell something he couldn't, but that might be why his wolf was so upset.

"I showered," he said, "and it's still here?"

Stefan grinned. "Don't worry, Mercy won't smell it, either. Some kind of vampire magic designed to keep some poor fool from taking a bite of a Master Vampire's prey. Vampires can smell it from the newest hatchling to the oldest doddering geriatric." His smile was real, but his eyes were solemn. "It's considered rude, unless it's one of your own . . . people, someone who has to go out and about among our kind, and you want to protect them from other vampires."

"What an interesting thing to do to a guest of Bonarata," said Marsilia. "I wonder what it means?"

Adam felt his mouth quirk up. "I guess we'll find out."

Marsilia narrowed her eyes at him.

"Come on out to the main room," he said. "I have a few things to talk over with everyone."

But when they made it to the main room, Honey was still getting dressed in Elizaveta's room. Smith was in the suite, and from the wide-eyed look he gave Adam, he'd heard about the vampire scent-marking him. Adam was pretty sure there was a glint of something in Smith's eyes, too, but the other wolf dropped his head like a good submissive, so Adam couldn't be sure.

Given that there were no bite marks, Adam could see why they found it funny that he, a werewolf, had been marked as prey by the stupid vampire.

The two goblins were pointedly looking at the window, their backs to the room. Presumably so that Adam couldn't see their wide grins.

Elizaveta looked from Adam to Smith to the goblins and said, in a voice with virtually no Russian accent at all so that Adam knew she was really angry, "Please tell me the joke so that I know what you and the vampires were conversing about. It seems that I am the only who did not hear what went on."

Adam bowed to her and said in Russian, "My apologies. It is a joke on me, I am afraid. Please let us wait until Honey is here, and I will tell everyone some information I've gotten while you've slept. And I think you may provide us with important information about what I have to say."

She arched an eyebrow at him, but he knew that by addressing her in Russian—which everyone here did not understand—he had given her a sop to her pride, because, in that case, she was not the one left out of the information flow. And letting her know she held vital information was a boost to her ego. She knew he was manipulating her, but she decided to allow it.

"Very well," she said in English, her accent back in place. "I can wait for Honey."

Honey came out, her short hair a little damp and her face freshly made up. She smelled, just a little, of rose petals. A human might not catch it, but the vampires would. She wore a rose-colored tank top without a bra and jeans that looked as though she wouldn't be able to draw a deep breath. Around her neck was a gold chain with a small wolf charm. He knew that Peter, her dead mate, had gotten her the necklace, because Adam had gone with him to pick it out for her birthday.

She looked like bait.

He smiled at her, and she gave him a toothy smile back. He was glad he'd brought her, fierce and strong. She was a good wolf to have at your back.

He told them about Mercy. Told them that Guccio had been walking around the villa with a spell bag that allowed him to roam during the day. And he told them that he'd been marked so that all the vampires would think that he was Guccio's food.

Honey stepped closer and sniffed him. "I don't smell anything?" She gave the vampires a suspicious look.

"I don't, either," said Larry. "But I know that vampires have a way of marking their prey. It's seen as crude, because usually, unless it's a Master Vampire, it's an accident. Proof that a vampire lost control when he"—he glanced at Marsilia and said—"or she found some food that appealed to her. Sort of like spitting into a drink that isn't yours."

Adam smiled grimly at the goblin. "Thank you. I'll store that image." He turned to Elizaveta. "The bag Guccio wore around his neck—it looked and smelled like a *gris-gris* bag. He said it gave him the ability to stay awake during the day, but it wouldn't protect him from the sun."

He closed his eyes and described it in as minute detail as he could manage, including a list of herbs and the other things he had picked up. "Whatever was rotting in the bag smelled vaguely rodent-like to me, but it had been dead and covered in herbs for too long. Mostly it just smelled rotten. He claimed that a witch Bonarata had once had made it and that it allowed him to walk during the day."

Elizaveta grunted. "Such a thing could be managed that way."

"Oh?" said Marsilia, a little too neutrally.

"I can do it for you for a fee," she acknowledged. "But such things are limited. A certain amount of time per day—and only for so many days."

"Could you do one for sunlight?" asked Stefan, but he didn't sound hungry, just thoughtful. "It would really suck eggs if Bonarata has access to something that allows him to run around in the sunlight."

He'd gotten that "suck eggs" expression from Mercy.

Elizaveta gave Stefan a shrewd look. "I can make you a *gris-gris* that will allow you to walk in the sun," she said gently. "Would you wear it?"

Stefan gave her an arrested look. "Never," he said slowly. "No tarnish to your honor, *donna*, but I would have to trust you a lot further than I trust anyone to venture out into the sunlight with a *gris-gris*."

Not at all insulted, Elizaveta gave him a slow smile. "That is good, Soldier. You are wise. I think that any vampire who has lived as long as Bonarata has lived would feel the same." She looked thoughtful. "Truthfully, I don't know that it could be done in any case. I would have to understand more about why sunlight—and not, say, full-spectrum light from lightbulbs—is fatal to your kind. The other—allowing you to walk during the daytime—would be a variant on part of zombie animation."

"So the *gris-gris* is a consumable," Adam said.

Elizaveta smiled at him. "A very expensive consumable, I think. It would take time to make, and its maker would have to be of a certain level of power. A lot of power and a lot of skill—you said the vampire claimed that Bonarata no longer has access to this witch?"

"That's what it sounded like," Adam said. "If this is a non-renewable consumable and valuable magic item, then Guccio was not casually strolling by Harris's room."

"No," agreed Marsilia. "It is a good thing that you were there, and a good thing you brought them back with you. Or maybe we wouldn't have had pilots to take us home."

"On Bonarata's orders?" asked Adam.

She shrugged. "Maybe. Guccio might just be trying to curry favor. Iacopo—Jacob—*Jacob* has always had a fondness for innovation."

"He probably marked you for spite," said Stefan. "It was a dumb thing to do, though. And dumb people don't tend to last long enough around Bonarata to climb the power hierarchy."

"A *gris-gris* such as the one he carried can affect people adversely," Elizaveta observed. "That is true black magic, and it tends to stain the user as well as the one who casts it." She glanced at her watch. "If we are to meet with Bonarata at the time specified, we should leave."

11

~~~

ADAM

*I could wish that Adam were more concerned with his
own life than with saving everyone else's. Since it is a
wish Adam has expressed (often) about me, I suppose I
have no grounds to complain. I do anyway, of course.*

BONARATA WAS DRESSED IN SLACKS AND A TURQUOISE
silk shirt that had been made for him. He was seated, doing paperwork, at a desk Adam had barely noticed the first time he'd been
here. "A moment, please," he said, without glancing up.

Adam's dad had liked to do that when Adam had transgressed in
some way. Invite him into his study, then sit down and do some other
work for a while so that Adam could think very hard about whatever
it had been that he (or one of his brothers) had done to get called into
the study. And let him know that neither he nor his transgressions
were as important as whatever else his father was working on.

It had worked quite well on Adam when he was eleven.

Adam strolled over to the desk and stood, looking down upon the vampire, Honey at his shoulder.

Marsilia gave him a horrified look. Stefan flashed him a quick smile before turning his attention to a painting hanging some distance away. It was *not* the painting of Marsilia. From his position, Adam couldn't see the subject other than there was a lot of blue, maybe a seascape. Elizaveta found an oil painting done in the classical style, the rape of Leda, Adam thought, because there was a muscled and naked woman grappling with a human-sized swan. The two goblins and Smith were on the far side of the room speaking softly—very softly if Adam couldn't hear it. If he couldn't, then neither could Bonarata.

Bonarata figured out what had happened pretty quickly, Adam thought. His intimidation tactic had been turned on its head. The minute Bonarata looked up, Adam had the upper hand.

Adam was fighting down amusement when the door next to the desk opened—and his wolf recoiled with horror and pity and revulsion as a dark-haired woman came in.

She could have been beautiful or ugly or anything in between, and Adam would not have noticed. Every hair on his body, every sense belonging to the werewolf and Alpha and pack understood that the werewolf who came into the room was *wrong*.

"Jacob," she said in a perfectly unremarkable tone as she set a large envelope on the desk in front of Bonarata. "Annabelle gave me this for you. She says that the architect has redrawn the section in the house in Seattle." She turned to look at Adam and stared blankly at him.

Her wolf was dead. And not dead. And so was the woman. Or not. Whatever she was confused his wolf and sent him into a frenzy of horror.

"Good," Bonarata said. "I've been waiting for these."

Adam thought that he was supposed to be nervous that the vampire was building a home in Seattle, but he had no emotion to spare for the vampire; his wolf was too focused on the damaged wolf. She wore a silver collar, though there was no marring of the skin where it rested—so it was not real silver. White gold, maybe. Her neck was covered with scars of bite marks and so was every bit of skin he could see that wasn't on her face. Her clothing had been chosen to display as much of that scarred skin as possible without being tacky.

Adam wasn't the only one reeling. On the far side of the room, Smith forgot himself far enough to utter a low growl.

"Lenka," said Honey, in a low voice that held the same horror that Adam felt.

While Adam had been paying attention to the broken werewolf, Bonarata had come to his feet, effectively putting an end to the dominance issue he'd begun. Adam was very far from caring about whether he or Bonarata had the upper hand.

"Lenka," said Honey again, taking a step toward the wolf, who looked at her without recognition.

Honey said something in a tongue that had a nodding acquaintance with German, her voice taut and frantic.

The broken wolf said something in reply in the same language, then turned to Bonarata. "I am sorry. You told me to speak only in English. You must punish me."

She sounded . . . eager, though her scent carried bitter horror.

Bonarata smiled. "It is of no matter. You were accommodating our guest." And then Bonarata made a mistake. He turned to say something to Honey.

Distracted by Marsilia, Bonarata had not paid much attention to Honey the day before, and he hadn't paid any attention at all to her while indulging himself trying to get one up on Adam. Honey was worth looking at normally—dressed as she was to attract attention, she could stop traffic.

"You—" said Bonarata, and that's as far as he got, because as well as traffic, she apparently was pretty good at stopping speech. But mostly because Bonarata was an addict—and Honey fit his craving like a bespoke suit.

Honey, uncharacteristically, didn't see Bonarata's reaction. She was only paying attention to Lenka. Adam wasn't entirely certain Lenka saw it, either, since he was watching Bonarata and Honey, but there wasn't a werewolf in the room who wouldn't have smelled Bonarata's sudden interest. Lust had a very distinctive scent, be it a human, werewolf, or vampire.

"Honey," Bonarata said slowly, his voice deepening. "Honey Jorgenson, correct?"

Lenka looked at Bonarata. Then she drew a knife from somewhere and struck Honey. Or rather she struck at Honey, who moved and thus caught only a thin slice across the front of her shoulder.

Kill that one, said Adam's wolf as clearly as he'd ever heard anything. He'd heard other werewolves say that sometimes their wolf spoke to them—and a couple of those he respected too much to discount their word. But in the nearly five decades he'd been a werewolf, he'd never had it happen to him. *She is broken. Kill her.*

Honey was a fighter, born and bred. Adam had spent the better part of three decades teaching her martial arts, but she'd had a good foundation before that. Lenka had no style, but, like some of the men he'd known in the Rangers, she showed every sign of having killed a lot of people. Honey moved prettier—but Lenka moved faster.

His people started toward them as soon as Lenka pulled her knife. But they stopped when Adam waved them away. "Honey was attacked. She has the right to finish this. Lenka broke the guesting laws." The rest of them could interfere, but then the expectation would be that they subdue Lenka. If he left it as Honey's battle, she could take it all the way to the death because Lenka had struck the first blow.

Bonarata moved around his desk. "Let me put a stop to this."

But Adam stepped in front of him. "No. She attacked Honey unprovoked. This is a legal fight by guesting law."

Bonarata snarled at him, "She'll kill your wolf."

Adam took a step backward and turned at the same time, putting some distance between him and the vampire and allowing him a clear view of the fight. Let Bonarata see for himself how likely Honey was to die in a fight with any werewolf, let alone one who was underweight and broken.

Lenka was changing, her facial bones moving subtly under the scarless skin of her face. She took a kick in the ribs and let her body move with it as her hands snaked down to grab Honey's leg. But Honey saw it coming and dropped her body into a shoulder roll that brought her back into the outer circle of combat.

Honey was holding back.

Adam told her the words the wolf was whispering in his head. "Kill her, Honey. The woman you knew is not in that body anymore and cannot be brought back."

Honey didn't look at him, though he could tell from the stiffness of her shoulders that she had heard him and didn't like what he'd said. Across the room, Smith met his eyes and nodded agreement. He, too, understood what Adam's wolf had known instinctively.

Bonarata turned to Adam with a hiss. "She is *mine*."

Adam assumed he meant Lenka, but given his addiction, he could have meant either one of them.

"Then you should have kept better control of your wolf," Adam told the vampire. "If she had not attacked Honey, we would have left her alone."

Bonarata growled soundlessly, but Adam heard it just the same. The vampire turned to the fighters and said, "Lenka, kill her for me."

Adam was pretty sure that Lenka was doing her best to do just that. Those words had been aimed at Adam.

After that, everyone was silent, only moving to get out of the way—and Elizaveta was both quick and graceful for a woman of *ahem* years.

The room was mostly empty of furniture except for the small desk Bonarata had been using. And the desk didn't last. Lenka ripped off a delicately carved leg and broke it over Honey's thigh—a hit that was meant for her knee.

It was the table leg that got Honey's head on straight. Up until that point, despite Adam's order, she had been fighting defensively, unwilling to seriously hurt the other wolf. Honey tore off a second leg. When it broke off with a sharp point, instead of using it as a club, she used it as a modified lance.

"Good," Adam said quietly. She'd hear him. "That's it."

She lost the table leg eventually. She brought it up as a shield when Lenka struck with her knife, taking advantage of an opening Honey had lured her into. The knife sank deeply into the wood. Honey twisted, and Lenka couldn't keep her grip on the weapon. Honey threw the table leg, knife and all, through one of the plate-glass windows, shattering the glass and leaving the knife out of play unless and until someone decided to go through a window after it.

"She is beautiful," Bonarata said, mesmerized, his desire scenting the room. "Like a tigress. All muscle and speed." Lust had changed his eyes, and not even the most mundane human would have looked into that feral face and thought anything but vampire. Even though vampires didn't need to breathe, he was sucking in great gulps of air, air now scented with blood and sweat and need. His need.

Across the room, Marsilia was watching Bonarata with sad eyes. Not hurt or brokenhearted or anything like that, just sad. The way someone would look at a fallen Ajax or Hercules.

She was wrong. Bonarata wasn't even down yet, let alone out. But there was no question that his hunger for Honey—for any female werewolf's blood—was driving him now.

He wouldn't like having Adam and his people see him like this. He'd remember it later. But so would Adam.

It took her a while—because Lenka was a hell of a fighter—but Honey pinned the other wolf to the floor in a wrestler's hold. Panting, blood dripping from her mouth and her nose, Honey looked, not at Adam, but at Elizaveta.

"Can this be fixed? I smell witchcraft on this band around her neck," Honey said.

Adam was starting to think that he should find out more about Bonarata's witches. According to Bonarata, he had a healer who had mended Mercy's near-fatal wound. Healing was not something black witches are supposed to be good at, and no white witch would have that kind of power. He'd had someone who'd made a *gris-gris* that had impressed Elizaveta—Adam knew how to read that old witch.

Elizaveta walked to where the werewolf was pinned to the floor. She sank to her heels and examined the metal band around the werewolf's neck.

Lenka bucked and struggled, but Honey held her fast. Elizaveta didn't seem worried.

After a moment, she stood up.

"No," she said sadly. "The band keeps her under control, but it is a simple thing, if powerful. It makes certain that she follows the orders she is given."

Honey looked at Adam then.

He said, "It is a kindness."

She nodded.

She had to let up, just for a second, to get the knife she kept strapped to the inside of her thigh. The one that she hadn't drawn during the fight because she needed to be sure that killing was the right thing to do.

Lenka almost broke free, but she wasn't quick enough. She was malnourished, and that had hurt her fighting abilities. She was neither as strong nor as fast as she could have been. Now she was tired, too, and her speed was half what it had been in the beginning, though the fight had been relatively short.

She couldn't avoid the small blade that slid into the joint between her spine and her head. She died when the blade slipped in, but it took a moment for the air to leave her lungs and her body to quit moving. Honey's blade wasn't silver, but it was deadly enough.

Honey pulled the blade out when Lenka was dead. He couldn't always tell with vampires, but werewolves were easy—their smell changed.

She wiped the blade clean on her pant leg. It wasn't a prudent place in a building filled with vampires, but he thought she was not in the mood for prudence. She sheathed the blade and accepted Adam's hand up. She didn't need his help rising, but he knew the touch of pack would center her. She stood, letting him hold her for half a breath before she slipped away.

As soon as she was standing, Adam turned his attention to Bonarata. Adam knew he'd been taking a chance by turning his back on the vampire. But Honey came first, and he had people in the room who would watch the vampire for him.

As it turned out, Bonarata had had other things to occupy himself with. The Lord of Night was staring at Lenka's body with an expression Adam had seen on junkies looking at a dime bag, a deep need that overwhelmed any other thought or emotion. But the expression faded as Lenka's blood died with her. Leaving Bonarata with an expression that looked very much like regret and relief on his face.

"Adam," said Stefan urgently.

"Beside you," said Smith, at nearly the same moment.

Adam reached out and wrapped a hand around Honey's biceps and blocked her with his body as she launched herself at Bonarata.

"Stand down," he told her, pulling her close to his body so she could smell pack and Alpha. So she could feel his command sink into her bones.

He felt her resistance, though she never pushed against him. She just leaned her forehead to his shoulder and said, "Lenka was a wolf I'd have hunted the moon with. Not a friend. But she was smart and tough. Peter had stories . . ." Her voice trailed off.

Adam didn't take his eyes off Bonarata, who was beginning to look at Honey the way he'd looked at Lenka. Adam didn't want to share intimate things in front of the vampire, but for Honey he'd do what he could. He put a smile in his voice. "Peter had a thing for powerful women."

She laughed wetly against him. "I guess he did. I miss him."

He kissed the top of her head. "We all do. You should go change your clothes and clean up." He looked around for someone to send with her.

Stefan said, "I'll go up with her." He was watching Bonarata's face, too.

Dressing Honey to seduce had, in retrospect, been a stupid thing to do. Adam glanced at the body on the floor. A stupid thing, but he couldn't regret it. This poor creature was free now.

Keeping his body between Bonarata and Honey, Adam turned her over to Stefan. They walked slowly, but no one in the room spoke or moved until after they were gone.

When the door shut behind them, Bonarata blinked and came back to himself. Ignoring the body, as though Lenka had not been his . . . "sheep" was the wrong word, and Adam couldn't find a right one . . . "victim," maybe. As though Lenka hadn't been his victim for centuries, Bonarata said, in a light, casual voice, "I had asked you to meet with me here to tell you that I have disturbing news."

Standing close behind Adam, Smith inhaled and made a sound, and Adam wondered if he was going to have to send Smith out, too. It was probably a good thing that they weren't pack; the two of them weren't connected at all really. Rage was one of those emotions that tended to snowball between pack members.

"What news?" asked Marsilia. Adam thought that she had decided to play mediator, then remembered that he'd asked her to do just that. To get them out of there in as short a time as possible, so he could go find Mercy.

He reached out to Mercy and found her. Just knowing that she was still okay was enough to settle his wolf a bit. But, like Bonarata, Adam made an effort not to look at the dead wolf on the floor. Impossible not to smell her, though.

A chime sounded, a slightly different chime than the one that had announced last meal.

"Ah," Bonarata said. "First meal. Why don't we discuss matters over food?"

"Agreed," said Adam. "We have news for you as well."

Bonarata led the way into the dining room. Marsilia and Elizaveta followed him. The two goblins, Harris slightly to the back of Larry—like a guard—fell in behind the women. Smith, taking up the tail end of the line, stopped by the dead werewolf. He went down on one knee beside her and touched her forehead.

He bowed his head and said, very softly, "What are you going to do with the body?"

Bonarata came to a halt and turned back. Adam would swear the sadness on his face was genuine. "She served me well for a long time. We will bury her in the garden where she liked to rest in the sun when she could. I think she would have liked that, don't you?"

Smith vibrated, his hand still on the dead wolf's forehead. Adam waited. Finally, the wolf said, "It sounds peaceful, I think. Thank you."

"Did you know her, too?" Harris asked.

Smith got up, sighed, and walked to the others. "Everyone knew about Lenka," he said.

"Then someone should have done something sooner," muttered Larry.

"Lots of someones tried," said Bonarata. "We did not bury them in the garden." His voice sounded amused. His public mask was back on and firmly in place.

Adam didn't think that Bonarata would have been so sanguine

if he'd been looking at Smith at that moment. But maybe he was wrong. People discount submissive wolves.

———————

ADAM HAD HOPED TO BE GONE BEFORE THE FIRST meal, but that wasn't going to happen now. Mercy was still on the other end of their bond, so he could manage another hour of negotiations as long as he wasn't the one doing the negotiating. Now that they were being honest in their dealings with Bonarata, he trusted Marsilia to reclaim her role as diplomat.

And there was still Guccio, who had marked Adam as his food. To get to Mercy an hour sooner, Adam would have forgone the pleasure of teaching Guccio why vampires didn't go about thinking of Alpha werewolves as prey. So he wasn't altogether disappointed with the delay.

They crossed into the dining room, and Bonarata stopped to speak softly to one of his vampires, who then walked quickly off without appearing to rush.

"Your witch wasn't careful," said Elizaveta as they started forward again. "That collar would not have . . ." She paused. "I think it was already no longer keeping her obedient."

Behind them, Smith growled again. It was a quiet thing, so maybe the vampire and witch didn't hear it.

Bonarata nodded. "It was becoming a concern," he said. "But I have not had a witch capable of that kind of work since before the Second World War." He smiled at Elizaveta. "Would you be interested in a job?"

When she didn't immediately respond, Adam looked at her thoughtfully.

"No," she said at last. "Though if you let us leave with Honey, I'll let you pay me to remove that unfortunate addiction you have." She pursed her lips. "It won't be cheap, I warn you."

"He could not keep Honey," Adam said coolly, because it had been obvious from Bonarata's expression at Elizaveta's reply that the vampire had been considering how he might do that very thing.

"No?" asked Bonarata silkily.

"No," said Marsilia.

He turned on his heel so that he faced Marsilia. Her shoulders were back, her weight was balanced over the balls of her feet: she was ready for a fight.

Bonarata's mask held for a heartbeat, then it was gone.

Adam realized that they had done what they set out to do—upset the Master Vampire in the middle of his own game. The bonhomie of their first meeting was no longer a solid disguise behind which Bonarata could run the show. Adam could see the monster quite clearly—and as Bonarata looked at Marsilia, Adam could see the man, too.

A man with a million regrets that mostly surrounded the woman who defied him.

Ironically, now that Adam knew where Mercy was and he just had to shake himself free of Bonarata, Adam would have been happier with the genial host. They could have taken care of business in a cool and logical fashion, and Adam would be on his way by now.

Instead, Adam could feel his wolf's satisfaction as it settled itself for the brutal fight the beast foresaw. Something would happen. The energy of the room had tipped into potential violence. Because if Bonarata said the condescending pablum Adam could see his mouth forming—Marsilia was going to hit him.

No matter how happy that would make his wolf, it would be faster to go if a fight didn't break out, so Adam broke up the moment between Marsilia and Bonarata by saying, "If you don't have a witch of my Elizaveta's power at your call, how did you heal Mercy from her 'near-fatal' wounds?"

His intention was to turn the vampire's ire from Marsilia to himself and to force Bonarata to backtrack. Because, logically, either Bonarata had lied about what he'd done for Mercy—and Adam *knew* those wounds had been bad, he'd felt her pain and seen the blood—or just now Bonarata had lied about not having a witch.

Bonarata dragged his eyes from Marsilia, and the look he gave Adam was almost grateful. It was a guy thing. He, too, knew whatever he had been about to say to Marsilia wouldn't have been useful. It had just been beyond his power to not say it. Adam was happy to help.

"We didn't have a witch mend your wife," Bonarata said. "A healer did it. Come and meet her."

A healer?

Bonarata didn't wait for questions. He looked around the dining room and led them to a back table with a soft-looking vampire male who was playing games designed to encourage the girl sitting next to him to eat. Adam recognized those games because he'd played them more than a time or two when Jesse was a toddler.

This girl was a lot older than a toddler. She was dark-haired and blue-eyed and oddly unfinished. A mundane human would look at her and think Down syndrome or something of the sort. *Adam* observed her and his nose told him that she was fae and human. She looked like she was fourteen or fifteen, but, having fae blood, she could have been four or five hundred years old and looked no different.

She was too thin, and there were circles under her eyes, but when she looked up and saw Bonarata, her face lit up. She left her place and trotted (there was no other word that fit the high-stepping shuffle) around the table and made happy noises as she raised her arms.

Bonarata laughed—a big booming laugh that suited him oddly well and was nothing any vampire had any business having—and wrapped his arms around her. He swung her around twice and set her down gently on the floor. He stopped her too-loud babbling that didn't, to Adam's ears, appear to actually be words.

She quieted and looked up at the vampire with the eagerness of a corgi awaiting orders.

"Stacia," Bonarata said, "Stacia, these are my friends. Marsilia. Elizaveta. Adam. Larry. Austin. Matt. People, this is my friend Stacia."

She gave each of them a cheerful wave until she got to Adam. She squinted, stuck out her tongue in thought—then clapped her hands suddenly and her mouth rounded in surprise. She looked at Bonarata and wiggled her fingers with such abandon it took Adam a moment to realize she was using a form of sign language.

She turned back to Adam and gave him a huge smile. She patted his arm, sending a zing of power all the way from the skin where she touched up to his nose. He didn't flinch. He took her hand in his and kissed it.

He knew what he was looking at. This child was the single reason Bonarata's machinations hadn't killed Mercy.

She blushed and clasped her hands together, pressed close to her stomach. But the smile she gave Adam was pure delight.

"She says that you belong to the pretty lady she healed," Bonarata said. "She thinks that you should go find her and give her a hug."

The girl patted Bonarata. He laughed. "Okay. A very big hug." She nodded firmly, apparently having no trouble understanding English, even though she apparently didn't speak it—and maybe no other language except her own. "And you need to go eat, young lady. You are too thin."

She gave him a sweet smile and took the hand of the vampire who was evidently her caretaker and let him lead her back to her food.

On the way through the dining hall, Bonarata said, "We found her in a ghetto in some little town in the middle of the Great War."

World War I, Adam thought, a century ago.

"She is fae," said Larry.

"Partly," Bonarata said. "Or so we think."

"More than half," Larry told him seriously. "Don't let the fae know you have her here. She'd be useful to them, and I don't think they'd treat her as well as you do. They've little patience with creatures who are not perfect." He spoke, as he often did, as though he did not consider himself to be one of the fae.

"So I have always thought," agreed Bonarata as he turned, presumably to take them to where they would be eating this evening.

He paused. Looked sharply at Adam and took a step closer and inhaled.

The vampire who'd brought drinks to their room earlier approached before Bonarata could comment on the scent he'd finally noticed.

"Your pardon," she told them. "Our seating arrangements had to be rapidly rearranged. Ms. Arkadyevna, Mr. Harris, Mr. Sethaway, Mr. Smith. I have you seated over there, the little table with the peach-rose flower arrangement. There was not time to find a cordial dining companion, so I thought it was best to seat you among yourselves."

Bonarata held up a hand. "One moment, Annabelle. Could you find Guccio, please, and bring him here?"

"Adam met Guccio wandering the hall with a witched bag that allowed him to walk in the day," Marsilia told Bonarata in a low voice, because people were starting to look at them.

"Ah," murmured Bonarata. "I'd been told that piece of witch-craft was no more."

They all watched as Annabelle walked quickly through the room and found Guccio talking to a small group of vampires near the table where they'd eaten before. Guccio looked over at Bonarata, then said something to Annabelle and patted her shoulder before breaking off from the others and weaving his way to Bonarata's side.

"Why is it that Adam carries your mark?" Bonarata's voice was almost cheerful.

And now the whole room fell silent. No one looked at Bonarata, but they were listening as hard as they could.

Guccio blushed and swore. Then he said contritely, "I am sorry, Master. I had hoped to have a word before this meal, but I was distracted with some confusion about a delivery of—I suppose that part doesn't matter. It was a stupid thing. I was going through an old trunk last night and happened upon this"—he pulled the *gris-gris* out of his shirt—"I didn't even know if it worked or not anymore. Mary made it for me a long time ago. I thought I'd try it." He took a deep breath, then said, in a voice that was raw, "I miss the sun."

There was a sympathetic echo that had no sound, but it swept through the room just the same. Those words found a home with every vampire here. A human might not have noticed it, but Adam's wolf was on high alert, and that left Adam taking note of everything.

"It still worked, but Mary's spells always brought out the wild in me," Guccio continued.

A second, lesser reaction in the hall. There were a number of people, Adam judged, who knew what Guccio was saying and agreed with it. He thought about Elizaveta's words—how such objects should be used with caution because the . . . evil could bleed through.

"I was just walking," Guccio said, his eyes half-closed, as though he was reliving that moment in his dreams. "I could feel the sun above me, reaching through the walls of the house, and suddenly there he was. I touched him before I thought." He gave Adam an apologetic smile. "I am sorry. It will fade in a day or two as long as I don't touch you again."

"It is of no matter," said Adam.

MATT SMITH'S SUSPICION TURNED INTO A CERTAINTY. He'd been concerned since this morning when Adam had come in to tell them he'd had a run-in with Guccio. It was not like an Alpha to allow another person to trespass—to mark him as if he were prey—then dismiss it as nothing.

Matt stepped forward and touched Adam on the shoulder. When the other werewolf looked at him, Matt dropped his gaze.

"I need to have a word, sir," he said. "It's important."

Bonarata frowned at him and said, "It will wait until after breakfast, I trust. I would not have my cook offended for a light matter."

Matt could have heaved a sigh of relief, but he didn't. If there were words better guaranteed to get him his five minutes alone, he wasn't sure what they were.

"Of course not," said Adam. "We wouldn't dream of offending your cook. You will start without us. I'll be back shortly."

"Adam?" said Marsilia.

Adam glanced at Matt, who shook his head. This was a matter for wolves.

"Start without me," he told Marsilia, and he headed for the nearest door, which happened to be the one that led back into Bonarata's art gallery.

Matt trailed after him, doing his best to look apologetic. He knew people well enough to understand that no one who wasn't seated at the table with the little healer half-blood would get to eat until he and Adam got back.

Adam shut the door behind them. "There are cameras in this room," he said. "And this model includes a mic, so don't say or do anything that you don't want Bonarata to know about." And Adam would know, wouldn't he? Security was what the Columbia Basin Alpha did for his other job.

Matt said baldly, "You've been Kissed by a vampire, Adam."

Adam stared at him. "No," he said without conviction. "I looked." His breathing grew rapid, and so did the pulse in his neck. "There were no bite marks."

He pulled up his sleeve, and there were two rough puncture marks on the inside of his arm. "See?" he said. "Vampire bites heal as slowly on a werewolf as any wound on a mortal. If I had been bitten, there would be marks." His voice was slowing, slurring, as something inside—probably his wolf—fought to uncover the lies he'd been fed, lies that blinded him to the red marks on his skin.

Matt wished there were pack bonds between them—pack bonds always made it easier to get an Alpha to listen to him. He raised his eyes and met Adam's.

"You were bitten," he said. "Without the pack here to anchor you, a powerful enough vampire can make you remember whatever he wants you to remember. You have to fight it, Adam. *Listen* to your wolf and fight it."

Adam held his gaze and broke out in a sweat as the brown lightened to gold. The wolf inside Adam, in another place and time, might have objected to another wolf holding his eyes. But this was not a dominance fight. Matt's status, instead of making this a fight, made it an offer of help acceptable to Adam's wolf.

Matt had hoped it would work. But dominant wolves were unpredictable. This could have ended in bloodshed.

"Shit," said Adam, the words dragging out of him like pulling a body out of quicksand. "Shit. Damn it to hell. I've been bitten by a fucking vampire."

"Change," Matt suggested. "That will help."

Adam shook his head and gritted his teeth. "Can't," Adam said. "Can't lose face with Bonarata. I have to stay human. I have to get out of here tonight to get Mercy—and before I do, I need to figure out why the *hell* Bonarata stole her in the first place. Stupid fucking vampires."

"Agreed," said Matt. "Though pretty undiplomatic if we are being recorded. Is there anything I can do to help?"

"Not now," Adam said. "I'll fight this out myself. Now that I know what's going on. I think I've got this." He took a deep, ragged breath. "This will teach me not to listen to my wolf. It's been telling me there is something wrong since"—Adam looked at Matt and flashed him a surprisingly sweet smile, given the sweat trickling down his forehead—"since Mercy disappeared, I guess. And that was the problem. Too hard to tell one hissy fit from another."

He fell silent. Matt put a hand tentatively on the other wolf's shoulder, and when Adam didn't shrug him off, he left it there. They didn't share a bond, but Matt was older than he looked, and there were ways to feed power through touch.

Adam lifted his head and opened blind eyes when he felt the initial rush. He sucked in two gulps of air, then said in a hoarse voice, "You'll have to teach me how to do that when this is all over. I can think of all sorts of times that would come in handy."

Matt smiled, though the other wolf couldn't see him. "Will do." And then he fed him more power.

It wasn't as much help as Adam's pack would have been. With a pack, Guccio would never have been able to get such a hold on an Alpha's mind. It said something about Guccio's ranking among the vampires that he could do it at all. He caught a whiff of Honey and knew that Adam was pulling on that bond, too.

He could tell when Adam freed himself because the Alpha wolf's body relaxed, and his breathing eased. When Adam opened his eyes, they were dark brown once more.

"I've left the tie in place," he told Matt. "I don't want to give Guccio warning. Let's see what he does with it."

Matt's eyebrows rose. "Is that wise?"

"Probably not," Adam said with a toothy smile. "But I've got it. Do me a favor, though?"

"Anything," Matt said.

"If I start doing what Guccio says, take that gun in your ankle holster and shoot me with it, would you?"

Matt grinned. "Sure thing."

———

ADAM TOOK THE LEAD BACK TO THE DINING HALL. THE filthy tie that Guccio had imposed upon him made him feel like

Little Miss Muffet on her tuffet—but he couldn't afford to react to the great spider.

He tried to look as if all that he'd been discussing with Smith had been the latest episode of *Doctor Who*, though he couldn't do anything about the sweat. Thankfully, his suit would hide any sign of dampness even if there was nothing to be done about the smell.

As he'd surmised, despite having told them all to eat without them, everyone was seated with food growing cold on their plates or in their glasses, depending upon what kind of monster they were.

Without saying another word, Smith headed to the table with the goblins and Elizaveta, who was frowning at him. He felt something, and a gentle breeze, that smelled of Elizaveta, brushed his skin. Her face went blank; and then she looked pleased. She greeted Smith with a pleasant smile.

Adam sat down opposite Bonarata, with Marsilia on his left and Guccio on his right. There was a warmish American-style breakfast on his plate, enough food to satisfy a werewolf. If he were to guess, conversation hadn't been going too well while he was gone. Marsilia's mouth was tight around the edges, Guccio looked amused, and Bonarata looked particularly bland.

"Sorry to keep you," Adam said to Bonarata. "Urgent pack business."

"I thought your pilot wasn't pack," Bonarata said.

"He isn't," agreed Adam pleasantly, dumping ketchup on his eggs. "But sometimes submissive wolves run into problems if they're around too much violence. Since he is here because of me, he has the right to ask me for help." Which was sort of true— violence became a problem for most people eventually unless they were true sociopaths, and there was no need to tell everyone that Adam had been the one in need of help.

The food was good, even cold, and Adam made his way through the meal with the dedication of a man drained from fighting off a vampire attack. As soon as he took the first bite, other people started eating, too.

A male vampire stopped by the table and handed Bonarata a note. He read it, frowned, and looked at Adam.

"This concerns the bad news I had," he said. "I sent out word yesterday that my people were to locate your mate and assist her if necessary and otherwise just keep watch and send me word."

As opposed to kill her on sight, Adam thought.

"My people have all been contacted except for one—and from him I have had no word at all."

"He is in Prague," said Adam.

Bonarata looked at him with narrowed eyes, and Adam knew he was right.

"Mercy has this . . . this uncanny ability to go where the trouble is thickest," Adam told him. He had decided a while ago that it wasn't deliberate, and that it had something to do with being Coyote's daughter. He was pretty sure that Mercy was completely oblivious. "My wife went to Prague. A city where, my people tell me, there are two vampire seethes in a place that should only be territory enough for one. Hopefully she is safe with Libor of the Vltava."

"You sent Bran's foster child, whom he loves, to *Libor of the Vltava,*" said Bonarata. Because, evidently, Bonarata knew there was something up between Bran and Libor.

"Do *you* know what caused the bad blood between them?" asked Marsilia with interest.

Adam had discussed his qualms about Libor with his people, including the secret trouble between Libor and Bran. Marsilia suggested asking Bran himself. Adam had just shaken his head and explained that Charles had told Ben that the secrecy was powered by an oath of silence. Taking their curiosity to Bran would be useless. Bran doubtless knew, Adam had told them, that Charles had told Mercy to go to Libor. If Bran had had objections, he'd had plenty of time to voice them.

Bonarata shook his head. "Libor doesn't talk much. He especially doesn't talk to vampires. He informed me so when I attempted to meet with him a few months ago to discuss why his city had two seethes—one of which no one can pin down, not even my . . . the Master of the city. I have a few ideas about it." He frowned. "It was probably a mistake to put it off, since the Master is no longer communicating with me. We tried him just before dawn, because we couldn't reach my hunter."

"Is the Master of Prague still Strnad?" asked Marsilia.

"No," said Guccio. "Strnad killed himself seventy or eighty years ago. Kocourek took over the city from him."

She frowned. "I don't remember Kocourek."

"After your time," said Bonarata shortly.

"Is this Kocourek a rebel type?" she asked. "Or is he in trouble? Or is he just away from the phone for a couple of hours?"

"Maybe Mercy did something to him," offered Adam dryly. "You can never tell with Mercy. I expect there are buses in Prague, too."

Marsilia raised her eyebrow at Adam—an admonishment to behave. Adam raised one back at her.

"It is unlikely that Kocourek is away from the phone," said Bonarata. "That is cause for concern, certainly. But anything further than that is speculation at this point."

He didn't sound like it was speculation. He sounded like he

was seriously angry about it. Adam suspected Kocourek was not long for the world, but that was Bonarata's business.

"I'm sure you will understand," Marsilia said, "that Adam is anxious to collect his wife. Especially if your vampires on the ground in Prague are not responding. Perhaps we should get on with business. You took Mercy. Why?"

Bonarata pursed his lips, took a sip of his wine as if he enjoyed it. Then he looked up at Adam.

"You have made a bold move," he said. "It was a brilliant move, perhaps, to claim your town as your territory and vow to protect all the people in it. You've made your town a place for humans to come and treat with the fae and the werewolves. A place where they feel safe. Humans come to see the fae, and the fae show their true faces—at least part of their true faces there. All because you have said you can keep them all safe from each other. It is a happy thing, a thing full of infinite possibilities and hope."

He played with the glass. It looked fragile in his big hands. Then he set it down with a sigh and said, "And when it doesn't work, you are going to spark a war with the humans that has not been seen on this planet since the Spanish Inquisition set off the Witch Wars. When I was a boy, every village had a coven of witches. Every city of any size had a witch as strong as Elizaveta in charge of it. The humans began it, driving the witches into breaking treaties that had been in place for centuries. By the time it was finished . . . I thought for fifty years that they had succeeded in killing off every witchborn person on the planet."

The vampire spread his hands, then set them on the table on either side of his glass. "I do not believe that you—a pup not even a century old—can do this thing you claim. Even the Marrok has pulled his support from you, though your mate is this woman you claim is the child of his heart. He waits for you to fail, because if he did not think you would fail, he would join you. You are no match for the Gray Lords. You are no match for the werewolf packs who will move in on your territory because the Marrok no longer gives you the mantle of his protection. You are no match for me." He gave Adam a sad smile. "No matter how much I wished it to be otherwise."

Adam waited until Bonarata seemed to be done. Then he cut into a crescent roll dusted with raspberry drizzle and ate a large bite. He made sure to chew it well and washed it down with a swallow of water.

"Point of fact," Adam said. "The Marrok broke with us because he thought we were going to step into the middle of a war the fae were courting with the humans. He needed to keep the rest of the werewolf packs out of that because, as you well know, if the fae turned their attention to eliminating the werewolves, they'd probably be able to do it before the humans managed to destroy the fae."

He took another bite and chewed slowly.

Marsilia said, "The question you should be asking yourself at this point, Jacob, is why didn't the fae destroy Adam and his pack out of hand? We all here at this table know they could have done it."

Bonarata looked at Adam and invited Adam to answer the question with a lift of his eyebrow.

Adam swallowed his food. "You are looking at this wrong. You think I hold my territory by the might of my fist. But that's not it. I hold my territory by consent of the governed. I think it is a very American concept, which might be why you never looked for it."

He ate another bite in virtual silence. The rest of the people in the room—and there were maybe forty people here outside of his—seemed to understand that something was going on, and they quieted to hear it.

Adam decided that he'd offered enough. If Bonarata wanted to know more, he could ask. This time it wasn't a dominance thing, a power play. This was for keeps. If Bonarata asked the questions he needed answers to, he was more likely to believe what he heard. The sooner he understood how their safe zone worked and why, the sooner Adam could get into the plane and fly to Prague.

"Explain it to me, then," gritted Bonarata, "who is hampered by being old and European. Explain to me how a single Alpha werewolf can dictate behavior to the Gray Lords. To Beauclaire, who has the power to level cities. To the children of Danu, who were worshipped as gods."

"Oh, that one is simple," Adam said. "They made me do it."

Silence.

"He's not lying," Marsilia said. "I rather enjoyed the show."

Adam tipped his water glass at her. "I'll remember that." Then he dropped his indolent air and sat forward, all business. "When they made their dramatic exodus, the fae expected to be able to retreat to the reservations and never deal with humans again. Three thousand years ago they could have done that, retreated to Underhill and lived happily for as long as they cared to do so. But that Underhill fell and closed her doors to the fae, forcing them to make their peace with the humans, who reproduce so very quickly and love the cold iron that is the doom of most of the fae.

"Moving to the New World was a desperate move, revealing themselves to mankind again was a desperate move, creating the reservations was an even more desperate move. The latter paid off, or so they thought. In the wilds of western North America, where cold iron doesn't have the weight of history that it has here, they were able to reopen the ways to Underhill in the territories they controlled. Places where cold iron and Christianity had no hold. So they flipped the bird at the humans and retreated, expecting that they could run from this world."

Arrested, Bonarata absorbed that. When Adam started to speak, the vampire held up a hand. "I had not heard . . . a moment, please."

Adam went back to eating. Maybe if he weren't hungry, if he hadn't been a soldier, the tension in the room would have ruined his appetite. Maybe.

"They opened the old ways," Bonarata said, "but they did not find what they expected."

Adam nodded. "Exactly. Underhill wasn't happy with them— wasn't entirely sane—and had no intention of allowing them to return and reign in their old, arrogant fashion."

"Leaving the fae trapped in a cage of their own making," the vampire said.

Adam nodded. "They had some choices. One of them was to go out fighting. Even a hundred years ago, they might have won a war with the humans, though I doubt it. They have the power, but the fae just don't have the numbers—and a fair percentage of them would rather kill other fae first, *then* go kill the humans. Now? With modern weapons? I don't think it is a fight they can win, and neither do most of them. But the fae still have the kind of power that could make it a war with no winners." He brought his fists up together, made a quiet explosive sound, and opened his fists like fireworks. "Everybody dies. Some of the fae find this a very attractive option, death in the glory of battle."

Bonarata snorted inelegantly. "Morons," he said. "Where is the glory if there is no one left to tell the story?"

"Thankfully, most of the Gray Lords agree with you," Adam said. "They had locked themselves in their fortress. But the fae are not vampires or werewolves, who can live in peace with their brethren." His wolf laughed at that. Fae living together in peace? Werewolves maybe, if the Marrok were there to bang heads together. Vampires? Still, one must flatter one's host, and the vampires were better, generally, at living together than the fae were.

"If they kept their people trapped in the reservations for much longer, they would die at their own hands." Adam only voiced what was obvious to everyone here who knew the fae. "They were already starting to murder and torture their own—out of sheer boredom, I think."

"If they are to return to the world, they have to negotiate with humans again," Bonarata mused. "But now they have thoroughly schooled their hosts in exactly how scary, how powerful they really are. How could they reestablish communications after that?" He gave Adam a doubtful look, clearly indicating he didn't think Adam was up to the task.

"I don't think you understand just what Adam is to the humans," Marsilia said. "He was a celebrity werewolf almost from the first moment the werewolves came out. He's good to look at, and he understands how to walk in the halls of power. He was respected by the military-industrial complex of the US before it was known that he was a werewolf. He was a person trusted by high-level military and political people. So he helped to weave relationships between the werewolves and humans." Here Marsilia paused to smile wryly. "And then Mercy took a handful of Adam's pack and killed a troll to save the humans. They risked their lives and were hurt in a battle they could have avoided. But they put themselves between the fae bad guys and the humans and turned themselves into heroes. They are celebrities."

"Stupid of us," Adam said. "Because it gave the Gray Lords an idea."

"You were set up," Bonarata said sitting forward. In a hushed, power-filled voice, he said, "They set you up. Set you up to be a hero, pretended to be afraid of you so that the humans would believe you could make the fae behave."

Bonarata was being surprisingly reasonable for a man who had just lost one of his pets. Elizaveta had said the collar was almost out of power, hadn't she? And the witch who had made it was no longer working for Bonarata. Maybe Lenka's death hadn't been as unplanned as it had seemed.

"The fact is," Adam said, addressing the issue at hand, "no one believes the fae are afraid of me. Not the fae. Not the humans. Certainly not me. What they believe, because we have done it, is that we will fight to the death to protect the humans in our territory. But, I can tell you that if a fae steps wrong in my city, I won't have to lift a finger to destroy him, because the fae themselves will do it for me. We have a treaty signed in blood to that effect."

Marsilia cleared her throat, and Adam thought back over his words.

"Destroy him or her," he said. "The humans believe that we can protect them—and we can. They are mistaken, a little, because they don't know about that treaty, about why we can protect them. The fae know that the Gray Lords will kill to protect that treaty. And the fae *are afraid* of the Gray Lords."

"Most important," Marsilia said, "is that the humans don't just think Adam and his pack can protect them—they *know* that

Adam *will* protect them. He is a superhero—like Wolverine or Spider-Man."

"And it isn't just my pack enforcing order," Adam said. He wasn't a superhero—but he could see Marsilia's point. "It's Marsilia and her seethe. It's Larry." He raised his water glass in Larry's direction and, twenty feet away, Larry raised his in return. "It is Elizaveta." He and Elizaveta exchanged the same distant toast. "It is the fae themselves. I am, for my sins, just the face of that protection to the public eye."

Bonarata stared thoughtfully at Adam. Adam met his eyes and held his gaze. This time, Bonarata smiled, a wide, generous expression that was as honest an expression as a vampire of his age and stature was capable of.

Yes, Adam thought, Lenka's death had been planned. Bonarata's sorrow had been real enough. But her death at the hands of Adam and his people had been planned. Maybe Bonarata wanted to use her death to justify killing Adam. That felt like something a vampire of Bonarata's reputation might engineer. It had been an accident that Lenka had struck the first blow—and that Honey had been entirely justified in killing her.

Bonarata glanced around the room, and people resumed talking and doing things other than paying attention to Bonarata. Sound reestablished itself comfortably.

In this semiprivacy, Bonarata said to Marsilia, "Recently, you lost several of your stronger people. If you would leave me a list of my vampires you would trust at your back, I will see who is willing to travel to you." He paused, then said, with evident sincerity, "You may account the gift as my endorsement of this idea of your safe zone." He paused. "Alternatively, you could return here, and I will send people to replace you so the werewolves are not left without support."

As an "I love you and wish you to return to me" it lacked both clarity and passion, Adam judged. If he'd said something that lame and uncommitted to Mercy, she'd make sure he paid for it. He didn't think Marsilia would be any more impressed by it than Mercy would have been.

Marsilia looked down at the table. "I loved you," she said in a very low voice.

"You defied me," Bonarata said in the same low voice. "You fought me. I could not let it go, no matter how much I loved you."

She gave him a hard smile. "You destroyed Lenka and her mate because it was easier than controlling your hunger for her blood. By destroying her, a strong werewolf, you demonstrated that you were still in charge—a very big lie. It worked only because people are willing to believe lies that are big enough. Because you did not want to control your addiction, not really. You enjoyed the power boost the blood of a werewolf gave you more than you recognized the addiction as a weakness that is more than a match for any strength it gives you."

"Yes," said Bonarata without apology.

"You loved power more than you loved me," she said. "You chose once as you would choose again." She smiled, and it was tender and sad at the same time. "I know you, Iacopo. I would not change you for anything. But I cannot live here." She waved her hand to indicate his home, his seethe, Milan. Everything. "I am useful where I am. There are people who depend upon me." She looked at Adam, who solemnly nodded. "It is then my choice to go back to my home. I will send you a list of people I might trust, and you may do what you wish with it."

Adam finished his food. He glanced at Guccio, who was watching the other two vampires. Guccio had managed the whole meal without saying more than a single sentence. Adam was a little, a very little, disappointed in Guccio, that the vampire was going to do nothing—leaving Adam in an awkward position. Maybe the story Guccio had told about marking Adam had been true—except that he'd bitten him and bound him instead. The marking could be overlooked as the bite never could. Should Adam let the trespass go if Guccio didn't make a move? Adam found that answer extremely unsatisfying, and so did his wolf.

"I regret what I had to do," Bonarata was telling Marsilia in a soft voice.

Marsilia lifted a brow in disbelief, and Bonarata gave a half-embarrassed laugh and spread his arms. "You are right. I needed the power, Marsilia. If I had not had it, we would not have survived."

She made a sound that might have been disagreement. "Did your werewolf blood give you more power than having Stefan and me by your side would have? More than Wulfe? You broke him, too, Iacopo. He is not . . . not safe anymore."

Bonarata nodded. "When they saw what I was willing to do, what I could do, they quit fighting me. It allowed me to take the reins here. To keep us all safe."

She looked at him. "Then, my once-love, what is it that you regret?"

"That I could not have just told you what I was doing and why," he said. "That I had to hurt you."

She shook her head. "Don't pretend that was part of your plan. You hurt me, I hurt you back. I broke your rules, fed from Lenka, and tried to break your hold on her. I failed in that, to my regret. You punished me for breaking your rules—but my real crime was hurting you. Was daring to tell you that what you had done, what you were doing, was wrong. I know you, Iacopo. You aren't sorry for anyone except yourself."

She didn't say it like she was condemning him, but she meant it.

His face lost all expression. "You don't know me, Marsilia. You knew the person I was. And call me Jacob."

"Fair enough," she agreed. "But I, too, have changed. I'm not yours through thick and thin anymore, I am not *your* Blade. I do not feel the need to forgive you anything, *Jacob*. I will never pine for you again, though I think I will remember you fondly. In a few years, perhaps." She glanced around. "And if you really wanted me back, we'd have had this conversation without an audience. Having discussed everything that needed to be said, Adam needs to leave for Prague to find his mate. Have we your leave to go?"

Bonarata leaned back in his chair, looking at Marsilia. His face was sad and hungry and lonely. "I believe our business is concluded." Bonarata looked at Adam for confirmation.

Adam considered the vampire. "Just to have things clear between us," he said. "You know what we're doing back home, and it isn't what you thought. The fae aren't going to suddenly kill a bunch of humans in a spectacularly messy fashion because it is not in their best interests. There won't be a second Inquisition begun because of us. You are now okay with this and won't send another crew out to attack me and mine." He took a deep breath and had to fight to keep his wolf from snarling. "If you do, I won't be coming over here on a diplomatic mission a second time. I am not a diplomat. Like you, I am a killer, and anyone who forgets that deserves what they get. That said, I am leaving as soon as I can get my crew packed and ready."

Bonarata said, very quietly, "Be careful, wolf. Remember what I am."

"Back. At. You."

"Adam," Marsilia. "Jacob. Perhaps we should just agree that matters have been settled."

Bonarata stood up, giving permission for everyone in the room to do likewise. Adam got to his feet, too, tucking his chair back under the table.

Bonarata rounded the table, his path taking him around Guccio rather than Marsilia. "I won't say it has been a pleasure," Bonarata said. "But it has been interesting. I wish you luck on your endeavors."

He held out a hand, Adam reached out and—finally, finally Guccio made his move.

"Hold him," Guccio said softly, sending the command up the blood bond he'd initiated when he had fed from Adam in the hall this afternoon.

12

MATT SMITH
(WHO IS NOT THE DOCTOR)
AND ADAM

Water is wet and vampires are treacherous.

MATT SMITH HAD BEGUN TO WONDER IF LENKA'S DEATH or something else had interfered with Guccio's plans. That Bonarata had people waiting to usurp his power wasn't a surprise to him. Werewolves were a little more honest about it, usually, but when a race was governed by the meanest bastard around, one generally had to prove that one was the meanest bastard over and over again. Until someday one wasn't, and someone else got to fight all the time.

Matt glanced across the room at Bonarata, who seemed to be giving the "good-bye and good riddance" speech to Adam and Marsilia. *Or maybe one finds someone else to take out one's enemies.* Just how likely was it that Guccio had managed all of this without Bonarata's noticing? Bonarata, the Lord of Night, who had been a prince of the Italian Renaissance, seemed unlikely to be the sort of man who overlooked an attempted coup.

If Guccio and Adam fought, thought Matt, watching Bonarata carefully not look at Guccio, then Bonarata could not lose. If Adam killed Guccio, he was down one rebel. If Guccio killed Adam, he would be considerably weakened.

Matt set his napkin on the table and started to get up at the same time Bonarata and everyone at the head table got up.

———

ADAM DREW IN A BREATH AS THE BOND BETWEEN HIM and Guccio tightened. He wondered, briefly, how long Guccio had been planning this moment. Wondered if he should kill Bonarata or let Guccio do it—and *then* kill Guccio.

Today wasn't going to be Guccio's day if Adam had anything to say about it. Not because he was a fan of Bonarata's—he wasn't. But Bonarata was the best path to peace for Adam's people. If Bonarata died and Adam was involved, even if only as a "blood slave," the same hell that Larry had promised if Adam killed Bonarata on his own would still rain down upon his family.

Quickly, Adam did as instructed. Maintaining the handshake, Adam leaned forward as if he were going to do one of those European manly hugs that were so popular on the mob movies he'd grown up with. He reached up and put his free hand on Bonarata's shoulder, feeling the vampire stiffen in surprise and the beginning of a realization that all wasn't well.

That Guccio hadn't been talking to some waitstaff or minion when he'd said, "Hold him." That he'd been commanding Adam.

Guccio also began to move.

Bracing his legs, Adam pulled Bonarata sharply toward him with their clasped hands. At the same time, he used the hand on the vampire's shoulder to push him into Guccio.

Surprised by the unexpected impact, Guccio hadn't managed to draw whatever weapon he'd been reaching for, and was trapped momentarily with his hand tangled under his jacket.

Adam used that moment to pull Bonarata around and into Marsilia. He trusted Marsilia would hold Bonarata off Adam long enough for it to be clear that Adam wasn't trying to kill the Lord of Night and wasn't under Guccio's control. He also hoped that she'd be able to keep any of Guccio's confederates from killing Bonarata while Adam was taking care of business.

To help that result along, Adam said, "Protect him, Marsilia." And also as he faced Guccio, who was rapidly recovering his balance in all senses of the word, Adam said, "Don't let him kill me, either, please."

The table erupted in a spray of drinks, crystalware, and dining utensils as Guccio seized the tablecloth (moss green today). The vampire cracked the cloth like a whip, turning the remains of the meal into airborne weapons.

A water glass hit Adam in the chest hard enough to hurt, and the pitcher of ice water shattered at his feet, making the footing treacherous. Adam trusted the soles of his shoes to protect him from the glass, but the water- and ice-covered floor would be slick.

Guccio smiled, showing white fangs. Then, instead of attacking, he began a slow, backward dance designed to keep Adam on the wet floor and allow Guccio to pick his strike.

Adam thought the fangs were intended as some sort of threat display, but, since they were only slightly longer than those of Mercy's cat Medea, they didn't do much to intimidate him. Guccio had kept the tablecloth in his left hand, gripped lightly near the fabric's center. More interesting was the dagger Guccio held in his right hand.

Adam knew weapons. This one was old and well made. The

blade bore designs in bright silver, and Adam assumed it was real silver. He was also pretty sure that the designs were probably a sign that the blade was—

"Careful," Elizaveta called. "There is magic in that dagger. Old and corrupted. I can't tell what it does."

Yes. That's what he'd thought. Probably it wasn't a problem—ensorcelling blades, no matter what D&D had taught a generation or two of young people, was no easy matter. That's why smiths like Zee had been so prized and feared.

———

THE FIGHT STARTED BEFORE MATT COULD PUT A WORD in Adam's ear—and he wasn't sure what it would have been, anyway. Everyone else got up from their tables, too. The little healer's people got her out of the room, though she didn't look too upset by the fight and kept turning around to get a look.

And it was a pretty thing, this fight. Matt thought of himself as a peaceful man. But he couldn't deny that there was beauty in violence, a battle between two well-trained warriors.

Guccio was typical of noblemen of his era. Flash and pretty words that sought to disguise just how dangerous he was. Becoming a vampire hadn't slowed him down or given his blows less power. He had been fighting for hundreds of years, and every moment of that showed, both in his movements and in the choreography that he gave this fight.

———

ADAM LET GUCCIO GUIDE THE FIGHT WHILE HE PAID attention to the vampire's fighting style. The most notable thing about it so far was how much the vampire liked to talk.

"How did you manage to slip my leash?" Guccio asked. He held the dagger low and centered, its tip pointed at Adam's heart. But he was being careful, choosing his strike, because even though Adam was bare-handed, he was still a werewolf.

Adam didn't answer, so Guccio found his own answer. "You belong to Marsilia," he said sagely. And also incorrectly.

Adam, who'd been thinking about ending this quickly, decided that maybe the vampires here needed a demonstration of what a werewolf could do. Bonarata didn't need to believe that Adam could take on a Gray Lord—but maybe he should know that Adam wasn't a weakling, either.

"No," he said softly. "I belong to Mercy."

Adam knew a little something about fighting with a blade. The Army had begun his education, but he'd had half a century to add to what he knew. The best knife fighter Adam had ever encountered held a knife just like Guccio did. Guccio was the product of an earlier age, with all of those years to practice.

While most of his attention was on his opponent, Adam was aware that the room had burst into motion as soon as the tablecloth had announced the beginning of the battle. Bonarata had taken control and was ushering his people out of the room as quickly as possible.

———

MATT HELPED THE NONCOMBATANTS—HUMAN, VAM-pire, and other—get out of the room. Interestingly enough, Bonarata was doing the same thing.

When they both helped a young woman to her feet, Bonarata tried to catch his eye—Matt supposed he couldn't help himself. There was always a lot of debate about what advantages the vampires might have over werewolves. Matt had always felt that it was the need most wolves had to establish dominance by meeting eyes. It was handy with other wolves, quite often preventing bloodshed or misunderstandings. But doing it with a vampire was a mistake.

Matt's beast was cannier than that. Matt said something to the sobbing woman and handed her over to another woman—and the two hurried out of the dining hall.

A vampire who'd been pulling a table out of harm's way bumped into Bonarata—and the Lord of Night grabbed the other vampire and broke his neck. Reaching out with a casual hand, Bonarata broke off a chair leg—there was getting to be a lot of broken furniture around—and stabbed the helpless vampire through the heart.

A second assassin launched himself from the top of a nearby table. But before he got close to his target, Larry the goblin, in a very ungoblin-like public display of why one should never underestimate goblins, leaped on top of the diving vampire and beheaded him with a garrote. The body, both parts, dropped to the floor just behind Bonarata, with Larry crouched on top of the biggest part.

Bonarata spun, already poised to kill whoever was behind him. Seeing the tableau there, the canny old vampire came to the right conclusion and stopped his attack before Harris had to give up his life by being stuck through with a chair leg that would otherwise have impaled Larry. Bonarata gave both goblins a shallow bow of thanks and turned his attention back to clearing the room of nonessential personnel.

———

ADAM'S ATTENTION WAS ON HIS OPPONENT, BUT HE was aware when some sort of scuffle around Larry erupted in blood, but Larry was still on his feet at the end of it. Adam had to trust he could take care of himself.

One of the diners, a human, passed by Guccio too closely. He casually backhanded her with his left hand. She collapsed to the floor in a broken heap. Dead, Adam judged grimly, before she hit the floor.

But he had no time to mourn for a nameless stranger. Guccio whirled the tablecloth quickly overhead and cast its spreading folds at Adam, then he rushed in right behind it.

It was a classic two-pronged attack: dealing with either threat left one vulnerable to the other, and if Adam tried to move fast enough to counter both, he risked losing his footing. Rather than trust the treacherous floor, then, Adam jumped backward, onto the table he'd so recently been eating at. He landed near the back edge of the table.

He leaned a little and added a little extra thrust with his legs, which pulled the table over with him on top. He grabbed Guccio's tablecloth and rode the table to the ground, putting the upended piece of furniture between him and Guccio.

The vampire leaped into the air like a demented ballet dancer, soaring neatly over the table. He aimed a kick at Adam's leg as he brought the dagger down in a sweeping slash at Adam's neck with inhuman speed.

Adam was happy he wasn't human, either. He twisted his hips and pivoted to avoid the kick and snapped the tablecloth at Guccio's blade. The kick missed completely, and the tablecloth fouled the dagger strike, so it missed its target and only sliced a burning line across Adam's shoulder.

Guccio's momentum carried him past Adam and he stopped a few feet away, raising the wetted dagger to his forehead in a mocking salute that claimed first blood. As he stepped back from the salute, he stumbled on an overturned chair and was momentarily distracted.

Adam moved in with a strong front kick, but the wolf, catching some motion that seemed wrong, warned him. Adam aborted just in time to avoid being hamstrung when the vampire brought the dagger up between them. The stumble had been a feint, and it had nearly worked.

Adam pulled the kick but had to struggle to control his forward momentum. Guccio took advantage of Adam's lost balance and used the pommel of the dagger to strike at Adam's head. Adam blocked the dagger, but not the knee that drove into his stomach.

It hurt, with a dull pain that built to a crescendo, darkening his vision in waves that ebbed and flowed. Vampires were almost as fun to fight as werewolves.

WITH THE ROOM MOSTLY EMPTY, MATT GAVE HIMSELF over to the spectator sport in the center of the cleared floor.

Guccio was an excellent fighter; there was no doubt of that. But once in a while there comes a fighter, human or other, so beautiful to watch that he turns the fight into great art, something that Matt felt a privilege and honor to watch. Sugar Ray Robinson had been such a fighter, both graceful and powerful. Matt had seen Robinson fight many times, as often as Matt could manage.

Adam Hauptman was another of Robinson's ilk.

He moved no more than he had to in order to avoid an attack, a half inch here, a quarter there. He stayed mostly on the defensive, letting the vampire give away his secrets. Neither Adam's face nor his body gave anything away, and he appeared relaxed and in control—not a usual sight for a werewolf in a fight against an opponent as good as Guccio de' Medici, who was from a cadet branch of that very famous family, Matt was given to understand. Harris had been a wealth of information about Bonarata's people.

"Hauptman can fight," said Bonarata quietly. For a moment, Matt thought he was being addressed.

"Yes," agreed Marsilia. "He is accounted fourth among all the werewolves in the New World. He is young for such a rank—but this is why it is his."

———————

ADAM NOTED THAT THE ROOM HAD EMPTIED WITH surprising speed, keeping collateral damage to a minimum. A handful of observers—among them Bonarata—spread around the room, careful to avoid the combat zone. He trusted they were all people who could defend themselves. One dead innocent in this mess was enough.

He and Guccio circled the room, hopping over fallen chairs and discarded tableware. Twice more, they exchanged blows, with neither taking any serious damage. Adam needed to end this decisively, but the vampire's dagger meant that he held that advantage in reach.

They circled for a few more seconds, then Guccio slid smoothly into a long, gliding lunge. Fast as a striking snake, the dagger flicked toward Adam's stomach. Only a shift in weight had signaled the move, but Adam leaped back a pace, forcing the vampire to either fall short or commit to an awkward running attack. Guccio, proving he was no novice, aborted the lunge before closing enough to allow Adam to engage.

Guccio sneered. "I see you have some training," he said. "Your teacher was inferior. Your footwork is wooden—"

Me and Muhammad Ali, thought Adam, though he didn't respond aloud. *We float like a butterfly and sting like a bee.* No one was perfect—and fighting was always one big compromise. But his footwork was fine.

Guccio was still speaking, trying to distract Adam with words. "You are too concerned with defense to mount a proper offense. I had expected more from you—the great Adam Hauptman. Allow me to educate you."

Guccio snatched another tablecloth and dropped it over his left arm. It hung at knee level.

"This is the cloak," he said. "Its use is to confuse and conceal." He gave the dagger a quick flourish, moving his dagger hand beneath the cloth. "The dagger hides behind the cloak," he said. "And now begins the game. Where is the dagger, and where will it strike?"

As Guccio moved, he made the cloth dance in a way designed to lead Adam into making assumptions about his movement and the dagger position. Twice Adam was sure he saw the beginning of an attack, but the wolf disagreed, reading the vampire's intention differently. Adam listened to the wolf.

Guccio moved the cloth in a fluttering swoop, while the dagger appeared in a reverse grip, slashing at Adam's throat. The blade lay backward along Guccio's arm. Most blocks or grabs would result in serious damage to Adam's hands. As it blurred across Adam's throat, the vampire bent his wrist back, allowing the blade to snap forward and take a wider path. Guccio's body was close behind it, sliding in an arc past Adam.

Adam jerked his head back. The blade sang as it passed by, slicing open nothing but air. Adam threw a hard jab. He hit, but the fluttering cloth had made him misjudge, and it was just a glancing blow, barely hard enough to make Guccio throw in a short step to regain his balance. The vampire whirled past Adam, discarding the tablecloth. The green woven linen fluttered to the ground to land across the dead woman's feet.

As Adam pivoted to face the vampire again, a sharp pain drew his attention to the fork sticking out just under his ribs on the left side. Guccio must have grabbed the fork with the tablecloth and used the cloth to conceal it.

Silverware, real silverware was sterling silver, 90 percent silver. Everything except the knife. Had Guccio stuck him with a table knife, Adam could have pulled it out and expected his body to heal in a reasonably rapid fashion.

The fork burned.

Guccio grinned at him, then tilted his head, listening. Adam heard it, too. The fork had penetrated Adam's diaphragm, allowing air to seep into his chest cavity. His left lung was slowly collapsing, and pulling the fork out would only serve to accelerate the process. Wounds made with silver had to be healed just like humans heal. This small wound changed everything, and they both knew it.

Adam backed up slowly, and Guccio shadowed him, the vampire's movements lazy. He was confident of his victory. Now that the prey was wounded, there was no hurry. Werewolves kill their prey quickly, but vampires, like cats, enjoy playing with their food.

Adam intended to use Guccio's confidence and eagerness against him.

He opened the pack bonds. Although the only one of his pack nearby was Honey, she was a deep well of power, and she gave it freely. Her energy trickled into him, cool and refreshing, swallowing pain.

Adam continued backing away, breathing shallowly. He angled along an overturned table until he bumped into one of the larger tables, where someone had been clearing the table and left one of those carts with a black tub on top, a tub filled with dishes.

Bonarata's people dined off fine porcelain china.

The busboy—busperson?—had kindly stacked the plates for Adam. He picked up several in his left hand and with his right he Frisbeed the top one at the vampire.

Guccio was less than ten feet away.

Some people might think a plate a poor weapon. Some people weren't werewolves who could launch the things at speeds a major-league pitcher would envy. The first plate hit the arm Guccio lifted to block it and exploded, sending sharp fragments of glazed porcelain flying like shrapnel. The impact also knocked the knife from Guccio's hand. It flew, hit a table, and fell to the ground a dozen feet away. Not entirely out of play but close enough.

The second plate took Guccio full in the throat, the narrow edge sliced like a knife, parting flesh and opening a second mouth that bled dark, viscous blood.

The third plate struck Guccio in the forehead, shattering on impact and leaving another bleeding cut with large shards embedded in his skull.

Staggered by the rapid impacts, Guccio took another couple of steps back. Blood from his forehead ran into his left eye. He wiped it clear and opened his mouth to say something.

And Adam pulled the H&K from his shoulder holster. The first shot took the vampire just below his left eye. A .40 wasn't the biggest caliber in the world, but modern ammunition made the most of it. Adam wasn't carrying target rounds.

A large portion of the vampire's head blew outward, fragments of bone and tissue flung eight feet or more.

The vampiric magic that bound Guccio to his half life didn't give up easily. Guccio wasn't dead; he swayed on his feet with a confused expression on his face. Apparently his high-velocity lobotomy had degraded his thinking skills because he just stood there. The raw tissue writhed and pulsed in the open wound as the vampire's body struggled to repair the damage.

"A gun?" said Bonarata quietly.

"Why didn't you shoot him earlier?" asked Marsilia. "You had time to do it after you sent Iacopo to me."

"Because," Adam said, "I needed Bonarata to know that I can defend my territory from vampires without any help at all. Guccio is one of your strongest vampires. He attacked me armed with a dagger—and I could have defeated him with a stack of plates." He put two more rounds into Guccio, this time between his eyes.

Guccio dropped bonelessly to the floor, faceup. There were three neat holes and only a little blood from the gunshots. The real damage was hidden from sight. He had been a pretty man, but his features were only visible for a moment.

Dead vampires as old as Guccio dry up and turn to ash pretty quickly.

"The gun just makes things quicker." Satisfied Guccio was permanently dead, Adam looked at Marsilia. "But if I'd used the gun right at the beginning, there would have been one less casualty." He looked at Bonarata. "In my territory, I'd have used the gun."

"Why was he fighting so hard?" asked Larry. "He acted like he actually had a chance. Once Adam saw to it that the assassination did not take place, Guccio was ended. Even if he had taken

Adam out, his element of surprise was gone. You wouldn't have let him live."

Bonarata looked around the mostly empty room and sighed. Besides Adam's people, there were five or six vampires.

"My people," Bonarata said. "How many of you were obligated to follow Guccio while he was alive?"

All of them raised their hands.

"Raising new children is troublesome," Bonarata said. "You all understand how it works? You collect sheep and tend them. And in a few years, five or six on average, if you are careful, you will have one prepared who can become your child. For that one, you will have tended a dozen who, for one reason or another, will never live to become vampires. Once you have changed your fledgling, for years afterward, sometimes decades and sometimes centuries, you still have to feed them and make sure that they are not misbehaving. Eventually, you hope, they will go out on their own and be able to produce their own children."

"I am Bonarata's child," said Marsilia. "And I know a few others, but there are only a few of us." She gave Bonarata a quick, affectionate smile. "He is too lazy to tend children."

It must have been an old joke because he smiled back. "We vampires are selfish creatures."

Marsilia completed it by saying, "It is the only reason vampires haven't taken over the world."

Bonarata said, "Stefan is the only vampire I know who never was tied to his Master by magic-driven obedience. I myself destroyed my maker when I decided what I wanted to become. I could not afford to have someone who I would have a hard time refusing."

Wulfe had been Bonarata's maker.

Marsilia said, "We believe that once a vampire can survive on his own kills rather than needing supplementary feeding from his maker or another Master to maintain their humanity, it is time to release them from obligation. When a child of mine quits feeding from me, the tie of obedience fades, though it doesn't disappear."

"Usually. Usually it can be revived," Bonarata said. He looked at Larry. "Which is the logical path for a vampire like Guccio to follow. He could force obedience not only from his own children, but their children, too. And through them, their children. All he would have to do is feed them from his own vein, and they would be his." He looked around the room, where people, mostly vampires, were returning now that it was as safe as anyplace vampires laired could be.

While Marsilia and Bonarata had been explaining things to Larry, Stefan had walked briskly into the room. He looked around, and his eyes found Adam's and ran down his body, taking in the damage. Stefan caught the arm of another vampire and listened to her intently. He turned on his heel and walked back out. Adam figured he'd been sent by Honey, who'd know something had happened but not what.

Smith, who'd appeared with a tablecloth that he'd ripped to pieces, produced a knife from somewhere and started cutting Adam's suit jacket off him.

Larry said, "So your people here, most of them, had to obey Guccio and not you—and you didn't think it was a problem until today? If Guccio had won, he would have turned your own people on you."

Bonarata smiled, but it didn't touch his eyes. "Oh, I knew it was a problem."

"And he decided to use Adam to solve it for him," murmured Matt Smith, sounding as though he might admire that.

Stefan said, "Being lazy. I expect he had contingency plans had Adam failed to eliminate Guccio."

He'd returned from a different door, and Adam had missed it. He had Bonarata's healer, Stacia, by one hand. She regarded Adam with big, sad eyes.

"It really was a compliment of sorts, Adam," Stefan said, his eyes steady on Bonarata's. "If he'd thought you would lose, he wouldn't have set you up—because then Guccio would have had nothing left to lose and Iacopo would have had to bestir himself. How did you arrange that Guccio 'discover' that *gris-gris*?"

Bonarata said, "You knew what I was when you brought your friends here. You have no cause to be angry." But there was a pleased air about the Lord of Night that told Adam he was happy to be discovered. He was proud of the play he'd engineered.

"He played us," said Adam.

Marsilia shook her head. "My life is so much more peaceful now that I do not live in your world, Jacob." She looked at Adam. "He arranged it all. Wheels within wheels. What if Guccio had managed to suborn Adam? Did you know, Jacob, that Adam's mate is peculiarly immune to vampiric powers? That she might pass that on to Adam?"

"No," said Adam grimly. "He didn't. Until you just told him. Thank you." Speech was a little difficult with a collapsed lung, and that wasn't improving with time as air escaped. He decided that he was okay if everyone in the room, except Matt Smith, thought that Guccio had never had Adam in his thrall. It might keep the next vampire from trying it.

Adam's jacket was on the glass-covered ground in shreds. Smith unbuckled Adam's shoulder holster and handed it, without a word, to Harris. He ripped the shirt around the fork but paused when Adam spoke.

"Is she?" Bonarata said, arrested. "She turned into a small dog, Lenka told me. A wild dog. Was it a coyote? Is your wife a walker, Adam? A descendant of Coyote? Fascinating. So Wulfe wasn't lying as wildly as I thought he was. If I had known, I would have kept her longer."

Adam raised an eyebrow. "Not likely," he said—and coughed, which really sucked. He didn't want to collapse in front of the present company, so he concentrated on breathing for a bit.

"Mercy is slippery," Marsilia said. "If you had kept her, you'd have regretted it. I'm sorry, Adam. Even if he didn't know, he'd have figured it out pretty soon. She did something as interesting as escaping his clutches. He would make a point of finding out about her—and what she is is no longer as secret as she kept herself before she joined your pack."

Bonarata smiled.

"What he knew," said Stefan grimly, "because he had opportunity to experiment on Lenka and her mate, was that a single feeding without consent would never be enough to hold an Alpha werewolf. I expect that he took great pains to make Guccio think that werewolves, for a vampire of his power, would be easy prey, without mentioning the little quirk that makes Alpha werewolves much trickier."

Unless they are traveling without their packs, thought Adam. He figured he'd keep that one to himself.

"So this was a setup," Smith said, returning to his self-appointed job of stripping Adam's shirt. He didn't bother with a knife. The silk was strong, but the stitches gave way to werewolf strength without trouble. "You kidnapped Adam's mate to take care of your little issue with your subordinate?"

"No," said Marsilia before Bonarata could say anything. "He's quite able to run twenty plans at the same time without a sweat. He was honestly concerned that our situation in the Tri-Cities might cause trouble for him. But once we were here, he decided to use one problem to eliminate the other. If he had changed his mind about what we are accomplishing, he'd simply have killed Adam after Adam killed Guccio for him. If Adam had really been caught up in Guccio's play, he'd have killed them both." She looked at Adam. "He is lazy—but that doesn't mean he isn't dangerous. Guccio was allowed to forget that. You should not be like Guccio."

She looked at Bonarata. "You are getting bored, Jacob." Interestingly, Adam thought, Bonarata was starting to wince every time she called him Jacob—even though he himself had insisted upon it. "Time was when such a one as Guccio would have been taken care of long before it got this far. You enjoyed playing with him, and that is dangerous. Not just for you—you can take care of yourself—but for those who depend upon you."

Bonarata looked at her. "Stay, my beautiful, deadly flower, my Bright Blade. Stay with me, please? I need you. You see what I am become without you?"

Marsilia shook her head, and said, not ungently, "Not for all the gold in the ocean or gems in the sea would I stay with thee more."

"This is going to be unpleasant," said Smith to Adam, reaching for the fork.

"Wait," said Stefan.

"Wait," said Adam. "Guccio wasn't coming for me. I found

him heading for Harris and Smith. Smith should have given Guccio what he wanted, a wolf under his control."

"Guccio just needed a werewolf," said Marsilia. "Any would do. Then he could cause a war in which the werewolves were the cause of Bonarata's death. If it became known that Guccio killed him . . . you wouldn't know it, but Bonarata has friends, many nearly as dangerous as himself. If Guccio and a werewolf tried to kill Bonarata? Then Bonarata could retaliate by moving into the Marrok's territory. Smith isn't one of your wolves, Adam, but he is one of the Marrok's."

"Would you have avenged me?" Bonarata asked Marsilia softly.

"I might have helped Guccio kill you," she said. "We'll never know now."

Bonarata laughed.

"His plans are like hydras," Stefan said. "With many tentacles woven together. He doesn't care which path is taken as long as all possible outcomes leave him on top." He turned to the fae healer, who had been swinging his hand in hers and looking at a broken table as if it were a Picasso. "Iacopo owes this wolf a big favor," he told her. "Would you heal my friend?"

"She doesn't have much power left," Bonarata said, though he didn't really protest. "She used a lot for Adam's mate, our little coyote."

"It's not a big wound," Stefan answered. "It's just in an awkward place."

He brought the healer to Adam and released her, murmuring something in Italian. She nodded, using those awkwardly big movements Adam had seen before.

Smith had backed up. Stefan put his hand on the fork. "Brace yourself, wolf," he said.

Adam nodded, and Stefan pulled the silver out of the wound. Almost immediately the little healer put her hands on Adam's side, and warmth replaced the burning of the silver. A moment or two, and he could breathe again. She staggered a little as she removed her hands. Her skin was paler than it had been a moment before, and he was pretty sure she was thinner, too. She reached up toward his burning shoulder, but he caught her hands before she could touch that one. There had been magic in the dagger, but his wolf assured him that it had only caused the wound to be slow to heal; there was no corruption in it.

"Enough, little sister," he told her. "That one won't trouble me much. You fixed the bad one. Thank you." He kissed her hand again because it had seemed to please her so much the first time. Then he leaned down and kissed her cheek. "Be well," he told her.

"Niki," called Bonarata. And when a roundish human woman came over to his call, he handed the healer into her care. "Take her to her room," he said. "But stop in the kitchen and see if Cook has some food for her."

People were moving about the room now, righting tables, cleaning up the glass—and the dead. Bonarata saw Adam look at Guccio's ashes, and said, in a pained voice, "Those plates were two-hundred-year-old Limoges. It will be very expensive to find replacements."

Adam would have said something scathing, but the woman who had led them to their table this morning stopped in front of Bonarata and dropped to her knees, spilling the tablecloths she was carrying as she did so.

"He wouldn't let us tell," she said in a whisper. "I tried, I tried to break his hold, Master."

"Annabelle," Bonarata said gently. "I know."

She sobbed, shuddering. "You are most gracious."

"No," Bonarata said, his voice still soft. "You misunderstand me, child. I know."

She froze. Bonarata sank the dagger that Guccio had been fighting with through her back and into her heart. She fell, hitting the floor as ashes rather than a body. Apparently the dagger was rather more deadly to vampires than it was to werewolves.

"Pity," Bonarata said. "She was useful." He looked around at his vampires, who were suddenly all actively engaged in whatever work they could find. "I trust that she will be the last I have to put down over this."

"Did you see him pick up that dagger?" asked Smith very quietly.

Adam shook his head, but Larry, who was too far away to hear something that quiet, caught Smith's eye and wandered over.

When he stood nearby, he said, "Elizaveta called it to her—and then gave it to Bonarata."

"Mmm," said Smith.

Adam looked at Elizaveta, who was seated at a table drinking a cup of tea. She met his eyes, smiled, and sipped her tea.

———————

BONARATA INSISTED ON TRAVELING WITH THEM TO Prague. He had still not heard from his man there. Since they were headed that way, it would be only courtesy to allow him to travel with them.

Bonarata spent the whole time they traveled in conversation with Marsilia and Stefan. Mostly Marsilia—and it didn't sound like business. The bits and pieces Adam overheard were more like old friends catching up.

Adam made sure that the Lord of Night stayed away from Honey. Upon being alerted that Bonarata was coming, she had dressed in jeans with an oversized baggy shirt that smelled like Smith's. She'd scrubbed her face of makeup.

When he'd first seen her new guise, Adam said, "You could wear a bikini, and I would not let him touch you."

She'd smiled grimly. "I'd kill the old bastard first. And we still need him alive. So I'll keep out of sight as much as I can."

"And if you kill him, I'll help you bury the ashes, and we can blame Guccio," Adam said.

Honey grinned at him and held up a fist, which he bumped with his own. But when she made explosive noises and let her fist open and drift down to her side, he just watched.

———

THEY LANDED AT THE FIELD DAVID CHRISTIANSEN HAD arranged for them. No questions were asked except those pertaining to the care and refueling of the plane. David's contact even provided them with two vans.

When Adam asked, Smith and Harris chose to come with them.

"Are you sure?" Adam asked them.

"You don't think Mercy is with Libor," Smith said.

Adam shook his head. "You heard Libor on the phone." Adam had phoned the other Alpha to tell him they were on their way. Libor had merely told Adam his address and hung up. "Did that sound like a gleeful arrogant bastard who has successfully babysat the woman another Alpha managed to lose?"

"Then you may need all the people you have," said Harris. "We'll come."

Bonarata had been speaking to Marsilia. He looked at Adam.

"It is nearly dawn," he said. "I had intended to go speak with Kocourek, since he has not seen fit to answer his phone. But people I sent here last night tell me that his seethe is abandoned—and has been for a few days. There is no one to question there." He smiled at Marsilia. "I did let this go too long. Kocourek was one of Guccio's making. I had forgotten, because it was so long ago. But since it is empty, there is time for me to accompany you to Libor's bakery, and I just happen to know the way there. We are old enemies, Libor and I. I can at least spare you the usual trouble when two Alphas meet. He'll dislike me more than he dislikes you. I will deal with the vampire issues tomorrow night. If your woman is still not found, I will help you then."

He seemed unworried about the coming dawn. Marsilia and Stefan could teleport. Maybe Bonarata could also. And wasn't that just a lovely thought.

Adam called Libor to warn him that he was bringing Bonarata, too. Libor was worryingly nonchalant about the Lord of Night invading his den.

———————

THE BAKERY WAS CLOSED, THOUGH IT WAS NEARLY dawn, as Bonarata had noted. Adam could smell the baked goods the whole quarter of a mile they walked from where they'd had to park the vans.

Honey and Smith both looked at Adam as they neared the front door. But Mercy was somewhere else. He couldn't talk to her through their bond, but he could feel it pulling him away.

"Let's go see what Libor has done with my wife," he said, and knocked on the door.

Since Libor knew they were coming, it didn't take a minute for someone to come to the door. A less dominant wolf—not quite submissive—answered, and he went white when he saw Bonarata.

"Libor knows I'm bringing him," said Adam. "Take us on in to him, and your part is done."

The heart of the building was the kitchen, and that was where the wolf led them. Neither Bonarata, nor Stefan and Marsilia, had needed an invitation—which was why Adam would never make his pack's home out of a business.

The big room was filled with people, mostly wolves but not all, mixing, rolling, and baking. Huge electric fans in the ceiling sent the warm air on out, but it was still ten degrees warmer in this room than it had been outside.

It might have been full of people, but when the broadly built man stepped out of a storeroom with a fifty-pound bag of flour on his shoulder, there was no question who the Alpha was in here. He felt them, too. He looked at them, set the flour down, and strode toward them, wiping his hands on his apron.

He took the whole of them in at one glance, his eyes lingering a little here and there. When he took his apron off, the work in the kitchen slowed. He hung it up on a hook on the wall and said, gruffly, "Get to work. There are hungry people who will be here in a couple of hours, and they expect us to feed them." He spoke in English, then switched to another tongue and, presumably, repeated himself. When he finished, his people went back to work, with only a few surreptitious looks at their visitors.

He caught the attention of the wolf who'd been their guide. "Go get Martin and Jitka, eh? Bring them to the garden."

Then to Adam and his people, Libor said, "Follow me, gentlemen." He saw Bonarata and grunted. "And you'll have to let me know how it is that the vampire who was trying to kill your wife is now traveling about with you. Though I know Iacopo Bonarata well enough not to be surprised."

Harris, Smith, and Larry took up the rear. The goblins liked it best when no one noticed them. Smith evidently felt the same.

The garden was an unexpectedly beautiful spot of nature in the center of the bakery. The Vltava Alpha walked to the end, then turned and faced them.

"I'm Libor of the Vltava," he said.

"Adam of the Columbia Basin," Adam responded. Then one by one he introduced his party, though he'd told Libor who would be coming and why. Since there were so many old beings in the court-yard, he began with the women, starting with Honey because she was the closest. Mercy would scold him for being old-fashioned.

"I have heard of you," Libor told Honey. "Peter was a good man, a good werewolf. The world is a darker place without him in it."

Honey blinked more rapidly than usual. "Yes," she said.

"Honey killed Lenka," Adam told Libor.

Libor looked at Bonarata with yellow eyes as he said, "Good. This is something that should have been done long ago. When I depart this world, not doing something about Lenka will be part of the cross I will bear on the way to Paradise." He turned, took Honey's hand in his, and kissed it. "If she could, she would thank you."

Adam moved the introductions along. Bonarata was on his best behavior—but that might not last.

"You are Bonarata's Blade," Libor said, after Adam introduced Marsilia. "I have heard many stories, enough to make me regret that we never met while you were here."

She nodded gravely. "I've heard stories about you, too, Libor. It is probably best that this is our first meeting."

He smiled. "Undoubtedly true. And still . . ."

When Adam introduced Elizaveta, the other wolf smiled with genuine happiness.

"Your name is well-known," he told her gravely in Russian. "And those who speak of you do not exaggerate your beauty."

"I have heard your name, too. And they who speak of you do not exaggerate your skill at flirtation," Elizaveta responded, but she was pleased.

Adam started on the men, but Libor said, "Iacopo Bonarata and I know each other well. I will have some words for you later about your vampires here in my city, and for this reason, I allow you here in my home."

"You will find me eager to listen," said Bonarata.

They exchanged toothy smiles. And Adam continued introductions.

"The Soldier," said Libor. "I have heard stories about you."

"Exaggerated, I'm afraid," said Stefan. "I have heard many things of you also. I would not want you for an enemy."

Libor smiled. "I would agree that it is good not to be enemies, you and I. Though I don't know that we will be friends."

Adam introduced the last three all at the same time.

Libor greeted Harris and Larry and said, "Goblins do not usually interest themselves in the affairs of wolves."

Larry smiled easily. "Usually you aren't so entertaining," he said.

"And I'm getting paid," said Harris. "When I get paid, I'm always interested."

"And Smith," said Libor, his body quiet and his eyes yellow. "Smith and I know each other." There was an edge in the other Alpha's voice—a lot of the old wolves had history.

Smith looked at his feet and smiled peacefully. "They needed a copilot who could haul around vampires and werewolves," he said. "Harris was fine, but he needed me to help out because the rest of his people are either human or they won't travel with vampires."

Libor stared at him for a moment longer, closed his eyes, and heaved a sigh. "It has been a long time," he said.

Then Libor looked at Adam and said, "Your mate brought trouble on her tail."

"She usually does," he agreed gravely.

A pair of people came into the garden then.

"Let me introduce you to my wolves," Libor said heavily. "This is Martin, my second, and Jitka, my third. I'll let them tell you how they lost your mate."

13

~~~

MERCY

I am pretty sure that philosophy was first developed by prisoners. Being stuck in a cage, unable to do anything more about my situation, left nothing for me to do but think.

ONE OF THE THINGS I'D LEARNED ON MY IMPROMPTU trip to Europe was that it didn't matter how frightened I was. If the bad guys didn't show up in a timely manner, eventually boredom set in. There was a kind of special-hell dimension that existed only when boredom and terror combined, because numbness never quite settles. I supposed I might die of terror just waiting for something bad to happen if my wait lasted a few hours more.

On the other hand, I wasn't alone. The weeping young woman had achieved near mortal solidity to me. I was studiously trying not to pay attention to her so matters didn't get worse. She didn't seem to mind if I was watching her or not. She spent a lot of time wandering around the room—then I'd blink, and she'd be right back with me. It took me a while not to be startled when she did that, but eventually I can apparently get used to anything.

I felt it when Adam set foot in Prague. He'd been growing closer for a while. I closed my eyes, resting my head on my dead companion's knee. Adam was here. Adam would find me. I could feel the fear and the horror just slide out of me.

And then the whole building shook.

I sucked in a breath and hopped to my feet before I realized it wasn't really the building, it was the witchcraft surrounding it that had taken the hit. A second vibration had me panting because it wasn't a good sensation, for all that it wasn't really physical. The ghost let out a gasping moan and plastered herself against me and dug her fingers into the ruff of fur around my neck, half choking me.

We both waited, motionless, for something else to happen.

There were about ten minutes during which nothing happened except that I could hear running footsteps overhead. Then another and another wave. That time the second attack—because it felt like an attack—sent agony shivering through my joints and muscles like a Taser.

About five minutes after that, the door to the basement opened, and seven people, humans, including the young man who had been down here with Mary, came stumbling and staggering down the stairs.

Three vampires shepherded them down, two men and a woman. They steadied the humans when they wobbled, crooning to them to keep them moving. But the people staggered to a stop at the sight of the girl's dead body.

Someone hissed impatiently from the top in Czech. So there was a fourth person up there, someone I couldn't see. One of the shep-herding vampires, the woman, vaulted off the side of the stairs (rather than pushing through the unwilling sheep). She picked the corpse up gently and carried her past the body of the vampire still chained to the wall, and set her in the shadows, where other corpses, mostly bones, were piled.

The she returned to the stairs, crooning soft words to the humans, standing between them and the corner where she'd put the body. The light wasn't that good. Likely, someone who was purely human wouldn't be able to see that corner well enough to know that the girl's body wasn't the only one there. Possibly— because I don't know exactly what humans see in the dark—even the dead vampire on the wall was beyond what they could sense. I could have been blindfolded and known there were bodies down here by the smell, but humans don't always pay attention to their noses. And most of the corpses were either done rotting or hadn't yet gotten a good start on it.

A skinny and worn-looking middle-aged man tentatively started down the stairs. As he did so, the female vampire said, in heavily accented English, "Are you sure this is the best place for them?"

"It will take her a while to look for any of us down here," said the voice of the man who'd translated for me earlier. Kocourek. I couldn't see him; he was still at the top of the stairs.

"See if you can get them to settle in under the stairs, then put them to sleep," he continued. "Smells so bad in here, I don't think she'll know the difference."

I had to agree. It was foul here, and the humans didn't help matters. Hygiene was apparently not something that this seethe valued in their sheep.

"Should we just kill them?" the female asked, her voice shaking with stress, I thought, though her accent made it difficult to tell. She changed the angle of her face, and I realized she was crying.

"It might come to that," said Kocourek grimly. "Anything would be better—*Lars*."

One of the other two vampires stepped over and caught a middle-aged woman who had turned to run back up the stairs. He caught her, stared into her eyes a moment. The terror and tension in her body relaxed.

He said something soft and sweet to her, turned her, and kept his hand on her shoulder as he took up the rear position.

The third vampire sighed.

"Let's get them as safe as we can, people. Dagmar?"

"Yes," the first vampire said.

She had a lantern, and she turned it on. It glowed red rather than white. She set it under the stairs, bathing the area in the gentle glow. From my position, I couldn't see the whole area, but it looked as though the only thing on the dirt floor was dirt— which made it a lot cleaner than most of the rest of the room.

She took those seven people, one at a time, met their eyes, and caught them in her hunter's magic. But instead of feeding on them, she sent them into the space under the stairs, where they curled up around each other for warmth . . . and slept.

The little man with the mustache, who was the only one whose name I hadn't heard, crawled in with them to tip one woman's head so she didn't snore. He did it with tenderness, and he kissed her cheek. He took the lantern out from under the stairs and left his charges in darkness.

There was a click as the overhead lightbulb was turned off. Kocourek came down the stairs like a panther, the red light of the lantern allowing me to see them well enough to judge where they were but not the expressions on their faces.

Without speaking, they all took up positions designed to allow them to keep intruders away from under the stairs, without shouting to the world, *Hey, I'm protecting the people under the stairs.*

I got it. What I didn't get was why. Who were they protecting them from? Mary? But that didn't really make sense because no one had protected that poor girl who died.

The double hit on the magic that surrounded this place happened again, and this time I wasn't the only one in the basement who felt it.

They staggered under the weight of whatever was bludgeoning the place. During the second attack, Lars, who was neither tall nor blond, though with a name like that he should have been, went down to one knee. Mustached man groaned, and Dagmar swore. I thought she swore, anyway. There was an emphasis to the words that just translated to swearing in any language.

When the second one let up, I shifted to human, startling the ghost—which was a switch. She disappeared for the moment, though I could feel her lingering nearby.

"Kocourek," I said quietly, because they'd been trying to be quiet. "How long have you belonged to Mary?"

The four vampires did that really chilling thing where they move at the same time, exactly at the same time, better than any award-winning dance team.

Lars said something. It sounded harsh and staccato, but it was still quiet.

"Mercy Thompson Hauptman, daughter of the Marrok, wife of the Alpha of the Tri-Cities, Washington, pack," said Kocourek.

"May I make known to you the few of my seethe who are left me—Dagmar, Vanje, and Lars."

"Close," I told him. "I was raised in Bran Cornick's pack, but he's not my father. And our pack is the Columbia Basin Pack. Werewolf packs are seldom named after a town. How long have you been Mary's minion?"

"Guccio's," corrected Kocourek mildly. "Never Mary's."

"She's not even her own person yet," said Dagmar. "She still needs to feed from us to stay sane. Sort of sane—as sane as that witch gets. She's a fledgling yet—and Guccio caters to her for her magic. He set her up here, with her own seethe made up of his children."

"Pretty Vampire's?" I said slowly. "The one who looks like he could make a living as a stripper? He's your Master?"

"Maker," said Kocourek shortly.

At the same time, Dagmar snickered. "'Pretty Vampire'? He'd love that. He'd *have* loved that."

"I thought that Master Vampires didn't have to obey their makers anymore," I said.

"Why are you answering her questions?" asked Lars.

"Because I think she's the cause of whatever is blasting away at Mary's spellcrafting," Kocourek said shortly. To me he said, "Mostly after we quit feeding from our makers, their influence over us wanes over years. I made a mistake. I welcomed Guccio into my home as a guest, and he caught me and rebonded me—fed from me and made me feed from him. And so he took me and my children, then he told me to listen to Mary as if she were he." The rage in his voice, for all that it was quiet, could have ignited diesel fuel. Not much ignites diesel, but it burns pretty well.

"For how long?" I asked him.

He smiled at me fiercely, the expression big enough I could see it even in the dim light. "Two years, three months, four days. Once she discovered a way to create new vampires more quickly, he decided to speed up his run to power. And that meant that our seethe had to be joined to Mary's. For two years and more, I have been his slave again. Ending this evening, two hours ago." This time they all smiled, but it wasn't that creepy thing where they all did it at the same time. They were alike, but only in determination.

"What happened then?" I asked.

"Guccio lost his bid for the Lord of Night's place, I expect," Kocourek said. "Someone killed him."

"Vampires," I said dryly, "are dead already."

"Are we?" he said. "Maybe. Then let us just say that someone destroyed Guccio today. And I and my whole seethe walk free." He looked at his comrades. "There were eighteen of us. And the five of us who were our own people, we had our households—our humans. When we came here two years ago, my seethe counted ninety-seven. Mary creates vampires quickly, but she destroys at an even greater rate. She is more witch than vampire, and that's why Guccio values her." He gave a curt nod to the chained vampire. "You saw what she does."

"Why are you hiding your sheep from her?" I asked.

Vanje, the mustache-wearing vampire, jerked his head toward me and growled.

Kocourek held up a hand. "These are not sheep, Mercedes. These are the last of our households. The people who served us well and faithfully—only to be turned into . . . what did you call them? Sheep. Mary's people call them *dobytek*. *Vieh*. *Cattle*. We called them our friends."

"Not all of them," said Dagmar pragmatically. "We just gathered up the humans and brought them down here. Two of them are a couple of people Mary collected last week—and why are we telling this to a naked human who is interesting only because she is the wife of an American werewolf, Kocourek?"

"Because it is good to talk," he said. "To remind ourselves of who we are, that we are no longer subservient to Mary. Because she is not a human—you must not have observed her change. She is a coyote shapeshifter. From America. And because I want her to answer our questions."

It came again, the double strike against Mary's magic, and this time the second strike lasted for a long time—ten or twenty seconds.

"That stings," said Lars on a gasp when it let up.

"What do you want to know?" I asked. I wiped my nose on my wrist because I thought it was running, but it was blood not snot. Less embarrassing, maybe. But I would have rathered it was snot. Blood meant these attacks were causing damage. Mary's bit of witchcraft must be drawing power from anyone who had magic inside her sphere of influence; otherwise, we wouldn't all be feeling it—and the mundane humans not reacting at all.

"Coyotes are tricksters," Lars said.

"That's not a question," I retorted. "But *Coyote* is a trickster."

"You are a death walker?" he said, suddenly very interested. "One who has power over the dead."

And that right there told me that this vampire from Prague knew as much about what I was as I did. Just like the golem had. I didn't say anything. This was bad. This was very bad. Because if he said what I thought he was going to say, it might mean that someone besides Bonarata was behind my ending up unexpectedly in Prague.

"One of your kind came through here during the First World War," Lars said.

"Don't tell me." I groaned. "His name was Gary Laughingdog." My very much older half brother whom I had just met this past winter. Hadn't he said he volunteered for the army in World War I?

"You know of him?" Kocourek said. "He caused a lot of trouble here, in this town. Afterward, he told me that it was a curse of his—to come and make havoc. He said he tried to leave things better than when he came, but he would not answer for the bloodshed, destruction, and mayhem that happened while he was here."

I hate coincidences. I don't really believe in them, less now than before I met Coyote. But what in the world made Coyote care about vampires in Prague? And why would he think I could do anything about them? Probably my being here was just a coincidence, and I was being paranoid.

"She can command the dead?" asked Lars. "Can she command us?"

"Can you?" asked Kocourek.

I suppose I could have lied. But being raised by werewolves meant I'd never made lying a habit. "I don't know," I told him. "Maybe. Sometimes. No." I shrugged.

"Gary Laughingdog could," Kocourek said.

"Scary bastard," said Vanje. "I was glad he went back to fighting Germans."

"So what did you bring down on Mary's head, Mercedes who walks with the dead?" Kocourek asked.

And then I knew what Coyote might find interesting about Prague, and it wasn't the vampires.

Before I had to work up an answer for Kocourek, the upstairs door blew open, and Mary turned on the lights.

"Kocourek," she said. And then she said some other things in another language—stuff that was obviously orders.

I didn't think she'd gotten notice that Kocourek wasn't hers to order anymore.

"She wants to know where our humans are," Kocourek said. "She needs to feed her witchcraft with them so she can withstand the monster at our gates. What did you bring down upon us, Mercy?"

"It's the golem," I told him.

He froze and turned back to me. "The golem?"

"The golem?" asked Dagmar. "Didn't Gary say something about the golem? He was always saying odd things." She frowned, then her face cleared. "I've got it. He said the golem wasn't dead, and someone should do something about that."

Lars said, "And he was sure glad his name wasn't someone because that was going to be a messy job."

"I *remember* the golem," said Vanje thoughtfully. "I'm not sure that was a good choice, Mercedes Hauptman. It took the good rabbi four days of work to put that thing down—and the rabbi was never the same afterward."

Mary said something sharply.

"She wants us to quit speaking English," said Lars. "I don't know about the golem—I wasn't here when the golem was active. But I think someone needs to do something about Mary. And I'm willing to be someone today. How about you?"

Kocourek said something to Mary in a conciliatory voice.

I don't know what it was, but I thought from the tone, he'd decided Lars was right. Instead of hiding their people from her, he was going to lure her down.

"Witch," I murmured. "Witches can kill you from a distance, and they are sneaky. Are you sure you don't—"

And the golem attacked her spells again. This time when the first wave hit, I blacked out. When I opened my eyes again, I could tell that I wasn't the only one.

Mary had collapsed on the stairs and rolled to the bottom. Lars was flat on his face in the dirt. Dagmar was getting to her feet. Vanje had a hand under Kocourek's elbow, pulling him upright.

Mary reached out and wrapped her hand around Lars's wrist. Her voice hoarse, she started chanting. I was pretty sure it was the same thing she'd used before when she tortured the screaming-clanking vampire with her magic. I couldn't understand her, but the rhythm was the same.

"Stop her," I said as Lars twitched convulsively.

And the ghost formed right next to Mary and dug her fingers into Mary's wrist. I don't think Mary saw her, but the ghost's fingernails drew blood as she wrenched at Mary's wrist, breaking her hold on Lars.

Mary stopped chanting to say something ugly. She flung her bleeding hand up, and a drop of her blood hit Vanje. It didn't seem possible that she'd done it on purpose—but I could feel the wave of magic that hit Vanje, sending him to the ground with a cry.

His skin erupted in reddish bumps with black centers that grew with hideous speed. The little black circles in the center grew, too, spreading out and lightening to purple on the edges. He thrashed and twisted, his movements sluggish.

My ghost hit Mary on the shoulder with both hands, causing the vampire to stagger. Mary turned to see who had hit her, and I could see by her face that she still couldn't see the ghost.

And the golem hit the spells again.

Mary screamed in agony—which made my own pain somehow hurt less. She reached out and pulled her magic back from Vanje, who lost his horrible, plague-like lumps. I couldn't tell for certain, but it felt as though she was able to pull more magic back than what she'd sent at him. She used that magic to do something that changed the shape of the power of the golem's attack for just a moment—enough to make my ears ring.

Then there was nothing. The golem's attack just stopped. I wondered if she'd destroyed him.

Mary rose unsteadily to her feet. She kicked Vanje and spat something at him.

Kocourek staggered out of the shadows near the staircase, sword in hand. With a lunge and a twist of his upper torso that would have done credit to Babe Ruth, he cut off her head while she kicked Vanje a second time.

We all waited for something to happen. In the movies, when someone killed the spell caster, all of their spells just go away. There were some magics like that. I'd seen them myself. But according to Elizaveta, if the witch was good enough to set spells that were self-sustaining, then they actually had to be broken.

I have to admit, I was waiting for her to get back up and kill us all. Even the ghost seemed to catch the worry; she kept touching Mary's decapitated head and making it roll.

The third time she did it, Vanje noticed and rose to his feet with a yelp.

"Don't worry," I told him. "It's only a ghost."

Galina, the ghost told me. *My name is Galina.*

And though I knew better, I said, "Galina."

"What?" said Dagmar.

Kocourek said, "Don't you remember Gary? He always was talking to dead people—and I don't mean vampires. Galina is the ghost."

Galina tried kicking the head this time, and it rolled about three feet, coming to rest about six inches from Lars.

"Tell her not to do that, please," said Lars. He was still sitting where he'd fallen, cradling the hand Mary had grabbed against his chest.

But I didn't have to because Mary's head and body collapsed into dust.

"Okay," Lars said. "That works, too."

The golem attacked again, and this time it broke Mary's spells. It didn't hurt this time. It didn't hurt me, anyway. The vampires all cried out. It didn't take them long to recover, but by that time the golem was entering the apartment house. He made a lot of noise tearing down the door.

"Can everyone see us now? The building, I mean," I asked. I was stuck in the stupid cage and unable to *do* anything. But if the humans could see us, then soon there would be police and fire-fighters and all the good people who help others. And they would be coming into a place filled with vampires.

Humans could not find out about the vampires. No one sane wanted a panic war where all the supernaturally gifted people—and anyone else who might be thought supernaturally gifted—were killed by their neighbors with whatever weapons they had handy. There was no way something like that would not be a total disaster.

"No," said Dagmar. "I don't think so anyway. Two different spells. Mary designed it so the veil magic would last a month or two before it faded. She was planning on moving into Kocourek's seethe, assuming Guccio killed Bonarata."

"You gave the golem back its body," said Vanje, listening, as we all were, to the sound of something very heavy moving over our heads. Then the screaming started.

"It won't hurt you," I told him. "You're the good guys."

Vanje looked at me. "We are vampire, Mercy. Not even when the rabbi first gave it life would it have tolerated vampires in its territory. At its end point, not even being Jewish and a decent person was good enough. It will kill us all if it can."

"Dawn is coming," said Lars, who had at last risen to his feet.

"How long do you have?" I asked.

"Not long enough to fight off the golem," said Kocourek. "Assuming we could. Less than five minutes."

"Get under the stairs with your people," I told them. "That will keep you out of sight. I'll do my best to keep the golem off you."

"You are in a cage," said Lars. "How is it that you will stop the golem?"

"Can you open it?" I asked, rattling the door a little.

Kocourek shook his head. "Mary spelled that box shut. She was the only one who could open it."

"The golem is only after the bad guys," I said, trying not to hear the screams. "I'll tell him you are the good guys."

Kocourek sighed, gave the other vampires a wry smile. "It has been an adventure, people. I am glad to have served with you."

While he spoke, his vampires had been following my advice.

Dagmar said something to him in a language I didn't understand, presumably Czech, but it could have been Serbian. Kocourek laughed, shook his head, and crawled under the stairs with them. They arranged the humans so that they were on the inside, protected by the vampires still.

I'd expected them to put the humans on the outside to shield the vampires from the light. But these were the good guys, right? Right.

The cries upstairs stopped at the same time the vampires under the stairs died in the dawn. As if in response, the destruction upstairs redoubled. The floor on the side of the basement where Dagmar had carried the girl's body collapsed with a roar of brick, stone, and rubble.

Coughing and choking in the resultant dust, I realized that it might all be over even if the golem didn't find us down here. Light broke through the rubble on the far side of the room in dim rays that illuminated the dust in the air.

The dust settled. The sunlight seemed out of place—and I was glad the vampires were under the stairway, or my saving them from the golem would have been a moot point. After a while, I wondered if the golem, like the vampires, was only active at night—or if it would leave me alone down here.

Galina seemed unaffected by the light, which was my experience with ghosts. Most people encountered ghosts at night more often than during the day. I suspected it was because if they see a ghost in the day, they don't recognize what they are seeing.

The golem came at last. It ducked through the doorway and started down the stairs. The stairs were sturdy, and they didn't even creak under his weight.

He wasn't the biggest monster I've ever seen. He was maybe eight feet tall and looked like an animated suit of armor made of red clay. His face had no features, no eyes, no mouth. There were also no letters on his forehead for me to erase if I needed to.

His magic felt different than it had before, which was only to be expected. He was different now. I'd given him the power to become real again.

"Greetings to the Golem of Prague," I said.

It paused on the stairs.

You do not belong here, he told me.

I couldn't tell if he meant here in the basement or in his city.

He clarified it for me without my having to ask, so I guess he was still in my head.

Your help was necessary. You should leave and not ever come back. I won't be so lenient again.

"I'm trapped here," I told him. "As you know very well. I will leave when I can."

Acceptable, it said. And it started down the stairs again. It was an awkward-looking movement. Since the stairs weren't wide enough for his feet, the golem leaned back to center his weight over his . . . over what would have been his heels had he been human.

"What are you doing?" I asked.

There are demons here. The last of the demons in my city.

The Jewish Quarter, I thought, not Prague. I hoped he didn't mean Prague.

"You've done your job," I told him. "The vampires left here are no villains. They mean no harm to the people here."

Yeah. I had a hard time with that last one, too, after I said it. Vampires ate people. It was what they did. But they had brought all the humans here to shelter them, and they were still guarding them to the best of their abilities.

They are demons, said the golem. *They must be destroyed.*

"What about the humans?" I asked.

They are not my people, he said—and I felt a cold chill. Because I knew what he meant.

Vanje had said that not even being Jewish had been enough to save people from the golem.

I didn't know what percentage of the people living in Josefov were still Jewish. But if Prague was like the rest of Europe, after the Nazis got through with the city, it was a far smaller percentage than it had been when this had been the only place in Prague the

Jewish population could live. And if being Jewish wouldn't save them anyway, it didn't matter because the golem would kill them all. If Vanje was right.

"What will you do to the humans who are not Jewish?" I asked.

They are not my people, the golem said. *None of the humans are my people. I have no people.*

"What if they are Rabbi Loew's people?" I asked.

It roared at me without a sound. I covered my ears, and it didn't do any good at all. In that sound, I heard a fury built up over centuries of frustration and rage. He didn't speak in words, but I heard him just fine. The rabbi had condemned him to that horrible half death, burdened him with the need to guard and no means by which to do it.

He didn't intend to stop at destroying the vampires. Or the humans. And being Jewish wasn't going to save anyone from him.

I drew a deep breath as the golem took the last step down.

"Stop," I said. *"Stop moving."* And I used the power that allowed me to give orders to the dead.

It stopped. It had eaten the magic of all the ghosts we could call here between us (except for Galina). That meant its power came from the dead—and the dead had to listen to me. And then it did to me whatever it had done to Mary's spellcrafting.

When I could open my eyes again, the golem had found the vampires. The space between the old furnace and the stairway was too narrow for the golem to get through, though he had pounded the furnace into half the size it had been. So he reached down and began tearing up the stairs.

When we'd removed the anchors that allowed the manitou of the volcano god to travel, it had been forced back to its original home. I had to do something like that here.

But though it was tied to clay with kabbalistic magic powered by the spiritual energy I'd given him, this manitou belonged here, in Josefov. Those weren't the technical terms, I was sure. But I wasn't a mage, and I was running on instinct.

The rabbi's problem was that he'd tried to stop it by killing something that wasn't killable. He'd managed to render it almost dead and to separate it from the physical body that allowed it power.

I couldn't kill it. Couldn't even fight it because I was locked in a cage. Couldn't free it—

I closed my eyes and stretched with my senses, the ones I'd used to contact Stefan, to find my pack and Adam through our bonds, but this time I directed my attention toward the golem.

He ripped at the bottom stair, and it gave with a squeak of nails and cracking wood.

I couldn't do anything with the spellcrafting that held the golem together. But the energy, the magic he'd stolen from the dead . . . that was mine.

I opened myself up—and found Adam. As if he were in the same room with me, I found Adam. He always had my back when I needed him.

There was no time to ask for permission, no time to try to communicate anything because the golem had grabbed someone and pulled them out from under the stairs. I couldn't tell who it was because the golem's body was blocking my view.

I centered myself, pulled on the connection between Adam and me, and spoke one word. *"Sunder."*

I hadn't meant to say that. "Sunder" means to divide, to part, to separate—I'd meant to try to do what the rabbi had done. I'd planned on saying, "Die." I'd hoped that with that command, I could force the golem back into the limbo I'd brought it out from.

But someone who sounded suspiciously like Coyote whispered that word in my ear as I opened my mouth.

I could not touch the manitou with my magic because it was not dead. I could not touch the kabbalistic spells because that was not my gift. But Kocourek had named me death walker, and the dead obeyed me, no matter how much I tried to ignore that. And it was the power of the dead that held the golem together.

My power, the power over the dead, driven by the energy I borrowed from Adam and focused by the single word I'd used, washed through the golem. He staggered, dropped his prey, then turned toward me. He took two quick steps and brought his fist down on the cage.

I think we were both surprised when his fist bounced off. It made sense because the cage had been built with steel, silver, and magic. It had been built to hold werewolves. But I was still surprised he hadn't killed me with a single blow.

I reached for Adam a second time, and this time he gave me . . . everything. The first time I'd tried this, he'd had no warning, and I had just taken what I could. This time he pushed power at me. I could feel his authority, built by the belief of the pack that he was the one who could keep them safe, as it settled over me. Belief is the most powerful magic of all. He gave me that, trusted me with it.

The golem was still waiting for the cage to collapse under his fist, his face not a foot from mine. His fist still on the top of the cage. I reached up and touched his clay flesh with a finger through the mesh. Then I used everything I had, everything I was, and everything Adam had given me when I repeated the word.

"Sunder."

I felt the word hang in the air for a moment; it was like waiting for the rumble of thunder after the flash of lightning. Then the magic of that long-ago rabbi shuddered under the weight of the command. The newer spells the golem had woven himself gave way as the power of the dead tore them to shreds, leaving chaos behind.

I'm a mechanic; I fix things that are broken. I turn into a thirty-five-pound coyote. I have powerful friends. But when it comes right down to it, my real superpower is chaos.

The golem's clay body fell to the ground and shattered as though it had been dropped from a hundred feet onto rocks. Clay shards bounced off the mesh of my cage, mostly harmlessly. One or two got through but only one caused me any damage. And for a very long moment, the reek of the mess that Mary had made of her seethe gave way to the smell of springwater, the kind that bubbles up clear and pure from the earth. And then it was gone, and the whole place smelled of the dead.

14

~~

MERCY

It was hard to look like I'd won when I
was still stuck in the stupid cage.

MINUTES PASSED. I GOT A GOOD LOOK AT THE PERSON
the golem had pulled out from the stairway. He was the middle-
aged man who had led the other humans. I was still trapped in
my cage. Galina tried to help, but her abilities to interact with the
real world were limited to rolling heads around.

I tried to contact Adam, but my bond had fallen silent again:
there but not there. As if I'd overloaded it.

The man moaned a lot. At one point, he started to crawl. I don't
know where he was going, but he didn't get there. And there was
nothing, not anything I could do about him. Nor could I do anything about the sunlight that entered through the broken corner and
from the open door at the top of the stairs. I watched, helpless, as it
crept closer and closer to the dead who waited under the stairway.

THE WEREWOLVES CAME JUST AFTER NOON. ADAM didn't bother with the broken stairs; he just jumped over the handrail at the top. He stepped over the rapidly rotting body of the man the golem had killed.

His bright gold eyes on me, he took a step toward my cage and stopped with a grunt. I felt the magic flare up as it had not for the vampires, the ghosts, or the golem. Galina petted his shoulder and looked concerned for him. He took a half step back, then he squatted so his head was level with mine.

He didn't say anything, just stared at me with those gold eyes, his hands clenched into fists.

If I had been free, I'd have climbed into his lap and buried my face in his shoulder and cried. It was probably better for my dignity that I couldn't do that. I reached out and put my hand against the cage where it was closest to him.

"I think Coyote sent me here," I told him. My voice was hoarse from the power I'd used to destroy the golem. "To fix things or make me crazy—it's a toss-up." I was almost certain that the reason I'd chosen "sunder" instead of "die" was because of Coyote. "I hope he's happy. I think I've ensured that all of the vampires in Prague are dead. Except for the four people under the stairs." Suddenly anxious for them, I leaned forward. "They are the good guys, I think. So make sure no one shines any sunlight on them, okay?"

He didn't say anything for a while, just put a hand up toward me and then pulled it back with a grimace.

"Who hit you?" he asked, his voice in that deep place it went when the wolf was riding him. He didn't say anything about the vampires, but I could trust him to take care of it.

Had someone hit me? I frowned at him, and he ran his hand down the left side of his face. I'd forgotten about that.

"Guccio," I told him. "The pretty vampire. I think he's been disposed of, though. That's what the vampires under the stairs said. It meant they could quit following orders."

"Guccio's dead," Adam agreed, so apparently he knew who Guccio was. "I killed him." His tone was satisfied, so I expected there was a story that went with that. There would be a lot of time for stories.

"It took you a long time to find me," I said. And it had. It had been hours since the golem had died—since the manitou who powered it had been freed at last to go and be what he was supposed to be and not what Rabbi Loew had turned him into. But my stomach was easing, and my body was starting to believe I was safe. Hearing Adam's voice, velvety soft, was better than medicine for what ailed me.

"Your power draw knocked me off my feet," Adam said. "I was out for an hour. No one could do anything until I was conscious, and it took a while for the bond to start functioning well enough I could use it to track you."

"Sorry," I said in a small voice.

"My love," he said, his voice intent, "you are welcome to all that I am, all that I have. I would destroy the planet for you. I was even diplomatic for you, which was a bigger sacrifice. A little power drain is nothing."

"An hour," I said. He was a werewolf, and I'd knocked him out for an hour. "You could have died."

"*You could have died,*" he said intensely. "What would I have done then?"

He took a deep breath. When he spoke again, it was in his own voice despite the gold in his eyes. "You are welcome to anything I have, my love. Martin and Jitka got us to Josefov, but only after I took them to the park did they remember they'd lost you here. It took Elizaveta the rest of the time to get through the veil spells without pulling them down entirely. She . . . Libor . . ." He grimaced again. "We all thought it might be a good thing to see what was inside the invisible wall before we exposed it to the good people of Prague—especially since there were vampires involved. But it took time."

"They might want to leave it up awhile longer than they are planning," I told him. "I think there are a lot of dead bodies here. Sixty years' worth or more."

He sat all the way on the ground. There were fine lines around his eyes and shadows that told me he was nearly as tired as I felt. People had started to filter down the stairs, werewolf people, presumably belonging to Libor.

Adam told them about the vampires under the stairs and requested, politely, that someone tell Elizaveta that he needed her.

"The cage is designed to subdue werewolves," I told him. "I'm not being hurt."

"When Elizaveta has a moment to spare will be soon enough," Adam told the wolf who'd started up the stairs.

"So you think Coyote sent you here?" Adam asked me. "Marsilia is pretty convinced it was a giant plot by Bonarata to get us to take care of all of his problems for him. He's not unhappy to take the credit."

"Marsilia?" I folded my legs more comfortably and leaned my forehead against the cage. I listened to Adam explain what had happened after they'd found the wrecked car and why he'd brought the people he'd brought.

"Larry?" I said. "Seriously? The king of the goblins is Larry?"

"Someone call my name?" A goblin bounded down the stairs, knelt by Adam, and handed him a bottle of water. He grinned at me, and I saw that there were a few too many teeth in his mouth. "I know," he said to me. "What *were* my parents thinking? Larry. Even worse, though, is that my full name is Lawrence—which makes me sound like a proper wimp." He had kind eyes. "We're pretty glad to find you more or less in one piece, princess."

"Not as happy as I am," I assured him, and he laughed.

He turned to Adam. "I'd hoped I might help. But this is witchcraft. I expect Elizaveta can take care of it as soon as she gets done with the wards she's laying to keep out the innocents. She says it will take her a while because something destroyed the ones the previous witch built."

"It was the golem," I told them. "And the witch is dead." I looked at Larry's shoes. "You've been wading through her. She was in love with Guccio, and he was in love with her power."

"Dead vampire dust," said Larry thoughtfully.

"Dead vampire witch dust," I said.

"I think we'll find that she belonged to Bonarata originally," Adam told me. "He had a witch go missing a while back."

Larry got up and went somewhere. I wished that I could drink some of Adam's water. Food would be nice, too.

"Was the cage dented when they put you in it?" Adam asked me.

I shook my head. "That was the golem when it tried to kill me."

Adam sat up straighter, and his eyes, which had just gotten back to the dark chocolate color that was more usual for him, brightened again.

"I killed the Golem of Prague—for real this time," I told him. "After I used him to kill all the vampires. I don't know how many he killed. Lots, I think. Mary figured out how to mass-produce vampires, though I gather they had quite an expiration date. The problem was he didn't want to stop with the vampires. Your help was the only reason all of the people in the Jewish Quarter aren't dead."

He looked around the basement. I saw him take in the scattered shards of pottery. He clenched his fists, then released them.

"It was my fault everyone died," I told him. "If I could have figured out a way to kill just Mary, I think Kocourek could have controlled everyone else." But all of those vampires would have known that Mary could make vampires in a couple of weeks instead of years. Stories would have been told. Someone would try it again. Kocourek understood what was at risk. He'd keep quiet—and he'd keep the others who survived quiet.

But so many people, and they were people to me whether they were vampires or ghosts . . . all gone because of me.

Adam looked at my face and deliberately let his anger of a moment ago drift away. He pursed his lips. "You beat us. We only killed two people. Lenka—Bonarata's werewolf—was the first one. He was losing control of her and used us to execute her for him." He sounded sad, then his voice hardened. "Guccio was the second. If I'd known he hit you, I'd have taken longer."

It was my turn to nod. I was so tired.

Even more people were tramping up and down the stairs, which, despite the damage the golem had done to them, were still working just fine. A werewolf in slacks and a white shirt and a tie lifted Elizaveta Arkadyevna over the wreckage of the bottom step.

I was very, very tired. And Adam was here. I was safe. I let my eyes close. Then I whispered, very quietly, "Is that Bran? Or am I hallucinating?"

Adam smiled at me; I heard it in his voice. "Of course not.

What would he be doing here? It's Matt Smith, our copilot and submissive wolf."

"Matt Smith is the Doctor," I informed him, then fell asleep with a smile on my face as Elizaveta started to unlock the magic on my cage.

I DREAMED I WAS SITTING BESIDE A FRESHWATER spring that bubbled up in a small garden. It was surrounded by stone walls and medieval-style doors that led into the buildings that enclosed the garden.

Except for the spring, it reminded me of the garden with the friendly mastiff. This garden didn't have a dog, though, only me, Galina—who looked as real as I did—and Coyote.

"It's happy," said Galina thoughtfully, leaning forward to touch the water with her hand.

"Yes," agreed Coyote.

"I wish I was happy like that," she told him wistfully.

"Do you?" he asked. He looked at me out of the corner of his eye. "Why don't you come for a walk with me?"

Galina touched my shoulder. "I can't leave Mercy alone. She saved me from the golem."

He smiled at her. "Did she?" Was there a bite in his voice? If there was, it wasn't directed at Galina. "She'll be fine here for a moment."

"Go," I told her. "You've done enough for me. I'm safe now."

"Okay," she said. She stood up and took Coyote's hand when he held it out to her.

I didn't watch where he took her. It was a private moment. Her private moment.

"Will she be okay?" I asked in a small voice when Coyote returned without her a long while later.

"Right as rain," he told me. "She's where she should have been now. Unstuck. I don't know why people get stuck like that."

"You sent me to Prague to free the spirit of this spring," I told him.

"I sent your *brother* to Prague to free the spirit of this spring," he told me. "Blame him for not getting the job done. I am impressed, though. I didn't expect you to resurrect the whole golem. Do you know what could have happened if you hadn't stopped it?" he asked. Then he threw himself backward on the ground, plucked a blade of grass, and stuck it between his white teeth. "It would have been glorious."

I woke up as Elizaveta broke the magic that surrounded the cage. Adam oh-so-gently moved her aside, then ripped the door off. His arms closed around me, so tight I could barely breathe.

Coyote's voice spoke in my ear. "Tell him to find you some clothes before you catch your death."

I ignored him.

———————

A FULL TWENTY-FOUR HOURS LATER, I WOKE UP NAKED in sheets that felt like silk and with the smell of my mate all around me. I sat up and rubbed my face, careful of the cheek that was sore. The shower was running.

Libor had offered sleeping space in his bakery, but we'd gone to a hotel. Adam had wanted me alone, and I wasn't arguing.

For the first time in forever, I wasn't exhausted and alone.

I walked naked into the bathroom. The shower was clear glass, and Adam had his back to me. I leaned against the doorframe and smiled.

"You going to watch my butt all day, or are you going to join me?" asked my mate.

"What if I had said I was going to watch your butt all day?" I asked curiously as I opened the door and stepped into the hot water.

"I've been considering belly-dancing lessons," he told me in a serious voice. His arms were tight around me, and he pulled me hard into him. "It would have given you something to watch. But I'm not sure if I could hold my head up around other Alpha werewolves if I did."

"Yeah," I agreed, the cells of my body both soothed and energized by the touch of his skin. "I know how much you worry about what other Alpha werewolves might think of you."

We made love under the water. He kissed my bruises and I kissed the healing slice over his shoulder. We said the kinds of things that wouldn't make any sense to anyone else. And when he was buried inside of me, his breath rough and his skin hot, that's when I knew I was home.

WE FLEW OUT OF PRAGUE THREE DAYS LATER. IT GAVE us time to do the diplomacy things that Adam pretends he isn't any good at. Bran stayed on the plane. With me safe, he didn't want to risk anyone's knowing he was there, because that would invite all sorts of random attacks of opportunity (Adam's words). Libor knew but had, for his own reasons, decided to keep his own counsel. I found out later that Bran had coerced Zack into calling Libor to request that his father take good care of me. I also found

out that Adam had done the same thing—all of this before Libor
had met me in the garden and made me bargain with him. Coyote
would like Libor.

Bonarata was charming, but I couldn't forget or forgive him
for Lenka. Honey stayed away from him, and I noticed that Libor
kept Jitka and the other female werewolves in his pack away from
the vampire, too.

Elizaveta was remaining in Europe, a guest of Bonarata's, for
a full month. He was paying her to remove his addiction to werewolf blood and to do all the things that Mary had once done for
his seethe. He was going to try to hire her away from us, Adam
said, but he hadn't sounded worried. She would come home—a
lot wealthier than when she'd left.

Marsilia had pursed her lips when Adam had told us what
Elizaveta intended.

"It won't work in the long run," she said. "Addicts have to
want to be clean. As long as Jacob thinks that it gives him more
power, he won't quit."

When she spoke of Bonarata, she didn't do it the way she used
to. There had been so much energy wound up in her voice, but
now that spring had worn down. He was someone she had once
known well, but now was an acquaintance.

Bonarata was staying at Kocourek's seethe, helping him rebuild.
I didn't think too hard about what that meant. Kocourek had
pulled me aside and asked me not to tell anyone about how Mary
had managed to create vampires so much faster.

"With her and the other vampires dead," Kocourek said, "no
one knows what she managed except for you, me, and my people.
It is better that way, no?"

"Agreed," I assured him. But part of me couldn't help but think of that saying about how two people can keep a secret if one of them is dead.

Adam and I spent two days playing tourists. We explored the castle complex, which included a cathedral and a church nearly as old as I think Bran is, and walked through the streets of Old Town. Adam bought me an amber necklace and matching earrings. I found an antique crystal goblet with the figure of a wolf on it.

———

ADAM AND I WERE CUDDLED UP WATCHING A MOVIE in one of the meeting rooms in the jet when Bran came in bearing a bowl of ice with three soda cans buried deep. He closed the door behind him, set the bowl on the floor, and watched the movie with us for about ten minutes before I couldn't take it anymore.

"Matt Smith?" I said. "Really? You are not the Doctor, Bran. At your age, it is important to keep a lookout for excessive hubris."

"Thank you," he said. He took a drink of his soda. "Your mother put you in my arms when you were less than three months old. I knew that I had no room in my life for such a fragile thing. I gave you to the best man for the job."

"Bryan was amazing," I told him, wondering what his point was.

Bran nodded. "Leah would have killed you if I had kept you."

"She almost killed me anyway," I said dryly. Bran's wife and I had a hate-hate relationship that worked quite well for both of us.

"And yet," Bran said softly, "you were mine from the day I first held you. No matter how hard I fought it. It isn't safe to be in my family, Mercy. And you were this fragile creature who put herself in the path of destruction on a daily basis."

He had abandoned me twice. First when he sent me away

because Samuel wanted me. Samuel was nearly as old as Bran, who is older than dirt, and I'd been sixteen. Bran could have sent Samuel away—but Samuel was his son, and I was only an annoying stray. It had taken an Adam to make me trust people again. The second time Bran had abandoned me was worse, because it was the second time. He'd cut his ties to my pack, for all the right reasons—and it had felt just as bad as it had when I was sixteen, only I felt stupider.

And then he'd risked everything he believed in—because if Bonarata had known who Matt Smith really was, all hell would have broken loose—to help Adam rescue me. He'd risked war between the werewolves and the vampires to keep me safe.

Carefully I said, "Thank you for coming after me."

"You rescued yourself," he said. "I should have stayed home."

Adam laughed. "I'd have been in trouble if you hadn't been there. And why do you think Libor was so cooperative? If it had just been me, we'd have had to fight it out before he agreed to go hunt down Mary's seethe—I know his type."

I sat up and looked at Bran while my body was warmed by Adam. "What did you do to Zack that made his father hate you so much?" I paused. "I think his birth name is Radim, right?"

"Zack?" said Adam.

Bran made a Bran sound. "Radim. Poor Radim. I can't tell you the details. Let's just say that being a submissive in Libor's pack would not be something I'd wish on my worst enemy. Particularly if, as in Radim's case, he was Libor's son." He tapped a finger on the top of his empty soda can. "I might have kidnapped him," he said finally.

"Okay," I said, and settled back against Adam.

"No wonder Zack doesn't like you," Adam said.

"That's a different story," Bran said. "You'll have to ask him."

We watched the rest of the movie without talking. When it was over, Bran said, "I love you."

I said, "I know." Adam nudged me with his shoulder, and I laughed. "I love you, too."

———————

WE TURNED DOWN OUR STREET JUST AFTER DARK. THAT made it easy to see the flashing lights of the fire department trucks. Adam didn't say anything, but he put his foot down on the gas pedal.

We parked on the lawn to avoid blocking the driveway for the fire trucks. The garage roof was a blackened ruin, and there was at least one wall that was a burned wreck. The whole house and yard were soggy with water. I could smell char and burnt things, but I couldn't see anything burning. People—werewolves and firemen for the most part—were wandering all over the place.

In the bustle and hum, no one noticed us except Aiden, because everyone else was focused on the garage.

He had his arms crossed and a militant expression on his face as he marched up to us.

"Hey, Adam. Hey, Mercy," he said in a tight little voice. "Welcome home. I stopped the garage from burning down, but that was after I started it. Apparently I burn down garages when I fall asleep doing homework. I'll find somewhere else to live."

"Hey, Aiden," I said. "I destroyed a whole apartment building." It had been the golem, but I thought I was entitled to claim his damage for my own. "Can I come live with you?"

Adam just laughed, reached out, and ruffled Aiden's hair. "It's good to be home."

"Yes," I agreed wholeheartedly. "I think I should go make some chocolate chip cookies."

CAST OF CHARACTERS

by Ann Peters

COLUMBIA BASIN PACK

Mercy Athena Thompson Hauptman, our VW mechanic and coyote shapeshifting heroine, mistress of snark and subtle revenge.

Adam Hauptman, aka Captain Larson, Alpha of the Columbia Basin Pack and married to Mercy; his revenge is less subtle than Mercy's.

Jesse Hauptman, aka Barbary Belle, Adam's human daughter by his ex-wife, Christy; Jesse's snark makes her worthy to be Mercy's step-daughter.

Aiden, fire-touched fae who looks like a young boy but is centuries old; Aiden and Jesse have reached a sibling-like rapport after a rough start of mistaken identity and grabbed bottoms.

Joel Arocha, tibicena member of the pack and not totally in control of his connection to volcano-god powers; Aiden is helping him decrease the number of fire department visits.

Ben Shaw, aka Sodding Bart, werewolf, our favorite British IT guy and world-class potty mouth.

Mary Jo, werewolf, a tough Pasco firefighter who doesn't like Mercy much.

Darryl Zao, werewolf, second in the Columbia Basin Pack; when not protecting Adam's back, he can be found using his PhD analytical skills on something brilliant.

Auriele Zao, werewolf, Darryl's mate; a chemistry teacher.

Honey Jorgenson, a dominant wolf moving up in the ranks and shaking up the hierarchy; she recently lost her husband.

Peter Jorgenson, deceased husband of Honey who still follows her in ghost form; he was the pack's submissive wolf before Zack.

Sherwood Post, the only three-legged werewolf; he doesn't remember his past.

Zack, the pack's current submissive wolf; he has a mysterious past and currently lives with Warren and Kyle.

Warren Smith, third in the Columbia Basin Pack and the pack's only gay wolf so far; he becomes very "Southern" when riled, and lives with his partner, Kyle, and their tenant, Zack.

Kyle Brooks, human divorce lawyer—partner of Warren.

TRI-CITIES SEETHE

Marsilia, aka Bright Blade; aka Queen of the Damned, per Mercy; Mistress of the seethe.

Stefan Uccello, aka the Soldier, a vampire with a heart who loves *Scooby-Doo.*

Wulfe, aka the Wizard, a powerful, magically talented, and bug-nuts-crazy vampire.

FRIENDS AND FOES

Tony Montenegro, bilingual Kennewick police officer and longtime friend of Mercy, even after recently learning of her supernatural nature.

Charla (Char), Mercy's college roommate and one of her best friends.

Gary Laughingdog, Mercy's sometime felonious, coyote-shapeshifting half brother who has a thing for Honey.

Coyote, archetype and sort of Mercy's father; he is the cause of much angst and ulcers.

Siebold (Zee) Adelbertsmiter, aka the Dark Smith of Drontheim, Mercy's mentor, who appears as a cranky old mechanic, but the Gray Lords walk carefully around him, as he has a habit of strewing around their body parts.

Thaddeus (Tad) Adelbertsmiter, Zee's half-fae son, who shares his father's affinity for working metals, even the cold iron that is normally lethal to their kind.

Elizaveta Arkadyevna Vyshnevetskaya, a powerful Russian witch with a fondness for Adam and also for money.

Austin Harris, extremely good-looking goblin pilot and owner of a small airplane company.

Larry Sethaway, goblin leader in the Tri-Cities; he has yellow-green eyes and four-fingered hands.

Matt Smith, not the Doctor, a submissive wolf and competent copilot.

David Christiansen, mercenary and friend of Adam's; David was the first werewolf to go public.

Gray Lords, the very scary and very powerful ruling class of the fae.

Alistair Beauclaire, a Gray Lord who declared the fae a sovereign nation and no longer under the rules of the USA after the justice system failed his daughter.

Underhill, a not-very-sane fae entity that is also a place, not subject to human physics.

Samuel, werewolf, Cornick Bran's oldest son and an early crush of Mercy's; he's now married to Ariana.

Ariana, silver-borne fae who is learning to get over her fear of canines, thanks to her husband, Samuel.

ASPEN CREEK PACK (MONTANA)

Bran Cornick, aka the Marrok, one of Mercy's foster fathers and Alpha of all the werewolves in America (except, recently, the

Columbia Basin Pack); Mercy would have given him ulcers by now if he weren't a werewolf.

Leah Cornick, werewolf, Bran's mate and a thorn in Mercy's paw.

Charles Cornick, the only born werewolf and second son of Bran; he has shamanistic magic.

Anna Cornick, Omega wolf with amazing musical talent; she's married to Charles and lethal with a rolling pin.

COURT OF THE LORD OF NIGHT

Iacopo (Jacob) Bonarata, aka Thug Vampire, aka the Lord of Night, Master of Milan; he is the European head vampire and ex-lover of Marsilia. He meddles more than Coyote.

Guccio de' Medici, aka Pretty Vampire, snappy dresser with a biting problem and a desire for power.

Lenka, beautiful but insane werewolf, Bonarata's "pet."

Zanobi, werewolf, Lenka's murdered mate.

Ignatio, one of the three vampire minions who hurt and kidnapped Mercy; it's only a matter of time before Adam finds a reason to pay Ignatio a visit.

Stacia, very young and sweet half (or more) fae healer.

Niki, a human sheep.

Cook, to be feared.

Annabelle, vampire, a servant.

CAST OF CHARACTERS

VLTAVA PACK

Libor, Alpha of the Vltava Pack.

Martin Zajíc, werewolf, Libor's motorcyle-riding second-in-command.

Jitka, werewolf, a sultry dominant who is Libor's third.

Pavel, werewolf, ex-lover of Jitka who succumbed to vampire lures.

Danek (Dan), poltergeist ghost of a traitor from World War II.

MARY'S SEETHE

Mary, Mistress of the seethe.

Kocourek, Master Vampire of Prague.

Ivan Novak, vampire.

Lars, vampire.

Vanje, vampire.

Dagmar, vampire.

Weis, the vampire hanging on the wall.

OTHERS

The Golem of Prague, animated by Rabbi Loew in the Middle Ages to protect the Jewish Quarter of Prague, and later destroyed—or so the rabbi thought.

Strnad, former Master Vampire of Prague.

Galina, a very sad ghost girl.

Jean Chastel, aka the Beast of Gévaudan, werewolf; thankfully this psycho is deceased!

HISTORICAL CHARACTERS

Reinhard Heydrich, assassinated during World War II.

Sugar Ray Robinson and **Muhammad Ali,** human boxers.